THE RATS OF HAMELIN

A PIPER'S TALE

Adam McCune & Keith McCune

MOODY PUBLISHERS
CHICAGO

Library of Congress Cataloging-in-Publication Data

McCune, Adam.
    The rats of Hamelin : a piper's tale / Adam McCune & Keith McCune.
        p. cm.
    ISBN-13: 978-0-8024-6701-0
    1. Pied Piper of Hamelin (Legendary character)—Fiction.
I. McCune, Keith. II. Title.

PS3613.C3865R38 2005
813'.6–dc22

                                                          2005007374

ISBN: 0-8024-6701-6
ISBN-13: 978-0-8024-6701-0

1 3 5 7 9 10 8 6 4 2

Printed in the United States of America

THE RATS OF HAMELIN

*To Grace Anne McCune,
with gratitude for bringing grace
to the process and the product*

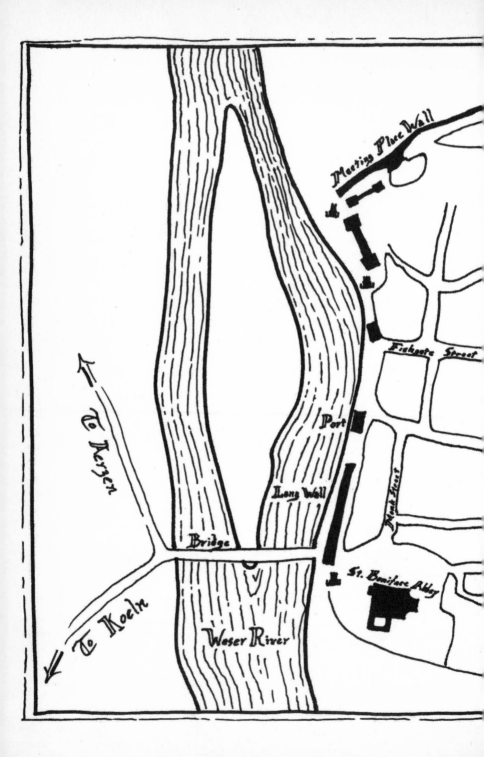

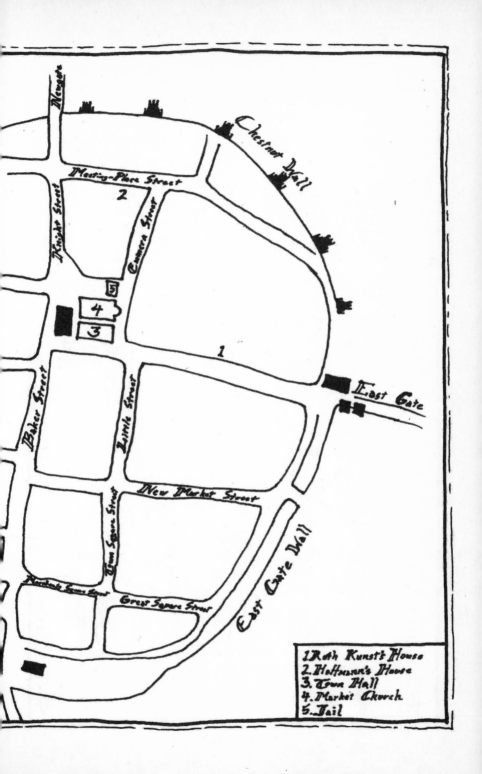

Chestnut Wall

Meeting-Place Street

Knight Street

Camera Street

Baker Street

Little Street

New Market Street

Town Square Street

Great Square Street

East Gate

East Gate Wall

1. Roth Kunst's House
2. Hoffmann's House
3. Town Hall
4. Market Church
5. Jail

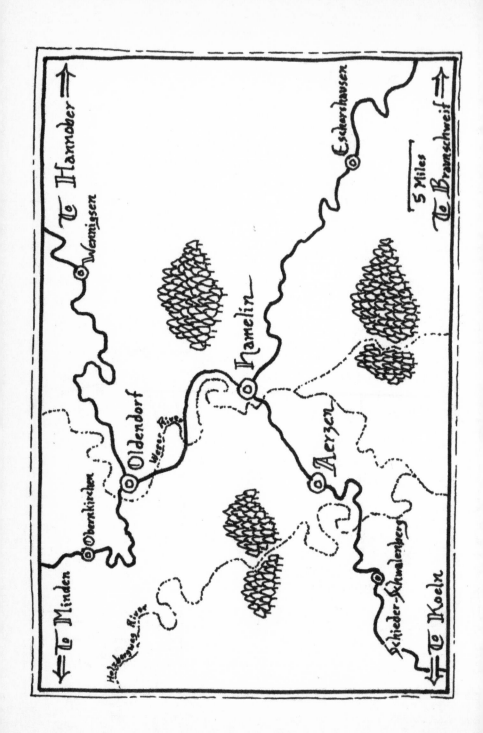

Contents

"In the year 1284, on the days of John and Paul, the 26th of June, a piper clothed in various colors came and led away 130 children born in Hamelin to Calvary on the Koppen."

—*The Lueneberg Manuscript, Hamelin, 1450*

ONE

The Musician's Son

Autumn 1278, Oldendorf

I CAN STILL REMEMBER WHEN MY FATHER WAS A GREAT MAN. I was nine, and Papa was strong, but me—well, I had fine bones. The girls in the next cottage called me scrawny, though how could you expect girls like them to recognize fine bones?

The lord of our manor didn't think much of Papa. But then, he didn't think much of anybody. I would say to blazes with him, and Mama would say don't talk like that.

Papa used to jump on me and growl, and I became the knight whose job it was to slay the dragon. I loved it, even though it was completely unfair—the dragon had a huge advantage. It should have been easy, stabbing a pretend dragon in the chest with an imaginary sword, but the problem was, Papa could hold me up in the air away from him with just one hand. We'd roll around till finally he'd let me stab him; then at last he'd die, twitching and roaring. It was my favorite game.

That was the year Papa made his flute. He'd hold it up to his nose, peer along that little curved surface, give a touch of the knife here, a touch there, and blow away the wooden curls. He played all kinds of tunes, and sometimes Mama would sing along.

> "Oh, where is my boy now, who went far away?"
> Asked the weeping old woman of Aerzen town.
> "For many a fair promise was made on the day
> When the children left, singing, with hardly a frown,"
> Said the weeping old woman of Aerzen town.

My father tried to teach me to play that song every time we took a break from plowing, but I just didn't have his flair.

The neighbor girls picked on me for making the flute squeak. Not that they even knew which end went up. The fact is, they picked on me about everything. If we were threshing barley, they'd say, "So were you swinging that flail, Joopi, or was it swinging you?"

That's another thing: they called me Joopi. I hated that more than anything. My name was Johannes, thank you very much. Joopi made me sound like Mama still wiped my nose.

One day Papa lunged at me, growling as he always did, and I charged back. Then, just as he was reaching out to grab me, he coughed, hard and long. When I thrust at him with my invisible sword, he fell over on his side and kept coughing. At first I figured the coughing was a new way of dying and letting me win. Then I asked if he was all right. He pulled himself to his feet, patted my head, said something funny about dragon sickness, and walked away, looking a little shaky. A few days later, one of his coughs brought up blood. We never played dragon again.

After that, Papa got real sick, coughing up blood almost every day. Soon I was doing almost all the farming, though I could barely manage that threshing flail. By the time I was twelve, we were way behind in paying our share of grain.

One day at suppertime a neighbor dropped by. He stood in the doorway and spoke to my father. "Brought some grain. We know you're having trouble making quota."

Papa laughed as if he'd just heard the funniest thing in the world, then straightened up and said, "Well, thanks a whole lot, but we're doing fine. I'll be better soon."

The neighbor looked at Mama, who was studying the ground. Eventually he left.

It happened again, and then again. When Papa said no for the third time, I saw Mama's mouth set in a hard line. Papa said we'd do fine. But I felt the broken blisters on my hands; I saw how Mama's back was bent at the end of the day. Papa might be fine, but we weren't. I was only twelve, but I could see it plain as day: there was something more important to my father than my mother was.

⊢——•——⊣

It was dark in the cottage the night the lord of the manor came; the fire was small. We were always short on wood. My mother laid a fragrant, cloth-wrapped bundle on the little table, then sat across from Papa. He reached around with his cold hand and squeezed my aching shoulder.

Taking the hint, I prayed aloud, "Our Father, who art in heaven . . ." And I thought, *Lord, when You give our daily bread, make Papa take it.* Then, as always, the part about forgiveness reminded me of the landlord. Amen.

Papa opened the cloth and lifted out the little brown loaf. Just by the way he broke it carefully into three pieces, I could tell: tonight Papa would not be crabby, as he sometimes was since he'd grown too sick to work.

"Well, now," said my mother, rubbing my back. "Eat up! You're a growing boy, Hannes."

I ate slowly, to make it last. Mama's bread was great, soft but solid, pushing back just enough against the teeth and tongue. All through that meal, Papa only coughed once, and there was no blood. And when we had eaten every crumb, my father took out his flute.

My mother and I scooted our stools together for warmth and settled down to listen. Papa hardly ever felt well enough to play. He lifted the flute with a flourish, pressed his lips together, and blew. The music rose, warm as a summer breeze, swelling and turning, rising and falling. At last the tune dropped down softly, pirouetted through one gentle trill, and faded into the dying firelight.

"I've got an idea," Papa began. His eyes were shining.

Mama looked at her hands in her lap.

He held up the flute. "I could become a musician up at the manor house. One little entertainment, and I could make more than a whole week in the fields. The lord might pay; the guests might tip. When I get stronger, I could dance. I'm not a bad juggler."

Still looking down, Mama asked, "Has the landlord ever shown interest in anything but getting more grain out of us?"

A quiet thudding came from outside—horse hooves on soft ground.

"And then," Papa went on, "what if a visiting troupe comes through Oldendorf, thinks I'm good, takes us with 'em to Bielefeld or Braunschweig or—"

Someone banged on the door with a stick. Mama jumped like she'd been hearing that stick in her nightmares. My father got up, leaning hard on the table, and opened the door. I could see the steward's horse. A voice said, "The master would like a word."

Papa turned to us with a grand smile. "It'll be fine," he whispered, and he was still grinning as he stepped out.

"Not enough grain," I said to Mama.

She folded up the bread cloth without looking at me and muttered, "Not for that landlord."

I unbolted the shutters as quietly as I could. I had never seen the lord of our manor, who often traveled between his various houses, including the one in Oldendorf. But some of my friends had seen him. He was a huge man, they said, and bald, with a wine-colored, crescent-shaped birthmark way up on his forehead.

I opened our little window. In the dark, I made out my father walking slowly by the steward's horse. A little ways away stood a second horse, larger, whose rider I couldn't see.

"Good evening, sir," said Papa's voice. Then he started to cough.

My mother's grip on my shoulder tightened.

"Sir," Papa wheezed, after a pause where all I could hear was a rumble, "this year was hard on everyone. I've been a little under the weather; my son's been helping out."

I saw my father listening.

"But, sir!" he stammered. "I've been right regular for—how many years now? We'll make it up next harvest, sir. I won't be sick forever; my boy's getting stronger."

The response was very short this time.

"Sir, I've thought of a way I could make it up to you. You have lots of visitors up at the big house. I could come play for your guests, often as you want. Folks say I'm not bad on the flute, sir. Here, let me—"

A laugh rang out like a thunderclap. There was a commotion, the horses turned, and the men were gone.

My mother and I ran out. Papa was lying full-length in the mud. He was coughing and coughing, with blood dribbled on his chin. I turned toward the sound of the horses riding away. I wanted to scream at the man who had hurt my father—the most awful, powerful curse in the world. I started to run after him, but Mama grabbed me.

"Don't be stupid!" she snapped. "Help me with your father."

We knelt beside Papa. He gulped air as Mama and I pulled him out of the mud. We could barely hear him as he gasped, "He's got someone else to work our land."

I pushed our wheelbarrow through the fog. My father had tried to take a turn the first day, but he collapsed onto the handles, coughing and shivering. And a week on the road had not helped, especially the night it rained. We were all but carrying him now.

"How much bread do we have?" he murmured.

My mother answered, "Two or three more meals."

"Not enough to get to Braunschweig," Papa said, looking at the ground. He shook his head, looking hopeless in the way that made my chest freeze up. "And there might be no more work in Braunschweig than there was in Oldendorf."

I felt the bite of the cold and hunched up my back against it. When I hit a pothole, I shoved the wheelbarrow out before my father could see and try to help. I pitied my father, but with every jolt in the road, another feeling was also growing.

Then I heard the sound of hooves battering through the fog ahead.

"They have horses; they'll have money," Mama said. The trotting got closer and louder, and she grabbed me with urgent eyes. "Hannes, get ready to wave and shout at them. Just say, 'Mercy, kind sirs.'"

"I'll . . . I'll play for them," said Papa. He pulled out his little flute.

My mother bit her lip when Papa raised the flute with a wave, as though hundreds were watching. He spread his stooped shoulders, took a step. He stumbled. When I jerked up my arm to catch him, the wheelbarrow tipped, heaving into the mud our cups, cook pot, blanket—everything we owned in the world. The flute slid from Papa's hand as he bent double with a racking cough.

My mother held a rag to his mouth and hissed to me, "You play! Quick!"

All I knew was "The Woman of Aerzen." As the pounding hoofbeats bore down on us, I raised the flute from the mud, wiped it frantically on my trousers, and tried to stop shaking.

But all I could see was that tipped wheelbarrow, and I started to cry like I had never cried in my life. As I cried, of course, every gasp made a little squeak on the flute. I tightened my stomach, breathed in deep, and sent some wavering music out into the mist.

Seven dark horses burst out of the fog, nearly on top of us, their riders surrounded by swirling cloth like wings. With all the shouting, swerving, rearing, neighing, and mud spattering, I jumped and bit my tongue but didn't miss a note of "The Woman of Aerzen."

One of the riders held up a hand, and the next thing I knew, a half circle of mounted men stood around my family. I looked down at the road and kept playing.

I heard the stretch of a saddle, the clink of a stirrup, and the squelch of a boot in the mud. The only other sounds were horse breath and that wistful tune coming out so feeble, note by note, from my father's flute, bearing the tale of failure: *He vowed they would win, but they vanished instead. . . .*

Clean hands reached down in the mud to pick up the pot. I stopped playing. White hair surrounded the rescuer's face. It wasn't fitting for a serf-boy to look a wellborn man in the face, so I looked down at his clothes, made of fabrics I didn't even know the names of. On a strap at his shoulder, nestled against his robes, hung a weapon. No, not a weapon—a long flute trimmed with gold, flaring like a trumpet.

The white-haired man righted our wheelbarrow, wiped the pot on the grass, and laid it in the cart. The other six riders swung from their saddles and began to gather our possessions. My parents rushed over to stop them, both from embarrassment and in the hope that the strangers' sympathy might take the form of coins instead.

Their leader walked over to my father, who had stopped coughing but was bent over, with blood flecked on his face and hands. The man said, "You're sick."

We were afraid to speak.

"Will you make a bargain with me?" he asked.

One of the riders, also wearing a flute, stepped up to the first man. "My lord," he said in a low tone, "we need to move on. Anselm has been gone for a week. Who knows what he—"

"I'll make this brief," said the white-bearded man.

He turned back to my father, held out his golden flute, and said, "If we take you to a place of healing, will you give me your son as my apprentice?"

Apprentice. The word drifted to me from another world, and for a moment I did not understand what he had said. Then hot and cold tingled through me and I saw myself, with my training finished, riding alongside this man with a flying robe and a golden flute of my own. I looked sideways at my parents, and my stomach sank. In the morning I would wake up, and my mother and father would not be there. And yet—the opportunity to be one of these men! I held my breath. Would Papa see this as charity and refuse it?

"He would have wages, payable to you," said the man, "as well as room and board. I am the Pipelord, head of the Pipers Guild; he would be well trained. And I swear to you on my pipe"—he gripped the golden flute—"I will treat him as I would my own son."

Papa straightened up as far as he could. "Sir, we're honored to have our son apprenticed. But as for the wages . . ." Suddenly he began coughing again.

My mother spoke up. "Thank you, my lord." And she bowed very low.

"Thank *you*," said the man. And so it was decided. "What is the boy's name?"

"Johannes," said my father, and coughed again.

I couldn't speak. My mother and father hugged me. I offered my father his little wooden flute, but he pressed it back into my hand.

"Son, I want you to have something to remember me by."

As my new master gave instructions to two of his companions, my mother cried on me a little, and still I said nothing. Then my parents got on horses with the two men, our things in a sack behind my mother, and I got on the horse of the white-bearded man, clutching my father's flute. My parents and I looked back at each other, then rode in opposite directions, leaving the little wheelbarrow by the side of the road.

◆———•———◆

". . . should have tested him," one of the riders muttered.

"Shhh! The boy'll hear you," another voice answered. "And we didn't have time."

"But the Pipelord's own apprentice?" said the first. "He could at least show some caution, after what happened to his *last* one."

"I can hear you," said the Pipelord above me, without turning around.

The murmurers fell silent.

"Did you notice that the boy kept piping, no matter what! We could all learn from that."

The horses clattered on.

"Don't mind Master Friedrich," the Pipelord murmured, his face upside down above mine. "He'll be your best friend by the end of the month."

The road below was a blur; everything else was rushing fog. I was dizzy from the height and a speed such as I had never known.

"Are you all right?" the Pipelord asked.

"Yes, my lord," I lied.

"You're my apprentice," he said. "Call me Master Josef."

"Yes, sir," I answered, and added, "Master Josef."

The ride was long and silent, except for the constant thudding of hooves. Finally my stomach quieted down, and I shut my eyes. The horses' feet went on beating in the darkness as I sank against the Pipelord's warm chest.

What seemed like a moment later, he was shaking me awake. I was very sore now.

"We've reached Hamelin," he said. "It looks like we'll have to open the gate ourselves."

I blinked. Behind us, I could hear and smell a river, the Weser. In front of us was a huge wall. Beyond it to the right I could see a golden spire shining—the ancient abbey of St. Boniface that my father had told me was the oldest thing in Hamelin. And directly in our path stood a gate, shut even though there was still daylight. I tried to imagine the five horses pulling it open.

I felt the Pipelord take a deep breath. He lifted his golden pipe to his mouth. As his fingers moved up and down the holes, a few hard, eerie tones came out . . . followed by one long note.

A rumble sounded through the gate.

The Pipelord leaned back, nudging the horse with his knees so that it moved back too. He repeated the notes he played at first, except lower, and then the long one again. He held the note, his face and hands perfectly relaxed.

Something large in the gate shoved and clicked. The gate creaked and slowly opened, as if the Pipelord had it on a string.

His face was very serious now. He slapped the horse with the reins, and we jolted forward into the city with the others close behind.

I heard a roar from up ahead and felt the Pipelord's muscles grow tense. The horses clattered along the cobblestones, and the city houses flew by. There were no people anywhere. When we turned onto another street and slowed down, I realized what the noise was: hundreds, thousands of human voices. Angry voices.

As we turned the corner, I saw a large open space boiling with people. They were all shouting and jostling one another to get a better view of something I couldn't see. The Pipelord's horse stepped slowly toward the crowd, and the other riders fell into place behind us. The people at the edges saw us first, and they froze.

Their faces were covered with gouges and three-rowed scratches, barely scabbed over. Silence ate through the crowd as more and more scarred faces turned to us. Amid the crowd a worried-looking girl about my age met my eyes. Surrounded by a waterfall of brown hair, her face was unscarred except for one small cut over her left eyebrow. Then someone moved between us, and I lost her.

At last the men in the center turned around, and I saw what all the shouting was about. A boy, twelve or thirteen, was locked, neck and wrists, in the stocks. His clothes were torn, and his dirty black hair was sticking up, with tufts of it missing. Blood and bruises covered him from his shaking knees to his cringing shoulders. But his eyes were hungry and burning.

As soon as the men stepped back, the boy's eyes pounced on us, and through cracked lips he shouted, "Master! At last! I knew you wouldn't want to see one of your own in the stocks."

"Be silent, Anselm of Aerzen!" the Pipelord shouted back, with echoes crackling from the walls around. "I don't want to see you in the stocks. I want to see you in court."

From the corner of my eye, I saw the people in the crowd look at each other, then look at the long pipes Master Josef and his men carried. The Pipelord turned away from Anselm toward the building nearby, which seemed to be Town Hall. In the dusk, its three stories loomed up, heavy and imposing, over the square full of people.

The Pipelord urged his horse forward. The crowd made way with doubtful faces, and we rode toward the bottom of the steps.

"O great Pipelord!" Anselm screamed, and we stopped. Burning anger forced the words through that thickened tongue and broken face. "You think you can just *replace* me? As if any of your *lackeys* could do what I've done. But you see, I know what you are. I know you've come to take Hamelin from me and run it for yourself."

The Pipelord's jaw tightened, but he never turned around. He dismounted and swung me down. As the pipers tied their mounts to a post, he said to me, "Stay here and watch the horses."

With his companions, the Pipelord strode up the steps of Town Hall two at a time and, flinging the doors wide, plunged into the darkness within. As the last of them disappeared inside, a murmur went through the square, and a few people ran up the steps. Soon the crowd followed, and Anselm got no more than a passing cuff on the ear from an old woman as they all climbed, jabbering, under the heavy archway. And the doors boomed shut.

I shuddered. I could feel Anselm looking at me, though with the setting red sun behind him, I couldn't see his eyes. At last he spoke.

"He blamed all this on me, didn't he?"

I put my hand on the neck of the Pipelord's horse.

"You trust him?" he asked.

I didn't answer.

"Why do you think he's here today?"

When I still said nothing, Anselm went on, his eyes pawing at me.

"It's all to keep his power. His reputation. Everything he says is just to sell the goods." He drew a breath, then groaned. "I'm innocent. The villain in this town is the man who put me here. You look . . . honest. Listen to me. The key to the stocks is in the vice-mayor's office. In that building, just down the hall—"

He stopped and turned his head as well as he could in the brace. Boot heels were clicking on the cobblestones. Anselm shrank. A four-sided stone pillar stood nearby, and I jumped behind it.

The clicking heels grew still. I peeked out from my hiding place. An enormous man stood ten feet from where Anselm's slight frame was bunched up in the stocks. He towered broad and black against the red sunset.

"Comfortable, Anselm?" he asked in a rumbling voice. He strolled closer. "Your hands look so empty without a pipe." Two feet away he stopped, raised his fist, and slammed it down on Anselm's head.

The prisoner choked for a long time.

"Your friend died before he gave anything away," the man growled.

Anselm's wide eyes rolled up at the man.

"But I hope to get more out of you. If only satisfaction." He crouched to look Anselm in the eye.

I did not move and barely breathed.

"Nobody gets back at me forever, boy. Nobody." He brought his massive hands toward Anselm's head.

A girl's voice rang out over the red-lit square. "Excuse me, sir!"

The man jumped and spun toward the voice. It was the girl with the cut by her eyebrow. She was standing on the steps, looking pale and thin as her dark hair and clothing stirred in the breeze.

"Sir, they're having a meeting about Anselm. They need you to come."

"I'll be right there," answered the man.

"But they need you now, sir," the girl insisted.

The man hesitated. Then he rose and marched up the stairs, his heels clicking all the way. One of the horses shied from the man as he passed, and though the pillar hid me, I shrank too. The girl watched him go until the sound of his boots faded behind the door. Then she turned, ran down the steps to Anselm, and pulled out a key.

Anselm wheezed out a little rattling laugh. "I knew it. I knew you loved me."

"I don't," she snapped. "I never did. And I never want to see you again."

I heard the key in the lock.

"And don't try anything now or I'll scream, and then you'll really be in trouble."

"If you don't care about me," Anselm croaked, "why are you letting me go?"

She was silent for a moment, struggling with the lock.

"Well?"

"What you did was horrible. But that doesn't mean they can do this to you," she answered.

With a click the top of the stocks opened, and Anselm carefully stood and rubbed his wrists.

"Go on, get out of here," she said.

"Which way is safest?"

"I'm not helping you!" she retorted. "I'm only here because one murder is enough. Go on." She pointed down a street. Just then she saw me and stood petrified.

At the look of terror in her eyes, I got up. "I won't tell," I promised. "Don't worry. I won't tell."

A shiver went through her, and she glanced back at Anselm. "Go!" she said. "Now!"

"Good-bye," he said. As he limped down the street, the girl ran past me, up and through the big doors.

21

The square was silent. One of the horses snorted. I heard the sound of running feet. Perhaps they'd caught her. But the sound wasn't coming from Town Hall; it was coming from around the corner.

The girl had had time to return the key. I sprinted up the stairs and yelled into the hallway, "Master Josef! Master Josef, Anselm has escaped!"

Soon the Pipelord, his pipers, and a crowd of men pushed me back out through the doors. About two dozen boys of Anselm's age, dressed in red cloaks and carrying long pipes, stood facing us.

At the sight of the boys, most of the Hameliners shrank back, but one yelled, "Go for the pipes!" and a few men rushed at the boys.

"Wait!" the Pipelord shouted, but already the boys had raised their pipes and played a burst of screeches.

The men ran faster at the boys, but I heard wings beating the air. In the fading light, crows appeared, black against the dark blue sky, with the sunset glinting red on their wings. They swooped over the buildings and down at the men like a pack of hunting wolves. The men waved, ducked, scattered. And the crows rose and fell in a relentless, bloody dance—dive, claw, jab, dive, claw, jab.

A long, deep note throbbed through me. The Pipelord was stepping out into the square, his pipe to his lips. The music pulsed in the air, the boys' hands shook, and thin smoke rose from their pipes. At last the boys yelped and dropped the steaming pipes onto the paving stones.

The crows slowed down. The Pipelord spread his feet and elbows. Abruptly the music tilted, and the crows swept away from the men, gathering around the Pipelord in a spinning ball. The music grew louder, higher. I could see only tiny glimpses of the Pipelord between the feathers as the crows raced around him in a whirling wall of beating wings. The music stretched and stretched until I thought the world would break; then, suddenly, it did.

A blinding flash of lightning cracked from the glowering clouds down into the crows. Fire burst from bird to bird, through the fluttering mass of them, and flaming crows were flung out in all directions. My ears rang, and my eyes were full of dancing light.

There stood the Pipelord, his pipe in his hands, the ground around him paved with dead, burning crows. He strode through the smoke and fire to the injured men. One of the pipers used the sash of his robe to snatch up the boys' pipes, then bound them together with a leather strap. The other pipers were already tying the boys' hands.

"Here," said the one with the bunch of pipes, looking my way. He held out the bundle at arm's length, as it swung, smoking, on the strap. "Put these in my pack." He nodded at the bag on his horse.

When I nearly toppled from the weight, he said, "Careful. They're still hot."

The boys were nursing their burned hands and stabbing at me with their eyes.

"Yes, sir," I said, and went over to the horses, bracing my left arm with my right. The pipes spun, glinting, with smoke trailing off them. I supposed I would get one soon. I shivered at the sight of so much power and lowered the pipes into the saddlebag.

The townspeople, who had retreated at the sight of the crows, were coming back out of the doors now, milling on the steps of Town Hall at a safe distance. The Pipelord found a doctor to tend the men that the birds had attacked, then turned to the boys. They did not meet his eyes.

"Why?" he asked after a long while. "Why did you listen to him?"

They did not answer.

"These people never did anything to you. How could you do all this?" He waved at the dead crows, the men with gouged faces.

The boys looked at their shoes.

The Pipelord breathed slowly in and out. "Take them into Town Hall," he said to the pipers. "We still have to negotiate their trial."

The pipers led the boys away across the smoldering square. The Pipelord's face fell as he surveyed the shuffling boys, the gawking crowd, the reeking ruin of the birds.

One of the pipers spoke to him. "My lord, don't punish yourself. It's over now. At least we've ended the Unbound movement."

The Pipelord said nothing.

"Except for Anselm," added the piper.

The Pipelord nodded.

He came over to me. "I'm sorry you had to see all that," he said. "Now help me put out the crows before a fire starts."

Even as he spoke, there was a cold breeze, and I smelled lamp oil. The Pipelord stiffened, and the crowd gasped. I turned toward the smell in time to see Anselm on the roof of a house, splashing

23

oil from a barrel on the walls below him. Already smoke rose behind him and an eerie light flickered from the windows.

"My *lord*!" Anselm made a mock bow, then dumped the rest of the barrel in a long arc to the nearest burning crow.

Flames leaped from the bird to the house, flowing into the windows and slithering up the walls. The crowd shouted. People ran for water. The roofs on both sides of the burning house were slate, but the one across the street was thatch.

The flames swelled, drawing in air, and the house glowed red against the gray sky. The fire welled up around the edge of the shingles, and we could hardly see Anselm through the red light and streaming heat. The Pipelord's eyes reached out to the boy on the burning house.

"Anselm!" he screamed over the rushing sound of the flames. "Anselm! Get onto the roof of the next house!"

"What's that, master?" Anselm hooted. He crouched down and put his hand to his ear. "Still giving orders to the very end?"

"Anselm!" the Pipelord repeated. "I can put out the fire, but what I do will kill you if you are in the way. Do you understand? You will die!"

"We will all die, master!" Anselm screamed back. "But I will die young and free, and you will die old, with nothing but a book of rules to keep you company."

The flying sparks were falling near the thatch now. Someone tried to dump water on the burning oil, and fire splashed everywhere. Some men were pointing at the roofs on either side of Anselm and bringing buckets into the neighboring houses below. Flames crept into the shingles.

"Anselm! Go!"

"Anselm, go!" the boy mimicked. "Master, surprise! I've learned to laugh at your orders. I see them now for what they are."

A man with a bucket poked his head out onto the roof beside Anselm's.

"You!" Anselm pointed a finger at him, and the man gaped. "Do you know what I would have done for you? For all of you!" His hand swept out over the crowd. "I would have made you a great empire!" He seemed to float in the red rippling heat. "Hamelin would have been my capital. One of you"—he squinted through the fire to scan the crowd—"one of you would have been my queen! And, master, I would have given you the crown. *If* you had been honest enough to admit you *wanted* it!"

The man with the bucket jumped up from the hole, and in the same moment, part of the wall between his roof and Anselm's collapsed. The roof warped, fire gushing from the wound. The man with the bucket fled, other firefighters scrambled from homes on both sides, and still Anselm swayed above the flames.

"Children!" he screamed. "You are all just foolish children!"

He crouched and, as dozens of voices screamed, he sprang into the yawning fire.

"Anselm!" the Pipelord yelled, and he ran toward the upward-streaming flames.

I saw him, small against the wash of fire, and I ran after him.

The wind whipped around us, sucking us to the red mouth of the house, and the flame beat us back. My skin went tight with the heat, but I plunged ahead and grabbed the end of the Pipelord's cloak just as he would have run through the glowing door.

He pulled against me. I fell to my knees and clung to his cloak, wrapping my whole body around it. I felt the cloak go slack.

"My lord," a piper was shouting, "Karl will look for him from the other side. Please, get away from the fire."

The blaze roared, and the draft lashed the Pipelord's hair about his face. He lifted me to my feet.

We trudged from the house with the crowd spinning around us, the roof of the house breaking and spilling. At last the pipers came and told the Pipelord there was nothing alive in the house. He nodded, and one of the pipers played a tune in a minor key. The fire swept out of the house toward us but gasped out at the last moment, leaving the rubble crusted with frost.

They called my master. With his hand on my shoulder, he walked into the shell of the first floor. There lay the body, a boy-shaped lump with the outer flesh burned away, covered with fine, white frost. I thought I would be sick.

The Pipelord kneeled in the rubble and ashes and put his hand on the charcoal forehead. "Good-bye, Anselm," he said. He nodded to the men, who carried the body away on a cloth stretched between them.

He looked up at me out of a weary face and said, "He was my last apprentice."

TWO

The Apprentice

Thursday, June Twenty-second, 1284, Aerzen

R ED FOOT, YELLOW FOOT, RED FOOT, YELLOW FOOT. I WAS ten days out from the guildhouse in the grand city of Koeln, but I still had a spring in my step. Not a swagger, a spring. I was a man with a mission. As I passed peasants mending fences and slopping hogs, I knew exactly where I was going. I had a scroll to deliver to a piper and a town to deliver from rats.

At age eighteen, a far cry from the undernourished, untrained boy Hannes who last saw these roads, I had come home to Saxony wearing my own impressive guild uniform. Almost a graduate of the finest training in the empire, almost a master in the much-honored Pipers Guild.

As I left the guildhouse, the Pipelord had given me further instructions. "First, confirm with Hamelin's council about your reward. Then go to Muender and find Master Friedrich. He'll remember you. He can help you guard and spend the reward. And give him this letter. It is for his eyes only."

Then, right into my ear, so I could feel the warm beating of his words: "It is extremely important."

So now I was going to Hamelin, to save them from their plague of rats. I was walking the long road alone—a dangerous business. But I held my pipe in plain sight, for bandits to fear and the world to admire. The elegant gold-plated pipe I'd received at the end of my third year at the guildhouse. I moved my fingers along the golden pipe, slipping them carefully into the familiar holes and fingering the edges, then sliding down to where it flared out like a lily.

Down in the bottom of my bag, I carried another flute, the one

I played on the night I had been apprenticed six years before. Without the Pipelord's urging, I'd never have brought this memento of my peasant childhood: the little wooden flute made by my father.

My father, who was healed at the monastery—then never regained his strength. My father, who refused the Pipelord's payments for my apprenticeship and insisted on earning wages—then couldn't. My father, who turned down the Pipelord's help in looking for work—then disappeared, two years into my apprenticeship. My father, who kept failing, no matter what.

⊢——·——⊣

Apprentices always got new clothes when they went with their masters to observe a mission for the first time. I had never worn dyed cloth in my life. When my time came, I ran to the Pipelord's room in my gray monklike uniform. I stepped through the door, and simply stared. Not only did my new clothes have color; they had two colors: red on the right side, yellow on the left.

"A pied outfit," said the Pipelord, his face very serious. "A many-colored outfit—or, in this case, two. Red for justice, yellow for mercy, so you don't forget either one." He touched my shoulder with his pipe. "I hereby dub thee Pied Piper of Oldendorf."

I nodded, too overwhelmed to speak.

When I went to lunch, the other apprentices, who had already gotten colored clothes, also stared without a word at mine. Finally I broke the silence. "Red for justice, yellow for mercy. That's what the master said."

"Really?" asked a senior named Otto.

"Yes. He called me a pied piper."

Otto and the others couldn't hold it in anymore. They guffawed. They pounded the table.

"What?" I asked.

"I've never seen anything quite like it," said Otto.

"But . . . noblemen wear different colors," I protested.

"Yes, but Hannes . . . you look like a jester!"

I thought of an excuse to leave, and I didn't have any lunch that day.

As time went on, it didn't help that the Pipelord kept calling me Pied Piper.

⊢——·——⊣

Today, on the day of my solo mission, I would not think about the Pipelord. I would not think about my father. I would think about my new life. I was about to become a master piper.

I lifted the pipe and played a light tune as I journeyed back to Hamelin, where my apprenticeship had begun. The only thing I hadn't figured out yet was what charity to give the reward money to. As Hamelin drew nearer, I'd asked questions at the inns along the road, sniffing for the sort of causes the Pipelord would approve of.

Fields of still-green grain spread out on one side of the road. Across the fields stood little cottages a lot like the one in which I was born. But no castle. Their lord must be a city dweller, like my childhood master. He probably lived in Aerzen, the town I'd just passed through.

Just ahead, the road bent sharply around a thick cluster of trees. I rounded the curve and stopped short. Twenty feet away lay a cart, tilted halfway into the ditch at the side of the road. A tired-looking horse was shifting its feet and whinnying with its eyes wide. Its reins were held by a girl of five or six. A second horse, sleek and well saddled, stood nearby. A man of about fifty, bent and bald, with thick eyebrows and thin clothing, stood in the ditch and strained to raise the cart, which of course was not moving. It would take a team of strong men with levers to pry it out of that ditch.

And on top of the cart, lounging at full length with a loaf of bread in his hands, lay a boy, eleven or twelve years old. He was handsome and, judging by the silk he wore under his riding clothes, must have been the landlord's son. The bread he held was not the black loaf of a peasant but a white, fluffy one that a baker would be proud of. He tore off a gold-white chunk of the flaky crust and flicked it at the old man's head.

"I'm going bald like you," the boy said through a mouthful of bread, "just waiting up here." The crust bounced off the old man's bald spot, and the girl picked it up, wiped off the dirt, and ate it greedily.

One good jolt by the old man, and the boy would topple into the mud, fine clothes, good bread, and all. I knew some pipe tunes that were just what he deserved. With an effort, I lowered my pipe into my bag, but I kept my fingers clasped around it.

I approached, and the boy looked up. "Who are you?" he asked, as though the road belonged to him.

I shrank. "Only a traveler," I said, and immediately regretted it. It was the sort of thing a serf would say, hoping to escape attention.

The boy's eyes locked on the man, who had stopped pushing and was breathing heavily. With a sudden snap and a thwack, the boy swung his riding crop and struck the old man in the chest. The little girl yelped, and the man bent over, wheezing.

Struggling to control my voice, I said, "What seems to be the problem here?"

Now the boy glared with suspicion. "This cart is my father's property. It must be in the barn tonight, and the one who landed it in the ditch must get it there."

"Where is your father?"

As the boy looked me up and down, I detected the first hint of uncertainty.

"Are you here to buy the manor?" he said at last.

"Perhaps," I bluffed.

The boy frowned, then sat up and slid onto his horse. "Wait here for my father's steward," he said, and rode past me and around the bend, back the way I had come, without another word.

I dug my fingernails into my palms. What was wrong with me, acting like a peasant? I was a piper now. I should have confronted him for his abuse of the old man and his rudeness to me. And if he refused to back down . . . well, I was a piper.

The little girl ran to the old man and clung to him, crying. He hugged her, rocking back and forth.

"Now, now," he said in a husky voice. "Why are you so upset?"

"Are you all right?" I asked.

He nodded.

"Here, let me help you up." I pulled him out of the ditch and stared at him. "Is this normal?"

"The young master learns it from his father," he answered, and shook his head. "Now there's a pair that deserve each other! Young master defies his father often as he can, and time to time we hear the father screaming at him."

He saw I was interested and warmed to the subject. "Oh, the stories I could tell you. We had a boy made a mistake once, shoeing the lord's horse. The lord beat him till the men couldn't stand to watch. And that boy's got a bad leg now—drags it along when he walks. That's the way of the lord of our manor." He sized me up and added a tentative "sir."

"Please, call me Hannes. I grew up working on a manor not far from here. I wasn't even very good at it."

As the old serf cleaned himself up a bit, I asked, "So does he beat everyone?"

"No, some get by without crossing him. But I'll tell you one thing—he's got every last one of us so tangled up in debts with all kind of taxes and fines that we don't know which end is up."

I nodded. I'd heard this kind of thing before.

"Sir," said the old man, then caught himself. "Hannes."

"Yes?" I decided it would be best to pipe up the cart's front end, angling away from the ditch.

"Were you really sent to buy the manor?"

"What?"

"Well, if you aren't here to buy the land, why'd you come?"

I shook my head. "How can your lord sell his manor? What will he live on?"

"He's got some land up north; that's where he started out. Got this place when he married, maybe twenty, twenty-five years back— his wife is nobility, see. He's not a proper lord, just rich. But we have to call him lord anyway."

An idea began to hatch. "How much is he asking?"

"I don't know. But he wants to sell it real bad."

What if the reward money from Hamelin were enough? I could turn the manor over to the serfs, set them free from their cruel lord and his brat . . .

"You gonna buy it, then?"

"Maybe." I walked to the front end of the cart, the little girl following me at a safe distance. "Look, let me see if I can help you with this thing."

"What? Move the cart?" The old man laughed. "Oh, you're kind and all, but it'll take more'n the two of us."

"You're right, but I have help." I reached into my pouch and pulled out the golden pipe.

The man's eyes widened.

"You'll want to move," I told the girl.

She trotted to the old man, then gazed at me with somber eyes.

I put the pipe in my mouth and placed my fingers, and my breath brought the metal to life. The first note bound me to the far front wheel of the cart with an invisible string. As each note helped me touch the cart, I felt its rough wood and its weight. I dropped to the long pulling note, leaned hard against the string, and backed away toward the trees.

The invisible cord between me and the wheel grew taut. Then the cart creaked and turned, and the far front wheel rolled up onto the road. At the same time, the back of the cart began tilting into the ditch. I moved my finger to cover a hole halfway, and a second string shot out from me to the far back wheel. The cart stood, poised, on the edge of the ditch, as I took a quick breath. I moved through the gripping notes, one octave lower this time, and drew out the pulling note again. I stepped backward into the forest, and the cart rolled onto the road.

I dropped the pipe into my satchel and bent, hands on my knees, catching my breath, as the old man and the little girl stared. In spite of all the pre-solo training, I was out of shape on lifting tunes; that was clear.

"You're a piper."

"Yes."

"What's your name again?"

"Hannes," I said, "from Oldendorf."

"Oldendorf. Hm. Oldendorf. You know, there's someone you got to see." He bent over creakily to look at the little girl. "Listen, sweetie. If the steward gets here before we're back, send him to Marthe's."

The girl nodded. The old man seized my elbow and pulled me after him, scrambling over the ditch like an oversized grasshopper. I followed him down a narrow path with a rippling lake of grain on each side, wheat stalks brushing my hosen. The grain stood tall; the man whose sweat had grown it stooped as he walked. I got his attention and pointed out over the field.

"Imagine if a piece of this land were yours, to do whatever you wanted with it, then give to your children. Say a new lord bought the manor and gave you a share. What would you think?"

He gave me a wary look. "You are a strange 'un." He snorted and spat. "That'd be like a holiday every day, compared to what we got now. 'Course it's about as likely as us harvesting barleycorns off this here wheat."

We walked through the wheat awhile—in silence, except for the old man's loud, extravagant spitting.

Maybe because we were near Aerzen, suddenly the song my father had taught me was running through my head.

"There came a fair preacher," the Hamelin folk said
To the weeping old woman of Aerzen town.
"He vowed they would win, but they vanished instead.
The children were lost by believing his vow,"
They told the old woman of Aerzen town.

On the steps of the church, with her fist to the skies
The angry old woman of Aerzen town
Found the preacher and screamed, "You are cursed for your lies!
Now the children of Hamelin will pay for your vow,
And be led out and lost by a man of my town."

I must have been singing out loud, because the old man frowned and set me straight. "She wasn't from Aerzen town proper. She was from right here." He waved at the cluster of huts ahead of us.

"It's a true story?"

"Of course. People all over lost their children. A preacher from Hamelin come. He said children would be the perfect soldiers to conquer the Holy Land. Pure of heart, he said they were. My great-aunt sent her son off. Her husband was dead; only her and her daughter was left. That son of hers never did come home. Well, she went and she cursed the town of Hamelin on account of that preacher."

"I never knew the song was about the Children's Crusade. I didn't know it was true."

"Oh, it's absolutely true." He nodded vigorously. "Absolutely."

"Except the prediction about children leaving Hamelin," I muttered, glancing over my shoulder. No sign of the steward.

"What was that?" asked the old man.

"Never mind. Where are you taking me, again?"

The grain ended. We had reached a little hut.

"Here we are," he said with a wrinkly smile.

When he nodded toward the door, I pushed it open and bent my head to get through. It all came back to me at once—the close little walls, the bumpy dirt floor, the withered-looking straw mats, the tiny, rough table, the oppressive heat and smoke of cooking, the smell of stale sweat, the windowless dark.

"Marthe?" the old man called, coming in behind me.

A middle-aged woman with a lean face appeared from a dark corner. Her bright eyes tensed when she saw me.

"Don't worry about him," said the old man. "Hey, I don't see little Gunter anywhere. Is he all better, then?"

"There was never much wrong with *him*," said Marthe. "But as for the other, bless him, I don't know if he'll ever be out of here."

"Well," said the old man, indicating me, "someone to see him, anyway."

"Go ahead, then. The more company the better, the poor man." Marthe nodded at a corner of the room partitioned off with a long rag. "He's had nothing but trouble since he came here. So far we've kept the master from knowing that he's not at work, but if he ever finds out . . ." Marthe shook her head.

I stepped among the sleeping mats, not breathing, and pulled up the rag.

Papa.

He was even thinner than I remembered him, dwindled down so far I could hardly tell where his legs were under the folds of the sheet. His hair was ashy gray.

My knees shook as I kneeled beside his bed. "Papa," I said.

His eyelids parted, and his bleary eyes welled up out of them and slowly focused on my face.

"Hannes?" he wheezed.

"It's me."

He reached out his spider-thin hand, and I took it in both of mine. He smiled, pressing wrinkles into his sunken cheeks. "Look at you," he said, blinking, trying to see better. "You're all grown up."

I held his hand and tried to think of something to say. "I still have your flute," I finally offered. "It's right here, in my bag." Leaving one hand around his, I fumbled with my satchel and brought out the little wooden flute.

"Oh, my." Papa chuckled, then coughed. "You've kept it."

Lifting his free hand with an effort, he ran a finger down the flute, pausing over the holes.

"Where's Mama?" I asked.

A hint of concern came into his eyes. "She's doing the laundry for Marthe. So that Marthe can care for me."

I felt my mouth harden.

My father fidgeted with his flute. "It bothers me to see her work so hard with me flat on my back . . ."

I couldn't keep the words out of my head: *If you make the decision alone, pay the price alone.*

"So . . . you really can't stand up?" I asked.

He shrank from me; his moist eyes swam away.

I lowered my voice. "You were sick once, Papa, but you got better. You got better, and you and Mama had plenty to live on . . ."

"Charity," Papa mumbled.

"So what do you call this?" I asked in a hot whisper. "When Mama does all the work, and this woman takes care of you!"

No response from the rheumy eyes.

"Papa, I don't understand; why did you have to go and disappear?"

"If I told you where I was, the Pipelord would keep paying me your wages. Apprentices don't get wages."

"Some do."

He shrugged. "I got sick."

"You got healed before. Look, Papa. Maybe you just need to walk a little every day. Get some fresh air."

He stared at the wall, ignoring me.

I couldn't stop myself. "Don't you want to get better?"

His wrinkled face twisted. "Hannes, I've had some time to think. Know what Mama and I need to do?" For a moment his eyes had some of their old shine. "We need to move to the eastern frontiers."

"In the meantime," I cut in, "you became a serf on this estate. How's it going?"

"Hannes, being a serf isn't so bad. You can't get kicked off. Supposedly." He flashed me a grin that baffled me. "You know, they're right there for you. They take care of you."

"I've heard how they take care of you," I said. "I've seen the landlord's son."

He didn't look at me, but he nodded.

"Papa," I said, my excitement growing as a plan took shape in my mind. "If you had another chance, if you could somehow just break out of all this and stop being a serf and stop being sick, would you do it?"

He cocked his head to one side, and then I heard it too: hoofbeats drawing up to the hut. Soon a dark voice shouted, "Where's the man who came about the land?"

My father's eyes widened, and he clutched at my hands. "Don't let him see me!"

"Papa," I said, looking into his eyes, "I'll get you out of here. I promise."

He pressed his flute back into my hands. Marthe and the old

serf were speaking with the steward. I wanted to push the flute under Papa's pillow, but ended up just stowing it in my bag instead. I stood up, jerked the rag curtain shut between my father and me, and picked my way across the floor.

"You *are* in there?" the steward shouted through the wall.

I had definitely lowered my standing by entering the hut. I opened the door and tried to look calm as I stepped out, squinting into the sunlight.

"So," said the steward, a lean, square-jawed man, as he looked me up and down from his horse, "who sent you?"

Marthe and the old man slipped quietly back inside.

"The Pipers Guild," I said, touching the pipe on my belt.

There was a flicker of uneasiness in his eyes as he peered down at it and frowned. "Well, then," he said. "Thirty thousand for the manor."

I clicked my tongue and shook my head. "More like five, you mean."

The man stiffened. "This estate is hundreds of years old. It feeds a whole city."

I swept my eyes across the fields. "Not very well, it doesn't. The serfs are badly overworked." I squinted back up at the man. "Nine thousand silver coins."

"Fifteen."

"Ten," I said.

He said nothing for a moment. Then he swung off his horse and yanked open the door to the hut.

"Who was he talking to in here?" the steward demanded.

The old serf frowned, and Marthe blinked. The steward scanned the room and stopped at the curtained-off corner. "Who's your patient, Marthe?"

"Just a sick old man," said Marthe, pursing her lips. "Please don't disturb him. He's resting."

The steward strode over toward the corner. I clenched my teeth as he quietly lifted the rag.

Papa looked as if he were asleep, with his shrunken chest gently rising and falling. The steward shot a look at me and dropped the rag back in place without a sound. He came back out of the hut and shut the door.

"You know," said the steward, a note of triumph in his voice, "if my master doesn't get that money by sunset on Sunday, he'll have to find a more profitable use for his serfs. Ten days' march away."

"What are you talking about?"

"Ten days' march. But I don't suppose that sick one would survive the journey."

My eyebrows furrowed. "Would you make a man march even if you knew it would kill him?"

"You are fond of your family, and I am fond of mine," the steward said with fierce calm. "My master has made some very clear threats. I *will* get him that money on time."

"Don't worry," I said. "I won't have any trouble getting the money. Ten thousand, right?"

"By sunset on Sunday," the steward answered. He thrust out his hand, and I shook it.

"Every last coin," I promised.

The man's eyes softened a little. "Well, then. Good day to you."

With a slight bow of my head, I turned and walked away from Marthe's cottage and back toward the road.

As soon as I was out of earshot, I laughed. This was too easy. Three days, three tasks: deliver a scroll, kill some rats, and set my father free.

THREE

Enter the Rescuer

Thursday, June Twenty-second, 1284, near Hamelin

HE WALLS OF HAMELIN ROSE GRAY BEYOND THE WESER River. Floating over the clustered roofs, the gold spire of St. Boniface Abbey welcomed me as though it were my war banner, flying over the place of battle.

Tugging like a dog on a chain to get at my mission, I forgot the Pipelord's warning.

"It may be worse than rats," he had cautioned, his hard mouth seeming to disapprove of my enthusiasm.

He had stood so close I could smell candle beeswax and sweat from his clothes as he grasped my shoulder with a tough grip. His eyes searched mine for something. If I had known what it was, I would have drowned all the rats in Christendom just to find it in myself and hold it up to him.

"Go well, Pied Piper. Stay alert."

A road by a dark forest should have put me on my guard. What's the point of years of combat training if one afternoon's good mood can erase it all? But so it was. My pipe was stowed in my knapsack. Behind me, the forest reached out with black branches and a smell of wet leaves and mold. Ahead of me, the city I would rescue spread warm and comfortable in the late afternoon sun.

I walked up to the edge of the steeply falling slope and leaned way out to take the city in. After the loneliness amid the crowded cots of the 'prentice house, I felt free as a bird, ready to fly to my city. I'd pipe the tune, gather the strings, and march down to the Weser leading my thousands of rats. The grateful townspeople would rush forward: streams of weeping grandmothers, shouting children, and admiring young ladies, merchants draped in multi-colored silk, artisans hoisting me onto their work-hardened shoulders. Released from a year of torment and starvation, they would hand over the promised reward with tears in their eyes. I would take the money back to Aerzen and set a village free. I would set my father free.

That was the Pipelord's plan and ten times more. Justice. I would go to Hamelin, and I would do justice. It was a kind of crusade.

My father's grandfather, Johannes, had crossed the Alps in the Children's Crusade. One of the darkest memories of my early childhood was his scowling, deep-lined face swallowing up the light, his thick eyebrows hanging over me, his beer breath mumbling how the heroes of the Children's Crusade ended up sold to Turkish brothels. I had no idea what a brothel was, but I knew it must be very bad.

Papa had named me for Great-grandpa Johannes, a man for whom *hero* meant "fool."

But there on the road overlooking Hamelin, I had no time for Great-grandpa Johannes. The first thing to step out and meet me there was a new song, and the failed men who shadowed me could not drown it out. I stood knee-deep in pungent-smelling wildflowers, surrounded by dandelion seeds spinning in the sunlight. Crickets hummed, and my march from Aerzen became a song. I had watched red foot, yellow foot, red foot, yellow foot, slicing along till I could feel the drum: *TUMtata TUMtata TUMtaTUM . . .* Now here came the pipe, stirring to life in my mind, with the eager working of the tongue and fingers. And words.

> *River of music—a piper's spell.*
> *River of rats—*

And then what? *A hideous smell? They came pell-mell?* No. I had it.

> *River of notes—a piper's spell.*
> *River of rats—from poor and wealthy.*

The last syllable gave an unexpected kick, all right. And that line would carry us from Hamelin to Aerzen, from the plague of rats to the deeper plague of injustice . . .

Suddenly, dry grass crackled behind me. I ducked and spun. Three men stood in a semicircle around me.

With a raspy voice the smallest one said, "Give us the bag."

"I'll give you all my money," I said. My voice cracked.

The biggest man's eyes showed some interest at the word *money*.

Keep talking; keep cooperating. I had to stay alive, to finish my mission. When the first numbness passed, thoughts came flashing.

Run down the slope? Too steep.

Quite a crossbow—not your ordinary bandit.

That one has a bad eye—get past him with a fake, a duck?

Spring sideways, and bang! A side kick to the top of that knee.

I shucked the bag off my shoulders. *Slowly. Don't upset them.* But there was something in it that I needed right now. The man with the crossbow raised it, and sweat burst out of me like juice from a grape.

"Easy," barked the rasping man, but not to me.

How to beat that crossbow if my first plan failed? *Sprint hard— to the left of that one, then run a tight zigzag and get out of range.* I could outrun them, at least those two. The small one was glancing back down the road; now he was smiling. He was used to hurting people. Well, I was here to deal out justice, and I was just inches from my pipe—that cool metal, flared end, fine openings. It would only take a few notes . . .

"Drop the bag!"

I yanked out the pipe.

They all shouted at once. The man with the crossbow fired, but his shot went wild as the rasping man knocked his hand.

The men surged forward when I pulled the pipe toward my lips. The small fellow drove his fist hard at my arm, in and upward, and the mouthpiece rammed into my teeth and mouth. I tasted blood, saw a blur of tears, dropped my pipe. Huge hands seized me from behind, pinning my arms. A blow to my cheek snapped my head sideways; a blow to my stomach knocked my wind out.

I jammed my foot down on the toes of the man holding me, twisted sideways in his loosened grip, and elbowed him in the chest. Then I smashed the back of my head into his nose, again, and again. I felt one of the others fumbling for me, and I kicked toward his hands. I must have connected, for there was a deep groan.

I was grabbed again from behind. Kicked hard in the groin.

Folding up, useless. *Whack!* Everything went black for a moment. Then, through watering eyes, I could make out the big fellow putting the pipe back in my bag, and *leaving* the bag on the ground.

Suddenly the air was full of shouting, running, hoofbeats, and neighing.

"It's all right, Wolf. Stop." This was a girl's voice, a voice that expected obedience.

As I lay tasting the dust, her horse thudded closer.

"They're not worth your time. Come help me with him."

"Miss Klara," replied a man's voice.

A fierce-sounding man, high up on horseback—a knight? Not with that accent. No, he was a commoner, like me. A bodyguard, then.

"Miss, they could come back—more of 'em."

Squinting through one eye, I saw my bag, flopped in the dust. Through the cloth I could make out the familiar shapes of my pipe and the scroll I must deliver, still safe inside.

The enormous voice pleaded, "Miss Klara, let's just leave."

"Wolf! We're not leaving him here." A soft voice, but she was stating a fact. It would be nice to see this Klara.

"Miss, look at him. He's just a commoner. He's filthy, he's bloody, he's . . . he's dressed funny." Then, in desperation, "He may already be dead."

"Wolf, look. *Crows, just waiting.*"

Wolf rumbled like a boulder coming loose. "Miss," he whispered, "I just don't like the look of 'im."

I managed a weak moan and heard a tight, dark *Tsk* from Wolf.

"He's alive, Wolf," said the girl. "Come *on.*"

Accompanied by a thunderous sigh, Wolf's enormous boots came crunching dangerously close to my head. His hand lifted my bag from the dust. Klara dismounted and knelt beside me. I felt skin like satin as gentle hands mopped behind my ear and tightened a cloth around my head.

"Wolf, what's the matter? Oh, your clothes. Use this to lift him."

Cloth rustled. I glimpsed crimson embroidered with gold. The giant's voice broke as he objected, "Miss, please, your cloak."

Then huge fingers wormed under my back and up onto the horse with me . . .

Now I was jogging along, sagging in the saddle ahead of the man named Wolf. As I leaned back, limp as a rag doll, on that burly

42

chest and those big shoulders, I felt blood caking on my face and didn't care. I felt filth covering my clothes and didn't care. I felt myself collapsing like a child on the giant who was saving my life against his will. And I didn't care. At first.

But once the free bleeding had stopped, once I had time to think about my position, it was humiliating to be helpless in the presence of this Klara, whose light hands had studied my wounds.

Klara, I wanted to say, *I am Hamelin's rescuer.*

A sound of riding came up fast from behind us. Wolf and the girl stopped.

"Good afternoon," said a rich voice, panting a little.

I turned my head, which brought on a needle of pain. As the newcomer spoke, I glimpsed a red beard.

"I saw blood. What happened?"

The three horses rode together, and Wolf and Klara told how they'd found me. Through Wolf's chest, I heard the story of how I should have died. His voice box boomed to the bones of my head; he cleared his throat like a cavern. As Wolf and Klara answered Redbeard's questions, the plodding of the horses, the smell of the sweet, hot grass and the conversation all swirled together in a pleasant mist.

". . . care for him at my house." This was the girl's voice, soft as a blanket.

"I don't know if that'll work, miss," Wolf growled.

The next time I opened my eyes, Redbeard's rich voice was rolling through my fog. He would care for me. The girl would visit; the girl would check on me. It all felt very nice.

Wolf's muscles tensed—he didn't think it was nice.

But Mr. Wolf, it is very nice. Bump along the road, bump against the shoulder. Someone said maybe the little sister could visit . . .

A sudden jounce of the horse brought my head up with a snap, recalling in vivid memory the explosion of the club on my skull. With a jolt I wondered if my toes and fingers still worked. I tried the fingers of my right hand. I couldn't feel them moving. Panic rose in my throat. I angled my chin to look at them, the five fingers that turned my breath into music and power, each one as precious as a child. Again I tried. They moved, just a little. I tested the other hand. It wiggled. I was entranced, watching my dirty brown fingers gloriously wiggling.

Now fear had cleared my head enough to grasp my new situation. The pleasure of returning to Hamelin, this time as savior rather than rescued—that was all gone now. I had meant to pipe through the city like a lightning bolt. Now I'd be lucky if I could hold the pipe.

───── FOUR ─────

Gudrun's Guest

Friday, June Twenty-third, 1284, Hamelin

HY ARE YOU HERE?" THE PIPELORD STARED DEEP INTO ME, and I began to sink.

"Sir, for justice. And mercy."

He raised his eyebrows. "Who needs justice and mercy?"

"Hamelin is suffering, sir. Aerzen too."

"Is that why you're here?"

"Sir, I want to bring honor to the guild. I want to finish my assignment. Please."

Again he asked me, "Is that why you're here?"

A child's voice woke me. "Oh, Miss Klara." The voice was growling. "He's all dirty, miss. Oh, miss. And he's heavy, miss."

I opened my eyes. I was lying on a mat on the floor, beside a kind of coffin with its sides gnawed. Nearby stood a walnut chest, lacquered and polished. To my left, a table, its legs covered with scrollwork. Twilight blue curtains with scenes from a hunt, leaping in gold. A deep fireplace set in a wall of dressed stone. Near the door of this elegant sitting room, a cunning rattrap—

And then I remembered everything: the bandits' hard blows, the girl's skillful hands.

The bandits had touched my pipe. I scanned the room for it, careful not to shift my pounding head. There. It lay peeking coyly from the old knapsack, where every rip and stain looked finer than the richest embroidery. And beneath the cloth, alongside the bulge of bedroll, slept the scroll I must deliver.

Meanwhile the voice continued, coming from a girl who sat at

45

my feet with her back to me. She looked to be about eight. Near her on the floor, cloths were draped over the brims of two basins, one with pink water and the other with red.

"He's hurt. He needs help," said the girl's voice, sweetened and pitched higher now. "Oh, he's bleeding. Oh, just look at the dirt!"

"Miss," answered the growly voice, "I can *feel* the dirt. What'll we do with him?"

The sweet voice spoke again. "Be nice to him."

Both voices came from the girl hunched in half profile. Unruly gold-brown hair that someone else had lavished time on spilled thick over her shoulders, with wisps flying this way and that. In one hand she held a toy bear with a clown doll flopping over his shoulder. In the other was a pretty clay doll with brown hair.

I held my breath and listened.

"He's a commoner," the bear spat out, as though the word had an aftertaste. The bear stomped up and down for emphasis, jingling the bells of the clown slung over him.

"Commoner or not, Wolf," argued the clay doll, "this man is dying."

The beauty and the bear debated my future, while exhaustion pinned me to my mat on the floor. Only my eyes could move. I let them roam for a moment over the field of play strewn on the floor around the child: dolls in various degrees of health, an acorn cap, a fine brass chain, a piece of chalk.

Meanwhile, with no agreement from the bear, the clay doll made preparations for her patient.

"Here. Put him here."

The bear lowered the clown to the floor, then retired offstage. Now the girl's free hand stretched out, and a tiny doll came onstage, a small, round girl doll with no legs, bobbing across the floor.

"What is that?" asked this newcomer doll.

"It's a man who needs help," the clay doll answered.

"He's dirty."

"I know," said the clay doll. Her voice grew motherly as she coaxed the new doll, "Gudi, could you please take care of him?"

"Oh, yuck." The legless doll jammed her face against the floor in despair. "Was he drunk and rats got him?"

"No. Listen, Wolf is going to clean him up. But can you feed him?"

The little round doll thought this over. She did this by bouncing from side to side.

"Well, all right. Because you know, actually I do feed my dolls."

"That's right," the clay doll agreed. "You are a very good mother to your dolls. And you *must* keep the rats away."

"Uh-huh." The tiny doll examined the clown. "Where'd you get him?"

"Beside the road."

"Will he die?" asked the Gudi doll. The clay doll heaved a sigh, as I strained my pounding head to watch. "I hope not."

The legless doll inspected the patient again. "How come his clothes are so funny?"

"I don't really know." Here the clay doll leaned close over the fallen clown, and her voice took on a quality I struggled to interpret. "You know, Gudi, a face can tell you more than clothes."

I inched my body upward to see the details, and my blanket rustled. The little girl turned, then sprang to her feet. I saw fear in her body and curiosity in her eyes.

"Good morning," I said.

No change. She stood there, ready to run.

"Can I play too?" I raised up the clown doll lying on the floor, stretched it near the footless doll, and wiggled its head. "Thank you, miss, for being kind to me." I reached the clown's floppy hand toward the footless doll. The girl watched me with eyes like a hunting cat's. The clown collapsed back on the floor.

"Help," I groaned for the feeble doll. "Heeelp. Where am I?"

The girl knelt down, her eyes never leaving me. She slowly picked up the footless doll, and her doll began speaking to mine.

"You are in Mr. Kunst's room."

"Are we in Hamelin?" wondered the clown.

"Uh-huh. What's your name?"

"Hannes."

"Hannes," repeated the girl. "Johannes."

"Yes. And you must be Gudi?"

Her eyes flickered over me. "Gudrun." She looked at my hosen. "Why are your clothes funny?"

"They're a gift from my master."

"You're not a jester?"

"No."

She considered this. "Oh. But actually your clothes are funny." Her frank eyes simply said, *In case you've never noticed.* With a deft motion, quick as a sparrow, she tucked a strand of hair behind her ear.

47

"Would you say these clothes are too bold, Gudrun?"

"I guess. Does that mean ugly?"

I burst out laughing, and she joined in, a little bit.

"Gudrun."

"Yes?"

"There was another girl." I pictured my rescuer on the trail, her serious eyes, her smooth skin, and a captivating frown when she concentrated. "The one who found me, Gudrun. I think—did she try to feed me?"

"No. *I* tried to feed you. Bread, and then later cheese." Gudrun smoothed her dress, clearly pleased with herself. "Actually Klara just felt your forehead. I brought all your food myself."

"Thank you. Thank you very much. Yes," I added, remembering snatches of my rescuers' talk on the road. "Her name was Klara."

"Uh-huh. And this morning—guess what? The housekeeper, Mrs. Rike, didn't feel good, and *I* had to make your oatmeal." Gudrun's face was radiant as she indicated a covered pot on the floor nearby.

But I was busy recalling the girl who had rescued me. "Mmm, that's terrible. Gudrun, she's not your sister, is she?"

"No!" Gudrun hooted with laughter. "Mrs. Rike's older than the Market Church!"

"No, no, I mean Klara. Is she your sister?"

"Yes." My caretaker sobered up completely and even looked a little unhappy with me, perhaps for my inattention to her story.

Now that I was hunting for it, I glimpsed Klara's shadow in the younger girl's thin lower lip, sharp chin, high forehead. But Gudrun's skin was the color of honey, while Klara's was cream.

"Klara saved me."

"Yes." Gudrun frowned. "You were by the road, with blood all over."

"And they brought me here to Mr.—"

"Mr. Kunst's house."

"Kunst."

"Yes, and I'm visiting you here, but actually this is not really my house. 'Cause like I said, it's Mr. Kunst's house. I check on your forehead too. And try to feed you. Wolf won't let you come to our house. He won't let Klara come here either, but she did come anyway. With me, of course. But she can't come today, because today she's at Town Hall."

Town Hall. I could go there, and—and what? I just wanted to see her. Was there a professional reason to do so? Well, I could thank her. The guild would approve of gratitude.

"What happened to you?" Gudrun asked.

"I was attacked. Three bad men beat me up."

Her eyes brightened. "Did you have any money?"

"A little."

"Did they get it?"

"I don't think so." As I twisted to reach for my bag, my leg thumped against the coffinlike thing. "Gudrun, did I—almost die?"

She launched into a laugh, then courteously stifled it to a quiet snort. "That's not a coffin. It's a rat box," she explained in a long-suffering teacher voice. "We put it over you when I go home."

Now I saw that the top was not solid but made of latticework.

She added, "The rats would've completely gotten you."

"Oh." I pulled out the pipe, its cool metal somehow reassuring, and held it to my cheek. I was still wondering what took Klara to Town Hall. Clearly a responsible young lady. Good. But of course wellborn. Meaning I could only be her charity project. I turned to Gudrun.

This leader of dolls seemed to be arranging her dependents at wood-block tables for a banquet. Gudrun did not see me as a peasant boy who lacked silver, land, and pedigree. She saw me as an adventure.

And yet Klara had visited me, herself.

With her banquet laid out, Gudrun turned back and observed, "They didn't get your flute, either."

"No. So Klara rides to other cities and visits patients and goes to Town Hall."

"Actually she can't go just anywhere, even though she thinks she should be allowed to go anywhere. Wolf always says, 'You're not just anyone's daughter.'"

On the last bit, Gudrun did the growly bear voice. It fit my memory of Wolf.

"So, Gudrun, whose daughter is she?"

"The mayor's, of course."

"The mayor is your father."

She nodded. That was all I needed. I had my mission; I had my pipe; I had my guide.

"Gudrun, may I ask your last name?"

49

She weighed my looks a moment. "Hofmann."

"Gudrun, I'm in a bit of a hurry. Could you take me to your father?"

"He's at Town Hall."

"All right," I chirped.

In fact, Town Hall wasn't just all right; Town Hall was perfect. I began to get up, with my arm, my abdomen, and especially my head throbbing at each twist.

Gudrun, however, wasn't going anywhere.

"So they didn't steal your money or your flute." This girl could hang onto a topic through a blizzard. "What did they actually want?"

I would tell Gudrun something that would make her take our trip to Town Hall as seriously as I did. "Gudrun, you know what? This is a special flute. I'm here to get rid of Hamelin's rats. And I'm going to use this flute to do it."

"Special?" She narrowed her eyes. "If you mean magical, we've had magicians before. About the rats."

"Gudrun, you haven't seen anyone with a flute like this."

"Can I hold it?"

"Sure."

She took the pipe and blew. A loud squeal came out, then rounded to a long, pure vibrato.

A well-fed brown rat entered the room with its ears flattened back and stared at us. The girl glanced back with no sign of surprise. But the rat began to creep in my direction and was joined by a second rat, long and gray. A third appeared, then another, and another, till Gudrun and I were in the center of a closing circle like a pack of wolves. Gudrun jumped up and hid behind me in a tight little ball. We could smell the musk of their fur and see their black eyes—and they looked *angry*.

I was up on one knee, swinging the pipe at them. They ducked but did not scatter. The largest one dashed in and leaped onto my foot. I knocked him off and was just putting the pipe to my lips when, with a thundering of padded feet, two enormous wolfhounds stampeded into the room, scattering the rats like chaff. Relief changed to terror in a moment, when the dogs turned on me, snarling and snapping. I chose my notes and gulped a lungful of air for my defense.

"Heel!" Though the word was not loud, it was spoken with authority. "Come here this instant!"

Panic drained from my muscles as the black beasts retired

meekly to the doorway, behind their master. It was the red-bearded man who had come along on the roadway.

Now I could feel Gudrun pressed shivering against my back, with her face beside mine. She whispered, "I've never seen the rats do that."

In fact, it had felt unnatural, like the attack on the road.

But our host was striding over to me. "Roth Kunst," he said, and grasped my hand in a warm, firm grip.

"My name is Johannes, sir," I answered, and added, "Hannes," the nickname that was the educated serf's apology for putting on airs.

"My pets been troubling you?" He kneeled and wrapped an arm around the massive neck and shoulders of each dog, nuzzling their ears and foreheads. "These foolish dogs have been a comfort in a town swarming with rats. And desperate people."

I told him his pets had defended me well.

"Enjoying my colleague's gear?" He indicated Gudrun's dolls, and my back and shoulders felt Gudrun wriggling. "Atmosphere's homier this way. And Gudrun's a fine nurse. Hm. She and I've had a time deciding what to make of you. She claimed you were a clown." His eyes took in my contrasting hosen.

Meanwhile Gudrun was gently bouncing side to side, reminding me of the legless doll.

"And what did I say, Gudrun?"

Gudrun pranced over to him, took his hand and, with an astonishing imitation of his voice and accent, declared, "Hm. More than a clown."

"And you said . . . ?"

Gudrun spoke into Roth's sleeve so I could barely hear: "Why would a clown carry a scroll?"

He tugged at a tangle of her dark-gold hair. "Johannes, this girl's a genius. She's a queen. Think I'll marry in Hamelin and adopt her." He cleared his throat. "Now, Gudrun, your friend and I need to be alone a moment. Take Thunder and Steel. See if you can keep them from liking you so much. I'm dying of jealousy."

Gudrun looked very important as she ordered, "Come," and the brawny dogs jumped to her side. She left the room, every third step a skip.

The door closed, and Roth turned to me. "How're you feeling?"

"All right, sir." Now it came home to me that in the rat-and-dog attack I had kneeled, I had crawled, I had swung my arms. My arms and legs were working, after all, but I felt sure that now I would pay for it.

"Never mind the 'sir.' Any pain?"

"My head hurts, and my arm . . ." I stopped short. "But my mouth . . ."

One of the most stabbing pains of the beating on the road had been that uppercut from the small man. He had driven the pipe up into my mouth. I was sure that I had chipped or lost a tooth, and my lip and the roof of my mouth had hurt and bled intensely. Now all of that was gone. I ran my tongue along the tops of my front teeth. No damage at all. I licked my lips. No hint of swelling. Yes, I could pipe now, with no problem.

"What about your mouth?"

"It's absolutely fine." So. Klara would see me not as a frog-lipped gargoyle but as a young man who on three separate occasions had been called not bad looking.

"Wonderful," said Roth. "Klara Hofmann did wonders with your cuts and bruises and whatnot."

I tested my memory out loud: "Bandits attacked me . . ."

"A man can't travel in these parts without bringing an army. Disgraceful. Lucky the girl and manservant came along—and me bringing up the rear."

"I am in your debt. Thank you for rescuing a total stranger."

"No need to remain so. You're not from Hamelin; that's clear. Well, neither am I. Hm. Now, who are you, exactly?"

"I'm an apprentice with the Pipers Guild. You may not have heard of them."

"I've heard a few stories." He knelt by a pitcher that stood near my mat and poured something bright into a cup, with a gurgling sound like music.

I sipped. With peasant instincts dreading things too fine for me, eager not to appear desperate in the company of a man of breeding, I reined in my desire to drain it all in one horselike gulp.

"Thank you. Anyway, the guild heard of the plague of rats. I was sent to help the town get rid of them."

"You were sent?"

"Yes. By the head of my guild." I nailed some emphasis on the word *head*.

"Hm. Well. Good luck. Seen enough rodents in a year to last

52

me a lifetime. So when're you going to send these rats back to hell, where they came from?"

"As soon as I've spoken with the mayor about the reward."

"Must be fascinating stuff—Pipers Guild work." He glanced at the pipe I held against my body. "Can't imagine the adventures you've had."

"Well, it's not really about adventure, sir. It's about justice."

"Hm. Doesn't the whole empire need more of that? And drop the 'sir,' by the way." He set down the pitcher. "All right. Let's say you drag off the rats. Why would you call that an act of justice?"

"Mr. Kunst, drowning the rats is the beginning. After that, I take the reward money; I march over to a town near here; I buy a certain manor. And my guild gives the land to the serfs who farm it."

"And that," he inquired, "that would be justice?"

"Their master treats them worse than animals."

Suddenly Roth's face turned grim, and his body trembled like a spring wound tight. "Johannes, anyone who talks the way you're talking, and does something about it—he'd better be ready for rejection. By *both* sides. Hm! You have any idea what justice costs the *judge*?"

He spat this out through clenched teeth—furious, but not at me. "Sorry," he said when he had composed himself. "Got carried away. You probably have no idea what I'm talking about."

Since he seemed to expect something, I hazarded, "Well, the guild does train pipers to . . . sometimes take up the pain of others."

He looked as if he were a thousand miles away.

Finally I said, "Mr. Kunst."

"Call me Roth."

I swallowed. "Um, Roth, what brought *you* to Hamelin?"

"Hannes," he said smiling and leaving his reverie, "I'm atoning for my sins." He jumped up and strode around the room while he spoke, making space for something large he had to say. "I've been in business, made some money, haven't always played by the rules. I won't bore you with sentimentality; here's the short version. I made a vow. Anyway, about a year ago, I heard of a massive need for charity: the Hamelin rat plague. I moved here."

"And how have you been helping?"

"Ah. Most business in Hamelin is tied to grain, and I can help Hameliners grow more of it. Most men don't know it's a new world out there. No idea how they're wearing out their own soil. And the biggest question of all . . ." He stopped and cleared his throat long and loud.

In the middle of my host's favorite subject, my head had dipped and my eyes had crossed. With a rich laugh, Roth clapped me on the shoulder and stood up.

"Welcome to Hamelin, stranger. You've had a nasty reception. Bandits, rats, dogs, and dull lectures."

When I tried to get up as well, knives of pain shot through my abdomen and head. Though I winced, I declined Roth's offer of help, gritted my teeth, and carefully sat back.

He moved the pitcher closer to my pillow. "I'm putting this where you can reach it. Now listen. Don't feel you have to hurry off to an inn. You need a full recovery. I'd be glad for your company."

At first I resisted, but in the end I simply thanked him.

He paused in the doorway. "One last thing. You and I both sound like good Saxons, all right, but the Hameliners'll pick up in a snap that you're not one of them. That may not open doors. And they don't love the Pipers Guild." He laid his hand on the door-knob. "All right. Get some sleep."

Roth left the room, humming an elaborate tune.

After a while Gudrun, my faithful guardian, tiptoed in, fortunately without Thunder and Steel. Seeing me burrowing into my pillow, she gathered her dolls, crept behind my head into the corner, and resumed her theater in intense whispers, which grew softer and softer.

With half-closed eyes I saw my bag. Suddenly I had to hold the scroll and know it was all right. Forcing myself against shooting pains, I stretched out my hand and lifted the bag. I breathed in its smells—a cheese I'd enjoyed in Aerzen, wildflowers picked before the attack—then loosened its leather cords, opened its neck, reached in, and drew out the parchment. The letter's seal was broken.

A plague on the bandits! Now I hated them more for what they had done to my mission than for what they had done to my body. Let them maim me if they must, but keep their filthy paws off my mission. Somehow in the fight the seal had cracked, and now Master Friedrich would think I had unsealed it myself.

Two lines of the Pipelord's sharp-angled handwriting were exposed. "*. . . compared to what this could mean, the suffering the rats have brought is child's play . . .*"

Compared to what?

Using my thumb, I unrolled enough to see the words above.

The phrases flashed: "*. . . problems far worse than its rats . . . the Unbound . . . fatal challenge to our guild . . . the other one . . .*"

What? My eyes were reading; my mind could not keep up. Before I knew what I was doing, I unrolled the parchment to start at the beginning. *My dear Friedrich . . .*

A small voice over my shoulder barged in on my whirling thoughts. "What's the Unbound?"

I froze, with my eyes locked on the phrase "*. . . worst trouble since the Unbound episode . . .*"

"Well," the voice insisted, "what is it?"

I tried to turn but felt a sharp twinge in my neck and hunched over. Gudrun knelt in front of me, felt my forehead, and gazed into my eyes.

"Gudrun," I murmured, "were you reading someone else's letter just now?"

She shrank as though I had struck her. I dropped the scroll and closed my eyes. The first wave of anger I felt was aimed at Gudrun. The second was aimed at me. I'd betrayed a trust with a confidential letter, and the Pipelord would hear of it.

"I'm sorry, Hannes."

Her fingers were stroking my ear, gentling the lobe. I was the clown doll.

"But actually there was one part I couldn't get." She took the unsealed letter from the floor, unrolled it, and pointed to a paragraph just past where I'd been interrupted.

. . . so perhaps you should keep an eye on him. Many brothers have questioned if I did right to choose him; many times I wondered if they were right. He has not been like other apprentices. This is connected to the question that you and I discussed last time, concerning the guild's future. Therefore I ask that you take . . .

The room fell away as I struggled to absorb the meaning of the words I was reading. Though I hungered to read to the end, I forced myself to roll up the scroll tight in my fist.

So—nothing was what it had appeared to be. I knotted up at the thought of more responsibility, more risk, more unknowns. I was facing some great danger alone.

"Gudrun, we shouldn't be reading this. I'm putting it back in my bag. I need to take it to a man and never touch it again. I'm already late. I'm very late."

I was sitting forward, slowly, pulling my feet under me. The back of my head throbbed where I had bashed the bandit's nose. I would not let myself think about Master Friedrich's reaction to the broken seal. He might discipline me by canceling my mission. Then my failure would be total. I couldn't think about it.

"Hey," she said. "They said you had to rest."

"I'm already late, Gudrun."

"But now I have to give you this oatmeal." Her eyes shone as she picked up the pot and lifted the lid to reveal a generous glop of porridge, hours old, now cold and well congealed.

"Gudrun, I'm really in a hurry."

She already had a large tablespoon loaded. "Mr. Kunst said feed you, and actually I have to feed you."

"Really, I feel full, Gudrun."

"I'm not taking you anywhere until you eat three bites."

I leaned over the bowl. I had never seen so much oatmeal riding on one tablespoon in my life. As I stretched my lips around it, Gudrun pushed it in deep in case I changed my mind. There was a crisis while I fought against gagging, then at last the spoon was out, the load was in, and the charge went down.

When I pleaded, Gudrun relented a little, and the next two spoonfuls were not quite as generous.

She stretched out her hand, pulled me up, and let me lean on her as I swayed. The pattern in the rug revolved a moment, and I spread my feet, fearing that I would be sick on priceless fabric.

"What are you late for?" asked Gudrun.

"I have a letter to deliver and a river of rats to drown." I clutched her shoulder, and she braced me. "But first I want to go to Town Hall and say thank you to Klara."

"Who wrote that letter?"

"Gudrun—"

"I won't tell anybody."

I sighed. "A man we call the Pipelord."

"He likes you, right?"

I looked into her eyes, which were curious about everything they touched. "Gudrun, I've been asking that question for six years."

My faithful nurse took the bedroll from my knapsack, put in the scroll, and reached for the pipe, but saw that I had no intention of parting with my weapon till we were past Thunder and Steel. She

56

shouldered the bag and slipped her arm through mine. "I can take you to Town Hall," she said. "Klara'll be happy."

"She will? Why?"

"To know she was right."

"About what?"

"You're not with the circus."

We hobbled toward the door.

Heavy footsteps sounded just outside it. The door opened and was filled by a man the size of a bear. I recognized Wolf, the man who had carried me to town on his saddle. He walked up to me and looked me up and down before he spoke.

"Where would you be goin'?"

Gudrun answered for me. "He wants to see Klara."

Wolf squinted at me. "Miss Klara is none o' your concern."

"I wanted to say thank you."

"I'll take her that message."

I tried to think of something wise like the Pipelord would have said, but all I could come up with was "She saved my life."

Wolf clenched his fists, as though he would rather solve this problem with his hands than with his tongue. In the end, he muttered, "She did that."

"And thank you, sir, for helping her save my life."

"Don't *sir* me." Wolf had two nasty puncture scars, one near each eye. "Bandits get anything off you?"

"I don't think so. You came just in time."

"They knocked you one good, though."

I smiled and wished I were sitting.

"Who are you?"

"My name is Hannes. I was coming to—"

Gudrun broke in. "He has a magic flute. Show him."

Obediently, I held out the pipe for inspection. The man's eyes never left my face.

"Miss Gudrun," he said, "I need a minute alone with your flute player."

I had no desire to be left alone with Wolf, but still I sighed with relief that Gudrun would not be talking to Wolf about my flute, after what she had just read.

"All right," answered Gudrun, transferring my support hand to Wolf. "But don't step on the dolls. Especially this one." She pointed to the clay doll. With a last look back at the flute, she scampered from the room.

Wolf dropped my hand, which Gudrun had so conscientiously placed in his, closed the door, and again stepped up so close I could feel the heat coming off him. With no change of his stony expression, he asked, "How you feeling?"

"I was just going to Town Hall," I replied, wanting to hold the doorjamb.

"You didn't answer my question."

"I think I can make it."

He snorted. "So where were you goin' out on the road? When they hit you."

"Hamelin."

"You're in Hamelin now."

"I know. I'm here to get rid of the rats."

Wolf pursed his lips. "We've had cartloads of rescuers. Most of 'em have done more harm than good."

I was too busy standing to reply.

He went on. "Have you seen the crusade memorial in Hamelin's Town Square?"

"No."

"Hamelin hates heroes."

"But I'm not . . . I'm not just here on my own. I'm from the Pipers Guild."

"'Course you are. You got any idea what happened here six years ago?"

"That was a renegade. The guild came to stop him and—"

"So you know what Hamelin thinks about your precious Pipers Guild?"

I was too tired for this.

"None of our saviors ever looked as young as you." He gave a withering glance at my stubble. "None of 'em was dressed in clown suits." His scowl took in the hosen. "None of 'em arrived in Hamelin on their backs."

He brought his face close to mine. He smelled of garlic sausage.

"Miss Klara picked you off the trail like a homeless puppy—it was mercy and nothing more." His eyes drilled into mine. "It's my job to protect Miss Klara from her mercy."

"And it's my job to deliver Hamelin from its rats."

"You can do that without her."

"The rat problem takes me to Town Hall in *any* case."

He furrowed his brow, backed up a half step, and expelled an enormous lungful of air. "We're tired o' fakes. What I mean to say is, sometimes a crowd gathers, and sometimes it gets ugly."

"I understand."

Wolf shook his head, rubbed his chin. I could hear the rasping whiskers.

"You'll need to meet the council, of course."

"All right."

"They need to approve you. That's the procedure."

"I'm ready."

He sighed. "And I got to find six witnesses."

"Fine," I replied. "I'll be waiting for you at Town Hall."

"Wait a minute. Today is a special meeting." Wolf's nostrils flared. "Listen, this whole business may have to wait."

"The people of Hamelin have waited long enough. And I *will* take care of the rats."

Wolf looked into my eyes till I grew uncomfortable. "Now *that* might be—" he began, then interrupted himself. "Unless you're lyin', in which case, pipe or no pipe, I'll beat you soft. But *that* might be just the present she needs today."

I said nothing.

"Sure you can walk?"

"Yes."

"All right then. Meet you at Town Hall—in the lobby, mind. Miss Gudrun!"

And so, with Gudrun taking me by the hand and Wolf leading me out of the hall, I resumed my mission, pausing every few steps as the world spun around. I was going to meet a kind, energetic young lady named Klara.

FIVE

Many Happy Returns

Friday, June Twenty-third, 1284, Hamelin

 T LAST I WAS UP AND OUT IN THE CITY OF MY MISSION. I PUT the bandits and the scroll out of my mind. What mattered now were three tasks: rats, coins, serfs.

After Wolf went his way, Gudrun led me through overhung streets toward Town Hall. The rats that wandered everywhere—those I was prepared for. But the sight of beggars at every major cross street—beggars too old or deformed or sick to survive long in a town that was hungry—that sight bore down on me. For so many, so weak, so poor, I had already come too late. Rats meant hunger, and already the cupboard was bare. Hamelin was a milling town, where a grain shortage was a deathblow.

Some of the people I passed were starved to the point of feebleness, skin stretched tight over bones. What could they do about the rats when they were too starved to protect themselves, and the rats, from sheer numbers, were too starved to feel fear?

We made our way down one long alley, all in shadow, with windows that never opened. Ahead, I noticed a low gray heap. As we drew nearer, I could see the twitching, seething motion that I was already growing used to: another tribe of rats scrounging another pile of garbage. But a few steps brought me close enough to see that the pale thing thrust from the mound toward me was a human foot, gnawed to the bone.

Gudrun, accustomed to putting these horrors behind her, tugged me forward. I felt weak; I closed my eyes. She'd led me through the miserable poor and their losing battle with the rats. Let her take me to the safety of Town Hall. I couldn't save them all;

I couldn't save from indignity those who were already dead. But as we passed the body and the feeding rats, I knew I had to stop.

"Gudrun."

She looked at me.

"Go up ahead."

She stayed where she was.

Swinging my pipe, I drove away the rats. Their reluctance filled me with rage. At last I could see the body. It was a woman, with the thinnest hand I had ever seen. Something was wrong with the face. Some of it was missing. I felt my feet and hands go cold, and I vomited, with spasms and coughing. I hung my head, panting and spitting and wiping my face. Under the woman I saw something, and my whole body began to tremble. I set my foot on her shoulder and rolled her onto her back. She was holding an infant.

I must do something. I could do nothing. I was frozen.

The mother had succeeded in protecting her infant's face. It was beautiful. The skin was clear and smooth. The eyes were large and blue. I bent closer. Even before I touched the child's cold and rigid neck, I knew. The mother's tightly curled body had protected her child but in the process had smothered her.

Gudrun pulled me away, and now I had no strength left to resist.

"It's been that way ever since the rats," she explained. "Klara says if you stop for every single body, you'll go crazy."

Hamelin was wounded deeper than I had thought. But I would *not* go crazy. No. My mission was back on track. I shook the darkness from me, clenched my fists, and counted out the steps to my goal, pushing my fingernails deep into my palms as I ticked off my objectives: Town Hall, permission, rats, reward, Aerzen, serfs.

From time to time the horizon tilted and Gudrun had to prop me, her eyes shining with pride. But suddenly I was really falling. I landed like a sack of flour, and my face hit hard. Something crunched—a tooth breaking? I tasted blood, as well as Hamelin's paving stones and Hamelin's dust, flavored with years of fine-trodden horse droppings. I licked my lips as I raised my pounding head. A group of children approached, laughing. I rotated my head till I could make out faces. There in the front stood the beautifully dressed boy from the Aerzen manor.

He stepped closer as if to study me. His shoes were of bright new leather.

"I thought that outfit looked familiar. In Aerzen you were pretending to be a landowner. Who do you think you are today?"

I said nothing.

"It's gotten lost on its way to the circus," cried the boy, turning to his friends.

The loudest laughter came from a pretty brunette, about ten or eleven years old.

The boy addressed her. "Frieda, do you think we can help it?" He shouted down at me, slowly, as if to a dimwitted child: "Hey! Where exactly were you going?"

I rolled over, away from the snickering knot of them. I would not give them the satisfaction of seeing me bloodied. In spite of my swimming head, I stood quickly and wiped at my face with my hand. Judging from the smear of dirt and blood streaked across my palm, I had only made things worse.

The boy's vast self-assurance unnerved me. I was faint-headed and looked strange; he was coolheaded and looked elegant. A great man like the Pipelord would have felt peace. I was not the Pipelord.

But I had no need to plan a response. Gudrun stepped between us, an egg-shaped stone in each hand.

"This man," she stated, "is a guest of Mayor Hofmann." Her voice, her stance, and her savage smile all told the same message: she could not wait for one of them to step toward me.

The boys, who seemed to recognize her, chose to pass up the challenge. The leader spun around with a snort. As though Gudrun and I were hopelessly beneath his interest, he sauntered off, and his friends with him. One of the last ones to turn away made a face as if to say, "Just wait till next time." When Gudrun raised her right hand, the challenger picked up speed.

When they had left, she dropped the rocks back into the leather bag over her shoulder, drew from inside it a clean cloth, and asked me to kneel.

"Muuud," she said, mothering me. "*Tsk*. And bloooood." Then, saving the worst transgression for last place in her list: "And vomit."

Using a kerchief and spit, she swabbed my face, especially the mouth and chin. I spat out a small piece of—gravel. Not a tooth after all. But what would my clothes and I look like by the time this mission was over?

"Gudrun, I'd like to talk to the council—"

"I know, but actually you walked *really* slow coming here, and we might miss Klara, and I do want to show you to Klara."

I muzzily agreed and stood. "Gudrun, who were they?"

"The leader's name is Strom. I've met him before," she answered, and clamped her jaw. "Well, Klara has Wolf, but I have these."

She chose one of the rocks out of the bag, took aim at a hitching post over twenty yards away, and let fly. The rock connected with a *ponk!* so high in pitch that I was sure Strom and his friends had made the right decision.

Gudrun had enjoyed the meeting with Strom and company. Even with the interference of me on her arm, I could feel her light body wanting to skip on every third step. My Hamelin family was full of surprises.

We rounded one more corner, and I stopped. For the first time in six years, I was looking at Hamelin's Town Hall, this time by daylight. On the broad post-and-timber façade, bright plaster set off the rich green of the shutters. Every corner was crowded with sculpture designed to impress. The building's size was suffocating; its color made the town feel shabby; its gaudy hodgepodge of shapes had nothing to do with the simple wood-and-stone rhythms of the homes around it. In a Hamelin wracked with hunger, Town Hall looked obese.

"Klara says it's the finest town hall in Saxony," Gudrun informed me.

I replied that it certainly made a strong impression.

"And so important for the morale of the city," Gudrun quoted, with an astonishing imitation of a smug male voice, as we headed for the stairs.

"Who says so?"

"Mr. Bauer. Vice-mayor." Her lips held the words like a mouthful of vinegar, and I found myself imagining: Bauer—*ponk!*

Halfway across the square, we came to two objects that were familiar and strange as though seen in a dream. Here was the pillory, from which the beautiful girl had released my predecessor, the rebel Anselm. When I touched its rough wood, I felt as though I had stepped into a shadow no one else could see. And here was the monument behind which I had hidden. It was a four-sided, shoulder-high block of granite, carved with words and images. I stepped closer to read it: *From this square our children set out and never came back: from*

Aerzen, Oldendorf, Muender, 130 children in all. God rest their souls. The Children's Crusade, Anno Domini 1212.

The simple legend hit me like a stone. Looking at the carving on the Aerzen face of the monument, I drew in my breath. There stood the woman of Aerzen, fist raised to heaven. Before her stood a crowd of people, cowering at her words.

Suddenly I remembered another verse of that old song from my childhood:

> *The people of Hamelin remember her still,*
> *That angry old woman of Aerzen town.*
> *For what if one day all her words are fulfilled,*
> *And their children go where they cannot be found,*
> *Like the son of the woman of Aerzen town?*

But I was standing at the door of Hamelin's Town Hall, thirty yards from my reward, surrounded by the victims I would rescue. I didn't want to remember the song my father had taught me, or the flute he had abandoned. This was a moment for pipe and drum, for feasting. The rescuer had come.

Gudrun was blinking at the memorial. "Great-grandpa was never the same after that."

"What?"

"My great-grandfather. They said he could preach like Peter the Hermit. Before, I mean. Oops—look, we better get up the stairs while we can."

She was right. As we had hesitated by the monument, a knot of beggars had come down the steps. Their thin hands stretched out toward us. Their thin voices proclaimed their desperation and their blessings on us.

Together Gudrun and I waded through them up the deep, high stairs and heaved open the vast wooden door. From an alcove a withered-looking man glared at us, stood slowly, then recognized Gudrun. With a voice so raspy I wanted to clear his throat for him, he barred the way.

"Mayor Hofmann is taking no appointments today."

"Good morning, Mr. Krueger. My father will be very glad to see this visitor. And actually we are in a hurry, and it is very important." She clenched her fists on the *very*.

"This is your sister's birthday party," intoned Mr. Krueger, his eyes gleaming. "I'm afraid your father won't be wanting to do any business today."

"Please, Mr. Krueger. It really is important. This man is my guest. And he's in Hamelin because Klara invited him, and it's her birthday and everything. Actually, Miss Hofmann will be *especially* glad to see him."

Mr. Krueger's raised brows and pinched lips showed his lack of enthusiasm for this unholy alliance.

Inspired, Gudrun added, "I've brought him here as a birthday present—to surprise her!"

Mr. Krueger sharpened his gaze as if he were about to pronounce sentence on a criminal. "You take him in. Then if they'll see your guest"—a dry glance in my direction—"you may leave him and come right back out. This birthday is an occasion for, ah . . ." And now at last he did attempt to clear his throat. "It's for adults."

"Thank you, Mr. Krueger."

We passed the desk, with the watcher glaring all the way.

At the end of a dim corridor, the left-hand wall yawned open suddenly to overlook a cavernous central chamber below. Laughter drifted up, growing crazed and ghostly in the stone-lined spaces. Below us stretched a long table surrounded by overfed men with fur at their collars and silver tankards in their hands. Between the slurring speakers and the echoing walls, I could make out every fifth word.

A moment passed before I noticed a slender young lady near one end of the table. Her eyes stared straight ahead. To her right, at the head of the table, stood a huge man dressed in an elaborate robe, with a heavy gold chain around his neck. He punctuated his speech with grand gestures, speaking toward the young lady, who showed not an ounce of celebration.

Gudrun punched me. "There she is."

In my first clearheaded look at Klara, I saw her dark hair flowing to a slim waist, a tide of skirt fabric draping about her, and long sleeves drooping from the hands clasped under her chin in a way that matched her melancholy face. Her pensive frown drew me like a smell from childhood.

Now the councilman with the gold chain chortled as one of his colleagues fell out of a chair. An uproar arose, and I made out the phrase *dancing girls*. The men somehow made it to their feet and began shuffling out, the man with the chain stepping over his colleague on the floor. Klara's head sank onto her hands, like a sail drained of the last breath of wind.

Gudrun and I wound down the stairs into the room below and approached her. Klara seemed small in the empty room, where already a few rats were sniffing at crumbs. Gudrun nudged her sister's arm.

Klara looked up. In her rich red and gold dress, trimmed in red velvet at the throat, her fair skin was stunning.

"Klara, here's the man you found. My clown."

Klara put out her hand. I clasped it, memorizing its five smooth fingers and its secret palm, and, with a prayer that I was not violating etiquette, raised it slightly toward my bowed head.

"Johannes of Oldendorf," I said. "Thank you for saving my life."

"Happy birthday, Klara," said Gudrun, giving her sister a hug, then me an over-the-shoulder wink.

"How are you feeling, Johannes?" Klara asked, offering me a chair.

As we talked about the attack and my recovery, her large gray eyes never left my face. And when Gudrun, swinging her feet in her giant armchair, related her adventures with her clown—our doll duet, our battle with the rats, our wobbling progress to Town Hall, our face-off with Strom and company—Klara Hofmann laughed. Her laugh soared to the high ceiling of that dark place and blessed it. I knew right then that Klara was a singer as sure as I was a piper. In my imagination she began singing a song I had written, as I accompanied her on the pipe.

I drifted back to the present to hear Klara praising my rapid comeback. And without commenting, I noticed hers: the Klara talking with me looked nothing like the miserable Klara that Gudrun and I had seen from the hallway above. Klara's eyes grew still wider when she learned I had come from Koeln, and she asked a number of questions about life in the city.

There I sat, a boy who'd grown up as a peasant with dirt under my nails, while a mayor's attractive daughter smiled at my jokes and admired me as the resident expert on big-city life. I completely forgot about Hamelin's needs till Klara said, "Well, then, is there anything I can do for you?"

Gudrun leaned forward. "Actually, Hannes has a plan to get rid of the rats. And he's *not* a fake."

"Really?" said Klara. She gave me a curious look, and for a moment there was silence. "Well, a happy birthday after all. But Mr. Bauer gave strict orders for only councilmen to be let in today. How on earth did you get past Mr. Krueger?"

Carried away with myself, I hammed looking this way and that and whispered solemnly, "Gudrun and I have our ways, but I won't tell."

Klara froze and stared at me.

"Miss Hofmann."

"Yes."

"Is something wrong? With my face?"

She apologized but kept studying me.

"I did fall on the way here."

"Oh," she said from faraway, and shook her head. "It's just . . . Is this your first time in Hamelin?"

"I was here six years ago."

"Six . . . ?" Her eyes widened. She shut them and shook her head.

"Miss Hofmann, what is it?"

She looked directly at me and said, with an intensity that almost embarrassed me, "I'm glad a man has come to Hamelin to do some good today."

I simply smiled, in no hurry to end this moment.

"You need to speak to the mayor—to register as an applicant for the reward."

"Yes," I replied. "That's why I'm here."

"I'll find out where the mayor is. Gudi, you must go home now."

"Whatever you say, Mommy," said Gudrun, and slouched toward the stairs.

"But *you* stay here," insisted Klara, beaming. "You shouldn't even be walking today. I'll try to find my father. He might be in his office getting ready for another meeting."

Klara left me there, in the dark belly of Town Hall. After some time, I grew curious about the sounds of music and raucous laughter coming from one of the side rooms nearby and went to investigate. Perhaps the mayor was there.

The door swung open farther than I'd planned. In the windowless room, torches flickered on the walls. Dancing girls, some scattered among the councilmen, turned empty faces toward the door and straightened up. As I entered, a hush spread.

Only one man seemed relaxed—the man with the gold chain, whom I'd noticed before. He took me in with a confident smile, then rose to an impressive height, shucking off like a napkin the young lady who'd been perched on his lap; she and her plate of fruit fell to the floor. He came and stood over me. Everything about him—head and hands and voice—was enormous.

"Permit me to introduce myself," he boomed, riveting me with his eyes while playing to the councilmen. He was handsome in an imposing way but had several scars similar to those I had noticed on Wolf.

"I am vice-mayor of the city of Hamelin," he said.

So this was Gudrun's Mr. Bauer. The dancing girls and council-men seemed to be holding their breath, watching the two of us.

"I am Johannes of the Pipers Guild," I answered. In customary guild fashion, I showed my pipe. The room grew cold. "I've come to apply for the reward—for clearing the city of rats."

The vice-mayor frowned as he sized me up. "What a disappoint-ment. I saw your outfit and thought you might be the next number in our program."

Snorts of laughter erupted around the room, and I shoved the pipe into my bag. I closed my eyes and saw the mother and child under the seething rats. I said, "I thought you might be a town council."

The vice-mayor's comedy vanished, and he stepped closer. "A member of the Pipers Guild lectures our council on the needs of Hamelin. Gentlemen, isn't it rich?"

"There was a promised reward," I said. "Ten thousand silver coins, correct?"

"Well, well." Mr. Bauer eyed me. "So businesslike for a clown."

The tension in the room dissolved in relieved laughter, and the vice-mayor, turning his back on me, slumped onto a couch. "That is the correct sum. How do you propose to earn it? Dance a jig till they follow you out of town?"

Once again a wave of laughter broke; even the dancing girls tit-tered. Then all went still.

"Yes, sir."

No one laughed.

"May I deal with the rats, sir?"

The vice-mayor looked directly into my eyes.

"Gentlemen," he said, with a lightning-quick glance at the pipe.

"If this street urchin, who seems to have made a point to roll in hog swill on his way here, were merely begging, we would show our customary compassion and give him a share of what's on the table. But no—he is a member of the Pipers Guild. Considering his tone, we have no doubt he has come to be our judge. We have no doubt he plans to use his little pipe for spells and blessings . . . and *curses*. We know what that means, don't we?"

Amid spilled drinks and rumpled clothing, faces that had been soft with festivity now grew hard. Once again I felt that sinking in the gut; my mission was slipping through my fingers. None of this was in the plan. The credentials I had hoped would buy me good will had made me a public enemy.

"Who on the Town Council of Hamelin wishes to sponsor this wayfarer on his mission?"

Deadly silence.

This was madness. I had come to rescue a city drowning in rats.

"Mr. Vice-mayor."

"Yes."

"I *will* take care of the rats."

"We do not recognize you. We do not give you leave. We do not promise payment to your kind."

"But, sir—"

"Surely," he interrupted, "surely it's obvious that you are not a welcome guest in Hamelin."

"Surely it's obvious, sir, that your people are suffering while you—" My voice rasped to a stop. In a moment I would be shaking. All the men in the room were looking at my right hand. It was in the bag, wrapped around the pipe, my knuckles aching from their grip.

I glanced around me. Here were the rats.

SIX

The Cupboard Is Bare

Friday, June Twenty-third, 1284, Hamelin

A HINGE CREAKED BEHIND ME.

"Excuse me," Klara said. "Where did my father go?"

"He's in his office working on his speech," said Mr. Bauer, smiling too much. "He declined to join this part of your birthday celebration."

Klara darted a red-faced look at me that said, *Let's go.*

The vice-mayor turned like an orator to the councilmen and their companions. "Gentlemen, I think we want to bid our guest a kind farewell. May God speed him elsewhere on his highly important business." He stood very close to me. "And now, if you'll excuse us, you have interrupted a birthday party."

"Excuse me," I said, turned on my heel, and strode from the room.

Klara followed me, popping through the closing door and over to me as though I were the last board left floating after a shipwreck. Through the door we heard the drum and lute resume. Someone inside made a loud comment, provoking hoots of laughter. For a moment we stood there, saying nothing.

"I'm sorry . . ." she began. The music behind us grew louder. "I've never seen them like this."

"Miss Hofmann," I said, dizzy again, "I think I'd better sit down before I fall over."

"Of course." Now she was my nurse again, her hands hovering over me. "You really shouldn't have come out for another day or two."

Through the door came rhythmic clapping and whistling, men's laughing and women's playful screaming.

"Let's not stay here. Can you make it upstairs to my father's office?"

I nodded, and we headed through the banquet hall toward the stairs.

"Oh."

At the sound of that one syllable, my eyes followed hers. A line of light from the high windows lit a path on the floor; everything else disappeared in shadow. To one side, half under the table, the councilman who had collapsed earlier still lay unconscious on the floor, where his colleagues had left him. The shadows around him were moving. Rats.

I sprang forward and kicked at the writhing mass. A rat smacked hard against the wall and lay twitching. The rest scattered with a clacking of claws on flagstones. My vision went black, and I fell to my knees, panting.

Klara rushed to my side and began examining the motionless man, who just then snored softly. We both laughed, and we both stopped ourselves.

"Doesn't seem to be any blood," I said. "Is there someone who can watch him?"

Klara straightened the man's shirtfront.

"This is Reinmar Lachler," she said gravely. "Grain merchant and town councilman. Last night I respected him and wanted to be like him. Then I turned eighteen." She shook her head.

Still hoping that Klara might remember our first day together as a pleasant one, I said, "Happy birthday, Miss Hofmann."

"Yes," she answered. She smoothed the man's wine-stained collar. Her face contracted, and she whispered, "I hate them." She jerked her head toward the room we'd just left. "I heard him through the door. The way he treated you . . ."

"Don't worry about it."

For a while we leaned together over the snoring, drunken councilman.

Klara flicked away tears. "You were great. With him in there."

As she looked toward the room with the dancing girls, her eyes, crosscut by a shaft of light, were so gray that I stared, and was still staring when those eyes turned and met mine. Klara Hofmann blushed. I memorized that moment. I memorized the way the mayor's confident daughter dropped her gaze, licked her lips, straightened her hair, ran her hand over her sleeve.

It took only three seconds, but I would review that scene in my mind twenty times a day, asking, *Why would a young woman blush while talking to a young man? Could it be anger? Could it be the temperature of the room?*

She said nothing for a long time, then finally asked, "Are you comfortable?"

"Excuse me?"

"You wanted to sit down. Are you all right?"

"Of course. I'm fine." In fact, the high ceiling was revolving.

Klara got up. "We better get you registered."

She offered me a hand, raised me more easily than I expected, and called a serving girl to sit with the unconscious councilman.

Now we were together on the steps. The last beam from the window struck highlights in her hair. In the stairway's darkness, the gold of her sleeve was disappearing from sight. Her footfalls were just ahead of me, now the flash of her white hand, now her silhouette. We were almost to the top. She turned. I still stood below her, on the level of her waist.

"I'm sorry about your birthday," I said. "But I'm going to give you a birthday present you'll never forget."

She cut me off. "Before we get to my father, I need to say something about what you've seen here today." She led me up the last three stairs to a bench in the corridor, and we sat.

"My father invited me to my first council meeting on my eighteenth birthday." She spoke in a low voice; we knew that the doorkeeper, Mr. Krueger, was likely at his post around the corner. "I was going to be part of my father's work, serving Hamelin. I couldn't wait. The party was a surprise. They asked me to sing. My heroes toasted me.

"Then my father had another event to get ready for, and he left. The party changed . . ." She shuddered. "But I promise you, my father will take these problems in hand."

I nodded wisely.

"So," she said with sudden, energetic brightness, "tell me your plan. For the rats." Her eyes were large and bright as she leaned toward me.

Here it was—the moment with Klara I'd been hoping for, the moment to whip out my golden pipe with a flourish, play a grand tune, deflect her admiration, celebrate the guild's might. But my moment had already been wrecked. One morning had taught me

73

that in Hamelin the empire's most honorable guild was as well respected as stable filth.

Still, Klara was waiting for my answer. I drew the pipe from my bag as though it were a diamond ring and whispered, "This."

Klara looked, then sighed.

"I'm with the Pipers Guild," I said stupidly.

"Well!" Her light tone was full of effort. "Have you ever played for rats before?"

"This will be my first time with a large number of them. I'm an apprentice. It's my first solo mission. Miss Hofmann, people in Hamelin . . ." I balled up my fists. "They shrivel up when I mention my guild. I'm used to that name *opening* doors. Look, I know what happened here six years ago. But that was a rebellion—it left scars on my guild as well as on your town. And the guild fought alongside Hamelin to deal with the renegades."

Klara studied the folds of her gown.

"At least," I added, "that's the way my guild sees it. Hamelin has a different view, I take it?"

Her shoulders went slack. With her eyes still fixed on her lap, she said, "Let me tell you about the Hameliner I know best: me. When I was twelve, two young men died in this town on the same night. It was a nightmare. They died . . ." Klara's eyes were steely but wet as she bit her lips shut. "I think they died because of me." The words landed like a stone in a pond deep inside her.

"I'm sorry, Miss Hofmann."

"But you already know this story."

"What?"

"One of the two young men who died was some kind of a leader in your guild." She gave me a strange look. "And you were here."

I stared at her. In my mind I saw a broken-looking figure limping down an alley, a small girl struggling with a rusty lock—and here she was, sitting in front of me, much changed. But I could see it now, that childish face hidden under this one. And something else: an inch-long scar near the left eyebrow.

Klara lowered her eyes. "Now it's my turn to be studied." She fingered the scar. "This scar is a gift. Without it the Hofmanns would have been known as the unscarred family, and that would be very bad."

"I've noticed a lot of Hameliners—"

"Yes. Theirs are from crows. Mine is from a flute." She went on,

"If I told my mother these two stories—that night and this day—she'd say you were an angel."

"What? The Hofmann family keeps pulling me out of the dirt. How could I be an angel?"

"On the two worst days of my life, you appear out of nowhere." She whispered, "You saw me release Anselm. Now here we are again."

And Klara Hofmann, even now that she knew who I was, smiled. We were old friends, sharers of an ancient secret. I wanted to say, *I have remembered your face and your kindness for six years.*

She stood up. "If you can make it, we'd better go see my father."

"Miss Hofmann."

"Yes?"

"I do need that reward money. Urgently. For a charitable purpose that is . . . urgent."

"Fine. We'll talk to the mayor."

"Miss Hofmann, I wonder if we could *look* at the reward fund."

"Why?" She glanced down at the pipe in my hand.

"If you prefer, you can go in the room alone. I just want you to look at the fund."

"Why?" she asked again.

"Something in the way the council reacted to my request . . . I just want to make sure it's safe and accounted for."

Again she offered the hand. Again I took it and memorized it.

"Let's go," she said, a little harshly, and hoisted me up.

"I'm sorry, Miss Hofmann. It seems I've offended you."

"Mr. Piper, I save your life, and you show up here, a complete stranger, and start pointing fingers. Who asked you to do anything but get rid of the rats?"

"I'm here by commission of the Pipers Guild."

"Did the guild commission you to insult my father?"

"Your father?"

"If the fund is empty, it would mean my father is an incompetent mayor—at best. I cannot believe that. But . . . Hamelin does have a rat problem." She sighed. "So all right. Come on."

I was standing inches from Klara Hofmann, my beautiful rescuer. And here was the outcome: she was unimpressed by my guild and insulted by my efforts to help her town.

To my relief, we turned the other way and did not pass the brooding eyes of Mr. Krueger.

"I certainly didn't mean to insult Hamelin," I insisted as I

75

hobbled. "Hamelin seems to be a nice little town, apart from the . . . effects of the plague."

"A nice town? I don't know." She shrugged. "A couple weeks ago something happened that's never happened before. Someone broke into my room. He took a few things, some earrings, but he turned the place upside down, like—he was angry or something. Wolf couldn't figure out how he got in."

"A lot of people are hungry and angry because of the rats," I replied.

I was sticking with a topic that we seemed to do well on, but she sank further into her dark mood.

"I've really enjoyed your sister Gudrun's company," I remarked, nodding and grinning like an idiot. "I had an extraordinary conversation with her this morning at Mr. Kunst's house."

"Uh-huh."

"She's an unusual girl."

Klara halted so suddenly I bumped into her, touched her clothes, and practically tasted her hair. Two huge men, one with a long scar on his face, were coming toward us. Their faces were so grim and cold that my pulse quickened until they passed us. They did not look like councilmen.

In a soft voice that once again made us coconspirators, Klara observed, "Mr. Krueger must be slipping . . ." She started to follow them, then stopped and shrugged. "After today, nothing would surprise me."

My head was pounding, and I had a hard time focusing on her face. Again I opened my mouth, but we had stopped at a door.

Klara knocked and without waiting walked in.

"Hello, Klara," said a middle-aged man, finishing up a sentence before looking up from his writing to beam at her. "How's the birthday party going?"

"Beautifully. You were very kind."

Mayor Hofmann rolled his finished parchment, rose, stepped over, and kissed the top of Klara's head while whispering something to her.

She looked at the parchment and nodded.

"And who's your guest?"

"This is Johannes of the Pipers Guild. He's here about the rats."

I braced myself to watch the mayor's face go cold at the mention of the guild. It did not.

"Wonderful," he replied. He smiled at me, his cheeks forming little bumps like plums, his slightly oversized teeth shining white in a very pink face. The mayor's plain features radiated warmth, honesty, and good health.

"Mr. Mayor, a pleasure." I bowed; amazingly, so did he.

"Pipers Guild," he reflected. "Well, it has been several years . . ." He shook his head as though to clear it. "You know, I . . . I wouldn't mention the guild in Hamelin, if I were you."

"Thank you, sir," I replied. "I'll be careful." Seeing that he was in no hurry to bring me back around to my business, I continued. "I was hoping to be registered. To remove the rats."

"Well, ah, normally one of our councilmen, Mr. Zimmer, takes care of that."

"Sir, the council is involved in a party. But I would like to get rid of Hamelin's rats this morning. Before—" I remembered the mother and child in the alley and was unable to continue.

Mr. Hofmann put an arm around me. "Good heavens, son. What have you been through?" He was looking at my lip, and now I felt how swollen it was. "Here, sit down."

Mr. Hofmann gently seated me in a massive armchair, liberally padded and elaborately carved. If I hadn't felt so weak, I would have refused out of embarrassment.

"Let me bring you—Klara, can you fetch us something to drink?"

Klara stepped to the door. "Daddy."

"Yes, dear?"

"Mr. Piper has something to say about the reward fund." She disappeared.

"All right," the mayor said, "I can write up your registration. Now what's this about the fund?"

"I was telling Miss Hofmann that I think it might be wise for you to actually look at it."

"Look at it."

"Yes."

He walked over to the window and gazed out over the town square. "You know," he said, almost absentmindedly, "a number of men on the council have urged me to discontinue the reward offer."

"Why would they do that?"

"Well, it's been quite a long time. The reward hasn't brought a solution. And some of my colleagues say the reward is having certain negative effects."

"Mr. Mayor, you certainly can't drop the reward today. Your town desperately needs to get rid of the rats. Your people are on the edge of starvation. I *will* take care of the rat plague. But I cannot do it for free, because the guild needs the money urgently for a charitable project."

The mayor looked me up and down and said, "I admire you, young man."

I grinned, maybe a little stupidly. In the mayor's comfortable chair and comfortable presence, I actually felt myself sliding into grogginess. I liked the Hofmann family.

"Mr. Mayor, as soon as you register me, I'll go do what I came to Hamelin to do. And sir, your people will remember you as the man who made their deliverance possible."

"God grant," he said, sitting at his desk and sliding open a heavy drawer. Pulling out a sheet of parchment filled in at the top like a contract, he added at the bottom, *To Johannes Piper of . . .*

"Where did you say you were from?"

"Oldendorf."

"Oh, a neighbor. Lovely town. What is today? June . . . 23." He finished writing, dated and signed the sheet, and added the mayor's seal. After waving it to dry, he handed it to me and said, "Best of luck. You'll need six witnesses. You know what? If you really intend to do it, I mean, if you really can—" He looked at me a moment. "Then include Klara as a witness. It would mean so much to her. She's taken this rat plague as a personal insult to her town and her honor."

Before rolling up the parchment, I read the words: *To the one who delivers the city of Hamelin from its plague of rats, the Town Council of Hamelin promises to pay upon completion of this service the sum of ten thousand silver coins. This we, the Town Council, do solemnly pledge to . . .*

In my hand was the certificate of my success. In front of me was the one man who believed I could do it. Let the fatted calves in the room downstairs stew in their own juices—together with their pathetic dancing girls. The mayor and I were up here having a party of our own. I was off to do battle with the rats. And as the rats poured into the river, everything would change between me and the mayor's daughter. The mayor had practically said so.

Klara reappeared in the doorway with cups on a tray. She saw our faces and the parchment in my hand.

"Daddy, did you talk about the reward fund?"

"Yes. Mr. Piper wants me to look at it."

Klara set down the tray with a clatter. "He thinks it's empty."

"Why should it be empty? Good heavens, we've been filling it with these damnable emergency taxes—that would be the limit, if after all the people's sacrifice, the pot turned out to be empty!"

"He says it's empty."

"Mr. Piper, how did you come to this conclusion?"

My head swam. The room tilted and nausea settled in me like a sour, heavy rag.

"Sir," I managed to say, "I didn't say it was empty; I just thought it *might* be empty. The councilmen were acting like—like they didn't want to lose the rats."

"What on earth can you mean?"

"I was sent here to rescue the city. I sensed that the council didn't want me to do that."

"But why?"

"Mr. Mayor, it wouldn't be the first time in history that one man profited from another man's misfortune."

"But these are my colleagues—the finest men in Hamelin. I would trust them with my life. Mr. Lachler convinced me to take the mayorship, when my father would have laughed at the idea. And, Klara, remember how Uncle Dietrich (that's Mr. Zimmer), how he used to bounce you on his knee? What was that little rhyme he used? And he always brought candy for Gudi . . ."

Klara's chin was raised and her jaw was clenched. I looked at the floor.

"Johannes Piper, you have come to me asking for an investigation. I have no objection to discovering the truth. But I must caution you about the temptation to hasty justice. Let me tell you a story from my life that will show you what I mean. Befor I was mayor, a teenage boy was caught stealing fruit in the market. There had been a lot of thefts, some large. The vendors were fuming. The mayor simply turned his back, knowing that the boy would be beaten, with months of bottled-up anger poured out on him. Johannes, that boy never regained consciousness. I stood over his body. His mother would not have known him. In his pocket, they found three plums." Mr. Hofmann's face trembled. "The former mayor would have said that his action, or lack of action, was just. But that is the kind of justice I fear."

79

Klara placed our drinks before us, and Mayor Hofmann raised his cup.

"I drink to Johannes Piper, the rescuer." He drained his cup in one swallow, then leapt to his feet. "Let's go look at the fund."

When I rose to join him, I staggered, and they both jumped to catch me. Klara reached me first; I fell heavily on her shoulder. She was stronger than she looked and set me back firmly on my heels.

"Are you up to this?" she asked.

"Yes."

"Daddy, I'm not sure it's good for Mr. Piper to come with us to the treasury room."

"Oh, I don't know. Is a treasury a graveyard at night? Johannes, are you afraid?"

"No, sir."

So the mayor took my arm, and Klara resigned herself to bringing up the rear. We made our way down the hall, down the stair, toward the treasury. When we reached the place where the corridor opened over the banquet hall, we heard Mr. Bauer's voice. I barely recognized it at first; it was so changed, so small and high.

"I promise I'll have it soon. Very soon. I have a meeting with a gentleman this—"

He was cut off by a snarling voice whose words I couldn't make out. It pulled at me like a magnet to think I might witness the humiliation of the man who had humiliated me. But Mayor Hofmann frowned and made two signs that said *Keep it quiet; keep moving.*

It turned out we had to walk past the men in order to fetch Mr. Zimmer. As we passed, they fell silent. Mr. Bauer stared at the floor, looking shaken. Standing, self-possessed, in front of him was the man with the long scar.

The party noise had grown loud by now and burst out when the mayor went into the room. There was a muting of the volume, then out came the mayor beside a small man with a comic face and a gleaming bald spot. This, apparently, was Mr. Zimmer.

He insisted on bringing out four goblets. "Absolutely no question, no—no question! No, birthday girl—got to have a toast, which the birthday girl, the father, father of the birthday girl, and her *eighteenth,* and also the, uh, our guest, the man who came to Hamelin about the, uh, need, have to drunk together, hee-hee, I mean drink together, on the occasion of the special, uh, yes, absolutely, there's no real question about that, no question, careful, that's good stuff, yes, sir. So."

Having distributed the cups, sloshing liberally, keeping one for himself, Mr. Zimmer now pulled himself up to his full height, bringing the radiant bald spot to my eye level.

"To Miss Klara Hofmann, fully qualified, fully qualified—" Here he put out a finger to suppress any gainsayers. "To be next mayor of Hamelin!"

Everyone laughed, Klara most of all.

"And I say, may Klara fulfill her, uh, her *dream* of Hamelin becoming the most blessed town in the whole entire—"

His face was such a sketch of goodwill and anxious effort that I could barely stifle a laugh.

"—in the entire kingdom!"

A bighearted but small-bodied man, Mr. Zimmer raised his goblet extravagantly high. He made to clink with me, fumbled, and dumped his very full cup down my front. I felt the wine trickling down the channels inside my clothing, seeping down my chest. Was there any indignity my bizarre outfit would not endure before I finished my mission?

The treasurer, grinning and reeking of wine and sweat, leaned close and put an arm around me.

"I am *terribly* sorry." He swayed. "But look! You're one of us now. How do you feel?"

"I feel wine running down my shirt."

He exploded with laughter. The rest of the contents of his cup now sprinkled my legs.

"Mr. Zimmer," said Klara. She glanced at her father, who nodded.

The well-wisher recovered himself with an effort.

"We need to see the reward fund."

A cloud overshadowed Mr. Zimmer's high spirits. "Well, now Klara, you've always been so clever with the books; of course they're good and also they're really quite *fine*. And really"—he turned to Mayor Hofmann—"really, I've become quite, uh, yes, dependent on your Klara. You should be proud. I've never seen such talent, such hard work, and, heh-heh . . . I feel she hardly needs an old man like me anymore."

"Mr. Zimmer," said Klara, with a voice that would stop traffic, "we don't need to see the books. We need to see the money."

81

Mr. Zimmer passed a hand over his face, leaving a trail of grease shining on his cheek.

"You know, Miss Hofmann," he said, looking at her hands, "I can't help but think it's a, it's a hard thing, doing business, you know, business, on this—I mean, it's your birthday. I had really meant to drink your health. But with or without my cup—oh, I know, the piper and I will share." He put his hand over mine and my cup and said, "To Klara Hofmann, and the most blessed town in the kingdom."

He contrived to drink at the same time as I, lips pressed beside mine. More damage to my clothing. It hardly mattered anymore.

"Ahh," he groaned. "A good wine. And a good man. Mr. Piper . . ." He squeezed my hand. "A pleasure to drink with you. And now if you will excuse me . . ." His hand was opening the door.

"Mr. Zimmer," said Klara, quiet as notching an arrow.

"Hang it all, we're in the middle of a party!" Mr. Zimmer was shaking.

The effect of these words on the two Hofmanns was remarkable. The mayor's face showed acute embarrassment, as though he had walked in on a stranger in a privy. Klara's face was the face of a hunter who has just heard a twig crack. The two spoke up at once.

"Naturally tomorrow would be soon enough to—"

"Mr. Zimmer," Klara said, "our guest is here for a short time. He wants to rescue our town from a *plague*. Compared to that, my birthday can wait till doomsday. And he will only do it if he can see the money first."

The treasurer sighed and stood looking vacantly at his hands, shaking his head.

"Excuse me," said Mayor Hofmann. "I'm sure Hamelin's treasurer and bookkeeper will be able to satisfy your curiosity, Mr. Piper. I trust them both. You already have my signature. And now"—he gave Klara a pained expression and held up his parchment like a flag—"I regret to say that I have a second invitation, far less important to me than my daughter's birthday, but important to my people. Klara, I'll be back here tonight. The council will still be celebrating. I wish you luck, Mr. Piper." He made the slightest bow, turned, and left.

"Strike me dead, I love that man," declared Zimmer.

Klara looked after her father till he disappeared from sight, then said, "Let's go."

Mr. Zimmer's face was a portrait of misery. "I don't know if I have the key."

"Is this it?" Klara pointed to a large key on a ring on his belt.

In the end, we dragged our way down the corridors and the stairs to the treasurer's office and stood in front of the door. Fumbling endlessly with his ring of keys, Mr. Zimmer finally looked at Klara's feet, gave a nervous shrug, and said, "Unforeseen expenses come up. Emergencies come up."

Klara said nothing but looked at the keys dangling in Mr. Zimmer's hand. He turned to me. "You run into cash-flow problems. You move a little from this fund to that fund. But we never worried about that, because we knew we had the best, the smartest bookkeeper in the whole entire kingdom!" His eyes shone with what was supposed to be ardor for Klara's bookkeeping.

"Mr. Zimmer, we'll count the money first and make explanations later."

After Mr. Zimmer had struggled with the key for some time, Klara offered to help and got the door open. Zimmer was keen to get the door closed and locked; then he withdrew to a corner and darted his eyes along the floor like a dog between beatings.

With his reluctant help, we located the strongbox and opened it. In the bottom lay a curled scrap of parchment with some figures in a row.

SEVEN

To Save a Thief

Friday, June Twenty-third, 1284, Hamelin

I T WAS ALL GONE—THE MONEY FOR MY GUILD, THE MONEY for my mission, the money for my father. Klara stared at the bottom of the box as though waiting for it to speak. Mr. Zimmer hung in the corner as though he'd been nailed to the wall. Pitiful as he looked, I wanted to hurt him.

He found his voice. "They made me do it."

"Who did?" asked Klara.

"I mean, it was a council decision."

"My father is the head of the council."

The treasurer sighed. He chose a spot in the floor and looked at it. "Klara, I can tell—and of course I understand, you're a brilliant girl, a committed girl, a girl who loves her father and her town —but I can see you're reading things into this that just aren't there."

Klara stepped closer to the man who had been her supervisor, the man she had grown up calling Uncle Dietrich. "Here's what I'm reading, Mr. Zimmer. There's no money." Each word was louder and higher than the one before. "A man has come who may finally be able to save our town from a plague of rats. And there is nothing to pay him with."

"Klara, we meant all along for the Hofmann family to have the largest share. It's been set aside in a safe place for your family's exclusive use."

"For my family's use? But it was for Hamelin."

"You can use your portion on whatever you want—on projects for social welfare . . ."

"But every penny—" Klara faltered, her eyes wide. "Every penny was intended for social welfare."

"It was for a rescuer who would never come."

"How did you know a rescuer would never come?"

"We—" He looked at us strangely, as though he had just remembered whom he was talking to. "We—well, I mean, after all these months it certainly seemed imprudent to keep waiting." Suddenly he waved his birdlike hand, brushing away Klara's questions like a cobweb. "Just let me give you the Hofmann portion."

"But this man is here to work on the rats. Today."

Mr. Zimmer looked at me out of large, frightened eyes.

"Mr. Zimmer," Klara repeated slowly, as to a child, "this man—"

"He will fail." He seemed to weigh the effect of these words on me, then added to me in a whisper, "You are in danger."

"Why will he fail?" asked Klara, as Zimmer seemed to shrink. She stepped closer.

I wasn't sure if she would put an arm around him or shake him till his head snapped.

She whispered, "Why is he in danger?"

I had one thought: this mumbler stood in the way of my task. The Pipelord had said, "Do your assignment, be wise, show mercy, pipe justice." This was no time for tiptoeing and sidestepping. I planted myself in front of the wretched treasurer, and he turned large, darting eyes in my general direction.

"Excuse me, Miss Hofmann. Mr. Zimmer, as a representative of the Pipers Guild that sent me and in the name of the people of Hamelin who have been robbed, I ask you, who is responsible for this theft?"

Klara spoke with a quietness that would break a bone. "Mr. Piper, please step into the hallway."

I looked at her and swallowed. I shuffled to the door as though I were ninety. I kept thinking, *I'll walk slowly; she'll apologize. She'll make me stay.*

She didn't.

A moment after the door boomed shut behind me, I pressed my ear to the oak and made out "Mr. Zimmer," followed by a few gentle syllables.

"Please don't tell anyone," he begged. "I'll pay it all back myself."

I didn't hear a reply.

"I swear, it will all be returned."

Klara's next words were again muffled by the door. Then came groaning and whimpering.

Please, I willed through the oak panel, *give that blubberer the interrogation he deserves—and let's find that money. And while we're at it, let's figure out what's terrifying him.*

Footfalls broke in on my angry eavesdropping. A man I did not recognize marched down the hall toward me, relentless as a landslide. I knew I must step to the wall or be shouldered aside. He drew up to me, never acknowledging my presence, and opened the door. Two faces turned toward the stranger and me. Klara looked puzzled at the interruption and showed no recognition of the intruder. Mr. Zimmer froze, with tears glistening on his face. In the center of this tableau was the cash box, open and empty.

The man frowned, squinted at Mr. Zimmer for a long moment, then turned and walked away.

Mr. Zimmer stepped toward the door and whispered, "Please. I have to leave. Now."

"Mr. Zimmer." Klara placed herself in his way. "You are Hamelin's treasurer. We are investigating a problem that occurred under your care. You are not going anywhere."

His darting eyes held hers for a moment as he appeared to think something over. "Miss Hofmann, please take me to the jail."

"I'll need to get one of the men-at-arms."

Zimmer fell to his knees and took her hands. His were trembling. "I am begging you. Don't waste a minute." He nodded his head in my direction. "He can guard me. Isn't he a magic piper?"

I studied the folds of his clothing for any sign of a knife. I wanted to ask him, and none too gently, why we should hurry, but I was still stinging from Klara's rebuke for my last intervention.

"Let's go," she said.

"Thank you, Miss Hofmann," said Zimmer, in a voice like a desperate prayer. "Now, just one thing. I am the one who understands the danger we are in. So please, please do as I say. There may not be time to explain. Can you agree to that?"

Klara nodded.

Zimmer turned his frantic, questioning eyes on me. "Please," he said.

"I haven't heard nearly enough about what we're doing, or why," I said, addressing Klara. "But if we have to hurry, then . . . I was sent to serve Hamelin. In this matter I will be bound by the mayor's trusted representative, Miss Hofmann."

Klara repeated, "Let's go."

"Good, good, good," Zimmer fawned. "We'll take Baker Street."

"That's not the way to the jail," Klara objected, but he insisted that the men who were now after him would be watching the front entrance. Klara nodded decisively, but the muscles around her eyes and mouth drew tight.

"Come on," whispered the chattering little man who was to be our prisoner and our guide.

The next thing I knew, we were creeping out of a servants' entrance, crossing the street as fast as we could without running, and plunging into a jumble of homes and shops behind Town Hall. We wound among vendors' booths, ducked under hanging merchandise—now a glistening string of fly-covered sausages, now a clanking chain-mail vest.

At one point Mr. Zimmer pushed Klara and me ahead of him into a shop, where we were surrounded by bolts of cloth. He strode up and down outside the door as though keeping watch, scratching his hands, darting his eyes. I kept an eye on him, sure that I could catch him if it came to a chase. With an eye on my stained outfit, the girl who was watching the store asked me to keep clear of the fabrics, please, but looked encouragingly at Klara, a promising customer.

In a whisper I asked, "We are taking this man to jail, right?"

Klara, with a face that pretended we were shopping together, replied, "Of course."

"All right," I pursued. "Say Zimmer is right. What if these attackers of his really show up?"

"Aren't you a magic piper?"

"I'm an apprentice," I answered, watching Zimmer enter the shop. "And you see the shape I'm in."

She frowned at a cuff that was not to her taste. "We'll be fine. It's broad daylight in my town, and I am the daughter of Mayor Hofmann."

"So why are we running like chickens?"

"I'm showing kindness to a member of my town's council who is also an old family friend. Call it humoring, if you like."

I stared at her. Zimmer was the one man in Hamelin who could find the money for my mission. Klara had risked losing him without even believing his danger was real. She sure wasn't humoring *me*.

Correctly reading my face, she sighed. "Do you wish I'd been more rational when you were the one in the dirt? On that day, for no good reason, with Wolf begging me not to take the risk, I saved a complete stranger. But now I'm supposed to play by guild rules and despise my father's best friend when he's terrified?"

"Miss Hofmann, I know you feel the need to help a friend, but I feel very confused about helping a thief. A crime against Hamelin needs to be investigated. We must take some kind of action."

She held the sleeve of an exquisite indigo dress against her cream-colored hand; the fabric was made for her. "Mr. Piper, that may take more than a few hours."

"So the sooner we start, the better," I urged, and continued in my sweetest tones. "Now, to start an investigation, do you think your father should contact the duke?"

"Do you always use a chair to swat a fly, Mr. Piper?"

Desperate to save my mission, I ventured another question. "Miss Hofmann, you do want to find out how the fund got emptied? And where the money is?"

She stopped her fiddling, turned to face me, and spoke through her teeth. "Why under heaven do you think I am taking my father's best friend to jail?"

"I'm sorry." There was no way I could win. The best I could do in Hamelin was to pick how I would lose. "So what do you—"

"I want this done quietly."

"All right," I said, "I'll confront the council privately, as soon as we can—"

"On what authority?"

"Well, with you, of course. With you—as the bookkeeper."

She directed those evening-gray eyes at me. "Prepare for a shock, Mr. Piper. Before you came to Hamelin, the council solved its own problems just fine."

How could Klara not see that in this war we were natural allies against all of Hamelin's rats? How had things gotten so twisted? I stood close enough to speak in an undertone.

"I'll be honest, Miss Hofmann. I can't understand you. How can you defend them, after seeing them today for who they really are?"

"Mr. Piper, no one in Hamelin, least of all an outsider like yourself, could feel more anger and betrayal than I did at the sight of that empty cash box. But I'm not going to let a sensitive investigation be put in the hands of an ignorant apprentice in a hurry—no more than I would put my sister's surgery in the hands of a drunk."

"I understand your desire for caution, Miss Hofmann. But you're not treating this like the emergency it is. There have already been victims—the men, women, and children who have died of starvation in this plague. You've seen them. Translate your compassion into action, Miss Hofmann. Today we saw that someone has grown fat on this blood."

Klara had graduated to the bolts of cloth now, fingering foreign stuff, studying patterns, pretending I didn't exist. My head was pounding, but suddenly my training spoke louder. Where amid all the glistening satin was Zimmer?

"Uh, Miss Hofmann, I'm sorry, but I'm afraid Zimmer may try to escape."

"You haven't been watching his eyes," she said breezily. "We're his guardian angels."

Sure enough, Mr. Zimmer's face suddenly emerged near Klara's, his mouth puckered with frustration. He laid his finger on his lips in a frantic plea for silence. His edge-of-tears panic, surrounded by the streaming gold and green of the crowded little shop, was so comical that I caught Klara's eye to share the joke with her. But her look answered, *How can you laugh?*

Amazing. Klara Hofmann, and all Hamelin with her, was blind. I looked up and met the amused, gawking eyes of the shopgirl. The three of us made a fair piece of comic pantomime, all right, and for her it was free.

After a furtive glance left and right, Zimmer beckoned us into the alley and whispered, "Klara, the Thiewall. Quick."

The two of them took off, with me barely keeping up. I needed to tell Mr. Zimmer I was still recovering. I was already short of breath when Zimmer cannoned Klara and me into a rich-smelling cheese shop. A barrel of cheese rounds, its bottom well gnawed, stood just inside the door; Zimmer pulled me behind it with trembling hands and pressed himself close to me. He pointed with his bugging eyes and whispered, "He's over there."

A thin man in a gray cloak had opened a barrel and was inspecting the apples inside.

"Can't you use that little, um, thingy of yours?"

"My pipe?"

"Shhh! Not so loud. Yes. Your pipe." He was whispering right in my face now.

"Mr. Zimmer, I can't pipe a man unconscious for buying apples."

In Zimmer's face, panic vied with exasperation. "He was looking at me."

"Maybe he was looking at Miss Hofmann."

"Good heaven above, young man, are you finding this amusing?" His lips were trembling. I had noticed in my years of training that members of our guild, when known publicly, tended to attract the insane. I scanned the councilman's face for symptoms.

"Mr. Zimmer," I replied, struggling to control my voice, "I hold the pipe when a weapon is needed."

But already he was ignoring my answer; his assassin had vanished from the apple barrels, and he was tugging me by the arm into the street, breathing hot into my ear that the town square area might be dangerous till tomorrow morning, that he had friends near the Thiewall, that the way there had plenty of people and places to hide. I reached out and clamped a hand on his shoulder, as though he were an unruly child.

"Mr. Zimmer."

He pulled me into the safety of a doorway, jumping with anxiety. "Yes?"

"If we are in danger, let's go to the Hofmanns'."

"His spies are everywhere."

"*Whose* spies?"

Ignoring me, the treasurer plunged ahead. "I think he's had my home watched. My wife . . ." His whole face contracted with a spasm. "And of course the mayor's home. Absolutely watched." He stared into space ahead of him and swallowed with difficulty.

"Mr. Zimmer, you must tell me who is chasing you, and why."

"They want me." He was bug-eyed and staring.

"*Who*? And why?"

"They want me dead."

"*Who does?*"

Like a boy blindfolded and spun in a child's game, I'd lost all sense of direction for my mission. What role would the Pipelord want me to play in this comedy? I felt like an idiot when I cooperated, and a villain when I resisted.

"I was told they would make it look like an accident. Now I don't think they care."

I could get nothing further out of him. I knew of some methods involving the pipe that I wished I had time to try, but we were dashing down the street.

My appeal for "action" back in the clothing shop now inspired a comfortable daydream. I would let Hameliners solve Hamelin's problems, just as Klara wished. I would publicly march a few of the rats—a hundred or so—into the river, then dangle the completion of the job before the harassed townspeople as bait. I would stand, calm and beneficent, and announce that all they had to do was encourage their beloved Town Council to relocate a few thousand misplaced coins. After the mob had finished a thorough investigation of the first councilman's house—

My head began to spin, and just then Klara drew up with me.

"Miss Hofmann, I need your arm."

No action.

"Miss Hofmann, I'm getting lightheaded."

"Are you making this up?"

"No."

She took my arm, with as much enthusiasm as if I were a leper, and we began to walk. We were being led across Hamelin by an exposed thief who wanted me to stun passersby for the crime of buying apples, and *I* was suspected of lying. This mission was cursed, that was all there was to it.

I put my face as close to Klara's ear as I thought seemly. Heaven help me, it was a beautiful ear. Even at that moment, it was a beautiful ear.

"Miss Hofmann, please. I have to ask you this. Have you ever doubted Mr. Zimmer's sanity?"

Except for the flaring of her nostrils, there was no evidence that she had heard me.

"Miss Hofmann?"

"No."

"Who was that man? The one who came to the treasurer's office."

"I never saw him before."

"What is Mr. Zimmer afraid of?"

"I don't know."

My headache was growing worse.

Mr. Zimmer's voice was in my ear again. "Please be more alert. You're the only one who's armed." Then, very intense: "It could be anyone." I heard a sharp inrush of breath, and he pressed us into a courtyard.

Just before I disappeared inside, I glimpsed a rough-looking, swarthy man who did seem to be looking for something.

After two minutes of listening to my heart beating, I felt Zimmer drawing me toward him again. "That was too close. Could you please hold the flute in your hand?"

"Mr. Zimmer," interrupted Klara, "you remember six years ago. If he walks around with the pipe in his hand, he might be attacked."

We reentered the street. Zimmer now refused to walk without touching me. Here the buildings and houses were smaller, older, and, for the most part, dingier.

Klara's voice pulled me out of a fog. "Mr. Zimmer, there's the Thiewall. Where do your friends live?"

I smelled the Weser River flowing just beyond the wall. My eyes throbbed. I hoped these friends were rich and owned a wagon with room for three.

Zimmer looked me over, licked his lips so rapidly I thought of a snake's tongue, and said, "You're tired. That's not good. Not good. You shouldn't be tired. What if . . . ?" He interlocked his fingers as for prayer, till the knuckles blanched. "You rest. Klara, our piper needs to rest. I can't be running around without a . . . You understand, don't you, Klara?"

My temples pounded. Klara gently laid a hand on Zimmer's shoulder. It was comforting to see one of us getting the encouragement he needed.

"All right," said Zimmer. "The two of you rest. I'll make sure the coast is clear." He nodded to himself, gave a grotesque smile that did not touch his darting eyes, and crept toward the corner.

As soon as he was out of earshot, Klara returned to our argument. "I can see you care about your principles, Mr. Piper. But can you love our people?"

I started to answer, but she cut me off. "Or does your passion for justice leave no room for patience? You got to Hamelin yesterday, and you're all set to fix something you don't even understand. It would be—"

"Miss Hofmann, we have to do something now." I clutched my

pipe. "I can't move ahead with my mission till I get answers. Who's Mr. Zimmer running from? Who took the money? The men who have the answers are powerful. They'll likely be as helpful as Mr. Zimmer has been. So how do we get them to talk? What would do that but a trial?"

Klara snorted. "Why are you so heavy-handed? My father will find the money. Without a trial. The only thing a trial would do is to make him lose face. Do you want that? To undermine the best man in this town?"

"Yes, of course he's the—"

With a cutting laugh, she interrupted me. "You think I can't see it in your eyes? When my father treats his friends with trust or mercy, you think he's stupid. But you don't know anything about my father or my town. I told you I once saw two young men die in one night. That night the old mayor didn't want a trial; he wanted gory entertainment. Over the priest's objections, my father buried Ans—" Her voice broke. "He gave the one man a decent burial."

Anselm. She had almost said the name.

"That is mercy. Mr. Piper, if you hurt my father, I will fight you with everything I've got."

Very softly I said, "Of course the first person I talk to will be the mayor. Before any kind of criminal investigation."

Her face gradually brightened as she asked, "Are you authorized to do a criminal investigation? No. You came to kill rats."

"What's your point?"

She took a deep breath. "Ask the guild to send a master piper to look into this thing properly."

"Properly?"

"Yes. You're an apprentice."

At my frown, she quickly continued. "Your guild had no idea you'd get attacked and find an empty fund. You're over your head. Just admit it."

"Miss Hofmann, this mission was entrusted to me, and I—"

"Yes. And then something bizarre happened; the money was gone. Would your guild blame you for that? Write them a letter. Calling a trial or blasting a town is not a decision for one banged-up young man a long way from home."

"I don't need a master piper's permission to stop a thief. I'm an agent of justice. I can't hold back from doing what's right when I see something wrong."

"But here's what I'm saying," Klara retorted. "Don't take on the job of judge without getting advice. Could you write a letter and wait for an answer, just as a favor for me?" She saw my hesitation and leaned forward. "Johannes Piper, as the one who saved your life, I personally request this: *Do not act* without the advice of your guild."

"Miss Hofmann—"

"If your ego demands that I get on my knees and beg for my family and my town—"

She fell to her knees on the flagstones, and my peasant instincts screamed *No!* This was shameful for her, dangerous for me.

"I'd hoped for better from an honorable guild," she murmured. "Mr. Piper, please wait till you can get advice from a master piper."

I wanted advice right now, on how to handle the wolfhound I'd once called my gentle nurse.

"All right," I conceded. "I'll write to a master piper who lives near here. Can you give me a courier?"

She nodded.

"I'll wait two days," I said.

Just like a man, Klara shook my hand to seal our agreement. She got up, dusted her dress, and suddenly stared down the very empty street. "Where is he?"

The hair stood on my arms when I realized what she meant. Mr. Zimmer had been "clearing the coast" for a very long time.

We hobbled to the corner. Rounding it, I had a glimpse of a gray cloak disappearing. And on the ground, poking out between a heap of building stones and a wooden wall, stretched Mr. Zimmer's legs in their elegant sky-blue hosen.

Klara was beside him in a moment, demanding, "What happened?"

"Get behind the stones," he barked.

Then I saw it. From the wall over his head protruded a feathered shaft. Adrenaline surged through me—now it was run, fight, or pipe. I tugged Klara down to a kneeling position behind the rock pile.

"Miss Hofmann, someone's taken a shot at him."

EIGHT

Butchers

Friday, June Twenty-third, 1284, Hamelin

R. ZIMMER."
Our prisoner's Adam's apple bobbed up and down on his stringy neck as he gulped back tears. I made him look me in the eye.

"Mr. Zimmer, two people are risking their lives for you. We need to know what's going on. Who is chasing us, and why?"

"Mr. Piper," he rasped, his eyes popping with earnestness, and he suddenly hugged me.

I felt the squish of the cloth that he had soaked with wine.

"You've saved my life. I feel safe now." He nodded at the pipe and swallowed. "I thought they'd cut my throat. But now, by heaven, I'm going to tell you everything." With a hand on each of us, he declared, "You are fine young people." He closed his eyes. "Someone brought the rats here. Someone keeps them here. It is no ordinary plague. That person is the one who wants to kill me."

"But why?"

Mr. Zimmer's mouth was smiling again, with no help from his eyes. It was like the grin of a panting dog.

"This person hates you, Mr. Piper. His people saw me with the empty cash box. We can just imagine, just imagine how that will look to him."

I opened my mouth to ask a flurry of questions, the first one being, *How does a man "bring rats"?* But Mr. Zimmer raised a forefinger to his lips.

"Please. We'll finish this later. We're in a very dangerous position. Very." His eyes grew bright. "But I know a place where I will be safe."

I stood and offered him my hand. Gawking down the street with bugged eyes, he creaked to his feet, then slowed down as he elaborately held his hat against his body. When I could stand no more dawdling, I jerked his hand upward; he lost his balance, and the hat fell. Mr. Zimmer had wet himself.

This was the last straw for the man, and he sobbed quietly. I took his cloak and draped him with mine, which was longer and would cover his shame. Inspired, I recklessly swapped my hat for his as well. Flying this flag meant risking my life for a Hamelin councilman—and proving Klara wrong.

She seemed about to object, but we were running openly now, forged by the undeniable arrow into a panicked family. Suddenly Mr. Zimmer hissed, "They're coming."

We ducked behind a large wagon stopped nearby. Seeing we were too far from the corner to get out of sight that way, Klara got the driver's attention.

"Sir, excuse me. This is an emergency. I am Klara Hofmann, the mayor's daughter. I need you to help me save this councilman from danger. May we ride in your wagon? I promise you will be rewarded."

The driver hesitated.

"Please. Let us get in the back, cover us up, and start to drive. I'll explain later."

Without a word, the driver jerked back the covering, we climbed in, and he threw it over us. We were bathed in the smell of cabbage. Near my head lay a specimen well past its peak of freshness.

The wagon began to roll, and with it, my cabbage. When we had gone a block and our rattling view through the slats showed no sign of pursuit, I heard Klara speak to Mr. Zimmer, who lay farthest back in the wagon bed and closest to the driver, asking him to direct the driver to the jail.

Mr. Zimmer made a slight opening in the old blanket that covered us and held a low-voiced conference with our driver. After we were all under the covering again, and the wagon was rattling over the potholes toward the jail, my grip on the pipe relaxed.

Klara's voice was near my head. "He could have been killed back there."

"Yes."

A silence, then: "What he said about the plague—"

"Miss Hofmann," I interrupted. I knew that the driver couldn't hear me over the sound of the rattling wagon, and I no longer cared about Mr. Zimmer. "The council stole the rat fund and knew someone brought the—"

"I will talk with my father about this. Immediately. But I have to ask you to forget what you just heard. For one thing, Mr. Zimmer is obviously upset. So we need to look at this thing . . . from different sides."

I struggled with the rage that flared up in me. Murder ran rampant in the streets, and Klara was still worried about people's delicate feelings. It was like my father, talking about flute playing when there was grain to bring in.

"Miss Hofmann, there are only two sides—one is right; one is wrong."

"There you—"

"Miss Hofmann, it's time *you* listened to me. If someone brought the rats here, what good would it do them? Who is it that benefits when rats eat all the food? You can count on this: If someone did bring the rats here, then someone is getting rich on high grain prices. That's a crime that will interest the duke, a crime worthy of the death penalty. And I for one would cheer at the hanging, because a leader who would do that is just a well-dressed murderer."

A dam had burst from the dark places of my childhood, and I was shaking. The wheels clattered and the axle groaned; then Klara's small voice floated across the darkness.

"What do you plan to do?"

"Well, whatever happened," I answered, "I feel that your father is innocent. As for the rest of them, after what we've learned from Zimmer, we can't avoid a trial. Probably with direct involvement of Duke Albrecht."

"But can you start by killing the rats?"

"Miss Hofmann, there's no money. We start by recovering the missing money."

"That could take a while. And Hamelin is suffering. Which you can cure."

"Would you be happy if I caught the rats but didn't catch the thieves?"

"The rats are your concern. The treasury is Hamelin's. Hamelin can find the money, raise the money, borrow the money, or even pay the guild on credit. My father will work it out with your master. But for now, just do your mission. Get rid of the rats and—"

Klara stopped short.

I was sure she'd been about to say, "And go away."

"My mission is to kill the rats and use the reward and *do justice.* I'm not free to pick and choose. Piping for free would undo the second half of my mission."

"Which is what exactly?"

I exhaled long and slow. "I stopped at a manor on the way here. The owner is savage to his serfs. He's eager to sell the land and the people, and he's agreed to the amount of the Hamelin reward. But I have to give him the money by Sunday, or the deal is off."

"You have no right to make Hamelin suffer for the sake of those serfs. They are your problem, not ours."

"I cannot pipe for promise breakers, and I cannot free serfs using warm feelings. As it now stands, neither Hamelin nor the serfs will get a bit of help from me. I might as well have stayed in the guildhouse. Then at least I wouldn't have a knot on my head."

I closed my mouth, long after I should have. The truth was I could have and should have asked for a master piper to accompany me. Then all this mess would be happening on his watch. As it was, here I lay, on my back, my favorite position since coming to Hamelin, like a bad character in a children's fable, paying for my pride in saying, "Sure, I can handle it."

"Mr. Piper."

"Please call me Hannes."

Silence.

"Or Johannes."

"Mr. Piper, you were sent here to get rid of rats. Please chase the rats as an act of charity."

The driver headed down a hill, and my cabbage rolled her way.

"My guild will not overlook a problem worse than the rats. Why can't you understand that?"

"I understand you." A dangerous-sounding pause followed. "And I understand your guild. Behind the slogans, it's all about how good you could look and how good you could feel about yourself because of those serfs that you freed! But I'll wake up here for the next thousand mornings and face the mess you made by being a hero."

I was speechless at her view of me.

"Mr. Piper, it's the people you can touch that you have to care for—even if your plans fly apart in the process. This is my family, this town is my world, and I would die for it."

I felt as though I were falling. "I've brushed death twice on this mission. You want to be useful, and I want to be useful. You have a family you love; I—" My voice stopped working for a moment. "I have a family. I have a father." I wiped at my eyes and nose. "He's one of those serfs."

"Your father," she replied, and her voice quieted to match mine. "I'm sorry." We lay silent for a while.

What I wanted to do, as we lay rattling in the stuffy blackness, was to ask a few questions of Mr. Zimmer, but he was on the far side of Klara. I didn't have the energy to talk across her, somehow. Or to raise her mother-hen hackles by bothering her baby chick. I lay staring into darkness, feeling every pothole, breathing tired cabbages, sorting out Klara Hofmann. She could be a voice close to my ear, her warm breath reminding me of the day I was raised from the dust of the road. She could be a sharp tongue making mincemeat out of what was left of my mission.

I was just too tired.

But Klara was squirming around to look through the slats. "Mr. Zimmer."

By now I recognized Klara's not-pleased voice, and this was it. "Yes? Yes?"

"We should have turned there."

"Oh, really? Ah, these petty vendors. Probably an out-of-towner. And didn't I smell wine on his breath?"

"Mr. Zimmer, I smell wine on your breath. Are we going to the jail?"

"Of course. Eventually."

"Where are we going now?"

"Please understand, Miss Hofmann. The jail is the first place they'll look. And jail bars don't stop these hired assassins. Quite the contrary. Quarry's treed. I understood this, back there at the Thiewall."

I heard her sighing in the dark. "So where are we going?"

"The Abbey. It's as safe as the day is long."

I lay on the hard planks, stunned. Zimmer was asking Klara to risk her life for him, then lying to her, playing tricks on her. At that moment—heaven help me—I wanted to straddle him, grip his bony shoulders, and slam his head on the wagon bed till I grew tired of the exercise.

But the driver was slowing. A peek showed we were rolling into the gate of an old cloister. The monk who greeted our driver burst out laughing when he threw back the cover and cried, "Welcome to St. Boniface. Good driver, I'd expected you might be selling cabbages to the brothers. But"—here he gave an enormous grin to Mr. Zimmer—"how much are you asking these days for councilmen?"

He pulled the treasurer up onto his knees and enfolded him in a long, back-pounding hug. "Dietrich, it's been too long. What on earth were you doing fellowshiping with cabbages? Don't tell me you've become a Franciscan?"

As he helped the mayor's daughter to the ground, he bowed deep, then helped me toss back the floppy-leafed cabbages we'd knocked from the wagon. Zimmer paid the driver well and spoke with the monk, Brother Neidhart, more candidly than I'd expected, saying he was in danger of his life and needed shelter for a while.

Brother Neidhart nodded gravely, then looked at Klara and said, "Follow me."

He led the three of us through a courtyard filled with a magnificent beech tree, whose centuries-old trunk rippled like molded wax. At last he brought us to the door of a cell, took Zimmer inside alone for a moment, and eventually showed us all in.

After we had thanked him and the door closed on us, Mr. Zimmer spread all ten long fingers out on the great stones in the wall and said, "Four and a half centuries of safety."

We had been alone just long enough for me to remember all the questions I wanted to ask him, when he jumped and made for the door.

"Good heavens! I have to get an urgent message to my wife. One of the novices can do it. Excuse me a moment."

At first I felt misgivings, with Zimmer out of my sight. But the ancient monastery breathed peace into us all. Zimmer had been acting calm, even happy, for the first time since the cash box. And how would his departure look to the brothers from whom he had begged sanctuary? It was impossible to imagine him fleeing from what he had found here.

Klara perched on a hard stool; I gingerly lowered myself onto the edge of a bare bed. I took in the simple cell with its incongruous red carpet, savoring the stillness of Hamelin's oldest building, wondering who had occupied this room and why, in all those hundreds of years.

"Johannes."

Klara had called me by my first name. I turned to her.

Standing and planting her feet solidly on the hard stone floor, she tried to convince me one more time. "Please chase the rats away. Hamelin is as needy as your peasants. And it has sixty times the people."

"Yes, Miss Hofmann, and sixty times the money. Don't you want to find the money?"

She crossed her arms. "Johannes, you can still do what you came to do. You can bless three thousand grateful people. You can change three thousand people's view of your guild. You can heal a sore that's been bleeding for six years. But if you abandon Hamelin, nothing you do with your serfs will impress anyone here."

I looked hard at her aggressive stance in that peaceful, ancient cell, and something in me snapped. "Miss Hofmann, I cannot betray the robbed people of Hamelin or the oppressed serfs on that estate. I cannot betray my guild, and I cannot betray justice." I rose and wobbled to the door.

"Mr. Piper, what are you doing?"

"I'm leaving."

"What?"

"I can't win, Miss Hofmann. It's too complicated. It's out of control. I don't even know what my mission is anymore."

"But—"

"I need to go back to the guildhouse, walk up to my master, and report. 'Sir, situation not as expected, conditions not suitable for apprentice, mission considered impossible. Request new assignment.'"

She rolled her eyes. "But think what that would mean."

"I know what it would mean. It would mean the council was in love with gold. And the town was in love with the council. And there was nothing I could do but let the pack of them stew in their juices till doomsday."

She looked at the rich carpet a long time. I had wounded her, but I felt no compassion. In fact, the phrase "nothing I could do" reminded me of my daydream, and I savored it: publicly drowning a fraction of the rats, informing the starving townspeople of the missing fund and the rat-bringer, letting the populace find creative ways to persuade their leaders . . .

"Mr. Piper, that's . . ." She stared at the wall for a moment. "That's just irresponsible. It's the choice of a coward. It might be easiest for Johannes Piper, but it would leave *both* the groups you came to save in misery."

I turned and took a step toward the door . . . just as Mr. Zimmer burst in.

"They're here. I don't know how they bluffed their way in, but I think they might have seen me."

"Then we're trapped," said Klara.

"No. Brother Neidhart showed me something special about this room." He bent over and grabbed hold of the carpet on the floor. "A monk might ask, 'Why a rug in a cell?' But a hired killer might not even notice." He pulled it aside. There was a trapdoor.

"Go on, hurry," he urged, and added, "Sorry there's no light," even in danger playing the gracious host as he had at Town Hall. "I'll go last. I know how to get the rug right."

I stepped down the ladder first into the growing coolness of the cellar, with its smells of damp stone and earth. At last my probing foot struck ground. The cellar reeked with a smell like a large wet dog in a small closed space. Klara clambered down beside me in the shadows, while Mr. Zimmer fiddled with the rug and the trapdoor.

As my foot touched ground, it all came to a head—my concussion and our escape, combined with the sudden coolness and darkness. I felt my lips grow numb and my head grow light. I had just time to groan and say one word. I think it was "Falling!"

I woke to Klara's hands, as I had on the road to Hamelin. She was shaking me.

"Mr. Piper. Please."

"Let the poor boy sleep. Heaven knows, with all I've put him through—"

"Mr. Zimmer, we need his pipe."

"Why?"

"Because I felt something."

It was so easy to imagine Zimmer's nervous, resigned shrug that for a moment I felt I could see in pitch blackness. And then—

"Aaaaahh!" It was my voice, ripping out of me in a strangled yell, stifled by the fear of our pursuers, but forced out by the unexpected pain shooting up from my ankle.

"What? What?"

My hand groped for my own ankle, and sure enough—blood.

"I got bit."

"By what?"

"A rat."

Suddenly the darkness changed. It was teeming with furry shapes. Now that I was listening, I heard a lake of them, chewing, sniffing, swarming toward my undefended feet. I remembered the rats' focused anger in my room at Roth's, and in this darkness, closed in with hordes of them and no way out, I felt weak with terror. I forced myself to kick across the floor in front of me, and my foot struck body after body.

"Friends, we need to climb the ladder."

"We can't leave," Zimmer answered in a hoarse voice.

"Not leave, just climb."

Soon the three of us were stacked close on the ladder like squirrels on a branch. I wrapped my legs and arms around the coarse wood for a long-term grip, certain that my thighs would get to know this rung very well.

"Now, Mr. Zimmer," I said, "it's pipe or get chewed."

"Well . . . all right. This floor is very thick; in fact it's . . . quite thick. I suppose until we hear them open the door, you could pipe softly. Go ahead."

I wrapped my fingers around the pipe and felt its kiss—the cool of its mouthpiece on my lips, the taste of its metal on my tongue, the rush of warm air from my lungs to its windway. I felt the sheer magic of doing to air what a potter does to clay, the shaping of vibrations that could shake the hearts of men.

The cellar was swallowed up, and I entered the Pipeworld, the place where I felt most alive. I was forbidden to go for pleasure alone, but almost always it was pleasure—a secret tower, a steaming bathtub, a waking forest . . . a taste of the union that most of life had lost.

Of course, with all the intensity of the Pipeworld, if contact with enraged rats was the assignment, then rats was what you'd get. The Pipeworld's perceptions are relentless, intimate, and unforgiving. It would be a contact close as licking—and the journey into Rat-soul would be more intimate than the touch of the wooden cart in Aerzen. With the far-reaching Pipeworld fingers, I felt the rats, and as I reached to them by the strings I had cast, I immediately knew that Mr. Zimmer had told us the truth: someone was keeping these rats here.

And I knew more than that. I was not the first person to place a piper's mark on them. They were leashed (how else to describe that feeling?) in just that way. As a dog sniffs and knows another dog has visited, I could sense the traces of guild piping. It was as though, on a deserted island, I had found another set of human footprints. For a moment the bandits, the rats, the empty cash box, the corrupt council, even Zimmer's assassins sank into the background. Here was a sign that brought the cold sweat to my body.

I held the rats at bay, gently, while my mind spun with the discovery: the plague was *piped*.

In that scented, touch-filled Pipeworld, where notes speak clear as words, where connections are thick and countless, I felt the chaining up and circling together of other traces in my head. I found and stroked the twining cord of rage: my rage at the birthmarked man and the landlord's son and the vice-mayor and the treasurer, Klara's rage at my guild and me.

And as the pipe amplified all sounds and souls, including mine, I heard my mind echoing: *The mission is dead.* No rat kill, no reward, no liberation. No home, no Hofmanns, no Klara. It was all an illusion. Like the blackness of the cellar and the smell of rat fur, this revulsion came over me until I swayed and could barely grip the ladder.

The pipe dreaming rendered the thick stone floor translucent. Suddenly I sensed our pursuers entering the cell overhead. By now the rat tune was so low only the rats in the cellar could hear it. My piping hands now spanned the two worlds—the swirling rats and the hunting assassins.

In came a thin man wrapped in coarse cloth—this must be the man in the gray cloak, so fond of apples. Another man followed him in, flicking his eyes around, hunting. It was the swarthy man we had passed on the street. They held their weapons openly: a crossbow and a sword. In spite of a day spent in wooziness, in spite of my cramped position, I was now fully alert. If these two cutthroats discovered us, I was ready to come at them with everything I had. I could hardly wait for the moment the Pipelord would have dictated: the moment of "imminent self-defense."

Their easy confidence as they discussed Mr. Zimmer, as though he were a rabbit to be caught for supper, infuriated me. *Come into my cellar.* I would give it three bars, and they would taste what they richly deserved. I would stand over these two monsters as they writhed on the ground at my feet and begged for mercy—they who had never given it.

Then, just as suddenly as they had arrived, they grew tired of the cell and vanished. My cellar mates had no idea that death had paid a visit and walked away.

I kept piping, holding off the endless, musky rats in the endless, moldy dark, and I had no idea how long it lasted.

Zimmer's bony hand gripped my shoulder.

"Mr. Piper," he whispered, "they've given up." And sure enough, there above me, framed in the square of our trapdoor, was the large head of Brother Neidhart, gazing down on us like a harvest moon.

———•———

When my head cleared somewhat from dizziness and from the toll taken by the time in the Pipeworld, we were walking very fast with a high town wall to our right. As soon as Brother Neidhart had told us the coast was clear, Klara had been adamant about getting Mr. Zimmer to the jail as soon as possible, and she overruled all arguments.

Zimmer wore a twitching smile. "I grew up near here," he was saying. "I know the good hiding places and shortcuts like the palm of my hand. Yes, yes, that used to be a good baker. Right. Now up to the East Gate, then left, and on to the jail . . ."

I stumbled. Zimmer caught me.

"Listen," I said, "if you need my help, then we have to rest. I'm sorry. I can't go on."

His face falling, Zimmer led us into a courtyard that seemed abandoned. On three sides leaned dingy homes, with sagging roofs and no windows. Since Hamelin was crawling with more dogs and cats than I had ever seen in my life, I was prepared to pipe away a pack of dogs just to get a moment's rest. But this impoverished courtyard lacked even dogs.

Thanks to an angle in the court, we were soon out of sight of the street, but Mr. Zimmer burrowed farther, as deep in as he could go. A shapely cherry tree, leaves bursting forth, bark glistening, rose out of the squalor. Near its foot was a pile of dirt left from some forgotten building project, and I fell onto it. I was long past caring about my clothes.

I was tired of running from hunters, tired of squabbling with Klara, tired of wrestling with the town I had come to rescue. At the center of my disgust were the shining eyes and shining bald spot of Mr. Zimmer. We were risking our lives for him, and he was still not leveling with us. We didn't even know who our pursuers were.

I reached into my bag and touched the pipe. At the touch of its metal mouth on my skin, I felt a sudden urgency. I had to get up and look. I reached the gate and peered into the street. All clear on the right. On the left—I froze at what I saw. It was the man in the gray cloak, with a dark-skinned man and two others, entering a courtyard not six gates away.

I felt my heart pound as I hobbled at top speed to tell Klara and Zimmer. For a moment I considered the doorways in our little courtyard, but then suddenly I understood. Our trackers had something better than a bloodhound: a purse. For houses this desperate looking, during a famine, there could be no sweeter music than the clinking of coins. Even if someone hid us, they would gladly betray us.

"Mr. Zimmer, they've found us. They'll be here in minutes. We have to run for it."

Klara took Zimmer's hand, and the three of us hurried to the gate.

"They're down five doors on the left, trying every courtyard. We have to run to the right and pray we make it to the corner."

"Wait," Zimmer said. His face was twisted with anxiety, but his eyes seemed clear. "If they're checking courtyards, we have our best chance right after they enter one."

Klara and I wordlessly agreed. Soon, from behind the plaster wall where I was kneeling, I spied the trackers emerging from one yard, felt my heart stop when it seemed the dark one looked right into my eyes, then leaned my cheek into the dirty stucco for sheer relief when the four men disappeared down another alley.

"Come on."

We ran as fast as I could down the filthy street. I panted along, slower than I'd run in my life, mad with fear yet moving at a snail's pace like a man in a nightmare. At any moment I feared an arrow in the back. Against all hope, we made it around the corner without being spotted and slowed to a walk. When I had just begun to catch my breath, Klara stopped and spoke.

"I should confront them," she said, and her eyes were flashing.

"What?"

"Look, they're not Hameliners. They just don't know I'm the mayor's daughter. If I stand up to them, they'll back down."

I couldn't believe my ears.

"Miss Hofmann, these men are killers. Who you are means nothing to them. Get in the way, and they'll take you down as well."

She began walking back toward the corner.

I grabbed her arm. "Miss Hofmann—"

"Get your hands off me." She pulled away and plunged into the street.

I looked, and there they were—all four of them. They had seen her and were breaking into a run.

"Klara!"

She stood firm, waiting for them. Already I foresaw the whole thing: how they would take her hostage and demand that I give them Zimmer in exchange. And already I had decided that I would hand him over in a heartbeat. Unlike Klara, I had no reason to believe anything good of the man. He was one of Hamelin's large-scale bloodsuckers, a confessed thief, a liar, a coward. If it was a choice between Klara and Zimmer, he'd better not count on me to be soft.

Just then, the man in the lead drew his sword, though only Klara was visible. He was closing on her. A stranger sprinting at her with a naked sword altered Klara's convictions about standing up for her rights. She turned my way, lifted her skirts to her knees, and ran.

All three of us took off. A terrified councilman, an overconfident girl, and a woozy piper, with four hired killers in hot pursuit. The way to win this fight was to run from it—if only we could reach shelter alive.

As we tore down the street, feet slapping on the cobbles, we could hear them gaining. With a look over my shoulder, I saw the archer raise his crossbow. We had to get indoors.

"In here!" I yelled at the sight of the first open door.

It was a butcher's shop, a rambling affair with a great slaughterhouse in the back, and rows and rows of tools for working on fresh-killed carcasses. The butcher was a portly, red-faced man who was cutting a mass of pork and bones into stew meat. After one look at our frantic, sweaty faces, he had no strength left for anything but an oath. He stood rooted to the spot, his cleaver hanging in his hand.

I turned to bar the door and heard another oath from the butcher at this liberty. Just then the man with the drawn sword appeared on the customer side of the counter, spotted us, and heaved himself up through the counter window into the shop. At this, after a third oath in which outrage vied with fear, the butcher flung down pork and cleaver and took to his heels, leaving through a side door. We heard the sounds of hurried barring and locking.

Meanwhile the swarthy man with the crossbow kicked the door open, banging me on the shoulder, and launched an arrow that just missed Mr. Zimmer and pierced a still-dripping hog.

The other two pursuers, a thin man holding a dagger and a thick one with a heavy club, burst into the doorway, and we scrambled for the back of the shop. That back door—we could escape and block it from the outside. We stooped behind counters and scuttled at top speed. Like naughty children we ducked and dashed through the dark, slippery shop, barely missing beeves and brains, blades and bones. I brought up the rear, fighting dizziness and nausea as I dodged the hanging carcasses of cows and pigs that Mr. Zimmer had set swinging in his escape.

As we dashed along, rats scurried out of our way.

Zimmer reached the back door first and clawed at it hysterically. The door was locked, with no key in sight. Klara and Zimmer kicked and pounded at the door, then, ducking all the while, turned to scavenge on the back table for weapons. I pushed a heavy cleaver into my belt but kept both hands tight on my pipe.

"We only want *him*," said the swarthy man, his hands confidently grasping the reloaded crossbow, his eyes never leaving Zimmer.

For a moment the thoughts flickered: Has Zimmer done something monstrous to deserve this? Should we just tell the men we give up? Then Klara and I could walk away, rather than bleed to death on the floor of a slaughterhouse. But I knew two things: Klara would not consider this option, and I should not.

For a moment of agonizing silence, flies buzzed on piles of coiled intestines, rats returned to their foraging, and the assassins approached us slowly, weapons raised, focusing on Mr. Zimmer.

"This man is our friend," Klara announced, in a voice big enough for a crowd. "He is a councilman of Hamelin, a close friend of my father, the mayor. Leave us alone, or you'll never get out of this alive."

At that moment, as though he feared more talking, the archer took another shot at Zimmer, and the dart sank deep in the door right where Zimmer had been standing. Klara heaved a meat-ax at the archer, and though he dodged, it struck his shoulder and drew the first blood.

110

He glanced at the wound, then swore at Klara in a dangerously quiet growl. He lunged, turning over a table, and bright red slabs of meat flew in all directions. He was soon entangled in sausages and pots, and I had a clear shot at him and at a large group of rats. Piping hard, I threw the pipe strings, tied them with two crisp notes, and ducked as the man with the club moved to corner me. I had a glimpse of the rats swarming straight up the archer's breeches as he grunted and bellowed like a trapped beast.

Klara fled to a safer position near the door with cover on three sides. Meanwhile two of the men surged forward, toward Zimmer. In desperation I piped a tune that set the carcasses swinging wildly on their chains. Still the two men, with the dagger and the sword, ducked, and kept closing on Zimmer. The treasurer of Hamelin pathetically threw two pans of entrails and then cowered, waiting for death as he had on the ground at the Thiewall. My shots, which needed eye contact, went wild in the mayhem of swaying carcasses.

Suddenly Zimmer popped up holding a chain with a cow's head hooked on it, the eyeballs gazing out forlornly. He drew it back and slung it with all his might. It caught the man with the sword square in the chest. He stumbled back into a pan of blood, sending up a scarlet wave, and bobbed up spluttering with a ghoulish face bathed in red. As he took a while wiping, the man with the dagger tore around the table at Zimmer.

I piped a shot, and at last I connected. His foot went wide; he slipped on a pile of pork fat that the rats had still not abandoned. With a grunt, a cry, and an oath, he came crashing down into a heap of hooves and tails.

Glancing around for the man with the club, I saw him closing in on Klara at the door. She held a knife in each hand but kept backing up. Her dress caught on a broomstick, and she fell. The thickset man stood over her, club raised high, and demanded she drop the knives. Next thing I knew, a thighbone with a cabbage-sized head of tissue sailed through the air. It hit Klara's attacker in the back of the head with a loud crack. Zimmer's work.

I was nodding my congratulations at him when I heard the zing of a bow shot. The archer had just missed me. I crouched behind a tub of livers, hearts, and pancreases, waiting for a pop at that crossbow. I had already picked my tune, but my target was continually hidden by standing pillars or dancing pigs.

Zimmer took aim at the swarthy man with a pot of tripe, which extravagantly splattered the wall. When the archer turned on him, Zimmer, who had found a pot bristling with knives, flung one after another, aiming carefully.

I heard a clank behind me and whirled around, low to the ground, pipe at my lips. It was the man with the knife—he had a second one in his other hand now. That spin had triggered a wave of blinding dizziness, and I lurched into a foul-smelling, fly-covered vat. When I leaped back to my feet, pipe at my lips, I was wreathed with intestines, fearing that my attacker had already been at me and that some of them might be mine.

The man with the knives, whose stance showed him to be the veteran of many knife fights, drew closer. He thrust at my stomach, and as I blocked with my hand, I felt the razor-sharp edge bite in— a long gash. Quick as lightning, his other knife made a short slash across the top of my head. He got his footing and rushed in once more. Concentrating on his target, he forgot the swinging carcasses, and one of them sent him sprawling.

My head was bleeding; my hand was bleeding worse. I wiped it, got a good look at the wound, and wanted to bind it. There was no time, as the swordsman saw me sucking a wound and sprinted at me.

I turned at a sound. Klara was standing beside me, with a sharpened hook in one hand and a cutting board in the other. She spread her feet and prepared for combat as though she did this every day.

The swordsman kept coming. I kicked a barrel of beef tongues at him, and they splattered at his feet. He stepped right through them and looked me in the eyes. That was all I needed. Maintain my gaze and four notes—the swordsman screamed in sheer terror. Good hit: he was blinded and would be for a while.

But Klara was still moving with the fury of a she-bear. Not knowing the advantage she had, with a grim face she struck the man a savage blow in the chest. He folded and went down. She was protecting her Uncle Dietrich, her father's friend, a Hameliner— whose guilt or innocence was not the point right now. The meat hook, already splashed with the man's blood, was raised high now for what might be a lethal hit.

"Klara, stop!" I yelled.

She looked at me.

"He's blind. Let him go."

The swordsman, his handsome gray cloak now soaked red,

began crawling on all fours back toward the street door. Then he did a terrible thing. He turned from a hired killer into a person. He began groaning, pleading with his companions, whom he could no longer see, to help him. When they did not reply, he screamed that he was dying.

Klara trembled. At any moment his comrades might begin skewering us, but now the man in the gray cloak had touched the nurse in her. As for me, I had never known it was possible to feel, all at once, such pity, disgust, and rage.

My earlier tune wore off, and the carcasses, chains, and chitterlings grew still. The two men with dagger and club were standing at some distance, sobered by their companion's fate. I had a clear shot now, and I lifted an arsenal of butcher's instruments from a tabletop and sprayed them toward the hesitating men. That was all the encouragement they needed; they grabbed the swordsman under the arms and, hauling him roughly, fled into the street.

But where was the one with the crossbow? When I turned, I saw Zimmer crouched behind a barrel, trembling. He'd gotten two innocent people entangled in this deadly mess, and now he was letting a dizzy stranger and an unarmed young lady face professional killers while he hid behind a barrel.

Just then I saw, from behind the knife cabinet, a crossbow being raised, aimed directly at Klara. Even as I lifted my pipe, hoping for a decent shot, Zimmer saw it too. With a squirrel-like speed that astonished me, he sprang and pushed her to the ground, just as the archer fired. It was such a near thing that I thought someone had been hit.

I heard the hidden archer reloading and thought of all the things I'd seen the Pipelord do to people without eye contact. What I would have given to know even one of those tunes at that moment! It was infuriating that I could lure out a hidden rat and yet be powerless against a hidden murderer. Even as I waited like a hunter for him to make his move, I felt my vision going black. Not again!

I felt the top of my head. My hair was matted with warm blood. I had to do something, or I would pass out. I grabbed the strung-up rear legs of the cow beside me, one in each hand, and hung on for dear consciousness. But I was sliding. I saw the murderer stalking toward Klara and Zimmer's hiding place, and there was nothing I could—

Bang! The back door was kicked open with a blow like a thunderclap. An arrow sliced through the air, and the assassin dropped his weapon, staggered backward, and went crashing down into a pan of innards. His limbs began a rapid twitching, and some poor woman's son ended his days on the floor of a slaughterhouse.

I tried to lift my head to see who stood in the doorway. Heavy footsteps crossed the plank floor. A voice that seemed familiar spoke with Klara. She was alive. I heard Zimmer's voice. He was all right. Footsteps again, shaking the floor under me. A foot rolled me over.

I looked up, and there hung the cow, its pink tongue lolling out and its hooves close enough to touch my face. The cow was pushed aside, and there in its place stood a large man.

"You again," he said. Wolf.

I tried to smile.

"By my head I swear, I'm gettin' tired of rescuin' you."

⊢——•——⊣

It was all happening again. I could feel Klara dabbing with a clean cloth and warm water at the cut on my head, saying, "He could have been killed."

I opened my eyes, and Klara actually seemed glad to see me conscious. I looked around without turning my head. We were in a humble peasant home, but with some fairly nice weapons displayed on the walls. That combination puzzled me till I saw, floating over me, Wolf's face. We were in his home. There he stood, arms crossed tight and huge across his chest as though he didn't trust what his hands would do if he released them.

As usual, Zimmer had shrunk into the corner. Across the room sat three small children, studying us but saying nothing. Meanwhile a round woman was scuttling to and fro between a large pan, where she seemed to be soaking Klara's garments in ash and soda, and a table, where she was scrubbing Zimmer's with warm wine and fuller's earth. I heard many an "Ugh!" and a "Tsk!" as she found fresh signs of pig entrails.

Once again I had awakened in a child's theater. This time it was Klara and Zimmer who seemed to be the players, dressing up in their parents' clothes: Klara's gray dress was sewn for a woman twice her width, and Zimmer's homespun brown tunic was designed for a man twice his height.

Water was steaming over a small fire. There was a smell of stew with beef bones and onions, a smell that made the assassins seem a thousand miles away. I knew from the furnishings that the whole family slept in this one room at night, and what I could see were the whole of Wolf's possessions on this earth. The floor was of tight-packed, clean-swept earth. That smell, too, a smell I had not slept with for six years, was utterly comfortable. This, and not Roth Kunst's house, was where I belonged.

"Miss Hofmann," I said. Almost no sound came.

"Yes?" She leaned forward, her eyes shining. Could Klara Hofmann and I make our peace only when I lost consciousness? That might get tiresome . . .

In fact, they were all leaning forward, eagerly, even Wolf. I pointed at Zimmer and said in the strongest voice I could manage, "He saved her. Twice."

Wolf stepped forward. "How?"

With many pauses to catch my breath, I told my version of what had happened in the butcher's shop. From Klara's face I saw that much of it was news to her. Then I was forgotten as Wolf hurriedly poured something into four cups.

"To the hero," he boomed, and raised a cup in Zimmer's direction.

Mr. Zimmer actually blushed, smiled skittishly, and clinked with them. He looked the happiest he had since toasting me, back in the Town Hall cellar. I felt tears in my eyes. We were alive, all three of us. Thanks to Zimmer. Heaven help me, I liked him after all.

Zimmer drained the cup, and his eyes bugged. "Oh," he said. His eyes stared, his face soured. "May I . . . ?" He raised his eyebrows and nodded his head toward the back of the house, suggesting the privy.

"Of course!" Wolf led the way, opened the door. In a moment he returned and heaved himself into a chair. "You stood me up."

I blinked.

"I went and got the six witnesses, just like we agreed." He scowled. "I come to Town Hall. Sit with 'em in the lobby. Decide I'll look in quiet on the party. Servant tells me Klara ain't been seen for some time. Since it's her party, I thinks, *Now that's strange.* An' 'e says, 'Mr. Zimmer's gone too. An' there was a funny-lookin' young man creepin' about here with Miss Hofmann,' he says. Well, 'at was it for me. I sent the witnesses home—and they just loved me for that—went askin' after Klara all over the place, came home, fearin' the worst; you can imagine. Just as I'm pickin' up my bow and gear, up runs my neighbor Heinrich the butcher and says, "There's a fight in my shop tearin' the place to shreds, and I swear, among 'em is one o' them cussed pipers, same as we had six years back!'"

We talked a bit about the fight. Wolf bounced back and forth between enjoyment of the details and a raging urge to beat someone to a pulp for allowing Klara to be one of the combatants. At these moments he would turn a dark eye on me.

"So," he asked, narrowing his eyes, "who were those people?"

We began to explain the little we knew about Zimmer's fears—how he had talked in riddles about threats of death, how it had all begun when one of the hunters saw Zimmer in the treasurer's office. When we explained about the empty cash box, Wolf's face turned strange, and suddenly he interrupted.

"Stop," he cried. "Are you sayin' Zimmer was your prisoner?"

"Yes," I whispered.

"No," said Klara.

He looked back and forth between us, then brought his fist crashing down on the table. All three empty cups jumped.

"Your prisoner's escapin'," he snarled, and ran out the back door.

NINE

The Trap

Friday, June Twenty-third, 1284, Hamelin

OUR BRIEF HUNT FOR MR. ZIMMER DOWN THE ALLEYWAYS behind Wolf's house was fruitless. We ended up at Roth's house, where Wolf insisted on remaining in the hallway, and Mrs. Rike was feeding Gudrun in the kitchen. So in the sitting room, which was also home to my sleep mat and Gudrun's toys, three of us were sitting around the table—Roth, Klara, and I.

Roth seemed as glad to see us alive after our ordeal as if we were his brother and sister, and ordered a delicious supper—a celebration supper, he called it—of the finest of his larder.

Mrs. Rike, Roth's housekeeper, laid out a masterpiece: a dish of succulent pheasant stuffed with cranberries, cooked with something called cloves and mysterious spices from places I couldn't pronounce. We nibbled on tender, pink ham with fine, white bread, pungent mustard, melt-in-your-mouth cheese, and a dozen other delicacies, some I'd never seen before.

Klara and I laughed at every trifle, downright silly with relief after the danger. Roth's house felt like an island of sanity where life might once again make sense. On that safe island, I told Roth about our strange afternoon—about Strom and his gang, the behavior of the council, the missing fund, the chase around town, the arrow, the cellar, the fight at the butcher's.

Klara said little, and Roth kept shaking his head, looking completely appalled.

When I finished my tale, Mrs. Rike set out a jar of a red, fruity beverage, confessing with an embarrassed smile that she had made it herself. At the sight of her simple joy, the realization sank in: I was alive. I was eating with friends. For a moment, let analysis wait.

I poured Mrs. Rike's creation in everyone's cup and said, "Friends, I must raise a toast to my Hamelin family."

They laughed, but I continued.

"No, really. That's what you are to me. Once again I have to thank both of you for saving my life, and for being with me in the strangest adventure of my life. So, here's to my Hamelin family."

I thought of the wreck of my father's life, of the loneliness I'd felt in the crowded 'prentice house attic. As we drank, Mrs. Rike's delicious concoction warmed me, I looked at Roth and Klara and felt some hope of finding home.

Roth raised the next toast. "To Hamelin's birthday girl. Congratulations. It's been a strange birthday, but whether the council recognizes it or not, you are Hamelin's heart! You have great dreams for your city. My wish for you, Miss Hofmann, is that one day you will earn a position that reflects your extraordinary heart." He beamed at the celebrant, and they clinked cups meaningfully, as Klara blushed and I hammered myself for forgetting it was her birthday.

The next thing I knew, she was crying and turning to wipe her eyes. On a chair in the corner, she spotted Gudrun's clay doll.

"Oh! That used to be mine," she remarked, and went to pick it up. "I haven't played with these since—" She dropped the doll back on the chair.

When she returned to the table, Roth intoned with mock seriousness, "I think we'd do wrong not to toast Hamelin's newest dandy."

Perhaps in hopes of concealment, Zimmer had escaped with my hat and cloak, leaving me with his. His hat was a thing of beauty, with an extravagant feather along one side. I wished I could read in Klara's face whether she thought it became me.

"Johannes," Roth went on, "we met yesterday. But we . . ." He paused, and the room was very quiet. "Hannes, you want to be useful to your guild. You want to be useful to Hamelin. Here's my wish. May you be both—perhaps in ways you've never imagined."

I drank, which was convenient, because with the lump in my throat I don't know if I could have spoken. A question occurred to me.

"Miss Hofmann."

"Yes?"

"It seemed to me that on the way here . . ." I suppressed a smile and went on in a low voice, almost mouthing the words, ". . . Wolf was *unusually* hard on me."

"No mystery," replied Klara. "He doesn't like the idea of my crawling all over Hamelin in your company." She must have seen the hurt rising in my face, for she added, "Don't take it personally. It would be the same with anyone."

"He resents any—" I began, and stopped, feeling my face go redder.

"Mr. Piper, as with so many things that surprise you in Hamelin, you would be well advised to ask and listen first. You might learn something."

"Miss Hofmann, I am your humble servant, asking, listening, and learning."

She flicked a cranberry at me. Our first cranberry.

"Six years ago," she began, "a young man was . . . interested in me. As I told you earlier, it ended badly, with two people dead. One was the young man's serving boy . . ." Klara shuddered. "The other was the young man himself. He committed suicide. So the answer to your question is: My father hired Wolf to 'help out.' Wolf is my bodyguard. He's practically a member of the family. And he's never going to let me get mixed up in anything like that again."

"Miss Hofmann, I remember that night—parts of it. It was my first night in the guild, and my first night in Hamelin, and it was terrifying."

"What a coincidence!" exclaimed Roth. "You could have met."

Klara's wary eyes reminded me of my promise to her six years ago. *Don't worry. I won't tell.* I shrugged. "A dark night, a strange town, screaming and fighting, hundreds of faces—a lot of it was just a blur."

"Hm," said Roth. "Shock for you, all right. How old were you?"

"Twelve. And it didn't stop there."

Klara was looking at her hands, but Roth's eyes invited me to explain.

"The suicide's name was Anselm; he was a rebel from my guild. Everyone who'd been leery of him now suspect me. I inherited his mantle."

Roth was listening with his mouth slightly open.

"A lot of people envied me for being the Pipelord's apprentice at a young age—just as Anselm had been. From time to time I over-heard comments on how my master was losing his touch, picking strange apprentices, overusing intuition, and so on."

Roth shook his head, hanging on my words. "Sounds lonely," he sighed.

I nodded.

"Well," said Roth, "I have a sad story to tell myself, a lot like yours. Miss Hofmann, it seems you and I are still recovering from the violent deaths of our childhood friends. In my case it was a friend I grew up with. He was the son of a lord . . . the, uh, illegiti-mate son. His mother was a serf. You know what was miserable? Realizing my love would never make up for his father's hate. A man can't bear to be helpless—especially to someone he cares about. And I was helpless to rescue him.

"My father would go to my friend's father. 'Couldn't you do a bit more for the boy? He's your *son*.' But the man was like granite. Wouldn't even acknowledge the boy. My friend grew up, a serf among serfs. All the hardships of serfs. All the diseases of serfs. And all the while he sees his father's legal son enjoying all he could ever want. Now, Hannes, look. My friend was an innocent victim, same as you." Roth shook his head.

"He never accepted his fate. The day came when he'd made as much of himself as a serf could. My father had made him a house servant; he had skills. I kept telling him, 'Look at yourself; you've already succeeded.' But that boy had only one definition of success. He dressed up, paid a special call on his father. Threw himself on his knees, begged to be accepted."

Klara and I waited.

"His father spat on him."

I winced. "What became of him?"

"I lost him. In the end, the young man took his life."

We talked about many things that afternoon, but eventually the conversation came back to Zimmer and the council and the cash box and what to do next. With Klara inserting lots of clarifying remarks, I told Roth the gist of our debate, and from time to time he would ask a refreshingly rational question. In the end Klara and I fell silent and turned to him as though he were the referee.

Roth looked evenly at us both. "You two don't need more dis-cussion; you need more information. You need definite evidence before you go to the duke or the townspeople, or even the council. Maybe I can help." He turned to Klara.

"You're right. It would be awkward for Hannes to go around asking certain questions. But I have business ties with councilmen; I'm popular with them at the moment. I know about some unofficial records kept at Town Hall, other than the treasury books you've been keeping. I think *I* could get at them safe enough. But after what's happened today, you'd be crazy to try."

Looking at me, he said, "The evidence I'm hoping to get will help us make a sensible plan, get the money, and punish the wrongdoers."

"Miss Hoffman," he added, "you and I will show what I find to the mayor. He can make all the decisions." He stood. "No time like the present. Let me slip off to Town Hall. See what I can see. It'll still be open—birthday, you know. I'll get back to you here as soon as I can."

And just like that, he left.

Soon Klara and Wolf did too. After saying good-bye to them, I shuffled back into the sitting-room and stared awhile at the crimson rug and gleaming floorboards. Where was my mission? Where was my reward? Suddenly I wanted to put my fist through a wall. I hated being stuck here, waiting.

I walked up to the ornately carved mirror. Wooden scrollwork I'd seen before, but what I had seen only two or three times in my life was the image of my own face. So this was me. This was what Klara saw when she saw Johannes Piper.

I rubbed my chin in a way that looked wise when the Pipelord did it. I hadn't shaved in several days; my beard was sparse.

The Pipelord had beamed at my two-tone legs, as though this outfit were a wise comment on my soul. There were times when I couldn't tell what the Pipelord was thinking, and even more times when I couldn't tell why.

I looked like a freak, someone who would never find a resting place, who would never fit in.

Otto, a fellow senior apprentice, once said to me with a knowing grin, "There are girls who would be drawn by the pipe—by the power, you know—even to a gargoyle. Or a man with a fuzzy little beard, or a man with red and yellow legs."

Otto had a magnificent beard, and forest-green hosen.

From the bottom of my backpack, I fished out a parchment

epistle by Anselm the Rebel, called *The Piper's Choice.* I stretched myself out on my mat and unrolled the scroll. *This is the piper's choice,* I read. *The guild has told you that you are a servant. I say to you that you are a king, destined to lead men as though they were sheep.* Comforting words, after the day with Bauer, Zimmer, and Klara. I read on, savoring the author's masterful turns of phrase, and welcoming the distraction, till finally the pressure of postponed duty was too great to ignore.

I gathered quill and inkhorn to write a letter to Master Friedrich. I made my presentation: moral problem, money problem, mystery piper. I explained the broken seal; I did not mention my father or my hard knocks. The letter was detached and formal. Guild masters issued decrees, changed lives, and behaved severely; they had to. And what if I disappointed them?

I lay back on my mat, stared at the ceiling, and wondered how it was possible for me to try so hard to do right, while Klara thought me so wrong. As my head grappled with that question, my hand strayed to Gudrun's dolls. I thwacked a particularly ugly doll against my palm and daydreamed of what I would do if I ever cornered the birthmarked man, the man who had broken my father.

I put the ugly doll down and twirled the beautiful clay doll absentmindedly over my head and imagined Klara relenting and proclaiming me her city's wise savior. As the doll swooped in my sky like a falcon, I heard a dry rattling. I sat up and looked the doll over. In the back was a little opening into the hollow body. Reaching in, I could feel a rolled-up piece of parchment. I wiped my quill and used it as a tool to coax the paper out from its hiding place. The opening was so small that I was perspiring and shaking by the time I drew it out.

I unrolled my little treasure. Before me lay a musical score, written as fine as ant tracks. I had never seen a score so complicated —my eyes crossed at the sheer quantity of notes, of thirty-second notes, syncopations, trills, slides, and runs . . . It contained difficult keys, difficult ornamentation. The notation and format, more detailed than any other in all of the empire, could mean only one thing: this music was from my guild. In fact, as I turned my attention to the encrypted markings at the bottom of the page, I recognized grim signs warning that the tune was powerful and dangerous. I set it down and stared at the doll. Why should a piping tune from my guild be tucked into the body of a child's doll in Hamelin?

I picked it up again, feeling my breath quicken, then put it down. The parchment looked as though it had been torn from a book. Torn by whom? From what book? I had to decide what to do with the score. For the moment I was stuck, alone in this room with this paper till either Roth or Klara called for me. This could not just be chance. Just when I didn't know where to turn or what to do, this scrap had come to me. I was meant to have and to use this thing, whatever it was. I was meant to be stretched by Hamelin's unforeseen emergencies, and to use this tool. And if the score turned out to be some spine-tingling judgment, maybe that was what Hamelin needed. Maybe that was justice.

In any case, this parchment must now stay on my person. I would learn this music, crack the coded instructions at the bottom of the page, and discover what it all did.

I heard a noise—probably Mrs. Rike leaving. Alone in the house, I could study my treasure with impunity. I took up my pipe and struggled to play this wild music, with its very high and very low notes, its continual movement between crisp and languid, until my mind and my mouth and my fingers were exhausted.

As I let my treasure fall from my knees, for the first time I noticed that something had been hastily scribbled on the other side. With difficulty I made out these letters: *H hshed E8stn.* I latched the door before any further work on the score.

And there I spotted Gudrun, sitting on the floor behind an armchair, surrounded by a tribe of dolls.

"Hello," she said, bouncing up.

"A spy!" I whispered, and she giggled. "Gudrun, what did you see and hear before I found you?"

"I saw you play from a piece of parchment. From my doll." She flounced down onto the mat and patted a place beside her. "How'd it get in there?"

"I was hoping you'd tell me."

Gudrun shrugged. "So you can read it? What does it say?"

I rolled up the paper and put it in my bag. "It says, *Dear Apprentice Gudrun of Hamelin, tell your friend Johannes he should be doing what pipers are meant to do. Please do not let him sit in his room any longer and wait for other people to fix what's wrong in Hamelin. Sincerely, Master Josef, The Pipers Guild.*"

"What's that supposed to mean?"

"Gudrun, today some men attacked me."

"Uh-huh. Wolf told me. That's what happened to Klara's dress."

"You know, your sister is a warrior. Almost as fierce as you with your stones."

Gudrun gave me a ladylike smile.

"But anyway, because of the bad men, I have to ask you to stay here and not come with me."

"Where are you going?"

"Town Hall."

"But you know, actually I do go there all the time."

"Please. Things have changed. Today Town Hall has become a dangerous place." I stood up to go.

"Maybe you need to lean on me."

I moved to the door. "Miss Gudrun, your care has completely restored me."

"Mr. Piper. That was my doll."

My heart stopped. What did she have in mind? "Of course, Gudrun. But this paper is from my guild. It's . . . it's got to be our secret." I knelt and looked straight into her eyes. "You can't tell anyone about it. No one."

"All right. Fine."

I patted her on the shoulder, said good-bye, and left.

———•———

Retracing my steps from the morning, hurrying past the nightmares along the path, I arrived at the town square feeling tougher than the first time. Still, the heavy-looking building seemed crouched to swallow me, and my first step onto the square actually took an effort. But this time, I had allies inside. The mayor would welcome me. Roth was in there somewhere, conducting the research that might put things right.

As I stepped into the square, a crowd of children looked up, shouted, and ran over to me. Remembering my run-in with Strom and his gang, I thrust my hand into my bag, wrapped it tightly around the pipe, and braced myself. But these were small children, most of them boys, giggling and gaping at me. I heard snatches of excited jabbering.

"That's him . . . They say he just played that thing and *pow*! . . . He's magical . . ."

They must have heard rumors about the skirmish at Heinrich's butcher shop. Most of them were staring at my right hand, concealed in the bag. As when I smelled the earth floor and the simple food at Wolf's, I felt a wave of recognition and reunion wash over me. This was more like it—like my training trips with the Pipelord. This was how the reception of a guild piper was supposed to feel.

I waded through the circle of boys, my spirits lifting, and by the time I reached the stairs into Town Hall, I found myself at the head of a chattering parade.

This time I got past Mr. Krueger simply by saying, with some distortion of the facts but with unfeigned urgency, "Miss Hofmann asked for me." I went to the last place we had been together: the treasurer's office, where we'd found the empty box that had spelled doom for my mission, and stepped in.

There was Klara, kneeling over something on the floor. When she lifted her head to see who had come, I saw something impossible: a man lying on the floor, dressed in my hat and cloak. In the back were three stab wounds, where the fabric of my cloak had been soaked in bright red blood. Mr. Zimmer.

The funny little man who had toasted me downstairs this morning. The old friend who had bounced Klara on his knee years ago. From Klara's expression, I knew he was dead.

"Miss Hofmann," I cried. "What happened?"

She shook her head. Her face was shiny with tears and streaked with blood.

"Miss Hofmann, you need to wash. Then we can go tell your father."

She rose as though in a trance and threw herself on me like deadweight. I struggled to support her as she wept in great, gulping sobs.

When at last she calmed herself and went to the banqueting room where she knew she could find a water pot, I stepped over to the treasurer's body. By his head lay a long knife. Three thrusts at the heart with such a weapon—Mr. Zimmer would have died quickly.

The door opened again. I turned to see Mr. Bauer, the now-sober Mr. Lachler, and Wolf regarding me and Mr. Zimmer with shock.

"What the devil is this?" whispered Mr. Bauer. He strode into the room. "Wolf!" he barked. Wolf threw me roughly against the wall, then drew his sword.

"And to think," said Mr. Bauer, "I considered you merely impudent!" His eyes were flashing. "Look at him, Lachler. He changed clothes with him before he—" To my amazement, Mr. Bauer choked and fell to his knees on the stone floor by Mr. Zimmer. He closed his eyes. When he opened them wide, they were turned on me.

"Dietrich Zimmer was my friend. And *you* killed him!"

TEN

Rats and Strings

Friday, June Twenty-third, 1284, Hamelin

O, SIR." I FORCED MYSELF TO ANSWER BAUER'S ACCUSATION. "I found him here. Miss Hofmann found him first, and I walked in."

"And where is she?"

"She is washing blood off her hands."

"Do you take me for an idiot?" Bauer snarled. He looked at the body, with its three crimson wounds. He looked at my clothing, streaked with the blood from Klara's face and hands. "Dietrich Zimmer was well loved. I don't know if the people will wait for legal procedures in a case so savage. Lachler," he said, "sound the alarm."

Lachler left, and the meaning of my situation crashed in on me.

Within a minute Town Hall's deep-voiced alarm bell was tolling out the news of Mr. Zimmer's cold-blooded murder. When I dared to look up at Wolf's face, I saw pure contempt and had no doubt that if I made a sudden move, he would use the sword now held against my belly.

Soon voices and feet were beating their way up the stairs and down the hall. Faces appeared in the doorway. The men carried clubs and brutal-looking homemade weapons. The scene was ripening toward mob execution of the prime suspect. Like a lightning flash, I remembered the face of young Anselm hanging in the stocks.

"This stranger," boomed Bauer's authoritative voice, "has the gall to wear the stolen hat of Mr. Dietrich Zimmer, our treasurer and friend. I found them like this when I came in with Mr. Lachler and this good man-at-arms. The foreigner was standing over Zimmer's body."

I had seen it before, during my training with the Pipelord, how a mob could behave like an attacking animal. A roar went up from the men in the doorway, and they poured into the office, weapons raised.

A man in a blacksmith's apron lifted a steel-headed club, aiming a blow at my head. This was the moment the Pipelord would have approved of—to reach into my bag and seize the pipe. But when I lowered my hand, Wolf pressed the sword and I felt its unforgiving point.

Suddenly Klara threw herself into the room and shrieked, *"Stop!"*

In that instant you could hear the creaking of belt and boot leather. My heart pounded with combat readiness.

"I am prepared to swear that this man is innocent. Put down your weapons and listen to me."

The men obeyed, as they would have stopped at the sight of a growling she-bear.

"I came and found Mr. Zimmer dead. Johannes Piper, the stranger you are prepared to kill without hearing proper testimony, arrived *after* I did."

"He may have been returning," retorted Bauer with a sneer.

"Can any of you," asked Klara, in a voice crackling with anger, "honestly imagine a stranger committing murder in Town Hall and then returning to the scene?"

Bauer approached Klara and stood looking down at her. Suddenly all of us were reminded how small she was.

"I will not stand here and let justice be obstructed by the testimony of a *girl*," he announced.

Tears of desperate fury came to Klara's eyes at this crowning blow to the morning's humiliation and betrayal. Mayor's daughter, Hamelin's finest citizen, leader in care for the sick, councilwoman-in-training—and now suddenly, when it came to a life-and-death decision, she was nothing but a "girl."

She faced Bauer. "I am the daughter of the mayor of this city. I worked day after day beside Mr. Zimmer, and no one in this town loved him more than I did." She turned to the crowd. "I have studied the laws of Hamelin more than many, and I know that they permit a man to appeal for trial by ordeal. As a witness whose firsthand testimony is being despised by this 'court,' I appeal for trial by ordeal for Johannes of Oldendorf." She reached a hand to me. "Give me your letter of authorization."

I did as I was told; I dug in my bag and drew out the rolled-up parchment, feeling at every movement a clear warning from Wolf's sword.

"This paper," she said, unrolling it before them, "is signed by the mayor of Hamelin and gives Johannes of Oldendorf the right to deliver you from the plague of rats. Baseless accusation by a mob does not remove that right from him. Assassinate him, and you lose forever the chance to be freed from this plague. I have seen all the liars and fakes who have come before now, just as you have. But I swear before you all that this man can and will do it!"

There was a murmur of assent from the crowd. They lowered their weapons, relaxed their faces and muscles.

"Will you let this innocent guest serve Hamelin and save Hamelin? For that is the only reason he has come. What do you say? Do we let him get rid of the rats?"

Mr. Bauer hissed, "He is not innocent!"

"Then," Klara answered, "let his work with the rats be his trial by ordeal. It is his right under law. If the rats are gone by this time tomorrow, Johannes of Oldendorf is innocent of all charges." She raised her hands and shouted to the crowd, "People of my city, let us go with our guest to Town Square, and see what he can do for us!"

The people drew back against the walls, and a path opened in front of me. I looked straight ahead and forced myself to walk slowly between those two rows of eyes, out of the room and down the hall. Klara followed me, and the crowd closed in behind.

Waves of cold and heat seemed to be moving over my skin. I could take away the rats, but if anything went wrong, if these people changed their minds, I might not be able to use my pipe in time for so many.

I pushed through the Town Hall doors, and Klara and I swept out onto the stairs.

Gudrun's anxious face waited at the bottom of the steps, all of Hamelin filling the square behind her. As I headed for the center of the square, with the crowd parting before me and closing in behind, she fell in step beside me.

"Hannes, what's going on?"

"They think I killed someone. This is called trial by ordeal."

Her eyes widened. "They're putting you in boiling water?"

"No. It's time to kill the rats."

I was in the center of the square now, with people in a ring ten feet away. Klara faced me from the crowd's edge, and Gudrun worked to free her hand from Klara's.

I turned to face the southwest corner of the square, where the pavement squeezed between Town Hall and the neighboring building. A movement caught my eye, and as I looked up at a second-floor window of Town Hall, Gudrun followed my gaze. Bauer sneered at me before closing the shutters.

On every side, the eyes of Hamelin were on me. And among the Hameliners scuttled the rats. One crawled up on Gudrun's shoe, and she kicked it off without even looking.

"Good luck!" she said.

My head cleared. I wasn't just saving myself. I was setting Gudrun free. I was setting them all free. I took a deep breath and pulled my pipe from my bag.

There were gasps as the people drew back.

"Hey!" said a man on the far side of Klara, taking a step toward me.

"Wait," Klara snapped, and blocked him with her hand.

I ignored them. I would save them whether they liked it or not. I shifted my weight to my toes, shut my eyes, and set the pipe to my lips. When the metal touched my skin and my breath stirred the pipe to life, the last of my weakness vanished.

Liberation.

That first note, I knew it well—soft, sorrowful, and piercing. Every rat in Hamelin halted. How many times had I dreamed of this moment—the pipe sounding, the rats turning, the town watching? I could feel the vibrating power of the pipe move across Hamelin like an earthquake.

As I played the first note, I could sense the rats, their weight tugging back a little, as if I had them on a thousand strings. That much was as it should be. But I felt another pull, another set of strings pulling them the other way. This was the hand whose fingerprints I'd sensed at the monastery. *So now we meet.*

The silence after the first note grew long.

I leaned against the pull and began to play. The music sludged out as if through mud. I stepped out and leaned again, but as I did, the strings cut into my shoulder and my feet slid back on the slick stones. I staggered and braced myself to strain against the strings again.

My eyes were closed, but I could feel the rats as clearly as if they were under my fingers. They were crouched, heads down, bodies quivering.

A drop of sweat trickled down my forehead, and I stood still a moment, with my muscles as tight as those strings. I knew this pipe work backward and forward But the counterpull was just as strong as I was. As I stood there, breathing the smell of them, I knew I could not budge the rats another inch.

I was afraid to open my eyes. I was failing at the one part of my mission I was sure I could handle. If I looked, I would see the crowd. They would see me failing. *I was a dead man.* The note I'd been playing faded into nothing. Faintly, I heard the crowd murmuring.

This was more pulling than I could do alone. This was the end of Johannes of Oldendorf, so it *had* to be the beginning of something greater. Through the pipe I could hear a thundering command like the crashing of ocean waves: *Free them. It is time. It is right.* Still hearing the surging waters, I opened my eyes and shot the tune out like an arrow.

The rats' heads jerked up, their eyes fixed on me, and they lurched forward, fumbling for balance. I marched ahead, playing on, taking up the slack, leaning against the leashes that bound ten thousand rats to me. And now the waters swept me on.

As I marched through Hamelin's dirty streets, the unseen strings cut deeper at every step. The rats were coming faster, massing in my wake. I glanced back and shivered at the sight of all those eyes. The music gushed from my pipe, drawing that enemy army ahead to its doom.

I was almost running now, though the strings cut like knives, and I saw the river. Under the music I heard the scrabbling claws of the rats keeping up. Under the music I felt the buzzing of the crowd's admiration. Such a short step from "Hang him!" to "Hurrah!" They wanted a circus, and I was their clown after all.

As I held that image, the counterpull overwhelmed me, and I stumbled down onto all fours. But as I panted with my fingers on the paving stones, I knew this: Liberation had a beauty that did not depend on the worthiness of the liberated. *Liberation.* I picked myself up for the last pull.

Suddenly the cobbled street was gone. I leaped into a boat that waited for some fisherman there, and the force of the jump carried me out into the river. My footing and my fluting faltered at an invisible yank, but I kept playing. The boat swung hard into the current, and I swayed. But still I kept on playing.

As I turned, the first of the rats rushed up to the brink, then wavered.

The strings strained back as never before, and I fell to my knees. The craft tipped so hard that water sloshed in, and my pipe slipped in my sweating hands, squeaking out bungled notes, then thunked in the watery bottom of the boat.

I shot my head up. The rats reeled back a few feet from the brink, catching their balance, then nosing about aimlessly. The shore was black with them.

I plunged my hands into the muck at the bottom of the boat, dredging till I felt the pipe, and pulled it out, spouting brown water. Finally I got it in my mouth, right side up, blew the water out, and with fingers slipping, managed to play another note. Instantly the bonds dug into me again. Onshore, the rats had already begun scattering, but now they stopped.

I tightened my jaw, planted my knees firmly in the swaying boat's filthy water, and played with all my might. The flood of tears and blood that I had followed here lifted me to the crest of an unseen wave and flung me full force against the weight of my enemy.

The first of the rats spun to the edge and tumbled into the water. I felt its string snap and go slack.

No pain could stop me now. I leaned against the pull and spouted my music into heaven as a waterfall of rats plunged into the river. They poured toward me, little streams from side streets gathering in the flood. As they fell one by one, they released me.

They made no sound but the clatter of their claws. On and on, row on row, they ran to the brink and toppled in. None rose to the surface.

Endlessly they came. My fingers flickered up and down my pipe, and I cried for the pain I felt and I cried for Hamelin, knowing that each of these thousands of rats had terrorized babies and starved families.

The sun was setting, and the water turned to gold around the boat.

Here, with feet scrambling over stones, came one last rat. He ran, leaped, and struck the water, just as the sun set and the water turned black. The final cord snapped; my song was over.

ELEVEN

Suspects

Saturday, June Twenty-fourth, 1284, Hamelin

 WAS BACK IN THE GUILD HALL, HELPING MY MASTER PREPARE for a journey, as I often did in the final year of my training. I held the woolen robe, I held the wide belt . . .

"Johannes," he said.

"Yes, my lord."

"You were sent to kill rats. You've killed them. Are you finished?"

The question terrified me. I could not meet his eyes. Instead of answering, I buried myself in the task of picking up his clothes. I picked up a shirt, but it turned out to be a winding sheet that had no end. I spooled it over my arm until the ball of it was as big around as I was. Now the whole room was an enormous sheet, mounds and mountains of it around me, white on white. So white, so shapeless. I would never finish.

I fell amid the linen, rolled in it like a dog, and banged the floor with my fists. As I grew quiet, I could feel a touch. What kind of touch? Suddenly I knew: I was being touched in the Pipeworld. By whom? By whom?

I heard a whisper: "Justice!" They were calling me. I leaped up but tripped in the tangle of cloth. I struggled and struggled. At last a door opened. Light poured from it.

I woke up, sweating, my heart pounding . . .

Gudrun was smiling at me.

"Good morning," she said. "Actually, it's afternoon." Sunlight that looked like four in the afternoon was streaming in the window. "So what were you dreaming about?"

"Huh?" What had I said?

"You kept mumbling 'other one.'"

As soon as Gudrun spoke those words, it all came back. I remembered that in my dream I had been touched in the Pipeworld. There is no mistaking the touch of a fellow piper.

And then I remembered the real world I was tangled in: the world where I'd been accused of murder in the town I came to save. I remembered that tomorrow was the deadline for buying the manor near Aerzen. I felt exhausted, ragged, and afraid. In spite of Klara's good intentions, would I be hanged? Or murdered in my sleep by the same killer who got to Mr. Zimmer?

"You were amazing with the rats."

Gudrun's smile crowded out my fears, at least for the moment.

"How do you do that?"

I shrugged stupidly.

"All right now," she said, taking me in hand. "First, how do you know what things to pipe?"

"Well, it's hard," I answered. "The guild has rules for what crime deserves which curse. But the curses are also supposed to teach a lesson, if people will listen. And if you pipe a curse before you've learned that lesson yourself, things can go wrong."

"Like what?"

"Well . . . what the masters say is the tune gets cracked. It's weak, like a wall that might collapse. Then bad pipers can get inside and change the curse, or take control of it. If there are any bad pipers around." I leaned close to her and asked earnestly, "Have you seen any?"

She considered a moment, big-eyed with concentration, shook her head, and went on with her interview. "Are there any things you haven't learned yet?"

"You mean magic things?"

"No," she said, twisting her hair. "I mean those lessons you were talking about. Like the ones the curses teach."

"Oh. Well, I don't know, Gudrun. I guess so. I'm not a master piper yet."

She shivered. "Still, it's amazing. How you do that."

On an impulse I asked, "Would you like to learn to pipe, Gudrun?"

The guild would have no problem with my giving ordinary music lessons.

"A little." She twisted the strap of my bag, working up to something. "But actually, if you give me lessons, everybody'll make me play for Klara."

"For Klara. What do you mean?"

"Everybody always talks about Klara." Her voice was suddenly that of a fulsome matron: "A voice like an angel—but dear me, what will we do with little Gudi?" She snorted. "Do you know how yucky that is?"

I remembered Roth's friend the bastard, gazing with longing and resentment at the well-clothed proper son. "I know what you mean."

"'Cause I mean, actually, I'm already Klara's shadow, and I already have a mother, and I just—" Her lip was trembling. Concentrating on not crying, she finished, "I just want something that's *mine*."

I held out the pipe to her, and her face lit up. With a savage wipe at her nose, she set her lips and fingers to the correct position. She blew three clear notes, walking smoothly up the scale. Roth's wolfhounds stepped gently into the room and lay down at her feet.

I gave her a brief lesson. Like a duck finding water, she quickly learned a simple melody using the three notes, and it was actually a pleasure to hear her play them.

"Ooo," she groaned as she thrust the pipe back at me, "what if I get stuck for the next five years accompanying Klara!" She imitated Klara's nervous in-focus smile; the likeness was stunning.

I stared at this eight-year-old girl, remembering how the attack of rats had followed her single note on my pipe yesterday, in this same room, and remembering gossip I had heard about the rebel Anselm entering apprenticeship at age eight.

"Gudrun," I said, "I want to give you something." I reached into my bag and pulled out my father's little wooden flute. "Take this. To remember me by. Would you like that?"

She nodded, pleased, and tied the flute onto the sash around her waist. "But anyway," she picked up her story, "people went absolutely crazy after you passed out."

"Really?"

"Really. People threw hats in the air; people hugged each other. Like all the holidays happening at once." Gudrun sprang over to her dolls, swept them all together, and heaped them in front of me to show me the celebration I'd missed.

They pirouetted and jumped. A cloud of them flung themselves into the air for me to catch and hug. In Gudrun's replay of the rat kill, this was Hamelin's first happiness in a long year, and Hamelin danced—almost everybody. One little greenish rag doll stood apart, though, with his back turned to the crowd, and suddenly a familiar, rich voice bleated, "My rats."

I howled. It was Bauer. I tasted the double pleasure of annoying Mr. Bauer and sharing that with Gudrun.

Oh. Here came the pretty clay doll. With the legless Gudi doll, and even the bear doll that was Wolf, there was jumping and hugging. And over by the cloth scraps that must be the Hofmann home, the clay doll said, "Mommy, he was so brave."

Gudrun reassembled all the dolls, the legless doll and the bear doll at the center of the heap. The legless doll pointed and asked, "What's this place?"

And the bear answered, "The Bull and Barrel."

I reached out and touched the woolen clown. It jingled to life. I repeated, "The Bull and Barrel. I love this place."

The three of us pushed into the mass of other dolls. My clown doll would enjoy the celebration that my passed-out self had missed. A faceless doll made of wood gestured in a clownish way and had the whole crowd laughing.

Mr. Wood was saying, "So then he comes up the street. He's playing that pipe all the way. And the rats march right after him. They're coming down the alleys. They're jumping out the windows. People are screaming and yelling and going crazy. My wife was scared half to death."

A short, pear-shaped stocking doll stood up, holding aloft one stubby arm that grasped an invisible tankard. "I give you the Pied Piper," he roared. "He's the man of the hour. He's the savior of the fine town of Hamelin. Every man admires his powers *(murmurs of 'Hear, hear' from the assembled company)*. Every young lady notices his rugged good looks *(elbowings in the crowd)*. So here's to our beloved rat-catcher *(the tankard now soared above the pear doll)*. May he live long and well *(all cups raised)* on the reward he gets today, which he will share *('Yes sir!')* with the Hamelin maiden of his choice *(hooting)* and with his faithful friends assembled here today *('That's right!')*. To the health and happiness of Hamelin's own piper!"

The circle of dolls arose in a mass, some raising invisible drinks, to honor the man who in a single day had delivered their town from the plague of rats that had been destroying it for months. All drank deeply, then sat down, plunging into conversation:

"How d'you reckon he does it? Is it a trick?"

"What? Don't you remember that business six years back?"

"Where on earth did he get that suit?"

There was a hush as the bear doll rose to an impressive height and said, "No disrespect intended, of course."

"No," said the questioner. "Of course not. Lovely suit. I was just wondering where I could, uh, buy one myself."

I applauded. As I did, it occurred to me that if Gudrun could imitate piping as she could imitate life, she might be a formidable student indeed. Gudrun seemed ready to understand the Pipe-world, if only I could introduce it by name—like a person who has already learned Latin, ready to pick up Greek.

"Klara was actually crying when the rats started jumping. Crying and hugging Wolf and hugging me and hugging a lady selling carrots."

"Crying?"

"Yes," she answered. Suddenly her eyes popped.

"What?" I asked.

"I didn't tell you the main part."

"What part?"

"About Wolf."

"What about him?"

She opened her eyes wider. "When the rats were dying and stuff . . ."

"Yes?"

"He looked at you."

"Yes?"

"And he *smiled.*"

The two of us sat there, savoring this moment. Gudrun tucked a strand of hair behind one ear.

"Is Mr. Kunst right, that you're a genius?" I asked her.

"Actually, you don't even know how smart I am." She looked at her hands folded in her lap, the picture of the ideal child.

"So tell me."

"Well, you know I do hear things when people don't notice I'm there, 'cause I'm little and stuff?"

"Yes?"

"Klara and Daddy talked about some money."

"Hm."

"And some man—she just called him 'he,' you know? He really needs it."

"Poor guy."

"But anyway it's really a lot."

"Uh-oh."

"And they went on and on and on about it, where are they going to get it and everything, but actually I know where to get it."

I lifted my eyebrows.

"The Ant's-hill Treasure!"

"Gudrun, is this some dumb legend, with a hero and villains and magic spells?"

"No. All the old people talk about it, the same way they talk about . . . about Great-grandpa Peter!"

"No!"

"Uh-huh! Some people get really cranky when they talk about it and say it's all stolen stuff, and some even say it's theirs!"

"Why is it called the Ant's-hill Treasure?"

"It's in an anthill. Actually under. Underground."

"Let's dig it up, then. Can you get a shovel from your father?"

" 'Course I don't know where it is." She laughed and stood up. "So, Mr. Piper, are you still sick, or can you be well enough for a dinner?"

"Gudrun, say the word and I will be healed."

She fluffed my pillow.

"Well, my mommy and daddy say come tonight." She explained the time and place, then said she needed to go home. At the door she added, "And Mr. Kunst is supposed to come too."

"You know, Gudrun, you are one of the people I trust the most in this city."

Her face turned serious as I handed her a bag containing the two letters to Master Friedrich. "I have to get this to your sister as soon as possible. She knows what it is. She told me she could arrange a courier to carry it to Muender. It's urgent."

Gudrun gravely agreed to carry the bundle and patted my shoulder.

———— • ————

As soon as I heard her leave the house, I reached into my bag and fumbled till my fingers closed on the parchment. The score had become a puzzle that my mind returned to constantly, like a wiggling tooth that the tongue can't leave alone. In a moment my pipe was at my lips and I was struggling once again with that impossible speed, that exhausting double- and triple-tonguing, those arpeggios I could not finger fast enough . . . Just hitting the notes wore me out.

As my cheek muscles wearied with failed attempts, my eyes strayed once again to those warning signs at the bottom of the page. What kinds of tunes were flagged like that? I once read of a tune that enabled the piper to change his appearance—used back around the Year of Our Lord 1150, by a piper-gone-bad named Heinrich the Wanderer. There were means to enter and divert another man's piping by accessing some key element in it. In 1212, Jurgen the Bold had broken into one of Pipelord Nicolas's most difficult tunes by discerning its central emotion. And then of course there was the oft-repeated ban on love piping: often repeated because there was not a single apprentice who had not seriously considered it. The threatened punishments were severe, as of course they had to be.

This parchment, plopped into my hands by wild coincidence—it just might be the key. The markings did show danger. But I was desperate, and what I read in the signs was *power*—and power I needed. Nothing but overwhelming power would save both me and Hamelin in the face of enemies known and unknown, in the face of Hamelin's incorrigibility, in the face of ruthless brutality. Nothing but overwhelming power would turn the tide against my devious enemy, who seemed to hold the town in his hand. I needed this power because the whole town hated outsiders, and pipers most of all. I needed this power because somewhere in Hamelin a renegade piper was watching me and thwarting me.

The material at the foot of the page was surely encoded verbal instructions: actions above and beyond the music that must be performed in the Pipeworld in order to complete the pipe work. I remembered brief training at the guildhouse in the breaking of codes. I took up my stylus and wax tablet to make the letter-number grids that I thought would give me the key to the cipher. I would use frequent repetitions to guess the code maker's original grid. It would be tedious work, but in my training I had shown a flair for it, and for the moment, I had the time.

After several failed starts, I remembered it was time to prepare for dinner, if I wanted to look my best. Mrs. Rike had outdone herself, soaking, scrubbing, and mending my cloak. I was a hefty laundry burden for the women of Hamelin; the thing had gotten two washings in two days. With a finger, I traced the stitches on the back and noticed the faint outline of a stain. Zimmer's blood. Who sent the man who saw Zimmer with the cash box, chased him, and killed him?

And who was this mysterious force—"the other one" from my dream, the other hand on the strings, the other piper who had piped against me?

Maybe I should shave. I hadn't asked Roth about gear for that job. Perhaps Mrs. Rike could help with some hot water and a sharp knife. But then, if I shaved, would it look as though I were declaring myself to be a suitor? It was way too early for that. I glanced in the amazing mirror. Oh no. I would definitely shave, not to honor the Hofmanns but to keep them from laughing.

The bandits, the rats, the mob—who was behind all that? Bauer, Bauer, Bauer. His arrogant face loomed in my mind: mocking, lying, accusing, sneering as I piped . . . Wait. Could it be some other member of the council? The mayor himself? Presumably he understood the Pipeworld about as well as he understood human nature. Wolf? Certainly Wolf had been hostile.

I lifted the lid from a jar on the chest. Inside, a clear oil smelled like the summer day of my walk to Hamelin—like honeysuckle and clover. It had been specially brought to the guest room; I was the guest. Was it meant for me? Was it for the skin, or for the hair? I would use a little on both.

Now let the investigation be fair. What about my allies—Roth, Gudrun, Klara? A piper up to no good would get close to any legitimate piper sent to Hamelin. But if Roth were fighting me, he'd had a dozen opportunities to simply finish me off while I was unconscious.

I was beginning to smell magnificent. Just a little more on the, uh, neck. Must ask Mrs. Rike about shaving. I still had time.

Klara was ambitious and clever. Hanged if she hadn't gotten exactly what she wanted—a free rat kill. And bound me to her with eternal gratitude by saving my life, again. She had also released Anselm the Rebel, six years ago. How did I know what had happened between the two of them? The three times I'd been surrounded—by bandits, by rats, by the mob—I'd had a Hofmann nearby. What should I think of Klara's skill as a healer? And what about Gudrun's strange success with the pipe?

And how to tie this in with the Pipelord's letter? "Worse than rats . . ." Had he planned all along for me to meet this other piper? The guild had accounted for every member of the old Unbound movement. But what if this were a dangerous new renegade from our guild? And what if my real mission were to catch him? If so, I was the—what?

I was the bait.

Would the Pipelord design a trap for a rebel or a test for an apprentice that might end in my death?

I pulled on the hosen. Yellow foot: maybe I *would* finish my mission. Red foot: maybe my mission would finish *me*.

Later, when I'd changed, assembled the shaving gear, and done my best with it, I went back to the parchment from the doll. I fiddled with the coded symbols awhile. It was like looking for a fingerhold in a polished slab of granite.

I decided to practice the tune. Slowly the accuracy and fluency of my playing improved, as I waded through time changes. I'd never felt such fatigue in the muscles of my lips and jaws. But wind and metal, mouth and hands were working well together now.

I went back to the code and was running through another series of possibilities for what the symbols could mean, trying each one and growing wearier by the minute. In the middle of the tedium, I felt a sudden impulse to pick up the pipe.

And when I played the opening phrase, for the first time something *happened*. In the flow of my breath through the pipe, I felt the flow of power.

Something clicked in my head, and in the string of meaningless symbols and numbers, I suddenly read a phrase: *the strings*. The strings. It *was* a guild score. It was a tune of power. And suddenly, barely checking the chart on my wax tablet, I was gulping down whole phrases: "from guilty, fearful . . . drawn through the children . . ." And there, at the end of the instructions, the word "Keychild."

I jumped to my feet, knocking the chair to the floor. I understood the code. I could pipe this tune completely, music and Pipeworld actions together.

I began to play from the beginning. My piping tongue on the familiar metal and the baffling language of the strange code came together in a current of power. The room fell away as that melody and its dance steps unfolded.

As it lurched in more and more angular, nauseating swoops, I was thrown from a rock-strewn desert to a staircase spiraling down to a suffocating dungeon, and down at the black bottom I fell in. Amid the rushing I saw or became an older woman terrified of her own home, a laughing toddler swinging a cruel club, a small foot crushing down on a large neck; then, as everything turned inside out, a chasm opened at my feet. I knew where this journey was going, amid burning homes and burning faces . . . faces of boys. There was a boy jumping into a blazing building—Anselm. There was a boy tossing bread crumbs at an old man—Strom. There was a boy giving away a small wooden flute—me. My pipe fell to the floor, and only the clatter woke me from the nightmare to which I had just given birth.

I had heard of this thing. Pipers who had used it came back to the guild grim and quiet and didn't like to hear its name. It was a curse for corrupt towns, a curse that for a time gave children the power to control adults. It was the Childrule Curse.

A gentle knock sounded at the door.

After a moment of pure stupor, I awoke to the room and time and my body and furniture and . . .

"Yes?" With new awe, I curled the parchment as I had first found it and tucked it deep into my pouch. "Come in."

Roth peered in cautiously.

"Hannes, what . . . ?" He looked exhilarated. "What . . . was that?"

"What was what?"

"That thing you were playing. It was . . . It was like . . ." In his love for the right word and his failure to find it, he threw his hands up in the air.

I was breathing like I'd just run from Oldendorf.

When I could trust myself to speak, I said, "It's a little thing I've been writing."

It was the strangest feeling, to have that statement hanging in the air between us, the most obvious lie in the round world, about as natural as a curled moustache on a girl's lip, and knowing he knew.

But all Roth said was, "Ah." His eyes were wide. "Hannes, you know what it was like? Instead of playing music, you were playing the thing the music is *about*."

"Thanks," I replied. A lame silence fell.

He shook his head again, and said, "Whew! Well, Hannes, I . . . I see you're dressed up. I'm glad to see—I mean, I'm glad to smell that you've made yourself at home with your room supplies."

"Thank you very much, sir," I replied, a little serf boy to the core of my foolish heart. Covering my embarrassment, I pointed to the jars and said, "Incredible fragrances in those things. Must be expensive."

"It's all rubbish, Hannes." He picked up the ointment and glared at me with a look so fierce I feared he would hurl the jar against the fireplace to prove he meant it. "I don't care a jot for any of this stuff. You and I—we'd both of us rather live in a barn and finish our mission than wallow all day in silk like these fool councilmen."

"Our mission?"

"What? You've forgotten already?" He grabbed me by the shoulders and beamed. "You chase out the rats; I bring in the silver. Together we're saving the poor folk of Hamelin."

I laughed.

"So what's your big event?" he asked.

"A dinner at Hofmanns'. You're invited too."

"Well! Do you know, I've been in this town how many months now, and this is the first invitation that didn't smell like business. Hm. All right. Time to decorate myself. Not to be outdone by my country cousin." He made for the door, then stopped and added, "Too bad you can't wear the Zimmer hat tonight—no, forget I said that. Family friend . . . tasteless comment. But for the record, Hannes, you look magnificent in it. It's the hat you were born to wear."

I spun and made a flourish in my twice-washed clothes, grabbed my own shapeless hat, jammed it on my head for a joke, and winced. Pain stabbed at me from both wounds now—from the bandit's club that had welcomed me to Hamelin and from the assassin's knife that had sliced me for protecting Zimmer. Breathing hard and clutching at my head, I knew the show was over. I was only a piper apprentice, playing at being a nobleman.

"Sit down," Roth ordered, and I sat on my sleeping mat. He tossed aside the hat, gently parted my hair, and examined the wound's edges with an expert touch. "Just a minute." He came back with a bowl and a cloth.

In a moment I could feel and smell that he was bathing the wound in wine.

"Now you need to keep this clean." He bared my wrist, felt the pulse, and asked some questions to assess my four bodily humors.

"Miracle you're still standing. After the welcoming committee on the road, and the butcher shop, and the rats. Hannes, hate to say it before a dinner party, but you look like the rat business took something out of you. How do you feel?"

I told him the truth: I felt terrible. I remembered the vision that had come when I piped from the scroll and felt more terrible still.

"Well, listen, Hannes, you're the piper, right? Did you come here expecting the rat piping to be . . . devastating?"

"No! I've practiced that tune; I've practiced with rats lots of times, and other animals; I've gone out in the forest. You think any apprentice worth his salt would go out on his solo without practicing? What I did today was supposed to be like piping a jig."

"So what went wrong?"

"I am going to tell you something, Roth, that no one in Hamelin knows."

"I'm ready."

"Roth . . ." I paused and took a deep breath.

"Forget it. You don't have to."

"No. Listen. When I piped the rats, somebody was . . . pulling against me."

His eyebrows said *Pulling?*

"What I mean is, it had to be a piper, but . . . how could that be?"

Roth stared at me. "Hannes, let me show you something. Didn't want to upset your dinner, but in a way it's good news." He fumbled in a pocket of his coat. "Found this at Town Hall. In a locked drawer of Zimmer's."

It was a signed letter from Hermann Bauer for Dietrich Zimmer to share with the council. Skimming past the formalities, I came to the substance: They were going to pay a man, and pay him well, to *bring* the plague of rats to Hamelin.

Now I had more than the mumblings of a frantic old man—I had something that would interest a judge. Now, in my hand, I held hard evidence.

TWELVE

Fine Dining

 HAT LETTER, STRANGELY ENOUGH, UNCORKED ME. After I had stared at it awhile, feeling hot and cold pass over me, Roth broke in on my thoughts.

"Hannes, it's proof. For someone interested in justice, that's a start." He studied me. "You wanted proof. So why do I get the feeling you're not happy?"

"Oh, I'm fine. After all, just look at the situation. The naïve little guild boy comes trotting into town to rescue the council from the plague they ordered themselves. No wonder they smirked!"

"Hannes, are you blaming yourself? How were you supposed to know the council was corrupt?"

"Because *my guild knew,* Roth. When they sent me. I read a letter not meant for me, and the Pipelord knew I was going to be up to my neck in manure. He knew there was something worse than rats wrong with Hamelin. He told a fellow master, but he forgot to tell *me.*"

"He's a busy man, Hannes."

"Too busy to notice that a renegade piper might be a bit much for one lone apprentice?"

"I think you're doing fine."

"Don't comfort me. I've been swimming in my own false comfort for days. It's time to face the facts. My mission will probably fail. And I may never make the guild."

Roth laid a hand on my shoulder. "I'm sure your master will be understanding."

"We have a fellow at the guildhouse," I said, panting. "His name is Jakob. He's already balding even though"—I laughed, hearing my voice get shrill but not caring—"he's still an *apprentice*. But, Roth, the Pipelord changed his title—out of *mercy*." I pounded my fist on the mat. "And I don't—want—his—mercy!"

"Hannes, there's no shame in taking help when you need it."

"I'd rather be honest and call a failure a failure. Of course the guild shouldn't give an apprentice more than he can handle. But if he really can't succeed, don't nurse him along in the charity ward. That may look nice, but, Roth, it's really a trap."

Suddenly I didn't want Roth to see me like this.

He was beside me—a merchant with a peasant sitting on the floor, his hand still on my shoulder, not hurrying me. "Hannes, you're all excited. But this is just one mission. You've got your whole life to look forward to—working in the guild."

"Roth, that's just it. What if I *do* make the guild? I mean, now that I know what it means to be a piper. It means getting attacked. It means feeling weak and looking small and losing control. I want to *face* that, Roth. My mission is out of my hands. And you know what's funny about that? I was so sick of my father losing. And afraid that because I was his son, I couldn't win either. The guild seemed like a place I could win. But if a piper's life is out of control, then . . . the last island has sunk."

"Hannes, I want you to know—you can stay in this house as long as you choose. And remember: the rats are gone. You've done everything that anyone asked you to do."

"Sure, fine," I replied, wiping my nose. "Right, fine. I'm a great errand boy. But my plans for Aerzen—I don't know. I didn't choose this life, Roth; it chose me, and I feel like a pawn. Or a victim. Which would be right in line for my family."

"Victim?"

"That's right. My father talks like a hero, but . . . I remember once his grand dream was beekeeping, and once it was moving to the eastern frontiers. But all the talk is just a way of not facing the facts, not *doing* anything. Instead, you know what happens? First, the grand gesture. Then—he walks away from success. It's amazing, Roth. He finds a place where he's a failure and he stays there, and if he gets taken away, he *goes back*. And every time he tries to play the hero, my mother ends up as the victim."

Roth was looking at me with an intense, unreadable expression.

"What to make of you, Johannes Piper? You're an unusual young man."

I shook my head to clear the fuzz out. "No, no, I said pawn, but that's not really it. I do want to please my master; I do want to join my guild as a full master piper; I do want to gain honor and finish my mission." My voice was smaller as I said, "I do still want that."

Roth said he was sorry and clapped me one last time on the back. He was kind, but I was pierced by the awful truth of my own words. How much of all this had the Pipelord *intended*? Did the guild exist for this? Was this suffering at the heart of a piper's work?

I thought of the appalling music I had piped, and I sank even further.

"Listen, Hannes, hate to say it now . . ." Roth spread his hands in a way that meant *after everything you've been spilling*. "But there's something else I have to tell you."

I sobered up instantly and felt my muscles contracting with that feeling of run-fight-or-pipe.

He looked at the ground and swallowed. "When I went to Town Hall, Zimmer was still alive."

I held my breath.

"Hannes, before he died he told me who killed him. It was Bauer."

"Oh, my." I groaned at the memory of Bauer's theatrical skills, so convincing *I* had almost felt guilty.

Roth went on. "I guessed the very thing you got hit with— Bauer'd love nothing better than to pin it on someone from out of town. Figured the best thing would be to go to the mayor together with Klara. Took me forever just to get to the back door—kept hearing Bauer and his cronies. Next thing I knew, here's a crowd coming to lynch you, and I ran up in time to hear them accusing you. I was about to speak up when Klara did the job for me. And listen; when it comes to a murder trial, I'm still an out-of-towner. I'm a more valuable ally to you the less we're together in public."

Anger boiled in me. Bauer had humiliated me. Bauer had brought the rats. Bauer had made a fortune on inflated grain prices. Bauer had led the way in stealing the people's money and my reward. Bauer had murdered Mr. Zimmer. Bauer had accused me of the crime . . .

"Roth, I have to go confront him. Now."

I slung my bag over my shoulder, grabbed my pipe, and headed for the door, the blood pounding in my temples.

147

Roth stopped me. "Wait. You know where he is?"

"You help me find him."

"He's a dangerous man."

"By heaven, tonight he's going to learn that *I'm* a dangerous man."

"You been *listening* to Klara?"

I stared at him.

"Be better for the town and for the Hofmanns if you do this thing legally."

"How?"

"Tonight after supper, tell the mayor. Take your lead from him."

I groaned and pounded the wall with my fist.

"Hannes, my friend, we got a supper to go to. Zimmer's not going to get any deader, and Bauer'll keep for one night. Is it a deal?"

I flung myself into the chair and stared into space as Roth made hasty preparations for dinner at the Hofmanns'. As he pulled his boots on, he reminded me of the good news—that now we had a definite direction and some hard evidence.

Before long Roth and I, dressed and ready to meet the rich and powerful, were stepping out the door into a beautiful deep-blue midsummer evening. The simple facts had eventually calmed my spirits—I had a plan, a piece of evidence, someone to take it to, and an ally in the fight.

Roth knew the way to the Hoffmans'. As we came up the walk, he stepped back to let me knock.

Mrs. Hofmann, together with a servant woman, opened the richly engraved door.

"Mr. Kunst, this is a pleasure? And, Mr. Piper, welcome?" Every line rose at the end like a question.

As we were ushered in, we passed the workroom with its heaps of wool and cloth, the counting room with its counting units, tablets, seals, and quills—the place where Klara had learned her bookkeeping skills. Our chattering hostess coaxed us up the steep stairway to the main room, hazy from the oil lamps along the walls and the hearth that spread under the hood of a generous chimney. The two levels of quality in the linen wall hangings were, I assumed, the handiwork of Klara and her mother. On a board in the corner stood a set of carved chessmen—apparently a game in progress.

Our host burst in, shook our hands, and seated Roth and me at opposite ends of a bench along one side of the long trestle table. Mr.

Hofmann squeezed his wife's hand and shared some joke with her.

Why must the Pipelord's zeal compel me to choose between himself and the mayor? I loved the Pipelord, but his standards of justice branded the mayor's sort of gentleness as a tragic wreck. It was too hard for me. I might manage such hardness for a week, but not for a lifetime.

Wolf appeared and sat at the end of the table, to my left.

Furrowing her brow, Mrs. Hofmann hovered as a cook carried in a pork roast with apples that smelled like heaven itself. I oohed and aahed with complete sincerity.

Next from the kitchen came a savory stew of larks with onions, brought by Klara. She wore a gown as blue as the midsummer sky, with a silver necklace, and her plaited hair was bound up behind her head.

Gudrun marched in, carrying the bread and looking solemn in a golden surcoat that set off her hair to dramatic effect. Being the youngest, she said grace: "Our Father . . ." She gave thanks for good St. John on his feast day, and the family joined in a jolly *Amen.*

When Mr. and Mrs. Hofmann sat down, with Klara and Roth on their right and Gudrun and me on their left, it dawned on me what this seating arrangement suggested. To the right of Wolf, who had his own chair, the arrangement on the bench was myself, Gudrun, Mrs. Hofmann, the mayor, Klara, Roth. Meaning: Roth was Klara's guest, and I was Gudrun's. I struggled to hold my face right as Gudrun and I washed hands from the same pitcher.

Mrs. Hofmann reached across Gudrun to hand me something wrapped in a small cloth. "This is a little meat pie from the Lachlers, especially for you, Mr. Piper? Mrs. Lachler said that it was for you and only you, as a small token of gratitude from her family and the Town Council? For your courage and your help?"

As I mumbled my thanks, the smell of fluffy pastry and savory filling overcame me; I could feel the saliva bursting into my mouth. It had been a while since I had eaten, and it was torture to smell that pie and not sink my teeth into it.

What seemed like a long time later, our hostess lifted her spoon, and we began to eat.

In answer to Roth's murmured praise of the stew, the lady of the house remarked, "I used lavender and—a little pepper?" Rotating her handsome head to take me in, she went on, "Have you ever had pepper, Mr. Piper?"

May God forgive me; I lied that I had. Perhaps pepper was what the black flecks were about. After Gudrun and I had shared the stew bowl, I brought a slice of the tender pork captive to the slab of bread that was my plate, delicately attacked it, and found that its aroma was only the beginning of delight. In the middle of my efforts, I noticed everyone sitting up to the table but not propping elbows, and immediately stopped leaning on my own. In a cold sweat I hoped no one had seen me.

While Gudrun, with a snicker, corrected me for biting my bread rather than breaking it, Mrs. Hofmann tried unsuccessfully to draw Roth into a description of marriage practices in the cities where he had lived.

With exquisite charm and a compliment to the wife he clearly adored, the mayor rescued Roth and led the four of them into a lively Roth-centered discussion of the economic future of Hamelin. Klara's eyes shone as Roth held forth on the benefits of eastward colonization, "Hamelin's young people heading out the Eastern Gate," and so on. I lost the thread.

A bit later Gudrun picked up yet another cue I hadn't noticed— that it was time to drink. Sure enough, the mayor raised his cup.

"I am only one man out of the thousands in Hamelin, only one man out of the dozen on the Town Council, but what I can do I must do, to show my gratitude to the young man who saved my town. Thank you for freeing us from oppression."

("He means rats," explained Gudrun.)

"Thank you for showing patience that many would not have shown. And please, sir, please forgive us for the ungracious accusation made against you in our town. As soon as we can add firmer proof to our words, we want to clear your good name fully."

("Hear, hear!" muttered Roth.)

The toast he had spoken was even sweeter than what was in the cup, but then—I noticed how Klara and Roth drank it together, and I could barely swallow. I was the hero being toasted, but I was watching that toasting pair from far outside. Suddenly I couldn't believe any of this was for me—the mouthwatering dishes, the lovely silver table setting, the evening with the mayor's family.

"May I have a bite of your pie from Mrs. Lachler?" Gudrun asked.

I said yes and sank like a stone into my chair. Mechanically I thanked both the Hofmanns for their kindness and assured them that I was only doing my duty, and all the while my heart was dropping out of the sky like a bird hit with a dart. The toast had cleared my head. What had I been thinking? The village idiot could see that as a suitor to Klara Hofmann, Roth Kunst outclassed me completely. I think I emptied my cup many times, and Gudrun, beaming up at me, refilled it.

The mayor brought Roth a lute, which he tuned and began to play. Klara rose and sang:

> *All that moves on earth so fair,*
> *All that travels through the air,*
> *All that rides in waves and streams,*
> *All that sings and rings in dreams . . .*

I had heard this song and knew where the next verse was headed. I was already dry mouthed at the thought of the finale when suddenly, in a surprising, clear tenor, Roth added the harmony. The two voices entwined with such power that everyone seated at the table froze.

> *All that's seen and all that's heard*
> *In this house we call the world,*
> *All beneath and all above*
> *Breathes the living breath of love.*

A creamy golden custard was served to the astonished audience. Its quivering mass looked like I felt. A bowl of walnuts appeared as well, and someone was cracking one, and Mr. Hofmann was saying how glad the family was to have us in their home. And now in a loud voice he was asking how it had felt to be the hero of Hamelin, marching down the streets with a parade behind me and cheers around me.

Too many cups from Gudrun, too many toasts, too many duets, too many beautiful duets, and to blazes with it all, and I replied to the mayor that I felt like his grandfather.

The hubbub around the table grew still.

Very quietly, the mayor was asking did I intend to lead away a herd of children.

I said no and he was smiling so I tried to laugh, but I was struck dumb because here came the memory: my sickening vision, and the chilling music from the doll.

I looked around the table for support. Wolf looked coldly amused at my performance. Gudrun seemed proud that I was quoting her story of Great-grandpa. Klara's tight face said, *Here it comes.* Her mother's face looked as though I had leaned forward and spat on the tabletop. Her father's face simply wanted this to end warmly. And Roth was trying to solve me, like a riddle.

"No, Daddy," corrected Gudrun. "Actually, what Great-grandpa did to the children is what Hannes does to the *rats.* That's how he means." She grinned at me.

Just then Klara giggled at some private jest of Roth's, and I could not take my eyes off her. When I turned away at last, I found Gudrun's eyes locked on *me.* In them I saw a deep and terrible understanding and a grim decision reached.

Her face grew hard, and she leaned over to her mother for a whispered conference, and I caught the words "duet" and "with our flutes." Then she asked me to come with her into the hallway.

Once out of the dining room, she put her head close, whispering right into my ear, "Do you know what happened, while you were sleeping, after the rats? My family doesn't even know this story. I didn't tell them 'cause I didn't want them getting upset with you. And I didn't tell you 'cause I didn't want you to *worry.*"

"What happened?"

Her breath poured hot and hard into my ear. "I was coming back from all the celebration. I turned down an alley. All of a sudden two big men stopped me. And they . . . they pushed me against a wall. And they were mean to me."

Her voice was near tears, and my heart was in my throat.

"You know what they said? They said, 'Tell your family to watch what side they take, or someone is going to get *hurt.*'" She swallowed, and the noise of it was like a storm in my naked ear. "They were mean to me. They were mean to me *about you.* They could have killed me."

My ear felt her hard breathing. I murmured, "I'm so sorry, Gudrun."

But she was talking again. "And you know that stuff Klara said about you drowning the rats? Later on she talked with my mommy and daddy about you and some other stuff, and everything she said then was *ter-ri-ble.*" Gudrun put so much venom in that last word that I was afraid.

"So," Gudrun said, with unsettling calm, "good night." She

wiped her eyes and nose and stuck her head through the door. "Mommy, I need to be excused. I don't feel very good."

After I made it to my chair, I was still barely aware of the room around me, still absorbing the shock of Gudrun's attack and making out its meaning, when a whisper from Wolf jarred me.

"You get the stew; I'll get the pork." My blank look brought an explanation. "Cleanup, my piper friend." Honestly, my first thought was, *No, I'm the guest of honor.* But one look at the other end of the table, where Roth and the three Hofmanns were deep into some detail of the town's charter, showed that by losing Gudrun I had lost my only real link to the cozy scene. It was in fact time for me to take my proper place as a peasant boy in a mayor's home.

I rose and grabbed the stew pot. Once we had set down our burdens in the kitchen, Wolf turned to me.

"You know what I don't like, Mr. Piper?"

"No. Tell me."

"I don't like it when a person pretends not to want something."

"Oh."

"Like for instance, the games people play at market. Me, I can't do that. I walks up to a man, I says, 'I'll give you two pennies for that knife.' It's what I honest-to-God thinks it's worth. If he says no, then to blazes with him; know what I mean?"

I braced myself to parry the thrust and said, "Where are you going with this?"

Wolf leaned very close to me, and with a strong odor of pork roast and something else that might have been pepper, he growled, "That Roth up there. You saw how Klara was meltin' on him like snow on a warm rock."

Once again I heard that fierce *Tsk!* so fondly remembered from the road to Hamelin.

"Meanwhile old Roth, he's makin' out he don't even smell the perfume, see. Like, 'What—is Klara a *girl*, then? Oh, I hadn't noticed.'" Wolf sucked air in through his teeth.

"Wolf, I think you could back down a little."

Wolf snorted a laugh, and I went on. "Why do you see enemies everywhere?"

He turned to me with black eyes that were on fire. "It's my *job*." When he saw my blank face, he went on in a furious pork-scented whisper. "To notice when the wrong sort is playin' up to Miss Hofmann. To spot the kind of fellow who would climb into a young

153

lady's window at night. And to break his fingers." Wolf's spittle was spraying me. "Ain't you heard anything about six years back?"

"No. But I can see what's happening four yards away. I saw a man being a polite guest; I saw a man honoring his hosts."

"Great heaven above, man, do you think I couldn't see you shrivelin' as you watched the two of 'em? I bet even Gudi noticed. I—I kind of, you know," he cleared his throat elaborately. "I feel bad for *you* into the bargain."

"Oh, how I was longing for your sympathy."

"You may be playin', Piper-boy, but *I* ain't playin'. Do you think I'm blind? Ever since this Roth fellow come to town, he's been settin' up this moment right here."

"Wolf, you have a lively imagination."

"Piper, you have a lively pig head."

I laughed. I just barely kept from spraying the man with walnut mush. I admit I was glad to find another man at my side who did not find the two lovebirds a pleasant sight. I wanted to whomp my ally's treelike shoulder but thought better of it.

"You're all right," I finally said.

His rumbling voice was loud and clear: "I guess you'll do, as well. I can take one look at you and tell you understand dirt, sweat, and hard work, anyhow." He took a vast drink from an earthen cup, and headed up the stairs. "I'll never forget my first sight of you. Ha. You weren't nothin' but a lump o' dust and colors."

"But you had mercy."

"Klara had mercy." His face grew stern. "And I like you all right, I guess, but she's miles out of your range."

Just after Wolf and I had taken our seats at the table, the servant-woman scuttled over to Mrs. Hofmann and spoke a word in her ear.

"Oh dear?" said Mrs. Hofmann, rising.

"What is it?" asked the mayor.

"Gudrun isn't well. She says her stomach hurts. A lot? And she's . . . she's vomiting, violently."

Klara and Roth got to their feet as Gudrun stumbled into the room, crying and holding her stomach, oblivious to the streaks and stains on her golden coat.

Roth put his hand on the mayor's shoulder. "Mr. Hofmann," he said, "I have some herbs at my house that will help. But we don't have a moment to lose. Let me borrow a horse. I'll take Gudrun to my place."

So. It would be Roth and not me saving Klara's sister.

The mayor nodded and rushed to ready a horse for Roth. Klara and her mother were examining and questioning Gudrun.

Before collecting the patient, Roth strode up to me. "Take that pie in its napkin," he said, speaking low. "Don't eat it, don't let anyone else eat it, and don't throw it away."

THIRTEEN

Diagnosis

Saturday, June Twenty-fourth, 1284, Hamelin

ROTH GALLOPED AWAY DOWN THE STREET, THE WIDE-EYED Gudrun doubled over his arm in pain. I stumbled into the Hofmanns' wagon with Klara and her mother.

"We'll get the doctor!" shouted Mr. Hofmann, already on his horse. Wolf, who was taking the mount that the doctor would ride, pulled up beside us, looking anxiously at Klara and at me.

"I'll watch her!" Mrs. Hofmann shouted.

The mayor jerked his head toward our driver. "Go!"

I heard the reins slap, and as the mayor and Wolf galloped away, the wagon jolted us in the other direction with a wild clattering of wheels.

Sitting across from me, Mrs. Hofmann rubbed her daughter's hands; Klara leaned against her mother with closed eyes. I thought suddenly of my parents—memories both sweet and bitter.

I looked down in my lap and saw the pie, wrapped in its napkin.

The pie. The one thing that only Gudrun ate. The one thing the Hofmanns hadn't prepared. I unwrapped the side Gudrun had bitten off and broke open the crust. By the midsummer twilight and moonlight, I made out chunks of meat, rings of onion, a thickened gravy, and small bits of . . . what? I lifted the sliver on my fingertip and recognized a slice of mushroom—the gray flesh, the darker gills. The mushroom was firmer than the onion, as though it hadn't cooked nearly as long. Or had my imagination grown overactive?

"What's that?" asked Klara, sitting up, her eyes now fully open.

"Piece of mushroom."

She took my hands, bending the pie and all the evidence close to her face.

I wanted to be the one to heal Gudrun, but if these were poisonous mushrooms . . . I hadn't been thinking of something so deadly. Pipe music couldn't simply heal; that wasn't how it worked. The harm had to go somewhere.

The wagon slowed, and the horses clattered to a halt. We were at Roth's house.

"Excuse me," I said, and sprang out. I ran across the stones and up the steps, holding the pie in one hand and pulling out my pipe with the other. As I reached for the door handle with my pipe hand, the door opened.

"Where's Gudrun?" I demanded of Roth, thrusting the pie into his hand and pushing past him.

"In the kitchen," he said, "but—"

Klara and Mrs. Hofmann came in behind me. I hurried down the hall.

"Roth," I said, "I'm bigger than Gudrun; I can handle poison better."

"But, Hannes—"

"Cure *me* if you can," I said, and darted into the kitchen.

Gudrun was seated on a chair, leaning over a bucket, her face puffy and pale, her hair plastered to her forehead with sweat.

I took the pipe in my mouth, looking into her eyes. My tune dropped deep.

I entered the Pipeworld, struggling to remember techniques of Pipeworld diagnosis as I fumbled. Gudrun's stomach was empty. The question was how much poison was in her blood. Dimly I sensed that between the poison and her body was some kind of a seal. It was as though a blanket had been wrapped around the poison, containing it. At first this containment felt like an enchantment, but I decided it must be one of Roth's herbs. With the musical cords of my piping, I laid hold of the bundled poison and began to draw it out.

I left the Pipeworld and laid down my pipe. I leaned over for the touch and transfer . . . The poison came into me with a jolt. I grabbed Gudrun's bucket and vomited. I spat till there was nothing left but a nasty taste.

Roth pushed a chair behind me, and I thudded into it as he hauled the bucket away.

"You already gave her something?" I wheezed. "To make her vomit?"

Roth nodded, handing me a cup of ale. I drank gladly, swishing it hard around my teeth.

"Well done," he said, "whatever it was you did. Now I hope *you're* not in trouble."

Gudrun was staring at me.

"How are you?" I asked her.

"Fine."

Klara and Mrs. Hofmann rushed to hug her.

"Thank you," said Mrs. Hofmann to me, with tears in her bright eyes. This fine lady was kneeling in front of me, a serf boy, and me sitting down. I tried to stand, but Roth pushed down on my shoulder with a warning not to rush myself.

Mrs. Hofmann thanked Roth as well, and he bowed his head.

"Let go of me!" said Gudrun, pushing Klara away. "I'm fine." She stomped out of the room and, without turning around, added, "I've been fine ever since *Mr. Kunst* cured me."

"I need to talk to that girl," said Mrs. Hofmann, pursing her lips and crossing the room in four strides.

"How're you feeling, Hannes?" asked Roth.

"Well . . ." I lifted my cup and found it empty.

Roth jumped up. "Let me get you some more." He took my cup and headed for the cellar.

Klara picked up the pipe I'd been reaching for and was about to give it to me when she stopped and ran her finger along its flared rim. "So much power," she said. "What do you do with all that power?"

"I do good," I said. "At least, I try."

She looked me in the eyes. "You've done nothing but good with it so far," she said, and gave me my pipe. "Thanks. For Gudi."

I nodded. Wiping my mouth, I played a few notes and felt through myself. Not a trace of the poison, or of the strange medicine I'd encountered.

"Looks like I'm fine," I said to Klara. "The poison's all . . . you know . . . out."

"Which leads to the question," said Roth, reappearing with a filled cup, "how did the poison get in—to Gudrun?"

"Oh! We need to get the news to my father," said Klara. "He still thinks Gudrun's dying."

"We'd only pass them in the dark," said Roth, handing me the cup. "Fastest way to find them is to wait right here. Besides, we still want the doctor to examine that pie."

"Why?" asked Klara, glaring at him.

Roth looked surprised and stepped back. "So we can prove Gudrun was poisoned."

"I want you to let me handle this," said Klara.

I stared at her. "What are you afraid of?"

"Hannes, Roth, thank you very, very much for saving my sister. But *no thanks* for accusing councilmen of murder."

"Miss Hofmann," I said, "I don't understand you. Two men who have shown themselves to be friends of the Hofmanns and friends of Hamelin are sincerely trying to help. And your greatest concern is how to protect yourself from help."

"I don't need you to solve Hamelin's problems."

"Really? Do you miss your rats?"

"We can handle our own criminals, Mr. Piper. We have a Town Watch. We have a Town Council."

"Your Town Council *are* your criminals!"

"Not my *father*!"

"And he'll 'handle it.'"

"Yes!"

"That's what I'm afraid of, Miss Hofmann. Your father 'handles' crime by abstaining from it. So is that the plan? Next time your sister gets poisoned, he'll go sign papers in his office?"

The blood was rising in her face, but I didn't stop. In the storm wind of my frustration with Hamelin's ways, I was utterly carried away, and I broke a six-year-old promise.

"I don't want to let you handle it, Miss Hofmann, and do you know why? The last time I know of, when somebody actually stopped a criminal in your town and had him in the stocks, along came Klara Hofmann, very quietly, and . . ."

Klara's eyes bulged, filling with tears, and I caught myself.

Roth looked from one of us to the other. He put out his hand to touch Klara's shoulder. She pushed his arm away and very deliberately walked out of the room.

"Well," said Roth, "you made your point."

Gudrun came in, looking down at the floor, with Mrs. Hofmann's hand on her shoulder, pushing her gently forward.

"Gudrun has something to say to you?" said Mrs. Hofmann.

"Sorry," Gudrun mumbled, without looking up.

"Let him hear you?"

"Sorry," said Gudrun, more clearly. "For being mean to you."

I kneeled down. "I forgive you, Gudrun."

She threw her arms around my neck, burying her face in my shoulder. It had been a very long time since I had been hugged properly.

Mrs. Hofmann beamed down at us and sighed, then asked, "Where's Klara?"

I stood up. "Miss Hofmann," I said, looking around the room myself, as if to find her there.

She wasn't in the kitchen. She wasn't in the hall.

I stepped into the doorway of the workroom. A few slits of moonlight came in around the shutters. But I heard her sniffling.

"Miss Hofmann?" I wanted to light a lamp; it seemed indecent to be alone with her in the dark. But she wouldn't want me to see her crying. The sniffling paused.

"Miss Hofmann," I said again, stepping into the darkness, "I was horrible in there. I broke my promise to you. I just . . . wanted to hurt you."

"No. You've been too polite for too long."

I moved closer now. Klara was huddled on a wooden chest, with the right edge of her silhouette traced in moonlight, her straying hair edged in silver, her wet cheek glistening.

"Please forgive me, Miss Hofmann."

She lifted her head and sniffled again. I kneeled and reached carefully into my pouch for the one piece of cloth I owned that was still clean—a white handkerchief, folded very small. I tried not to touch it too much with my dirty hands as I held it out to her.

Klara laughed, a laugh still wet with crying, took the handkerchief, and thanked me.

At that moment, Roth and Mrs. Hofmann came in with candelabras in their hands. Moonlight vanished as the candles threw our long shadows on the walls. Mrs. Hofmann raised her eyebrows, while Roth's face went slack. With a wipe at her eyes, Klara stood, and I got up too.

"Mr. Piper was kind enough to bring me a handkerchief," Klara explained, and left the room.

Now Gudrun appeared between her mother and Roth. "Mommy, where's Daddy?"

Mrs. Hofmann stirred and looked down at her daughter. "I don't know," she said. "It shouldn't have taken him this long."

Roth frowned. "Mrs. Hofmann, who did you say sent that pie?"

It seemed to take her a moment to hear what he had said. "Mrs. Lachler," she answered at last. Then her face changed. "But, Roth, Mrs. Lachler is such a sweet woman? She wouldn't hurt a fly."

"Then someone got in her kitchen," said Roth. "Who?"

Klara reappeared, no longer sniffling.

"Now, Roth," said Mrs. Hofmann, "I'm not prepared to go through all the people I know in Hamelin. And suspect them of attempted murder?"

"Mommy," said Gudrun, tugging on Mrs. Hofmann's skirt, "I'm hungry."

"Oh!" her mother said. "Of course you are. And, Johannes, you must be?"

Roth fished on his belt for keys. "Chicken and bread in the pantry . . ."

"Oh, thank you, Roth," said Mrs. Hofmann. "You'll just let me get it? Now all of you go into the sitting room; there's a dear?" She bustled off, carrying her candelabra.

Roth held his own light aloft and motioned us into the sitting room. We followed in his pool of light. He set the candelabra on the table as we sat around it, with me facing Gudrun and Roth facing Klara.

Klara gave her sister a meaningful look. "Gudrun," she said in a honeyed voice, "Mommy may need some help in the—"

"Mr. Bauer did it," said Gudrun.

"Gudrun!"

"I heard you talk about how mad he was at Hannes."

"Gudrun, you should be ashamed! You're accusing a councilman of attempted murder with no more evidence than a few ugly words."

"But that's what you all want to talk about," said Gudrun. She turned to me and Roth. "Isn't it?"

"Well, Gudrun," I said, "until we have solid proof, all we can do is ask questions."

"All right," said Gudrun, "I'm *asking* could it be Mr. Bauer. Because actually he knows Mr. Lachler really well."

"Gudrun," Klara tried again, "you really need to go help—"

But Roth cut in. "Gudrun, we're going to tell secrets now. You can't be talking to anybody about this. Either you promise that, or you go cut bread."

Gudrun's eyes in the candlelight were enormous. She whispered, "I promise."

"Listen," said Roth. "I'm going to put this straight. I don't want any more simpleminded thinking like what Gudrun just said about 'Bauer did it.' It's time to talk openly about the fact that we're fighting against a small army here."

"What?" asked Klara.

"Listen to me. Bauer's always had help. Someone else actually brought the rats. Then, as I've learned, the rats ate all the grain in town except for Bauer's and his partners'. Don't suppose you believe Bauer hypnotized the rats himself? And other *councilmen* helped hire this rat-bringer; the letter shows that. Bauer proposed a reward, then stole it himself, with Zimmer helping all the way. Then Zimmer got chased by thugs, presumably on orders from Bauer, who wanted to protect his secrets. Quite a little gang of accomplices. And all this time no one said a word. Though I'd bet money Bauer hoarded grain and then overcharged for it—"

"Crimes a man could hang for," I put in, "especially during a famine."

"Wait," interrupted Klara. "He never raised the price of his grain."

"He didn't raise prices for *you*," said Roth. "You're the mayor's daughter. That's the other thing—nobody in this town breathed a word of the price change to your father. Bauer threatened to stop grain to whoever said anything. Not to mention that the whole town is scared of his henchmen."

"Oh," said Gudrun.

We looked at her.

She shrank back a little bit. "All my friends' parents talk about how hard it is to get grain, and when I ask them why, they get all quiet and won't tell me."

"Roth," Klara demanded, "why didn't you tell me this?"

Roth paused, then said quietly, "The last time I pointed out a problem to someone in Hamelin, I was called a meddling outsider."

Klara stared. "Roth! Mr. Bauer may be a scoundrel, but we have no reason to think that he's a murderer."

"Miss Hofmann," said Roth, "I'm afraid we do."

"What do you mean?" asked Klara. When Roth and I exchanged glances, she turned to me and demanded, "What is he talking about?"

I said flatly, "Roth told me before dinner that he found Mr. Zimmer before he died."

"What?"

"And," I forged ahead, "Mr. Zimmer said that it was Bauer who stabbed him."

"Then the swine blamed it on Hannes," Roth finished.

Klara sat stunned. Gudrun's face hardened, and I remembered that the mayor had said that Mr. Zimmer used to give Gudrun candy.

Mrs. Hofmann walked in. "Well, I'm almost ready," she said, wiping her hands on a towel. She looked around at us all. "Well, what's happened to the lot of you? You're not still talking about that pie, are you?"

None of us met her eye.

"Now, really," she said, hands on hips. "Surely it was ordinary food poisoning? You don't really think there was anything . . . funny in there?"

Roth cleared his throat. "I was hoping the doctor could make sure when he comes."

"Oh, dear?" said Mrs. Hofmann. "Where can they be?" She frowned, shook her head. "Roth, is it all right if they eat in here?"

"Absolutely," said Roth.

Mrs. Hofmann left the room.

Klara stared at the floor. "We haven't had murder in Hamelin for years and years."

"Even when the Unbound were here?" I asked.

She frowned. "You mean the boy pipers? They hurt a lot of people, but they didn't kill anyone."

"There was someone else, though," I said. "Six years ago, I heard him tell Anselm that his friend—Anselm's friend—had died without telling him anything."

"Franz?" Klara said. Her eyes were wide, and she was clutching the folds of her dress.

"Who's Franz?" asked Gudrun.

"He was my friend," said Klara, "a very good friend."

Roth raised his eyebrows.

"Until Anselm took over. He was Anselm's friend too, right to the end. But I don't think he really understood what Anselm was doing. Franz always meant well, but he believed anything Anselm told him." Her hands twisted in her lap. "Men in masks dragged him off. I was so afraid . . ." And she stopped.

"I'm sorry," said Roth.

Klara nodded. Then she gave me a piercing look. "Who was it?"

I blinked. "The man talking to Anselm? I never saw his face. But it looked like he was going to kill Anselm, or hurt him anyway. Then he got interrupted."

Klara froze. "You mean . . . that was right at the end? Right before Anselm was alone in the square?"

Gudrun and Roth looked as puzzled as I was. "Yes," I said.

Klara said nothing.

"Do you know who it was, then?" asked Roth.

Klara frowned. "It was Mr. Bauer," she said.

We were silent.

"This is ridiculous," said Klara suddenly, waving her hands as if she were swatting away flies. "What we're doing here is no better than gossip. Someone needs to talk to Mr. Bauer."

"Fair enough," I said. "I'll talk to him when I get the reward from him tomorrow."

"Reward? You piped the rats for free! You did it to save your neck! Now you want the reward again?"

"Miss Hofmann!" I sprang to my feet. "How can you say that? How can you *say* that? Bauer blames me for the murder he committed —and this gives him the right to keep the money he stole? *I* have done nothing wrong, *nothing*. Why am I getting punished for what that"—I caught Roth's eye—"what that scoundrel did?"

There was a moment of silence.

"Because," said Roth, "suffering for others is what pipers are supposed to do." He held my gaze a long moment, then asked, "Didn't you tell me that?"

I sank into my chair as he continued, "Rotten way to handle a murderer, though."

Klara sighed. "Hannes, you're right," she said quietly. "You do deserve the reward. But couldn't you wait for a while? To spare this town?"

I said nothing.

"To spare me?" she said at last.

"Miss Hofmann . . ." I looked at the perfect paneling of the floor, searching for words. "How would I be sparing you if I left a man like Mr. Bauer on the same council as your father?"

165

Mrs. Hofmann entered the sitting room, bearing a well-heaped platter. On it was a golden roasted chicken, now cold but still savory smelling, and half a loaf of white bread, sliced thick. When she set it down, I realized how hungry I was.

Eating from the same plate as someone else, a person has to pace himself, so as not to seem greedy. But Gudrun was a stiff competitor, and I soon lost myself in the smell and taste and chewing and gnawing of cold roast chicken. When at last the bones were sucked bare, Gudrun and I sank back in our chairs with sighs of unspeakable contentment.

Mrs. Hofmann and Roth, now discussing the wool market's future after the rats, carried all but our two cups to the kitchen. In a minute, Gudrun followed them. Klara was sitting back in her chair with her lips pursed, looking at me.

"Miss Hofmann," I said in an undertone, "if I just left tomorrow, what would you do? About Mr. Bauer, I mean."

"I would tell my father."

"And then?"

"And then what?" she said.

"What would your father do?"

She tilted her head. "I don't know."

"What if he didn't do anything?"

"Then I would wait."

"Wait. For what?"

"For him to do something," she answered. "It's my *father's* job to do something about his own council, you know, not mine. I don't have the right to just deal with crime however I want to. That would make me a criminal myself."

"I see that. But *I* have been given authority by my guild. How can I let Mr. Bauer do as he pleases when I could try to stop him? It's not about my having the *right* to do something, Miss Hofmann. I have a *duty* to do something."

"Because you *can* do something, you should," she summarized. "Isn't that the way a criminal thinks?"

"Miss Hofmann, I'm not trying to criticize your father. But please try to understand what I'm thinking. My father was a serf. I was a serf."

Klara said nothing. The voices of Mrs. Hofmann and Roth, now on to the grain market, wafted in from the kitchen.

I continued. "Our lord violated every rule of a lord's duty to his

166

serfs, and every rule of ordinary human compassion. There was nothing we could do. My father was slowly broken down from a man into a . . . a shambles. So I can't understand why a man like your father, who is a good man and has the power to change things, *doesn't*. I want to change what needs to be changed. I have to. Do you understand what I'm saying?"

"I understand," said Klara. "You're angry that your father couldn't change things. You hope that when you do change things yourself, it will fix his life and yours."

"No," I objected. "That's not what I said."

"It's all right. My father . . ." Klara reddened. She glanced at Gudrun, who was snoring peacefully, before whispering, "I sometimes feel that way too."

Heavens. The efficient Klara and her smiling, ineffectual father. She was good at defending him—maybe it sounded well rehearsed because she worked so hard to convince herself.

"Miss Hofmann," I said, "all I ever wanted was to be on Hamelin's side. On your side. If we find out for sure that Mr. Bauer is an enemy to all of us, will we be on the same side against him?"

"Not unless we agree who's leading the attack," said Klara.

"All right," I replied, "I'll make a deal with you. The lord whose serfs I promised to free—he demands payment by tomorrow. I can still make it if I borrow a horse. Otherwise, I break a promise I made in the name of my guild. I betray my mother and father. I leave them and all their fellow serfs under a man and a boy who treat them worse than animals."

"But there *is* no money."

"*Somebody* has it; it didn't just vanish. If we apply the right pressure, I'm sure the council could remember where they put it. And Mr. Bauer has to be brought to trial for the murder of Mr. Zimmer before he tries to kill anyone else."

"So what's the deal you're making?"

"If your father does those two things—if he gets the reward back from the council and gives it to me, and if he accuses Mr. Bauer of murder—then I will do nothing else till he asks me to."

"And if he doesn't do those two things?"

"Then law has failed in Hamelin."

Klara opened her mouth to object, but I pressed on.

"What else can we call it, if members of the council rob and murder, and the mayor fails to act? If he fails here, then I will have to enforce your laws myself."

"And what will you do?"

"I will appeal to the people of Hamelin."

"And if they won't listen?"

I took a deep breath. "Whoever sides with crime will be punished."

Klara looked at me with horror. "What are you going to do to my city?"

I frowned. "What is your city going to do to itself?"

Mrs. Hofmann bustled in, drying her hands on a towel. "Oh, look?" she said, waving at Gudrun. "She's gone to sleep, poor dear?"

Gudrun had in fact slid so far down on her chair that she was lying on the seat of it with her head propped against the back.

"I'll get a bedroll," Roth whispered.

"Don't bother," I whispered back. I stood and gathered Gudrun carefully into my arms. She shifted a little in her sleep, and her head bumped against my chest. "She can sleep on mine for now."

Carefully I carried her to my mat, laid her down there, and pulled the covers up around her. I knelt at her side and looked at Gudrun Hofmann and prayed that, somehow, I would not have to act against her city.

We heard the front door open with a thud, and voices rang down the hallway. I stood and crossed to the door just as the mayor burst in, dragging a thin old man behind him.

"Where's Gudrun?" demanded Mr. Hofmann. He was alive with fury, and the thin man swung from his hand like a rag doll.

I motioned behind the chair, where Gudrun lay, and Mr. Hofmann charged past me with the thin man in tow.

"Oh no," he said, stopping and staring at his motionless daughter.

"Mr. Hofmann—"

"Oh," said the thin man, who smelled of wine. "What's happened here?"

The mayor spun around. "The *doctor's* late."

"Mr. Hofmann!" I broke in.

But the thin man was already backing away. "I had no idea! Why should anyone get hurt today? Finally no rats to bite them . . ."

The mayor's hand was tightening on the man's shoulder. "The

other doctors are all out of town," he said. "You knew that. We agreed you would be on call to the Town Council. But you left home; you went to a party; you got drunk."

"Mr. Hofmann!" I shouted, and I ducked under his arm to get between him and the doctor. "Mr. Hofmann, look at me. Gudrun is fine. We cured her. She's sleeping."

Mr. Hofmann looked into my face, shaking. Slowly the doctor's collar slid from his fingers, and the mayor crushed me to himself with a strength I hadn't expected, repeating, "Thank God; thank God."

When he had recovered, he kissed his sleeping daughter, then sat awhile and watched her breathing. Eventually he turned to us— me, Wolf, his wife, Klara, and Roth— asked our story, and then told his.

He and Wolf had first gone to the doctor's house, where they were told that Mr. Bauer had invited Nikolas ("That's Mr. Klein, the doctor") to dinner to celebrate the death of the rats. Bauer and Klein also planned to pick up Mr. Lachler on the way, so the mayor's next stop was Lachlers'.

There he and Wolf had found the lady of the house alone. Yes, Mr. Bauer had already dropped by with the doctor, noticed the "Pied Piper pie" that she was just tucking up, and admired it so much that he took it out to show to Dr. Klein. The two of them asked if her husband could be the third member of their little celebration, and Mrs. Lachler had heard them mention Mr. Bauer's best wine.

Finally, at Bauers', Wolf and the mayor had found the three men quite drunk, especially Lachler and Klein. It had taken them some time to make the doctor understand what was needed and to drag him outside.

"I was so afraid I'd be too late," the mayor finished, shivering.

Roth and Dr. Klein came into the room, the doctor leaning a bit unsteadily on Roth, his wine-muddled features wearing a puzzled frown.

"Mr. Mayor," he said, with an effort to speak clearly, "that pie is packed full of poison mushrooms. The kind called the Destroying Angel."

"What? Are you sure?"

"Positive," said the doctor. "I'd know that type of mushroom even if I were ten times this drunk. You know I was selling them dried for rat poison. But who would put them in a pie? I mean, Mrs. Lachler can be a little odd at times, but . . ."

The mayor looked at the table and frowned. "Thank you, Nikolas," he said to the doctor. "Wolf, will you take him home?"

Wolf inclined his head and stood. He and the doctor began to walk from the room.

"Oh, Nikolas," said the mayor. "I'm sorry. For . . . for blaming you. And losing my temper."

The doctor coughed. "You're too good a man by far, Mr. Mayor." And, still weaving on his feet, he left, and the front door shut behind him.

"Mr. Hofmann," I said, "I know this is a bad time to bring this up . . ."

"Hannes, you helped cure my daughter," he said. "Speak."

"Thank you, sir. Roth told us something about Mr. Zimmer."

When I turned to Roth, he had a frozen look. I hadn't thought Roth feared Mr. Bauer, but maybe when it came to actually telling the mayor . . .

"Don't worry, Roth," I said, touching the pipe tucked in my belt.

"I found Mr. Zimmer," Roth said. "When he was dying. He said it was Bauer who stabbed him."

Mr. and Mrs. Hofmann both gaped at Roth.

"That's not all, Daddy," said Klara.

And she told him about the cutthroat grain prices, and I told him about Franz and then showed him the letter about the hiring of the rat-bringer. I started to tell him about the empty fund, but Klara said she had already explained that.

I nodded. "All right. Sir, I do still need that money. In fact, the man I need to pay wants it by tomorrow."

"Tomorrow?" said the mayor, raising his eyebrows. "Tomorrow's Sunday. He does business on Sunday?"

"I would have paid him today, but I didn't have the money, sir."

"Oh, I don't blame *you*, my boy." He frowned, staring at the tablecloth. "I just can't believe all this," he whispered.

"Sir," I said, as gently as I could, "what are we—?" I caught myself and stopped. Desperate as I was for action, I would not bully this good man, and I would not make the guild look like money-grubbers. Let justice and the need of the oppressed speak for themselves.

He looked up at me, clear blue eyes framed in furrowed eyebrows. "I'll get you your reward, my boy. I'm going to have a talk with my vice-mayor."

Just hearing those words, I felt my muscles relax as if I were in a steaming bath. I offered my thanks, and I saw pride in Klara's eyes. Mrs. Hofmann took her husband's hand and squeezed it.

The front door creaked open, and a moment later, Wolf stepped in.

"Well," said Mr. Hofmann, standing. "I think I've intruded on your hospitality long enough, Roth. We'll take Gudrun home."

"Oh, let the poor dear sleep?" protested Mrs. Hofmann. "If that's all right, Roth?"

"Fine," Roth answered. "I'll fetch Mrs. Rike; she'll be glad to stay overnight with Gudrun. We'll put the two of them in the workroom, eh, Hannes? And I can take Gudrun to church in the morning."

Mr. Hofmann nodded. "Well, then. Thank you, Roth. You've taken such good care of her." He gave the two of us a good, hard hug.

As we all said our good nights and they moved toward the door, I said softly, "Miss Hofmann?"

Klara turned as the others moved on. Wolf squinted at me from the doorway.

"Miss Hofmann, it's good to be on the same side."

"Ah," she said in a low voice, with a face as if something bitter were in her mouth, "now that my father's measured up to your qualifications?"

I looked at her in disbelief.

"Look, Mr. Piper," she said, and her face seemed gentler, but as if she were working at it. "You risked your life; you helped save my sister. My family will never forget that. But I get the feeling there's something going on here that you don't really understand yourself. Am I right?"

The enemy piper flashed into my head, but I pushed the thought back out. I had to solve one thing at a time. The guild could deal with a renegade piper later. Besides, I'd beat him last time.

"There's a lot I don't understand, Miss Hofmann."

"Thank you, Mr. Piper," she said, and with a quick good night she left, followed by Wolf, who had never taken his glittering eyes off me.

I turned and slumped back into my chair, and gazed at the two cups standing among the crumbs.

I heard Roth making his farewells. At last he came back in and looked at me.

"Now what are you so downcast about?" he asked. "Didn't the mayor just fulfill your wildest dreams?"

I picked up an unnoticed crust of bread and nibbled it. "Oh, I don't know."

He sat beside me. "What, are you afraid that Mr. Bauer will kill the mayor?"

"Good heavens, Roth. D'you think he might?"

"Wolf and Klara are with the mayor tomorrow," he said. "They won't let him take too many risks. Besides, if Bauer even tried to harm Mr. Hofmann, I expect you'd pipe him one good, right on the spot. Am I right?"

I nodded, fidgeting with the edge of the tablecloth.

"You better just be ready for anything, Hannes," said Roth, standing up. "Bauer's quick on his feet."

He picked up the two cups, carried them toward the kitchen, and raised his voice. "You may have to deal with new enemies. Bauer'll be recruiting. Mayor'll need all the backup he can get."

I had told Klara that if her father took action, I would wait for his permission before using the pipe. But what if the pipe could not be avoided?

"Roth, what if my new enemy is Hamelin?"

"What?" he yelled from the kitchen.

That was it. What if the town sided with the criminals? Suddenly I saw Hamelin's view of my guild for what it was—not innocent confusion but monstrous ingratitude to the ones who had saved them. There was something twisted in the way this town viewed the world. They might just choose blindness again. Then what would I do?

There was the tune from the clay doll.

Surely they would pay me and deal with their criminals.

Suddenly I wanted not to be alone with this decision, and I wandered into the kitchen with its comfortable flagstones, hearth, and hanging copper pans, and the comfortable presence of Roth Kunst washing up a few dishes that had miraculously escaped Mrs. Hofmann. He was standing over a full basin, sleeves rolled up to the elbow, wiping the chicken platter.

"Roth, what if Hamelin sides with Bauer?" I asked in a soft voice, fearing the answer.

He looked up from the dripping platter. "Hannes, I want you to do for the souls of this town what I'm doing for their bellies. I'm sick to death of people taking the short view. Think of *ten years* from now."

My vacant face told him to go on.

"Johannes, here's the question: When Gudrun grows up, will she have a council of men like her father, or a council of men like Bauer?"

Dread began creeping up my arms. I knew what curse I had to use.

FOURTEEN

Paying the Piper

Sunday, June Twenty-fifth, 1284, Hamelin

N St. John's Day, Year of Our Lord 1284
To Friedrich of Muender, Master Piper
From Johannes of Oldendorf, Apprentice of the Same
Dear Master Friedrich,

Some of the choices I wrote about have made themselves.

The rats are gone.

An unknown member of our guild was paid by the council to pipe the rats to Hamelin. He fought me when I drowned the rats. Will he continue to fight me? How?

Councilmen have committed other gross crimes, including murder.

The mayor has promised to investigate and deal with these matters. But if he and the people do not side with justice against their corrupt council, then I believe the correct piper's choice would be the Childrule Curse. The conditions have been met: those in power grievously abuse their positions and crush the poor. I was not trained for this ministry, but the score came to me providentially.

The problem is that I am afraid. I spent most of the night looking for a different response. I looked in Just Pipe *under "Corruption, Governmental, Punishments for," as well as "Incorrigibility, Matching Level of" and "Complicity in Crime, Curses for Varying Degrees of." The Childrule is the last thing I want. In fact, this assignment is turning out to be not at all the mission I had dreamed of, nor the mission that M. Josef had prepared me for.*

Did you know how much Hamelin *already* hates *the guild? Besides this, I face the problem of hurting certain people whom I have come to love. So I am desperately hoping I won't need the curse, but I am prepared if the need arises.*

175

I have chosen a Keychild who should restrain things. Gudrun Hofmann shows an amazing understanding of adult life, of Hamelin's needs, and, incidentally, of piping.

Your advice, whether in person or by letter, would be most welcome.

Your humble servant,
Johannes

I opened my eyes. The shutters were still closed, but bright sunlight slanted in through the cracks. I had missed the church service. I jumped to my feet and stumbled from the kitchen, where I'd spent the night thinking and writing my second letter to Master Friedrich, into the sitting room.

The mayor would talk to Mr. Bauer—and I still needed time to get to Aerzen before sunset. I was late. Finding a courier for the letter would have to wait.

As I splashed my soggy face in the basin, I remembered the night. I had wanted to spend the lonely hours with Roth, but he was sleeping. Or with Gudrun, or Wolf. With Klara, or the mayor. With someone who could stand with me and help me make this choice. My guild was committed to justice—no matter what the cost to me and the people I loved. If I didn't have to be alone with this secret, I'd throw open the windows and beg for help; I'd tell my friends everything. But this had to be the piper's choice. It was my decision to make, even though my heart was screaming for a companion.

What if the impossible had suddenly happened, and old Master Friedrich had limped into the room? He'd have quietly advised me, "Justice, Hannes. If you do nothing, what will break the cycle of Hamelin's evil?" And I'd answer, "You do it! The Hofmanns and Roth and I will float down the Weser in our little boat, and you can do whatever you want to Bauer and the council and this grubby little town that just loves the way they operate."

I combed the hair of the still-unfamiliar-looking Hannes in Roth's clear mirror. I looked like I felt. All night I had tossed and turned and yawned, while my eyes burned wide awake. The choice dangled in front of me like a hangman's noose.

I had seen the evidence, the arguments for and against, and knew the time had come for my choice. But I would rather do anything else in the world. At one point I had begun feverishly polishing my pipe. I had suddenly remembered to air my bedroll. In the end, I had caught myself sweeping the room . . .

In the hours after midnight, I'd imagined Master Friedrich battering me with questions. *Hannes, do you see these councilmen? Do you see the townspeople who call this situation normal? Who will ever tell them this tumor is not normal, if you don't? Who will speak for the poor who have been crushed by this plague and this corruption? Who will open the eyes of the oppressors so they can understand how they have humiliated, rejected, and abused the poor? Hannes, they will never understand any language but pain. They will never understand till they taste the cup they've been giving to others. They must be humiliated, rejected, abused—by their own children.*

I held the Childrule score in my hand. On this paper was the nightmare Hamelin wouldn't be able to wake up from. I put it in my bag.

It was strange, being in such a comfortable room for such an uncomfortable business. But ever since I'd first come to Hamelin six years ago, I'd been preparing for this moment. Everything I'd tasted of oppression and justice, everything I'd learned from the two men who had been fathers to me, had ripened me like a grape for this squeezing—this long night, this dry mouth, these sweating hands holding this pipe, facing this choice.

I hurriedly pulled on my hosen, dancing on one foot and nearly falling in the process. First the red, then the yellow. Justice and mercy. *Hamelin, as I bring down justice on you, have mercy on me.*

I picked up my cloak and saw again the faint stain of Dietrich Zimmer's blood. Someone must pay.

Something good had happened on this miserable night. I'd faced the fact that this choice would make Klara hate me once and for all. And as I'd said good-bye to her in my mind, I understood that my feelings for her were solid and good. Now, when it didn't matter anymore, because the curse would kill any hope that was left, I saw clearly that the reasons I was drawn to her were good reasons. Klara Hofmann understood that life was too important to spend living for oneself.

But now, of course, all the Hofmanns would hate me forever. I'd be the bogeyman of Hamelin. I would scar the lives of Hameliners, including children, including Gudrun. All the work I'd done, building trust and winning respect, would be wiped out as though it had never been. And so I let it all go—the townspeople, Roth, the Hofmanns, Klara . . . I had to do what Hamelin needed, even if Hamelin hated me for it.

I ran out of the house, barely stopping to shut the front door behind me. The sun was already low in the sky. How could it be afternoon already? Three days, and I still didn't know what morning in Hamelin was like.

Down the street I ran, twice almost slipping on the muddy stones. I could hear noise now, the rumble of a crowd and the ringing tone of someone calling out over it. It was the mayor's voice. At last.

"Hamelin has suffered," Mr. Hofmann was saying.

I ran to the edge of the crowd that filled the square, but the mayor was looking the other way and didn't see me. He was standing in his Sunday best on the steps of Town Hall, with Mr. Bauer and the other councilmen standing nearby, and the townsfolk spread out beneath them. I saw Klara, also dressed for church and standing on the church steps. She looked angry.

"All of us have suffered," said Mr. Hofmann. "And even though the rats are gone now, our city is still worn down from the fight. I think the excitement of getting rid of the rats distracted us from that." His understanding eyes radiated hope over the people; his brow furrowed with sympathy. Behind him, Mr. Bauer contrived a solemn smile.

A cold tickling spread across my back.

"You know," said Mr. Hofmann, "many of the good things we had hoped to do for you were postponed during our time of trial. At last, we can give these our attention." He paused and beamed at his council. "As you know, several months ago the council established a fund whose purpose was relief from the rat plague. But this morning, I ran into my colleagues on the way to church, and we spoke about this special fund. I realized there are two choices."

The crowd watched him, caught up in his earnestness. I couldn't move.

"One choice is this. We can use the fund for the purpose we chose when our town was mad with pain. And that was: a reward for removing the rats. But if we do this, then all the work of caring for your needs and doing everything we postponed during the plague can only be funded by keeping up regular taxes. Yet, after the plague, and after all the special taxes for the emergency fund, you, the people of Hamelin, are wrung dry!"

A murmur of assent rippled through the crowd.

"We can't ask more of you now," said the mayor, holding out his hands to them as if they didn't believe him and had to be convinced. "Not when you simply need to rebuild your lives. Not when we have a huge fund, already gathered, meant for that rebuilding. No. We will rise up! We will rebuild! We will have a whole year completely free of taxes!"

The people raised their hands with a deafening roar of approval. The mayor seemed to float above them, tears in his eyes and his arms stretched out in benediction. Behind him the council applauded.

I began to push through the crowd, working my way around the edge of the square.

The mayor gestured for silence.

"After we decided this, we asked the good men of the Town Council how much each one of them, at this difficult time, could spare from his family's own means to express our city's gratitude to the Pied Piper. My colleagues were generous. I was touched."

I fought my way to the bottom of the steps, and Mr. Hofmann turned to me.

"Johannes!" he said. "At last!" He waved me up toward him on the steps. It was so quiet that I could clearly hear my footfalls on the stone. Beaming, he held out a bag that clinked in my hands. "We gave as much as we could, Johannes."

The council smiled behind him. Mr. Bauer was solemn, overcome with the needs of his fellow citizens.

"Mr. Hofmann," I said in a low tone, "what is this?"

"Your reward, my boy," he answered.

I clenched my teeth and swallowed. "What does this bag hold?" I asked. "Two, three hundred coins?"

The mayor raised his eyebrows.

"Mr. Hofmann, you promised me ten thousand."

"Oh," said the mayor, "you haven't heard what I've been saying. These people—"

"I heard your speech," I interrupted. "But I need full payment today, to help people who are suffering more than Hamelin."

"Johannes, I understand," Mr. Hofmann said, stretching out his soothing hands.

"No, sir, I don't think you do." I reached into my pouch, pulled out the mayor's permission sheet, and held it up to him. "Let me read: 'This we, the Town Council, do solemnly pledge to the bearer, Johannes Piper of Oldendorf.' *Ten thousand silver coins.* Your signature, sir. You promised me this money."

179

Suddenly Mr. Bauer was towering over us. "Is there a problem?" he rumbled.

I laid my hand on my pipe.

Mr. Bauer stiffened, and the crowd gasped. I took my hand off my pipe and tried to speak too low for the crowd to hear.

"Mr. Hofmann, what is this man doing with you?"

"Now, Johannes," said Mr. Hofmann, "he's my vice-mayor."

"You remember what we discussed at Roth's," I replied. "About the vice-mayor. And you remember that we have a witness."

Mr. Bauer looked confidently at the mayor.

"Yes, Johannes," said Mr. Hofmann. "People make mistakes. Roth must have been frantic when he found the man dying; his judgment was clouded. He misunderstood when poor Dietrich gasped out the name of his friend."

I stared at him. "And now you trust Mr. Bauer to administrate the fund? There *is* no fund. If he won't empty his pockets for me, in spite of my contract, why should he empty his pockets for the town he's been deceiving for almost a year?"

"Johannes!" said the mayor, looking shocked. "Johannes, this is all a misunderstanding. The fund was moved to a safer place."

"That's not what Mr. Zimmer thought."

"Johannes," the mayor began.

"Enough of this, Walter," said Mr. Bauer, stepping between us and raising his voice so the crowd could hear him.

"Mr. Hofmann, you promised me the full reward," I said.

"You have your reward," Mr. Bauer snarled, nodding at the bag in my hand. "Now get out of here."

The mayor was silent. I turned to the sea of frowning faces in the square. Above them, on the church steps, I saw Klara, and she looked back. I placed the bag of coins in Mr. Bauer's hands.

"Could you let me through?" I asked the people.

They parted for me, and I began to walk across the square.

"People of Hamelin!" I shouted, as they drew apart ahead of me. "You know what suffering is like. Until a few days ago, you were fighting with rats for your own food. So I know that you can understand the suffering of others."

"What is this?" Bauer demanded behind me.

"Mr. Bauer!" said Klara. "He saved us from the rats. The least we can do is let him finish what he has to say."

I was halfway across the square, surrounded by a crowd of hard-faced Hameliners. "On my way to Hamelin," I said, "I stopped at an estate where the serfs get harsh, brutal treatment from their lord, even from his son. I agreed with the steward to buy his lord's manor, so that my guild can give the land to the serfs and set them free. They are waiting. Hamelin owes this money to the Pipers Guild. Your leaders made a promise."

As I spoke, I turned back toward Town Hall. Mr. Bauer was staring at me as though he'd seen a ghost. There was silence in the square.

"Hermann," murmured the mayor, "don't you own—"

"Mistreated serfs! A manor for sale!" Bauer shouted to the crowd. "What proof does he have of this?"

"I have proof of one thing!" I yelled out. "The rats that terrorized your homes and starved you were brought to Hamelin by Hermann Bauer."

Someone in the crowd laughed and stopped short. The rest seemed shocked and puzzled. I pulled out the letter Roth had found and lifted it high so they could all see it. Climbing the church steps, I held the letter out to Klara. "Miss Hofmann?"

She turned to her father, then back to me, and took the letter.

"Miss Hofmann, do you recognize the signature at the bottom of this letter?"

"Yes," she said in a flat tone. "I see it all the time, on council paperwork."

"Whose signature is it?"

"Mr. Bauer's."

The crowd murmured.

"Could you please read the letter, Miss Hofmann? From here." I pointed at a spot near the middle.

"Don't think about the rats," she read, in a voice that rang. "Think about selling hundreds of rattraps. Think about grain prices at unheard-of heights. Think about raising a huge reward fund, completely under the council's control, for a rescuer who can never succeed. *That* is what the gentleman I have met will bring to Hamelin. He is simply a business partner, and he is asking a very reasonable price."

The square was completely silent.

"Look," said the mayor, "I was shocked, too, when I read that. It's unspeakable. But Mr. Bauer explained everything to me."

Klara's face was motionless. The crowd's eyes rested on the mayor.

"There was a day," the mayor said, "when Mr. Bauer was writing a letter, and he wrote a perfectly friendly first paragraph, and signed his name at the bottom of the page. Then he went to get some sealing wax, but when he came back, it was gone. Someone must have stolen it and added the rest, including that heartless paragraph. I can tell you, it was a relief to hear that I hadn't been mistaken about my own vice-mayor all these years." He gave a nervous little laugh.

The crowd was silent.

"Mr. Mayor," I said, "all the handwriting is the same."

"Why bring up the rats?" asked Bauer, his face full of fatherly disapproval. "The rats are gone, Mr. Piper. We have to think about what this town needs *now*. Why do you want to rob us of the little we have? Why are you stirring up trouble, like the last piper who paid Hamelin a call?"

I was speechless.

"Trouble," Bauer repeated, his eyes on the crowd. "That's what this piper brings and calls it proof. But people of Hamelin, what we need today is to leave our trouble behind. We *need* this relief fund. We need it for our starving families; we need it for loved ones who are sick; we need it to repair what we lost under the rats. We need it to celebrate our new freedom from the plague." His voice was rising and falling with a kind of magic in it.

The crowd stirred.

"That is what *I* offer you!" Bauer said, his voice soaring. "And unlike this pipe-toting foreigner, I have proof! Here is my proof!" he boomed. And he held up the bag of silver I had put back in his hands, opened it, and heaved its contents out over the crowd.

Silver fell like rain, and the people charged toward it. Klara and I were alone on the church steps, watching the waves of people scrambling and stooping. For several minutes, all that anyone could hear was babbling and fighting as Hameliners harvested coins.

As soon as I could be heard, I shouted, "Enjoy your silver now, people of Hamelin. It's all you're going to get. The fund they are promising you is empty!" I whipped around to Klara. "Miss Hofmann, tell them!"

She looked straight at her father, then turned to the crowd and said, "I saw the empty chest."

"But, Klara—" the mayor began.

"Daddy, it wasn't just moved." She faced the crowd. "Before he died, Mr. Zimmer told me what had happened to the reward fund. It went into the purses of some of the councilmen."

"What?" said Mr. Bauer, with a look of horror on his face. He turned to the council on the steps behind him. They looked back at him, some of them with anger and shock.

"Why are you surprised?" asked Klara, with an edge in her voice that I was glad to hear pointed away from me. "My father already told you about it this morning. Didn't you, Daddy?"

"Well, yes," said the mayor, with a puzzled face.

Mr. Bauer spoke to Klara, his face twisted in fury. "You side with this outsider? This troublemaker? This *piper*?" His hands clutched at the air. "His kind have brought our town nothing but pain. Remember six years back. And think: ever since *this* one set foot in Hamelin, we've had nothing but trouble." Bauer's voice swelled to fill the square as he raised his finger to point at me. "He killed Dietrich Zimmer!"

Anger awoke in the faces of the crowd. On the edge nearest us, a woman clutched her daughter closer at Mr. Zimmer's name. Then I saw who her daughter was. It was Frieda, the girlfriend of Strom. Now I saw that she had her father's eyes and mouth. She was Frieda Zimmer.

"No!" I said, pointing back at Mr. Bauer. "*You* killed Mr. Zimmer! I have a witness who spoke with Mr. Zimmer before he died!" I scanned the crowd, but I couldn't see anyone as tall as Roth. I looked at Klara.

"He wasn't at church," she whispered, and there was worry in her eyes. I looked at Mr. Bauer.

"So where is this witness?" he snarled.

"Mr. Bauer!" I shouted, shaking with fury, "What have you done with Roth Kunst?"

A flicker of puzzlement crossed his face, followed by anger. "This is preposterous!"

"I heard him!" Klara shouted. "I heard Roth Kunst testify that Mr. Zimmer named you as his murderer."

"Lies!" Mr. Bauer roared. "I am your vice-mayor!" he called out to the crowd. "This boy is a *piper*!"

The frowns of the people deepened.

"I have the council behind me!" he announced, and then spat out, "He has the testimony of a *girl*!"

Klara's lips were white.

"Hermann!" said the mayor. "She's my daughter. She's kept the council accounts for years . . ."

"Walter," said Bauer, and the mayor stopped.

"Mr. Hofmann," I said, "you know I won't let Mr. Bauer harm you or your family."

The mayor looked at me in bewilderment. "He hasn't threatened me," he said.

"See!" said Mr. Bauer. "He imagines villains around every corner."

The faces in the crowd showed confusion.

"Why do you listen to Mr. Bauer?" Klara screamed at the crowd. "He starved you with illegal prices all through the plague!"

There was a murmur in the crowd.

Mr. Bauer flicked his eyes over them, then back at me. "Why, you scoundrel," he said to me. "You've bewitched Miss Hofmann!"

The eyes of the crowd turned on me and on the pipe at my side.

"Enough!" I said. "We can't deal with all these accusations here. We have accused each other of murder. Murder trials are for the duke to judge. But this much is clear: this town promised me the reward, and I earned it. Or do you miss your sea of rats? Let the council dig deep in their pockets, return the fund, and deliver it— as they *promised.* You may send as many guards with me as you please to make sure I use it only to free those serfs. Then I will return with the guards and let the duke judge between me and Mr. Bauer. That is my proposal."

There was silence.

"All in favor of my proposal," I said, "come over to me."

No one moved.

"People of Hamelin," I called out, "this is the last chance for those serfs." In my mind, I saw my father—thin, sick, crumpled in the sheets.

The mayor took a step toward me, but Mr. Bauer glared at him and he stopped. Then Klara took a deep breath and stepped down to stand beside me.

"Leave, outsider," Mr. Bauer growled. "Hamelin's justice is for Hameliners, and Hamelin's mercy is for Hameliners. Hamelin," he intoned, "is for Hameliners."

There was a moment of silence, then someone cried, "Hamelin for Hameliners!"

"Hamelin for Hameliners!" the crowd shouted, lifting their fists into the air.

I saw Frieda Zimmer, her jaw clenched, tears in her eyes, glaring at me in triumph.

"Hamelin for Hameliners! Hamelin for Hameliners!"

I looked out at the roiling mass of people, and I shivered. I took out my pipe and held it high in the air. The shouting died.

"People of Hamelin, I warn you," I said. "If you break your word and side with the wrong that's been done here, I am *bound* by the laws of my guild. I will curse this town until you change your minds."

Klara turned to me, then stepped back, staring. She was pale.

"People," I called out, "do not make me do this."

"Grab the pipe!" Bauer shouted, and several men charged forward.

I thrust the pipe into my mouth and blew two notes. In the Pipeworld, I felt a mighty wind flooding out from me. People reeled back all around. All but Klara. She had stood by me, and the wind did not touch her. She reached toward my pipe. I didn't move. Her fingers were almost around it, and our eyes met. As the men in the crowd lunged forward and slipped back, Klara stopped. Her hand dropped to her side.

I turned back toward the crowd and shut my eyes to play the twisted notes.

One: Gather the adults. As the jagged tilts and swoops of the music moved through my lips and fingers, I reached out in the Pipeworld and swept my right hand across Hamelin, catching the threads of its inhabitants. I kept in my grasp only the thicker strings of the adults. I could feel every fiber—here was Bauer, a greasy string; Wolf, one that scratched my hand; the mayor, thin and soft. Klara's string, which I felt embarrassed to touch, was silky but strong as an iron chain. Her string I let go. As the only Hameliner who had sided with the right, she'd be immune, like me, to the Childrule Curse.

I felt a twinge of worry when I couldn't find Roth's string, but I kept playing till I felt against my hand the pull of them all—the weight of their minds.

Two: Gather the children. As the harsh music streamed on, I moved to the next step in my decoded instructions for the Pipeworld. My left hand swept the city for the children's hands—

the hands that in the Pipeworld meant control. In a moment, I held their fingers. There was Gudrun's hand. She was still at Roth's house, asleep on my mat. I gave her hand a squeeze and let it go.

Three: Give the adults to the children. With a jolt in the music, I passed the strings of the adults over to the hands of the children. I felt a crackle like fire as the children's fingers closed on the strings. I remembered Strom sneering at the old serf, and I shuddered.

Four: Give the children to the Keychild, the one who would rule the new rulers. On and on I danced in the Pipeworld, diving behind the children as the music dived, pulling and gathering their strings into Gudrun's hand. My fingers wrapped her fingers around them, and her fist tightened well against the tug as the song's last unresolved note faded. The world of Hamelin, bound in strings, was frozen, and I stepped behind Gudrun's mind to rest my hands on her sleeping shoulders. When I felt her breathing, and the pull of the whole city on her, I knelt and gave her a hug.

I held that note for a moment, when suddenly a current passed through the Pipeworld. I felt a distant music playing a counter-melody to my song. I sprang to my feet, but at that moment, scorching hands seized Gudrun and ripped her from my grasp.

FIFTEEN

Out of Control

Sunday, June Twenty-fifth, 1284, Hamelin

GUDRUN!" I SCREAMED ACROSS THE DARKNESS, AND I RAN after her. I was suddenly cold, and the space around me seemed strangely empty. My foot missed a stair in the outside world, I lost my balance, and I jerked out of the Pipeworld to topple down the steps and bang my head on them. Colored splotches swam over my eyes, and my head was filled with a splitting pain. The men who had been held back by my piping toppled to the cobblestones.

A cold morning breeze drove through the narrow streets, but that wasn't why I was trembling. The people in the square were shuffling around in a daze. Klara looked down at me with a strange expression and turned away.

Feeling limp, I raised the pipe to my lips again and softly played a few notes, groping in the Pipeworld to find what I had stumbled over. Klara's string, perhaps? Odd. Her string was gone.

Here was what had tripped me. I felt the cord in my hand, but at the same time, I felt my hand through the cord. Then this had to be *my* string, loosened from me. Conclusion: Both Klara and I were now under the curse.

I staggered to my feet in the Pipeworld, my notes falling around me as I fumbled for the strings. They were gone; all those minds were out of my reach.

The flaming hands had not only taken Gudrun from me; they had taken the curse from my control. I fell to my knees, and the Pipeworld wavered and vanished. I was back in the mud.

"Listen!" Klara called out to the crowd. "If Mr. Bauer is innocent, the trial will show that. Do what the piper says, and he'll take the curse away."

I shivered. I could *not* take the curse away. Now, even if they did everything I asked, I couldn't do what I'd promised.

"Ha!" Bauer scoffed. "This girl wants us to lower ourselves and appease the piper at any price. Fine! People of Hamelin, let us put our leaders on trial for him! Let us strip the last coins from our rat-starved citizens for him! Anything to remove the curse!" He laughed long and loud, then turned to Klara and roared, "What curse? Do you see a curse? All I see is an arrogant pup whose screeching would wake the dead."

I struggled to my feet in the mud, using only one hand, holding up the pipe.

"Miss Hofmann," I croaked. I stumbled up the steps to her, trailing mud. "Miss Hofmann, something's gone very wrong."

Her eyes were puzzled. I turned to the crowd—a sea of anxious faces. Even Mr. Bauer's defiant gaze was tinged with fear. Out near the edge of the square, a few men were turning slowly around in circles. I had no idea why. I focused on the others and spoke.

"People of Hamelin," I said, "something's gone wrong."

Silence.

"The curse has been taken away from me."

A man called out, "You mean the curse is gone?"

"No!" I said. "I mean I can't stop it."

At that moment a boy sprang up on the Town Hall steps, so suddenly that I jumped. The boy from the manor. Strom.

"You!" he said, pointing at the man who had spoken. "Suck your thumb!"

A strange expression snapped onto the man's face, and he obeyed.

Klara looked at me, first with shock, then with anger.

"You!" Strom said again, pointing at an old woman. "Bark like a dog!"

An indulgent look broke over her face, though she was blushing, and in a moment, she was doing a credible imitation of a dog. Now almost a third of the crowd were spinning in circles, flapping like chickens, reciting nursery rhymes. A shifty laughter moved through the children. The adults began backing away. I could see in their eyes the same fear I felt: it would be minutes before the crueler children thought of things even more debasing and dangerous. Some of them looked to me and shouted, "Do something!"

I couldn't meet their eyes. I couldn't break the curse.

"Are you just going to stand there?" Klara demanded.

I could hardly face her. This much was my own curse.

I saw Mr. Hofmann, torn with a parent's pain over the pain of his city. Then Strom saw him too.

"Mr. Mayor," he said, stepping closer, with some hesitation in his face.

The mayor saw this predator approaching and stepped back.

As on the first day I'd met him, I felt a zeal to give Strom what he deserved. He commanded the mayor to crawl and babble like an infant. Just then I felt another current pass through the Pipeworld. It felt like Gudrun. Before it could dissolve, I thrust my pipe into my mouth and played. The kneeling mayor, the frenzied crowd, and Klara running down the stairs—all faded like a dream.

I leaped onto the ripple, spreading my limbs and fingers to float, and caught the wave, sliding down the back slope as if it were a moving hill. I skimmed toward its source. Here it was. I found my feet. Heat was all around me. And since I had a nose like a bloodhound in the Pipeworld, I could smell Gudrun. The ripple had been sent out by a meeting between Gudrun as the Keychild and the new keeper of the curse.

I stretched my hand to feel Gudrun's mind, and my hands brushed a flaming net. I could sense what she was thinking, but I could not talk to her or touch her. She was opening softly, like a flower, slipping out of a dream. She turned, sleepy, surprised, but not afraid to face her host, who was wreathed in flame. I was like someone watching a dance through a thin curtain, or hearing a song through a door. I felt Gudrun's drowsy question, but the older voice's answer was so twisted by the fire I could only sense its quiet urgency. I reached out to touch my enemy's face but couldn't stand the heat.

Gudrun's strange, fiery keeper was showing her something, and her careful curiosity emerged like a snail from its shell. No, it was more than curiosity; she was amazed, she was honored, and yet she drew back.

The flaming person was offended but knew how to be gracious. After all, this was a child, and the thing being offered was a hard thing.

"Gudrun, don't listen!" I tried to call to her, but I only cut my hands on the burning web. She didn't move.

The blazing hands that had seized her for the curse stroked her shoulders, reassuring her. With her left hand holding the strings of Hamelin's childrulers, Gudrun extended her right hand to seal their agreement with a handshake. I lunged forward, but as I touched the web, a shudder went through me and flung me back. The Pipeworld vanished again as I tumbled from the steps.

"Stop immediately!" It was Mr. Bauer's voice. "I'm warning you, young man!"

I blinked to clear my eyes and saw Mr. Bauer standing at his full height at the bottom of the Town Hall steps, the one unmoved tower in a chaos of adults and children. Strom, on the steps above, turned slowly to look at him. There was some fear in Strom's eyes. But in the middle of the wreck of people around him, Strom stood tall as well. The cold wind rose, and Strom's jacket spread behind him as he and Mr. Bauer faced each other.

Then Strom looked down at Mr. Bauer and said, "Father."

My head spun. The manor—*my* manor—belonged to Mr. Bauer? So when Bauer robbed the fund now owed to me, he had robbed *himself*. The whole mission was insane, a snake eating its tail.

"Father," said Strom. "Give me your wig."

A contortion passed across Mr. Bauer's face. Then he reached up, lifted the false hair from a bald head, and held it out limply to his son, who set it on his own head like a crown.

"Kneel."

Mr. Bauer knelt on a lower step. Strom lifted his foot and placed it on his father's shoulder. Mr. Bauer quivered and lowered his head.

At that moment, I saw something high on his forehead, something the wig had hidden from me all this time. A wine-colored, crescent-shaped birthmark.

Then I hated him as I had never hated anyone before in my life. This man deserved to be tortured by his son. He had broken my father. He had crushed us all. How many people like us had he ground to powder? And this son of his, who had tormented people too—how kind had Mr. Bauer been, even to his son? I struggled to my feet, forgetting everything else, and strode toward him with my pipe gripped hard in my hand like a sword, breathing like a bull, ready to pay Bauer the wages he had been earning for six years.

"Stop!" came a girl's voice from behind me.

Though I was a piper and should have known better, I didn't realize at first that she was tugging my string.

The poor girl, I thought. *She needs me.* Immediately I stopped and turned to her.

It was Frieda Zimmer. She looked at me solemnly, wisps of blonde hair sticking to her tearstained cheeks.

Oh, don't cry, I thought.

"He *obeyed* you!" Strom exclaimed behind me, with a voice full of discovery and triumph. "Frieda, don't be scared," he said, talking faster. "There's no way we're getting in trouble now. This boy doesn't have the spell anymore."

Frieda eyed me. "Mr. Piper," she said softly, "give me your pipe."

What would it be like to lose a father? No one to protect her. Frieda had to protect herself—better than I had protected her father. She needed my pipe. I owed it to her.

I laid it on my open palms and held it out.

Klara's voice screamed, "Hannes, no!"

I jerked back, but too late; Frieda had snatched the pipe from my grasping hands. I ran for my life.

"Seize him!" yelled Strom, and toppled as his father ran forward with the rest.

Before I'd taken three steps, I was surrounded by the mothers and fathers of Hamelin. I crouched and flung myself where the wall of legs was thinnest, knocking over a councilman and a blacksmith. Somersaulting through the mud, I sprang to my feet.

"Hold still!" Strom commanded, clambering out of the mud.

I was a piper. In control of the curse or not, I had a chance at resisting . . .

How this boy must have suffered.

The adults were turning toward me.

If he was cruel, it was only because his father was cruel to him.

They surged at me, splattering mud.

All Strom needed was love. Couldn't I do this one thing for him?

Their hands stretched out.

"No!" I shouted; I yanked on the cord that bound me and found myself free. I ducked under the arms of his army and pelted down the block.

"Klara!" shouted Strom. "Come here!"

I stopped running and skidded in the mud.

191

Klara stamped over to Strom. "What do you want?" she demanded, but her voice was not steady.

"Leave her alone!" shouted the mayor.

A boy standing by the mayor squinted up at him and said, "Slap yourself."

The mayor furrowed his eyebrows and struck his own face.

"Stop it!" yelled Klara, a feeble adult in a child's world.

The mud-stained villagers turned where they stood, then came charging at me. Strom looked at me and grinned. A good anger filled me, and I ran a wide circle around the running mob, then sprinted at Strom.

"Hold still!" he told Klara.

I swept down and threw Klara over my shoulder, shoving Strom out of the way. I turned and ran toward the mayor.

"Punch him!" Strom yelped, pursuing us, and the mayor raised a fist. But I spun hard. Klara's feet slammed into Strom, and as Strom went down, the mayor's head seemed to clear. I grabbed the back of his coat and dragged him with me.

"Come . . ." Strom wheezed, but the mayor couldn't hear him.

We fled down an alley. As soon as we had rounded a corner, I put Klara down, and the three of us ran. We passed houses and streets, the empty faces of parents, and the unhappy laughter of children. We ducked behind door frames, around corners, and always Klara was whispering *right* or *left* until I had no idea where we were.

Suddenly it was quiet. I leaned against a whitewashed wall to catch my breath and glanced up between dark buildings at the strip of sky over the street. My pipe was gone, the town was cursed, the curse was stolen, and I had only a few hours to get ten thousand silver coins and set my father free.

"So Mr. Bauer owns the manor by Aerzen, right?" I asked.

"Yes," said Mr. Hofmann, puzzled.

"If he's really the one who got the council to steal the reward fund, then he owes me the reward. He owes me ten thousand in silver."

"Now, my boy," the mayor began with a dubious expression.

I dug my fingers into my palms. "I think I can prove that to you later, Mr. Hofmann." (And I thought, *Yes, all over again.*) "The point is, ten thousand is the price Mr. Bauer's steward asked for the manor. It was Bauer's manor I was going to buy with the reward."

"Ah," said the mayor, as comprehension dawned.

"But Mr. Bauer already has the money, so it's as though I've already paid him. So . . . by rights, the manor is already mine."

"But there's no proof that he took the reward," said Mr. Hofmann.

"Daddy!" said Klara.

"Never mind," I said. "My point is, what Mr. Bauer owes me now isn't the reward; he owes me the Aerzen manor. If he signs something saying that I own the manor and sends a message to his steward, that would be Hamelin's payment to the guild. And if he would submit to a trial as well, then he would have done everything I asked for." In my mind, I ran through the checklist one more time. "Yes. I could offer to remove the Childrule Curse if he would just do that. I mean, as soon as I get my pipe back. And control of the curse."

"It's always been about Aerzen," said Klara, looking as if she had just bitten into something rotten. "You've let your obsession with that skew everything you've done in this town."

"What?"

"You didn't give us enough time! You pushed ahead with this curse because *you* had a deadline! A deadline that had nothing to do with Hamelin! And now you want to bargain with the man you denounced. You're as willful as the people you want to punish."

"Maybe I'm closer to them than I thought," I said. I was silent for a while. "But, Miss Hofmann, I have kept my promises. And I'll make another one. I won't just leave after I have helped my father. I will stay here till justice is done. I promise."

Klara gazed into my eyes and nodded slowly.

"I'm sorry," I said. "You were right. I should have waited until I knew more about the other piper."

The mayor cleared his throat. "I am completely lost when you talk about this other piper and curse stealing. But—what do we need to do now?"

"I have to get my pipe back."

"The *next* thing to do is find Gudi," said Klara. "Dear God, please let her be all right."

"She's fine," I assured them, but I wondered. "Whoever stole the curse needs her as the Keychild. You can only change the Keychild if you cast the curse yourself."

"Keychild?" asked Klara.

Footsteps sounded close by. We all froze. With all the echoing,

I couldn't tell where they were coming from, but I took a guess. I edged away from the corner toward a door in the wall.

I mouthed to the others, *We can hide in here,* pointing at the wooden doorway of a tavern. The footsteps sounded very close now. Then suddenly they stopped. I reached for the door handle . . .

The door swung open, straight into me. A jolt went through my blood, and I shoved back. Someone stumbled free of the door.

"Hm," he said. "There you are."

"Roth!" Klara gasped. "Thank goodness you're here."

My knees almost collapsed under me.

"Follow me," said Roth, holding the door. "On the way, you can tell me what's going on."

"Where is Gudrun?" Klara asked. "Is she all right?"

He shook his head. "Haven't seen her since last night."

We went through the building onto another street, and I repeated for Roth what I'd said about Gudrun being the Keychild of the stolen curse.

"So, your curse got stolen," Roth said. "What does that mean?"

"And what is a Keychild?" Klara asked.

"Shh . . ." said the mayor, glancing up and down the street.

"Where are you taking us?" I whispered.

"My house," said Roth, and he smiled grimly. "Take more than a few children and their parents to break down my doors."

We crept down the street and around the corner without seeing anyone. There stood Roth's house, the one solid thing left in my dissolving world. There were the doors, closer, closer, and suddenly we were inside, and the massive bolt slid into place.

"Come on in," said Roth, leading us to the sitting room. "We need to talk."

I explained what had happened, and Roth said, "So you can't end the curse?"

I shook my head. "Even if I had my pipe."

"Couldn't steal it back?" Roth asked.

"Yes," said the mayor, and his face relaxed a little. "Just steal it back."

"I don't know how to steal it!" I said. "We didn't do that in school. There aren't supposed to *be* enemy pipers stealing curses."

"Figure out how he stole it," suggested Roth. "You could just do the same thing back to him, couldn't you?"

I shook my head.

"Johannes," said the mayor, "what if you played it again from the beginning? Maybe then you could break back into the code."

"I . . . I don't think so."

Their suggestions told me that they were imagining the theft of a pastry. That wasn't the way the guild or the Pipeworld worked; that was all there was to it.

"Please just try," Klara insisted. "Play it. What could it hurt?"

"You play the same tune to do the same thing, like doing the curse over or changing the Keychild. Taking control back is a different thing. I need a different tune."

"Harmony!" said Klara.

"Well . . ."

"You can figure out a harmony," she pushed. "Maybe we can work together. How does it go?"

They all looked at me.

"That tune is a closely guarded guild secret," I said.

"Oh, honestly," said Klara.

But the very mention of the word *guild* cleared my head.

"I need to take a fast horse to Muender and talk to Master Friedrich."

"Take a lot of time," Roth said.

I looked at him. He was right about that. He and Klara did know about music, if not about magic. If I could remember at least some bits of the countermelody my enemy had played, could they help me prepare an answering tune? The score was still rolled in the pouch under my shirt—the one place I hadn't fallen on. I lifted my hand for it.

A knock at the door interrupted us. After Roth peeked through the shutter, we heard him opening the door and a light voice saying, ". . . so hard!" Gudrun bounded in, looking at Roth, then the rest of us. "Klara, you're covered in mud and stuff."

"Gudrun!" we burst out together. The mayor and Klara jumped up and hugged her, and I stood there melting with relief.

"Gudrun!" said Roth. "Thank goodness you're here."

"Not now," said Gudrun, squirming out of Klara's arms. "I'm busy. Actually, these kids *are* hard to organize. Especially Strom. Every time I get some of them together, the other ones go all over the place. And Strom—"

"Gudi," Klara broke in, "what are you doing with the children?"

"Actually, *you* don't have to worry about this, because *I'm* taking care of it!"

"Gudi," said Mr. Hofmann.

"Daddy," said Gudrun, "let me finish."

Roth sketched a gesture of resignation and sat down.

Gudrun took a step toward Klara. "You think it's just a mess out there? Like you say about my room. But you're wrong. Those kids aren't being mean for no reason; they're only doing the same things grown-ups did to them."

"Well, they can't!" Klara said.

"You're right; they can't!" Gudrun shouted. "Because *I* won't let them."

"Then . . . good!" Klara faltered. "I mean, what are you saying?"

"It's all going to be organized," said Gudrun, folding her arms in an official-looking pose. "It's all going to be legal. We're going to have a court. Instead of just breaking things, the kids can make accusations, and cases get judged—by me and the Boss." She nodded at Roth.

"Roth?" Klara looked horror-struck. "You're helping her do this?"

Roth exhaled and tilted his head to one side. "Listen, Miss Hofmann. May seem strange, but the best way to deal with this Childrule business is to organize it. When the whole thing just goes wild—that's when real harm is done."

"What—" I began. My head was spinning with what I was hearing. "How do you know the curse's name?"

Gudrun said, "The Boss is from your guild, Hannes. He's the master pip—"

"*A* master piper," Roth corrected. "Hannes, I was going to tell you later. I'm the examiner for your final test."

My eyes widened. "You stole the curse from me as a test?"

"Yes."

All the strings were twining into one rope. I suddenly had a vivid memory of receiving my solo mission assignment, leaving the room, and thinking, *There is no way they're sending an eighteen-year-old out on first solo without a master piper!* I almost laughed. "You pulled on the rats against me as a test?"

"Yes. And after the bandit attack, I healed your mouth."

"So I could still play my pipe," I said.

Roth nodded.

"But who—" I began.

"Healed Gudrun too," he said, and put his hand on her head. "You noticed a spell holding the poison?"

I felt like an idiot as I replied, "Noticed, then ignored." With a rush of relief, I went on. "Well, I suppose you'll take care of this mess, then?"

"I will."

Salvation. I licked my lips and rushed ahead, like a runner sprinting for the finish line. "Master Roth, could you . . . free the serfs down near Aerzen? It should be easy to negotiate with Mr. Bauer now."

"Yes, it will," he said.

"I guess I've failed my examination," I said, sinking. The truth was, if the replacement solo was harder, I was done for.

"Hm. We'll see," said Roth. "Not just any apprentice could've done what you did with those rats. I kept waiting for you to pass out."

"I did pass out."

"Yes. *After* the rats were dead." He grinned and laid a hand on my shoulder. "Hannes, you were fine with the rats. You passed out, but you passed. There was a sort of second test going on—extra credit, you might say. Test on detection and deduction. See if you could figure out what in blazes was really going on here in Hamelin town—with Bauer, and with me. And on that second test, you were . . . slower."

The two of us laughed.

"What on earth is going on?" Klara demanded.

"You can stay out of this," said Gudrun.

A muscle in Klara's face twitched, but she fell silent.

"Hm!" said Gudrun, drawing herself up to her full height. "Klara, go in the hall for a minute. I have some important things to discuss with the Boss."

"Gudrun!" I said.

Klara clenched her fists and a spasm crossed her face; then she turned and walked stiffly from the room.

Gudrun's eyes softened as she watched, but she pressed her lips together just the way Klara did, and turned to Roth. "Boss, it'll be best if we start close to home, she said, standing very straight. "I think we should start the trial with her."

"Are you supporting this?" I demanded of Roth.

"Hannes," he answered, "have you worked with the Childrule Curse before?"

I said nothing.

"Afraid you'll need to trust my judgment," he said softly.

I nodded. "All right, Master Roth."

Roth turned to Gudrun. "Yes, we should begin with Klara."

"You're all bewitched!" said the mayor.

"Mayor Hofmann, would you like to be the defense?" asked Roth.

"No," said Gudrun. "He might have to be a witness. Hannes, you be defense."

Roth caught my eye, and I nodded. "Could you get that table out of the way?" he asked.

I pushed it against the wall.

"Accused may enter," said Roth.

"Come in, Klara," said Gudrun.

Klara entered, still walking as though pulled on a leash, with fists at her sides and jaw clamped tight. She glared at her sister and demanded, "What is this about?"

Gudrun's eyes never left Klara's as she said, "Mr. Hofmann."

The mayor blinked. "What did you call me?"

"Mr. Hofmann," Gudrun repeated. "Do I have a mother?"

"Yes, of course," answered the mayor.

"Where is she?"

"She's home, pulling supper together," said Mr. Hofmann. "At least—at least I hope she's all right."

"Actually I told the kids to leave our house alone," Gudrun replied, with a satisfied look. "Now, Mr. Hofmann, are you saying the, um, the accused is actually not my mother?"

"Of course not! Gudrun—"

"But does she *act* like she is?" Gudrun's voice rose, and Klara's eyes widened. "Does she boss me around? Does she pretend I'm a baby who can't think or talk or put on my own clothes without her telling me what to do? Does she treat me like a doll—okay for games, but clear out of the room when anything important happens?" Gudrun's fists were clenched now, and her voice trembled. "Is she a good mother if she steals my friends and makes them ignore me?"

My insides shrank. Mr. Hofmann was speechless. Klara's eyes were wet.

"Your witness," whispered Gudrun, and sat down.

I shook myself out of my stupor and wondered for a moment what to do. "Could Miss Hofmann sit down?"

Roth nodded, and Klara turned and stepped carefully to a chair, easing herself into it as though she might break.

"Mr. Hofmann," I said. "Would you say that Miss Hofmann— that is, Miss Klara Hofmann—" I gave up. "Would you say that your daughters love each other?"

His eyes were still puzzled, but he nodded. "Yes. Yes, absolutely."

"Does Miss Klara want the best for Miss Gudrun, even if she doesn't always act like it?"

"Yes," said the mayor.

I turned to Gudrun. "I'm the one who should be on trial. I'm sorry for ignoring you."

"Are you finished with your witness?" Gudrun asked.

"Forgive me," I said.

"It's not just you," said Gudrun. "Klara treats me like a doll. She orders me around."

"So now she's your doll?"

Gudrun frowned. "I thought you liked justice."

I shook my head. "This isn't justice; it's revenge."

"You made the spell," she said. "You made it so I could do this."

I sighed. "When Klara bossed you around, you wanted something different. What did you want?"

"I wanted her to treat me like a real person. The way she treated you, and Mr. Kunst, and her friends." Gudrun paused. "I wanted to be big, like her, and do things with her—important stuff."

I nodded. "Gudrun, I think the first step to getting that is to forgive her. And let someone else be her judge."

Gudrun's eyebrows pressed together. At that moment, we heard the scrape of a key and the back door banging open.

Roth's eyes widened as he hissed, "Hide!"

SIXTEEN

The Devil to Pay

Sunday, June Twenty-fifth, 1284, Hamelin

UDRUN STOOD UP. "I'LL TAKE CARE OF IT," SHE MURMURED. Heavy boots scraped at the lacquered boards of the hallway floor, and the back door slammed shut.

"It's Bauer," Roth whispered, glancing at the doorway. "Hide!"

Aerzen, I mouthed at him. *Serfs at Aerzen.* He nodded and waved me away.

Gudrun was crawling under the table. My father's flute was still hanging from her sash. I followed, then lifted the tablecloth for Klara and the mayor, Klara angling about awkwardly in her dress, the mayor puffing as he eased himself down.

Hiding seemed to take forever. Already the lock had clicked and the boots were coming our way. Bauer's voice was wheezing as he shouted, "Roth!"

The mayor joined us just as Bauer's footsteps approached the room. Before the tablecloth fell, I glimpsed Roth's face—a mask of calm. I laid my eye to the slit under the cloth.

"Lord Hermann," Roth said, as though he had found him at a business meeting.

"Don't 'Lord Hermann' me!" Bauer fumed. "What the devil is going on around here?"

Roth's huge table felt too small to shield us from that anger.

"What's going on?" Roth repeated. "An emergency, I suppose, since you used my back door key without knocking."

"Don't toy with me, Roth!" Bauer bellowed. "I hired you to flood this town with rats, not fill the kids with devils!"

My eyes widened.

"I'm not responsible for this curse," said Roth.

"Not resp—" Bauer spluttered. "Roth! This pimple-faced upstart was not supposed to be a problem for you! You were supposed to keep the rats here! You were supposed to keep him from doing anything important at all!"

"And keep him from noticing the empty fund?" Roth answered, not even trying to hide his sarcasm now. "And hide your illegal grain prices? Maybe convince him that he killed Zimmer? Am I the one who's been careless?"

"*I* am paying *you;* don't forget that!" Bauer growled. "*You* depend on *me! You* answer to *me!*"

"I depend on you, Lord Hermann? Tell me, how well was your grain selling before the rats ate all the grain but yours? How much defense against pipers did you have before I came? And who do you come crawling to when all your natural powers are exhausted?"

"Crawling?" Bauer rumbled. His face was as red as if he had been slapped. He drew himself up to look Roth in the eye. "I command you to disenchant this town. Now!"

Roth smiled. "I'm afraid that's not possible, Lord Hermann."

"Not *possible?* What kind of magician *are* you?"

Roth's face looked kind, except for a deathly cold in his eyes. He reached into his coat and drew out a long flute made of a deep red metal, covered in strange shapes and flared at one end.

"I'm a piper, Lord Hermann."

The red faded from Bauer's face as his eyes widened. He took a step back. "You— When we first talked, I demanded that the Pipers Guild be kept out of this."

"Hamelin is terribly important to the guild, Lord Hermann." Not taking his eyes from Bauer, Roth said, "Go ahead, friends. You can come out now."

Bauer swung his head around to look at every corner. Klara's face disappeared from my sight as she extracted herself and stood up slowly. Bauer backed away from her, turning from her to Roth and from Roth to her. Gudrun hopped out next, then the mayor. Bauer backed up into the wall. Then I crawled out and carefully straightened my back.

"It's true?" said the mayor. A look of horror glazed his eyes; his face was creased with puzzlement and anger. "You really killed Dietrich?"

Bauer looked at him. "I did *not* say that."

"You really did have the rats *brought* here?" The mayor was speaking louder.

Bauer waved his huge hands in front of him as if to wipe the questions away. "This whole situation is *absurd*. The mayor's family crawling from under a tablecloth . . ."

"You made this town *starve!*" Mr. Hofmann shouted, stabbing downward into the air with his finger. "While enriching yourself? You robbed the reward fund? You gave them hope of deliverance, then hired Roth to *prevent* it?"

Bauer's eyes darted to the door. But Roth was already saying, "I wouldn't try that, Lord Hermann," as he walked behind me, behind Klara, and stood at the mayor's shoulder, fingering the pipe in his hands. Bauer's eyes followed him at every step.

Roth whistled, and I heard heavy footsteps on the cellar stairs. A moment later, two men appeared in the shadows of the sitting room doorway.

"Before you go to jail, Lord Hermann," Roth said quietly, "there's something you should know."

He stepped slowly around to stand where all of us could see him, wearing an eerie smile. He raised his pipe.

He played two light notes, then a low one in a different key that seemed to squash them. Then two more high notes, and another deep braying sound. At each low note Bauer shivered.

But the power of this music was directed at Roth himself. In a few moments, a lump appeared on Roth's cheek, not far above his moustache. It swelled and burst. In a moment, Roth's face was boiling; his hair and beard were writhing.

We gaped in horror and fascination. Roth's mouth clamped hard on the pipe, and his eyes squeezed shut with pain. The bubbling mass of face and hands was collapsing. Now the bubbles cleared, and I saw that his face was narrower, the cheeks sunken, the clothes loose on a thin body. His hair was black, and all that remained of the fine red beard was stubble. He was not much older than I was. And what's more, I recognized him.

Staring at the sharp-featured face and thin hands, Klara looked as though a nightmare had come to life.

It was Anselm the Rebel.

His twisted smile widened, but he never took his eyes from Bauer. Bauer seemed to be trying to melt into the floor.

"No one, my *lord*," Anselm whispered to Bauer, "no one gets back at me forever."

We all stood frozen to the spot as Anselm played a torrent of notes. Bauer was flattened against the wall as if by a gale. His face was crumpling, straining; Anselm's eyes were wide open, drinking. I knew the music. It was two tunes mixed together—one to throw Bauer against the wall, and one to enter his mind.

I looked at Anselm in horror. With eyes still fixed on Bauer, he nodded his head toward the wall. The music twisted, and suddenly Bauer was hurled toward the other wall, slamming into it face-first.

Anselm took his pipe from his mouth. Bauer slid down a little, his legs shaking to hold him up.

Anselm chuckled at what he had learned from probing Bauer's memory. "So that's where your wig went. How did it feel to have your son throw you around like that?"

I took a step forward, but already Gudrun was running across the room. She stamped on Anselm's foot. "Liar!" she yelled.

He gave a grunt of surprise, and she fled for the door. The guards lunged at her, but she shouted, "Get away from me!" and they stopped instantly. In seconds, she was out of sight, and the front door banged open and closed.

Gudrun had waked me out of my stupor. I charged at Anselm, but his eyes turned on me, and in a flash his pipe was in his mouth.

The music hit me like a wave, and for an instant my feet were swinging free. I slammed up against the wall. As my head spun, the guards pointed daggers at Bauer, the mayor, and Klara. A rushing wind held me where I was, and my ears were full of the shriek of it. At the other end of the wind was Anselm, making music with the seriousness of a concentrating child.

Words formed in my mind, words with the sound of Anselm's voice. *Don't do anything you might regret,* he said.

What could I do? He had his pipe, and mine was gone. But he was helpless too.

You're finished now! I shouted above the roar of the wind. *You've stolen the curse, but Gudrun's still the Keychild. You can't change that without playing the whole tune over—and you don't know it. You had to steal it. And now Gudrun knows just how much of a liar you are. The curse will do you no good at all.*

Anselm's voice was quiet inside my head. *I'm sorry, Hannes. I never wanted to lie or steal from you. I had no choice; you still trusted the Pipelord.*

Over you? Yes, Roth—I mean, Anselm. Yes, I trust the Pipelord more than I trust you! You tried to pass yourself off to me as a master piper. I laughed through clenched teeth. *And I believed you!*

A master piper is exactly what I am, Anselm replied, his fingers moving up and down his pipe. *The only piper who understands that we would make better masters than these filthy lords. Hannes, you know this. You were a serf.*

Stop! I screamed back at him. I dragged up my right hand, pushing with all my might against the wind. *Don't pretend you know what it's like.*

Anselm looked back into my eyes, and the words entering my mind were sharp with anger. *I was a serf, Hannes. I was a serf under Bauer, just like you. I was at Aerzen. I was treated like dirt, just like you. And I've been the Pipelord's apprentice too. We're more alike than you can imagine.*

My hair lashed my face in the wind.

Look, Hannes, said Anselm. *What does the Pipelord do about the scum that wear silk and beat us down? Compared to what's needed, he gives a slap on the wrist.*

I said nothing.

But it doesn't have to be that way. Do you know what we could do for the serfs? Do you know what we could do with the vermin that crushed our parents? Hannes, think. He stepped toward me, eyes full of excitement, his fingers seeming to caress his pipe as he played. *Think what we could do.*

I tried not to think—about my father, or about the mass humiliation that was serfdom. But suddenly my mind twitched, and one memory kept flinging itself at me—that stroke of Strom Bauer's riding crop across the old serf's chest, again and again.

We can strike back, Anselm whispered in my thoughts. *We've always had the power. All you need is a plan. And I have one.*

What's your plan? I asked.

You teach me how to play the Childrule Curse, said Anselm. *I change the Keychild to Strom Bauer.*

Strom?

Wait. Then I twist the spell so it thinks I am Strom.

Making you the Keychild?

Exactly.

You can't fool the Childrule that easily. You're too old. And what makes you think you could pass as Strom?

Leave that to me.

But what would you do with that power?

Hannes, don't you want to bring people like Bauer to justice?

Yes, I said. *I do.*

Good. When I am Keychild, you and I will have the chance to bring many to justice.

Klara was looking straight at me. The guards had backed her and the mayor against the wall. I clenched my teeth.

You think they're innocent, don't you? Anselm's words were almost a snarl. *You think I'm the enemy and they're wonderful? My friend, you trust all the wrong people. It's time for you to know the truth.*

The wind faded, and I slid down to land shakily on my feet. My head spun, and my ears were ringing.

Anselm stood on his toes, with his eyes half shut, as the song slid from his pipe, gliding from one note to the next.

It was the tune for a waking dream.

The room was melting like wax. All I could see, solid against the swirling, was Anselm.

SEVENTEEN

Jury of One

Sunday, June Twenty-fifth, 1284, Hamelin

I COULDN'T FEEL THE WALL ANYMORE. THE AIR WAS HOT. Anselm's voice floated across the dark. "Welcome." With a deep roar, a flood of fire washed up all around. I jumped. In the red light, I saw that I was in a broad circle of dried, cracked mud. Outside of it, flames ten feet high gushed from fissures in the earth. The fire swept away from us, as though a strong wind flowed out in all directions from the center of the circle. Anselm and I were dressed in long black robes. He stood facing me on the other side of a black stone pedestal in the center of the circle.

He waved a hand at the towering flames. "This is where I test the words and deeds of men."

To my left, only a few feet from the flames, Klara was on her hands and knees, feeling around on the cracked earth. Her eyes were shut. Over Anselm's shoulder was the mayor, and behind me, Bauer, also with closed eyes.

"See!" said Anselm, in a ringing voice. "Hear!"

Their eyes opened and they jumped, as I had done, backing away from the roaring fire.

Anselm's voice tolled out over the circle like a church bell. "Face me."

All of them looked at him. "This," he said, looking at each one in turn, "is my land. Here, I am the lord. I am the law. Here you will be judged." His eyes rested on me.

"Where to begin?" he said softly. "The story of their crimes, Hannes, is the story of my life." He paused. "I will begin at the beginning, then."

I nodded. The longer this took, the more time I had to think of a way out.

Anselm stepped off the stone pedestal and walked past me, toward Bauer. "The saying goes that the lord of the manor should be like a father to his serfs." He looked back at me, and his eyes were hard. "We were abandoned children, of course."

He turned back to Bauer. "From the moment I was born till the moment I left the wasteland of his manor, I never saw him treat the farmers under him even as well as his horse. The man could never get enough grain." Anselm stood right over Bauer, holding his mouth as though he were about to spit. "Slowly but surely," he continued, "the land and the workers withered under the strain. He beat down or used up everyone I knew. My friends. My *mother*. He did it to me until I got away."

Bauer's shoulders slouched, and his eyes were large.

"When I was six I ran away," Anselm went on, "with the one merchant clever enough to cheat Mr. Hermann Bauer out of some of his grain profits. Mr. Kunst, God rest his soul. The man whose surname I took as my own. Ha! I impudently paraded my history under your very noses, confident that you would be completely blinded by my trappings of social class. And of course I was right."

With his hands clasped behind him, Anselm paced the broken earth. "Mr. Kunst and I stopped in many places," he said, "but we eventually returned here. It's good grain country. And who did we find in Hamelin but Hermann Bauer, still living as a law unto himself. Grain prices were as high as he could get the grain guild to push them. He kept some key families in terror of his thugs. There were spies; there was blackmail. His fingerprints covered the city."

Bauer clenched his teeth, his eyes wide and fixed on Anselm.

"But soon after I came to Hamelin," Anselm continued, strolling across the scorched ground, "Bauer ceased to be the focus of my attention."

He was looking at Klara, his eyes gnawing at her till she turned away.

"Hannes, it's time we talked about the Hofmanns. Now, I know it will be hard for you to understand the innocence of Anselm and the guilt of this family. So I need to make something clear to you about loyalty. Mr. Bauer loved to talk to his serfs about loyalty, though he was loyal only to himself. But I was loyal to my mother, until he starved her to death. I was loyal to Mr. Kunst; I was loyal to Franz.

"Klara Hofmann was loyal also—but only to her family and her city. She talked about mercy, but she had none for me when I poured out my heart to her. I ran into that stone wall of family loyalty, which was all she really believed in. Notice this, Hannes. The people I trusted were quite ready to *replace* me—the Pipelord with a new apprentice and the Hofmanns with the next suitor who showed up, as long as he had the proper background.

"And so I understood something." He looked into Klara's eyes. "You can only be loyal to your family if you have a family. You can only be loyal to your friends if you have friends. There came a day when I was left for dead, lying on my face in dust and blood, and I knew I was *alone*." He reached out a finger and softly stroked Klara's cheek.

She shuddered at his touch.

His eyes glinted in the red light. "Mr. Hofmann didn't even *see* me. I was just an object to him—for pity at best, or for contempt. I wasn't someone to take seriously as a suitor simply because I loved his daughter and had a good head. Good heavens, no." He walked toward the mayor. "I was lowlife, riffraff, a traveling merchant's apprentice who didn't know his place."

The mayor's round eyes and soft features showed that, with characteristic empathy, he was shamed and shocked at the Hofmanns portrayed here.

"How," said Anselm, in a low, tight voice, "how could I know my place?" The muscles around his mouth contorted as he looked at Klara. "My place was always being taken. By someone more pitiful, like Franz. Or someone richer, more respectable, like that mask named Roth. It was the same me, but, Klara, you felt different, didn't you? Do you like older men, Klara, or just their *money*?"

The fires around us roared up for an instant, and Klara jumped.

"Leave her alone!" I said.

Anselm turned his eyes on me. "Don't be fooled, Hannes. You're not good enough for her either."

He stepped away for a while; then, without turning around, he began to speak again. "Eventually Mr. Bauer found me alone. I'd made the mistake of running off with the man who cheated him. He took me out to a deserted stretch of road and had me beaten to a pulp and left for dead."

Anselm glanced over at Mr. Bauer, who met his gaze with a boldness that was chilling.

"I was discovered in that condition by the man who calls himself the Pipelord. My experience was much like yours, Johannes, except I was younger." He turned back toward me. "What an opportunity! I loved it. The Pipelord was my hero, and I was his star pupil."

I raised an eyebrow.

"Just ask him," said Anselm. "That is, if you're still ready to trust his answers, after the way he stranded you out here. Yes. I outjusticed justice and I outmercied mercy. But it wasn't long before I caught on to the scam."

I frowned, and Anselm stood over me.

"Who decides what's 'just' or 'merciful'?" he demanded. "The Pipelord, of course. He offers you power, but if he controls how you use it, who's really got the power?"

"The Pipelord lets us join him in—"

"—the great adventure!" Anselm finished for me. "No one knows those lines like me. Heaven's buttons, Hannes. I know them all." He strode over the broken ground, just as he had earlier strode around his sitting room unfolding ideas that intrigued me. "But you listen to me now, Johannes of Oldendorf, my fellow serfboy. All those principles—they're nothing but an excuse to drop you like a bad plum the minute you take some initiative."

He thrust his face close to mine. "Why did you and I join the guild, Hannes? To *do* something! To do justice to the predators"— he stabbed a finger at Mr. Bauer—"the men who brutalized our families."

Anselm leaped up lightly on the polished stone. "I can imagine the versions you've heard of the Unbound movement, Johannes. But do you know how Hamelin was run before I took it over? Just as it is *now*—the laws were a joke; it was men like Bauer who were really in charge." Now his voice rang as he shouted for the world to hear, yelling out each word as a challenge and a boast: "*I changed that!* Me! Nobody before me! And, Hannes, for this crime I was abandoned to the wolves! For this I was *replaced.*"

"By me," I murmured.

Anselm nodded. His breathing was heavy. "Watch out, Hannes. Don't start thinking. If you think, you might question his way of doing things, and you'll be thrown out as I was."

I said nothing.

"Of course," said Anselm, "by the time the Pipelord disowned me, I had already been disarmed." He turned around and stepped toward Klara. "Deceived on the very night I would have honored her most highly, the night I brought back something I had found in the closed section of the guild library. I had learned everything about the Childrule Curse except the notes themselves. But Klara betrayed me."

Suddenly the roaring fires were silenced, and for an instant I could see nothing. Then the darkness above me filled with stars, and I was walking down a street in Hamelin. The buildings were strangely tall.

—— • ——

I was in Anselm's body, in Anselm's memory. He was thirteen years old.

I walked as quickly as I could through the chilly air, down the empty streets, till I came to a house I could barely see in the starlight. With the help of a vine, I found a grip and began to climb up toward a window on the second floor. I pried back the shutters as quietly as I could and stepped through the curtains. Slowly my eyes adjusted to the darkness.

Klara lay asleep in bed, wreathed in blankets. I watched her breathing. At age twelve, she was beautiful.

I knelt by her bed, pulling out my dark red pipe. Suddenly Klara moved. A wrinkle appeared between her eyebrows. She yawned and opened her eyes and looked straight into mine.

She jolted up and threw herself against the headboard, clutching her blankets around her. She seemed about to scream, so I reached out to calm her.

"Shh!" I said.

Her eyes flickered to the pipe in my hands.

"It's all right," I said in Anselm's jarring voice. "I won't hurt you."

She sat blinking, still pressed against the headboard.

"Haven't you noticed, Klara? The crows haven't gone anywhere near you. Or your family."

Klara was silent a moment. "Why are you here?"

I smiled. "I'm taking the crows away."

Mild interest kindled in her eyes. She wrapped the blankets around herself till she looked like a big pillow.

"Klara, I don't need crows anymore."

She wasn't happy. She was supposed to be happy.

"Don't you see?" I said. "I'll have a peaceful empire. Nobody has to get hurt. And we can do all this the right way. I know you always wanted that. And it's all thanks to this thing that I've gotten hold of. It's something I've been waiting for years to hold in my hand."

"What is it?"

"It's called the Childrule. You wouldn't—"

"How'd you get it?"

"That doesn't matter, Klara. This is a huge victory for me, for *you* and me! The other pipers are out celebrating at the pub, but the person I wanted to celebrate with was you."

"Good," she said. But her eyes were still not happy.

"There are some instructions, in code. But soon I'll have it figured out, and that'll be . . . the beginning of a whole new world for me and for you."

"Why me?"

"I'm too old to be Keychild, by one year," I said. "That's the most powerful person in the spell, Klara. I want you to be the Keychild, and the queen."

My queen put one hand out of her blanket cocoon and tucked her hair back.

"You won't believe what Franz said to me tonight." I laughed softly. "'How could Klara be ready to be your queen, when she still loves little-girl games?' I told him *you* were my favorite game. He got all worked up. He says I'm thinking about ruling kingdoms and you're still playing with dolls."

"So what did you say?"

"I said, 'Then dolls are my favorite game.' Klara, it doesn't matter! I have what I want! Klara, it's the beginning—"

But Klara thrust out her hands, snatching the pipe from my fingers. As she grabbed and yanked, the mouthpiece hit her hard over the left eyebrow. Blood welled out. As I stared in horror, on my knees, she flung my pipe out the window. Klara was pushing me away with disgust; my pipe was clanking on the cobblestones below; she was screaming. In moments, her screams were mixed with sounds of running feet in the house and on the paving stones outside.

The screaming faded into the rushing sound of fire. I was back on the broken earth, near the circle of flame, trapped in the trial where Anselm had made me the jury of one. My whole body was clenched tight, and I was looking straight into Klara's terrified eyes. I looked at the scar above her eyebrow, first noticed on the night when I entered the guild and Anselm left it.

Anselm stood over her and quietly said, "Traitor."

"Why should she help you?" demanded the mayor from his corner of the triangle. "Anselm, tell me this: What laws were you upholding when you were jabbing at people with crows? How were you different from a criminal?"

Anselm shoved at the air, and a blast of wind flung Mr. Hofmann upward. He hung thrashing like river weed in a strong current. The fire soared up around him, inches from his skin, and shimmered on his sweat.

"Roth!" I yelled, then, "Anselm!"

"Order in the court," said Anselm placidly.

"Anselm, put him back!"

"As you wish," he answered. He dropped his hand, and the mayor drifted out of the fire and landed, stumbling, on the ground. Klara rushed to his side.

"We will finish his trial," said Anselm, walking past the mayor. "Which is more than anyone did for me." He stared into the flames for a moment. "Hannes," he said, "you're wondering how *I* passed through the fire, the first night you ever saw me." He reached his hand into the wall of fire, and the flames shaped themselves like a bell around his fingers.

"You're wondering about the body, aren't you?" Anselm pulled his hand from the fire and turned to face me. "I'd used my piping skills to build up some wealth. When the mob got hold of me, Franz hid it—though we hadn't agreed on a place. Bauer tortured Franz, trying to find out where it was. I found his body in the dump. I thought he'd be happy to help me out one last time."

His voice shook. He swallowed and walked toward Bauer. "Franz was my height. I took him into the house and drenched him and the whole place with oil. After my jump, I slipped out using a getaway trail I'd made with water, hid in the alley, and later vanished while people were busy elsewhere. The body of Anselm pulled from the burned building was really my friend Franz, whose death had given me a brand-new life."

Anselm stood over Bauer, who looked back with wide, defiant eyes.

213

"You know the rest of their crimes," he said to me. "Do you still believe I'm the villain here?"

I swallowed. All eyes were on me. "I can't decide."

"I see," said Anselm. "Very well, Hannes. Since you have doubts, I will defend myself to you. Here is the rest of my story." He paced again.

"I escaped from Hamelin and eventually found Mr. Kunst again. I grew rich. I came back. I came back to be a piper again, to bring justice to a town swimming in injustice. But to do this, I needed two things.

"When Klara screamed on the night of my visit six years ago, my old enemy, Lord Hermann Bauer, who was just then leaving a little entertainment at the Hofmanns', was the first one on the scene."

Anselm faced Bauer. "You took my pipe. Maybe hoping to figure it out? But one night, many years later, it mysteriously disappeared. And a month or so after that, a strange magician offered you a plague that promised profits like you'd never seen."

He turned to me. "It was only right that Mr. Bauer be given the chance to prove, one last time, that he cared about no one but himself. It was only right that he should bring about his own downfall. But my pipe was not enough. I needed one other thing. There was only one just curse for this town: the Childrule Curse. I had left the score with Franz, and he hid it, along with my treasure, right after I was captured. Then Bauer's men found him, and he only had the chance to scream one clue to me as they dragged him across the square: *It's all in your favorite game.* Klara was my favorite game. The scroll had to be in Klara's room. So I ransacked the room about the same time I got my pipe. I found nothing.

"That's when I had an idea: get another piper to come to Hamelin to cast the Childrule Curse for me. In the news that I arranged to reach the guild, I painted a picture so horrific I was sure the guild would send a master. A master of the Pipers Guild might see a town led by Bauer and consider casting the Childrule. I never dreamed I'd get an apprentice. They must have great faith in you, Hannes. But you took a lot of convincing. Fortunately, Bauer didn't need much help showing how guilty he was. Stabbing Zimmer and poisoning you were never in my plan. Even though he called me his partner, Bauer never told me what he was up to."

Anselm turned back to me. "Anyway, you came. I knew you were fresh from the Pipelord's propaganda against me. You wouldn't trust me if I told you who I was. I had to find another way."

Suddenly I realized what riddle had been gnawing at my memory for the last several minutes. Though I had never seen the faces of the two guards, their *silhouettes* were familiar.

"The henchmen," I said. "The ones you whistled for—they were the bandits who attacked me on the road."

Anselm sighed. "I told them not to hurt you. They got carried away. The point was to see how well you fought with a pipe—"

"And to give you a chance to rescue me," I said. "Except Miss Hofmann got there first."

Anselm nodded. "I would have rescued you, Hannes. In fact I'm trying to rescue you from the real criminals right now."

I said nothing.

"After all," said Anselm, "I did heal you afterward."

"So I could play my part in your theater," I said. "You needed the Childrule Curse."

The fires around us leaped higher.

"Hannes, you think I was using you. What do I have to say or do to convince you? I was only protecting myself. All along, all I wanted was to do what I'm doing now—to explain everything and ask for your help. But you make it hard, Hannes, with your blind faith in the Pipelord."

"Blind? He's taken care of me for six years!"

"Just wait till he's finished with you!" Anselm snapped. "Hannes, I arranged everything for you. I handpicked the perfect Keychild and introduced her to you. Unfortunately, now she's been turned against me too. But you can change that. You could help me become Keychild and fix all of this."

I compressed my lips tight.

"But you wouldn't trust me!" said Anselm. "I knew the Childrule was the right curse, but you were slow to come to that conclusion. You knew the tune, but I knew the town. I knew how to use the curse here. I live here. I know this town better than any other piper. If you had trusted me, we could have been a team. As it was, you forced me to work single-handedly—to borrow the curse from you. It was a boost when I learned things we had in common, things that helped me understand you. Hannes, when I found our common ground, I hoped it would help you understand me and be my teammate. But I knew that might fail. So I explored further, looking for weaknesses that might appear when you finally piped the curse. So I could take control of it.

"So you see, I couldn't let you cast the Childrule Curse until I found some key to the cracks in your piping. And you were bound to act as soon as the last hope of the reward died. But it would look rude to pry into your personal life at our first meeting, so I bided my time. When you learned about the empty fund, I was afraid I had missed my chance. I advised you to wait for evidence and work with the mayor."

He glanced at Mr. Hofmann with a knowing smile. "*That* would buy plenty of time. But then, at Lord Hermann Bauer's independent initiative, my piper was accused of murder, and suddenly you were going to try to kill the rats. I couldn't let that happen. Once the rats were dead, you'd demand the reward, they'd refuse, you'd cast the Childrule, and I still had no way to borrow it from you." Anselm glared at Bauer. "Of course, Bauer neglected to tell me a mob was waiting to kill you if you failed with the rats. Hannes, I was impressed when you managed to kill the rats after all. Just think what you could become if you would leave the guild behind." He frowned. "So much talent, going to waste."

Still shaking his head, he went on. "Soon afterward, Hannes, I understood our common ground quite well, and it was just a step from there to guessing what kind of cracks I'd need to look for. Once that was clear, all I had to do was convince you that Hamelin deserved the Childrule Curse.

"You know the rest. Bauer lied to the mayor, and the mayor broke his promise to you. Along with the rest of the town. As always, Hamelin looks out only for its own, so you had to curse them. And before you become too angry with me for taking away your child curse, remember: you took away my rat curse."

The flames swept up around us, reflecting on the black stone at my feet.

"It's time to make your judgment, Hannes. Are they innocent or guilty?"

I said nothing.

"Let's start with the easiest," said Anselm. He turned to Bauer and snapped his fingers. Bauer shut his eyes, stood, and marched toward the flames. The fire parted in front of him, showing black stone stairs, which he climbed.

Anselm motioned toward the steps. "Shall we?" he said. "We can discuss this on the way."

I glanced at Klara and the mayor.

"We'll deal with the Hofmanns later, Hannes. After you."

I walked to the stairs, Anselm just behind me and Bauer a little ways ahead.

"I said that Bauer was the easiest to judge," said Anselm. "Would you agree?"

"I would," I said, looking up the dark stairs at Bauer's retreating back.

"He's been a plague to his own people. He's hurt me. He's hurt you."

"He has," I said.

"Well, then," said Anselm. "Is Bauer guilty?"

Bauer was disappearing from view as the stairs curved between walls of fire.

"Yes."

"Of what, Hannes?"

Hermann Bauer, I thought, with smoldering rage, was guilty of throwing my sick father down in the mud. Throwing him down so hard that, in my father's mind, he never got up.

"Of cruelty," I said. "Of murder. Of breaking lives."

The stairs ended. From their top, a slope fell down to a cliff. Bauer lay on the edge, with his eyes shut. My enemy.

"He deserves death, doesn't he?"

"If he dies," I said, "Strom will be my father's new master."

"Come on, Hannes!" Anselm scoffed. "We're pipers! Do we have to let that happen?"

I said nothing.

"No, Hannes! We don't. It wouldn't take you five minutes with your pipe to take over that entire manor and set your father free."

"That's true," I said. "But there are guild rules, and there's the law of the land . . ."

"Forget the law, Hannes. What good has it ever done you?"

I thought of my sick father on the road, abandoned—in the teeth of every law about a master's duty to his serfs.

"Bauer never followed the law," said Anselm.

I nodded.

"Does he deserve to die, Hannes?"

"Yes," I said. "Yes, he does."

The flames roared up in a gust and swirled into a ball. In a moment, the ball was the sun, sinking behind the houses of Hamelin. We were on Roth's roof, with a trapdoor behind us, and

Bauer was lying asleep on the lowest shingles, with an empty road far below.

I blinked as Anselm pulled his pipe from his mouth and said, "Gudrun found something of yours." He reached into his coat, pulled out my pipe, and offered it to me.

"Here," he said. "Kill him."

Invitation to a Killing

Sunday, June Twenty-fifth, 1284, Hamelin

FTER THE DREAM FIRE, THE BREEZE ON THE ROOFTOP WAS cold. I took my pipe from Anselm. It fit perfectly in my hand, heavy with power.

I walked carefully down the shingles, leaning backward, till I was halfway down.

Mr. Bauer lay alone on the edge, his ponderous head lolling forward on his chest. With the wig gone, I saw the wine-colored birthmark that had come into my life twice before: in stories about the man who broke my father and in the spectacle of that man being broken by his own son, Strom.

I piped a few notes, and he woke. Our eyes met.

"Mr. Bauer, hello. You remember me. I got rid of the rats that you helped bring to Hamelin to line your pockets."

His eyes cleared completely—one predator smelling another, with instant understanding. He shot a glance at the street below and gripped the shingles.

"I saw the townspeople you threw to the rats. I saw the peasants who lived their short lives under your heel. One of them was my father, and you broke him, body and soul."

Bauer pulled a stern face, but his hands were shaking. "You'll be lynched if you lay a hand on me."

"Lynched?" I said. "The street looks empty to me."

Bauer's eyes flicked up to Anselm.

"And nobody will take *his* word for it. Not Hamelin. Not the guild." I came very close. "A suicide, Mr. Bauer. After what Strom did to you today, that's what everyone will think. I won't leave a mark on you, Mr. Bauer. I'm a piper. I can throw you off the edge without even touching you."

"No!" said Bauer. "I'll give you anything—money, power . . ."

"Anything you have, I could take from you," I snapped. "But that's not why I'm here. You deserve to die, Mr. Bauer. Give me one reason why you deserve anything else."

"Please," he said, "mercy."

"Didn't Franz say that, six years ago, when his bones were cracking under your blows? Didn't Mr. Zimmer say that as he crawled toward you through a puddle of his own blood?" I could hardly keep from hitting him as he cowered in front of me.

"Didn't my father say that? Six years ago, on the estate in Oldendorf. A man was sick, coughing, too weak to bring in the harvest. He begged forgiveness, he begged for time, he begged for work as a musician, and he played a tune on a pipe. He begged for *mercy*."

Bauer's mouth and eyes showed that he remembered.

"Do you remember what you did? You laughed." The memory rose in me like bile. It had to go somewhere. "Do you find flute music funny, Mr. Bauer? Because I've brought you a tune." I lifted the pipe.

Bauer leaned forward, eyes riveted on me.

This was what I had sought for six years. I focused. The image was my father, struggling up from the mud on the night Bauer crushed him. I felt the power I had dreamed of since I first met the Pipelord, and a drunken sweetness rose in me. I would be the hand of God. Time to pipe the last rat into the river.

I paused just as the metal touched my lips. The Pipelord had rescued my family, not by striking down Bauer but by whisking my father off to a place of healing and me off to a new life in the guild.

As I looked down at Bauer, crouching wide-eyed on the roof's edge, I remembered the words written by Anselm the Rebel: *This is the Piper's choice.* . . . I lowered my pipe.

"I don't want to see you murdered, Mr. Bauer," I said, and my voice broke. "I want to see you in court."

Bauer just stared at me. I turned away and began to walk up the roof. After a few steps, I began to sob. I crumpled to my knees, with my shoulders shaking and the tears streaming down my cheeks. I cried for my father, for his music that was silenced, for all that he could have become and didn't. I cried for Mr. Zimmer, and for his wife, receiving her husband's bloody remains. I cried for Klara, watching as Franz was dragged off to be killed.

"Hannes!" Anselm was standing over me. And from somewhere below, the sound of many voices was coming closer. "Hannes! Get hold of yourself. We have to finish up here."

I looked up at him dully. Behind him, the sun was setting. My father would never be free. He would die, because I had not saved him.

Anselm dragged me to my feet. Below us and beyond Bauer, people were swarming down the street from Town Square.

Anselm's jaw clenched. "We have to deal with our enemies one at a time, Hannes. Kill Bauer now, and we'll have Strom right where we want him."

Bauer was crawling toward the trapdoor.

"Lord Hermann!" said Anselm, backing away from me to stand in his path.

Bauer froze on all fours.

"Do you know what is about to happen?"

Bauer slowly shook his head.

"I am going to kill you," said Anselm. "Then I will give Strom the thing you always wanted—total control over Hamelin."

The sunset turned Anselm and the roof a deep red.

"Then I will replace Strom," said Anselm. "I will take everything that is yours, and everything you strove for. And then I will kill Strom, and the illustrious house of the Bauers will be swallowed up by one man—*me*."

Bauer collapsed on the shingles like a puppet when its strings are cut.

Below us, the adults of Hamelin were passing by, jostling along with their heads down and their shoulders rounded, a few with torches as evening came on. Children were running alongside, climbing up the front steps of houses to see over the heads of the crowd, and every once in a while shouting in flutelike voices, "To the East Gate! Keep it moving!"

"Father! There you are."

My eyes found Strom in the river of people, standing on the stairs of the house across from Roth's.

"He's calling you," murmured Anselm.

"Father, come down here this instant!"

Bauer stiffened and tried to get to his feet.

"Let's try a faster way," said Anselm. He placed a foot on Bauer's shoulder and shoved.

"Hey!" shouted Strom.

I ran across the shingles as Bauer tumbled, threw out his hands, and stopped himself right at my feet, on the very edge. One shingle broke off and fell to the street. The crowd looked up, and the screams began.

"It's Bauer!"

"Saints preserve us; it's Anselm, back from the dead!"

Anselm ignored it all, stepping purposefully down the roof. "Good-bye, Lord Hermann," he said, and put his pipe to his lips. The music tumbled out of it.

"No!" I shouted, and jumped between the two.

The force of Anselm's piping hit me instead. I was knocked off my feet; my whole body was tingling; I was toppling from the roof.

Then, with a jolt, my fall was broken. I was hanging by Anselm's hand.

"You idiot!" he said. "Am I going to have to rip the Childrule tune straight out of your memory? Every last note?"

My arm felt as if it were on fire. Noise and color swirled in the emptiness around me. I rose, scraping over the roof's rough edge, till my tingling face dropped onto the cold shingles. As I lay in a daze, I looked at my hand. It clutched my pipe. Then Anselm's foot pinned my wrist to the roof.

"You will teach me the Childrule tune now," said Anselm. "And we will kill Bauer now. Or you're going back over the edge."

I gathered enough strength to lift my still-tingling head and look at him. "No," I wheezed.

He kicked me, and I rolled a few feet till my feet dangled over emptiness. Something lay curled on the roof between me and Anselm, something that had fallen from my clothes. It was the scroll.

I thrust out my hand, but Anselm had already snatched it up, unrolled it, and gulped it in with his eyes. He turned to me.

"You had the score all the time. And ripped out of a book! Here I was, thinking they'd taught it to you. That you were *important* enough for the Childrule." He laughed. "This is *my* score, isn't it, from all those years ago? You had to get it from me. Well, Hannes, it's mine again. Now all I have to do is—" He looked up, and his face contorted. *"Bauer!"*

"My father went down through the trapdoor," Strom shouted up to us. "He's joining our procession. And you'll do the same."

Anselm whirled and sprang toward the opening.

As I reached the roof peak with him, I saw below me a dozen men in the backyard, led by a man a head taller than the rest, entering Roth's back door. Anselm looked with me.

"So. Bauer's men are here." He sneered. "Let them try to save him."

"Keep moving!" Strom shouted to the gawking crowd. Spasms crossed their faces, and they turned from us, trudging with the shadows ahead of them.

"Hamelin's youth are the lords here now," said Strom. "Hamelin is our castle, and the serfs"—he waved toward the parents of his comrades—"the serfs live outside. Join the procession," he called up to us, a metal edge to his voice. "Both of you."

Anselm had already entered the trapdoor, but he paused at the top of the ladder, turned to Strom, and called, "There's no need for you to give me orders."

I wanted to follow Strom. The trapdoor was full, but there was a shorter way—off the roof. The crowd needed me. My feet dragged, step by step, down the shingles.

"You're commanding the wrong person," Anselm said to Strom. "I gave you your power. And soon I'll give you more power than you can imagine. But there's no point in trying to command me."

Strom said nothing.

"I'm going to speak with your father," Anselm said.

I clamped my jaw. It wasn't right for me to follow Strom. It wasn't best, even for Strom himself. I turned around.

"Anselm!" I shouted, as my head cleared. "End this curse!"

He turned around. "Not for the world."

"Then I'll have to steal it back from you."

I lifted my pipe, and Anselm did the same. The gale of his playing blasted at me, but this time I kept my feet. I threw a torrent of notes back at him and bound myself to his body with a dozen Pipeworld strings. As the wind drove me and I dragged him, we both began to slide down the roof.

I thrust my question into his mind. *How'd you steal it, Anselm?*

His tune jabbed up and down, snapping my strings, but I tied on more.

How'd you steal the curse? What were the cracks in my piping?

"Come down!" Strom shouted from the street below. "Come down now! I command you!"

Anselm's song rose to a crescendo. Then the wind stopped suddenly, and Anselm yanked back on the strings. I stumbled forward onto one hand, just managing to keep my pipe in my mouth with the other.

"Fine!" Strom spluttered behind me. "I know how to change your minds. Where are the Hofmanns?"

Anselm's thoughts were in my head. *Was that the best you could do, Hannes? Looks like the Pipelord's lessons won't get you very far.*

His music dived, then surged, and the shingles around me broke up and flung themselves at me. I wavered a moment, ducking, getting battered by some smaller chips. Then the shingles under my foot shot out, and I fell through the plaster ceiling and landed in Roth's bed.

For a moment, all I could see were clouds of plaster dust. My eyes watered; I coughed and coughed. Anselm sprang down onto the foot of the bed and stepped to the floor.

"Can it be?" he said, twirling his pipe in his hand. "The great Pied Piper? The one the Pipelord chose from the side of the road to replace me?"

I kept coughing.

"You poor, sick fellow," said Anselm. "Let's give you some air."

He put his pipe to his lips and played a haunting tune.

At first, nothing seemed to change, but then the wood in the walls began to rot. In moments it crumbled as though from years of rain, mold, and neglect. Ugly vines crawled in the window, cracking the plaster. The wall warped and all at once gave way. Now I lay in a cloud of plaster dust, hearing the yells of people below as chunks fell.

All of Hamelin could see me now, fallen and helpless. I tried to put my pipe to my mouth, but the coughing wouldn't stop. I lay there feeling Anselm's contempt—so great that he never troubled to disarm me.

"This is the third time you've been flat on your back in my house," said Anselm. "Look at you. Watery-eyed, coughing, sick, bedridden. Remind you of anything?"

I said nothing. The red sunlight slanted across the room.

"Wasn't wise, making me your enemy," said Anselm. "Now your father will die. And you will die, with the weakness he passed on to you."

224

"Hofmanns!" shouted Strom. "Mr. Hofmann, Klara, whoever's with them—come out! Come out of there!"

A moment later, we heard the bolt thrown open. The Hofmanns and Anselm's henchmen came out, dragging their feet.

"You," said Strom, pointing at one of the men, "hold a knife to her throat. Klara, don't fight him."

Klara twisted her face, pulled away once, then gave in and let him hold up the knife.

"Johannes Piper! Roth Kunst!" Strom shouted. "Come out now, or the Hofmanns die."

The crowd murmured.

"Silence!" yelled Strom.

Frieda Zimmer appeared at Strom's side. "Strom," she said, "what are you doing?"

He answered, "Crushing rebels."

I began to sit up, but Anselm put a hand on my shoulder.

"Strom," he called out, "when you are ready to follow me, I will negotiate with you. Though Hannes may want to protect the Hofmanns, I don't. I was about to deal with their rebellious ways myself, but you'll do a fine job. And I'm not letting Hannes go just yet." He turned to me. "Johannes, we have to discuss your future."

"Now you listen!" shouted Strom. "I'm burning you out. And I want my father out."

Anselm sat on the edge of the bed and put the back of his hand to my forehead. "You're not much good with that pipe, Hannes." He checked my pulse. "If the Pipelord replaced me, he will definitely replace you. All you'll have left is what your father put in you. Which reminds me. I still haven't told you about my judgment on you."

He took up his pipe and played the memory tune.

I was cold. We all pressed close to the small fire—my mother, my father, and I.

"This is my judgment on you, Hannes," said Anselm. "As your examining master, I see the failure of your mission, and the failure of the guild's investment in you. And so I will simply undo what the Pipelord did. There are plenty of Lord Hermann Bauers out there, short on unskilled labor, who would check your teeth and take you on at the going rate for a plowboy."

The room was cold and dark. My stomach was empty. There was not enough grain to give the birthmarked man.

"Your pipe would make a nice . . . threshing flail. Think, Hannes —you can be all your father was."

My father was sick. He was shivering, thin, and pale.

"Your past and your future," Anselm murmured.

The vision was fading into darkness, but I held it. My father shuddered, then reached down and pulled out the little flute.

"Here comes the great deliverance," said Anselm.

My father raised the flute to his quivering lips. He played for us. The notes soared. I soared with them and left my hunger behind. My mother shut her eyes and leaned on my father as he played. Her anxious face grew smooth.

At last the music faltered, with a quiet cough. A single red drop appeared on the mouthpiece of the flute.

"The man refuses success," said Anselm. "Like father, like son." He looked at me questioningly. "So do you enjoy watching him deteriorate? No. Admit it. His failures once shamed and terrified you. Now they anger you." Anselm shook his head. "And yet, such is your destiny. Your *choice*."

My father held a finger over his lips. He hurriedly wiped the blood from the flute and, with his other hand, smoothed my mother's graying hair. I leaned on him, as she had done. The vision faded. All that remained was the warmth of my father's love, the drop of his blood, and the Pipelord's words: *He kept piping, no matter what!*

I sat up in the bed and looked Anselm in the face. "My father gave us all he had," I said. "He was poor; he was sick; he kept giving. That's what I'm made of. That's who I choose to be."

We sat frozen for a moment. Then we both sprang to our feet and began to play, pipe to pipe.

What have you done to the Childrule Curse? I demanded in his mind.

His music suddenly crescendoed, and the mattress flung itself at me. I ducked and piped—the mattress exploded in a storm of feathers.

What did your father ever really give you? Anselm asked.

I repeated his vine tune, and the vines that had broken the wall stretched in and began to wind around his legs. A few dark jabs of sound from Anselm's pipe, and one by one the vines withered on the floor.

He gave me life, I said. I had just enough time to dodge as the whole bed frame rose and came soaring toward me. I managed to plant a string and twist; the bed spun longwise and slammed against the wall.

Life!

I heard the grinding disgust in his voice.

They give it; they destroy it.

The long note trailed out, and we stared at each other.

This isn't about my father, I said.

Anselm raised an eyebrow.

This is about your *father.*

Anselm's eyes blazed. He played a series of screeches, and frost spread across my pipe. My fingers stung with the cold, but I kept playing.

Anselm. My notes tugged at him. *Who is your father?*

I reached out in the Pipeworld toward his mind. I felt him push me back, but the rhythm of his thoughts was too familiar. I fit into his mind like a hand in a glove and could not be pushed out.

Fire convulsed in his thoughts; I could feel the waves of heat.

You hate him. Right now, you hate him.

Stop it! Anselm snapped, the thought crackling inside my head.

He changed tunes, and I heard his vines growing under the floor. I walked toward him.

In his thoughts, I felt my way around the edges of the fire. I was moving toward an innermost place covered in something like dry, cracked mud. The fiery courtroom of bitter judgment I had seen was the core of Anselm's soul, shadowing his entire life. I thrust my fingers into the cracks and began peeling away the crust.

Anselm screamed, a thin wail that cut me like the wailing of a child. The skin beneath was soft, like flower petals. I kept groping. The fire was leaping from a long gash, swollen with infection. The fire that flowed out burned me, but I pressed in.

The wounds. Anselm's music came in gasps; his thoughts sounded as if they came through clenched teeth. *You have them too. If only you could see yourself.*

I worked till the sweat stood on me just to speak back into that solid darkness. *Anselm, who did this to you?*

His music jabbed, and in the outside world, the floorboards warped apart as a vine sprang up to twist around my ankle. I kicked, but it squeezed and slithered up my leg.

Who did it to you? he replied, looking straight into my eyes. *Or does that matter? What matters is what we do now.*

That's why you've always wanted the Childrule. The vine wound its way around my chest. What notes had Anselm used to wither it? *You want to hurt your father back.*

For a serf, you're quite a doctor of souls. Very deep, Hannes.

I could hardly breathe. The vine was reaching up my arm toward my pipe. I found the tune I needed and played. The vine paused, quivered, and burst suddenly into bloom. Petals drifted down around our feet as the vine slid to the floor, heavy with fruit.

Who is your father, Anselm?

Anselm clamped his jaw shut. *That is of no importance.*

Answer!

No!

I thrust my hand back into his mind, into the fire, and deep into the wound. Anselm shrieked, and his whole mind shuddered, and suddenly I found myself in rags, a serf-boy's rags, running hard across a field of mud. Serf huts stood scattered around me, and beyond them, plowed fields, a road, and trees. It was somehow familiar.

My pumping fists were small; my running strides were short; the huts and trees were tall. I was very young—about six.

I was running toward a massive white stallion that blocked the whole street just by standing sideways. Its rider, well dressed and gigantic, like the horse, was facing away. The stirrup straps were stretched tight with his weight. It was Mr. Bauer. Lord Hermann Bauer.

As I drew closer, my feet dragged to a halt. I was under the mountain of horse and man, in their cool shadow. I waited.

Finally Bauer sensed me there. A shudder went through his body as he turned toward me, with his chin raised and his eyes lowered. I went cold as the purple mark blazed out from under his receding hairline.

I had tumbled into my own memory somehow. But no—I had never seen his face as a boy; this had never happened to me. This was not Oldendorf; it was Aerzen. And I was in little Anselm's body.

I could feel the tangle of questions that chafed inside Anselm, but now that he faced the lord of the manor, he couldn't speak. After a moment, Bauer turned the reins to ride away.

"My lord!" Anselm's voice came out thin.

With his massive back still turned, Bauer paused.

"My lord . . . my mother told me . . ."

Bauer's horse moved on.

"She said I'm your son," Anselm blurted.

The rider never turned; the horse never stopped.

As the vision grew faint, something moved in me. I heard my own voice now, shouting, "Wait!" and I was running after the fading horse.

But it was my own legs running, back in a bedroom in Hamelin now, nearly falling out into the street as I caught my balance. I was staring into Anselm's eyes again. He was pale and shaking.

Down on the street, a group of shamefaced men stacked wood and straw against the wall below us.

One of the boys nearby was saying, "I don't know about this, Strom. Kicking them out of town for a day was one thing . . ."

"Silence!" said Strom.

"All right," said a very different voice, a bright, familiar voice. "Who actually *doesn't* want to set the house on fire?"

I recognized that voice and yelled out, "Gudrun!"

She waved at me, then turned to the crowd she had to manage. "Now listen. Everyone stop moving around; you're making me dizzy."

The adults slowly creaked to a halt.

"So, who doesn't want to set the house on fire?"

A lot of the children raised their hands. So did all of the adults.

In the twinkling of an eye, Strom seized a torch from one of the passing men and flung it over the heads of the crowd. Spinning like a wheel of fire, it landed in the straw heaped against Roth's house, and in moments, a huge mass of flame was lapping up the wall.

Adults yelled; younger children squealed.

"Quiet! Quiet!" shouted Gudrun. "Kids, let's stop giving orders; the grown-ups know what to do with the fire better than we do." Most of the children grew silent. "Everybody do what the mayor says."

All eyes turned to Mr. Hofmann.

"Everyone get back away from the fire," shouted the mayor, then turned to the man holding a knife on Klara. "Give that to me, sir."

Meekly, the man passed his dagger to the mayor.

"Gudrun!" called Mr. Hofmann. "Organize a bucket brigade."

"They're back in charge!" shouted Strom. "How could you let them get back in charge?"

"You be quiet!" said Gudrun. And Strom was.

A tall man pushed toward the flames, and the crowd parted before him like water. This bear-sized newcomer went straight up to the man who had surrendered his knife and gave him a blow like a battering ram. The dagger man sailed three yards through the air, landed on the stairs like a sack, and lay there in profound repose.

"Wolf!" cried the mayor. "Help these men round up any tools that will help us save these houses!"

Wolf turned to the men, who now looked to him. "Don't stand there chewin' your cuds," he said. "Go to every house and bring every tool you can find. Go on! Shovels, axes, poles—anything."

The new fire brigade shook themselves, nodded, and set off.

The mayor's voice rang out. "Karl, get everyone out of this row of houses as quick as you can! Wilhelm and Gunter, you and your friends—throw dirt, sand, mud, anything but fuel on the fire!"

"Come on," I said. "Let's get out of here." I turned back from the street to the room, but Anselm was gone. The door to the room was open, with staircases right beyond it.

I looked down one, then sprinted up the other. Anselm was sitting on what was left of the rooftop, with the rising flames behind him. He was reading the music from the scroll, holding it on his lap as he played. And he was halfway through the Childrule tune.

In a moment, Anselm said into my mind, *Strom will be the new Keychild. Then I will kill Bauer and replace Strom for the last time.*

In the Pipeworld, I reached carefully into my own mind. It was harder to reach into myself, but I stretched as far as I could go. I felt the skin of my memory and found a long, deep wound. I already knew what was inside.

Anselm smiled. "You're so predictable. You obsess on my past and forget the immediate future."

Even as he spoke, I blocked him. His enchantment ground to a halt. He played a few slow notes, pushing against mine. I pushed back with all my might. Neither one of us budged.

I found it, I thought to Anselm. *The weakness in my piping, the weakness you've been using against me all this time. And you have it too.*

"Let me go!" Anselm snarled. "Do you want to sit in this stalemate till we burn alive?"

At that moment, the front door of Roth's house burst open below me, and out through the flames charged Bauer, with more than a dozen guards. Anselm and I touched both the Pipeworld and the world of Hamelin. Through the shattered roof and wall, we watched the scene on Hamelin's street.

"Don't panic!" Bauer shouted. "I am here to protect you!"

His guards wedged a path through the crowd.

"Look out there!" someone called to Bauer and his men. "You're in the way of the buckets!"

But Bauer and his guards didn't seem to hear. They charged straight for Strom.

"Hold it right there!" Strom commanded.

His father kept coming.

"Stop right now!"

Bauer shoved through the crowd. Strom's eyes widened and he turned to run, but Bauer pounced on him and shoved a large handkerchief in his mouth. Each of the guards grabbed one of Strom's friends and gagged them too. Then Bauer pulled little wads of cloth from his ears and held a knife to his son's throat.

"Now all you children listen to me, and listen good," snarled Bauer. "You try to give a single order, and you'll have Strom's blood on your conscience."

The children stood silent as the grave.

One of the men below gave a tense laugh. "Mr. Bauer," he said, "it's all right. Most of the children are on our side now."

"Forget the children!" Bauer snapped. "Don't trust them. I'm the only one standing between you and the hellish chaos you saw today."

Strom gagged at the tightness of his grip.

"Listen to me, people of Hamelin. You'd better be careful. Don't listen to what that piper tells you, or the mayor and his family—they're all in it together! I'm the only one you can trust."

Mr. Lachler stepped forward. "No, Hermann."

Bauer's eyes bulged with fury. "What did you say?"

"I've had enough of your tricks. We have our mayor to lead us, we have Gudrun to fight Strom, and we have Hannes Piper to fight Anselm—"

"Hannes Piper!" scoffed Bauer. "I've seen with my own eyes that he and Anselm are partners all the way."

"I heard the new piper tell Anselm to end the curse!" a woman shouted. "And I saw him fight Anselm!"

There were murmurs of agreement in the crowd.

"You're mad to side with him," said Bauer. "You'd have to sell everything you own to raise his precious reward!"

"He's the only one who can fix what's wrong," the woman called.

Here and there, people were nodding.

"The point is," Mr. Lachler said, "we have good help. We don't need you, Hermann. We don't need your lies."

"Don't listen to him!" Bauer roared to the crowd. "Lachler's one of them. He wants to ruin me because I found out about his embezzlement—he's the one who's been robbing the fund!"

"Yes," said another councilman. "He and half the council, including me. We were all following you."

Mr. Lachler looked around at the crowd and called to them, "It's true. I'm sorry. Forgive me."

Other councilmen nodded and echoed the words.

"And I am sorry," said the mayor, in a voice grim with determination. "I let this happen." He paused. "I will never do that again. Seize him."

Several men rushed toward Bauer. His guards hesitated, then let them pass.

Bauer tightened his grip on his son and held the knife closer to Strom's throat. "He'll die!" Bauer said. He backed toward the doorway at the top of the steps and fumbled for the handle. "Don't anyone move."

Ponk! Something hit Bauer between the eyebrows. He blinked, then dropped his knife and toppled down the steps, unconscious.

Gudrun smiled.

While the crowd stood in shock, Strom jumped through the flames, jerked the door open, and ran inside. I heard the sound of the back door opening and slamming again.

Anselm's eyes were burning into Bauer as he lay unconscious on the ground.

"Anselm," I said. "You know about my father."

"Just let me kill Bauer," said Anselm. "Don't let them take him to trial. He'll bribe his way out."

"I resented my father," I said. "He didn't stand up to Bauer; he didn't make life work for Mama and me; he disappeared halfway through my apprenticeship. He should have been the man I wanted to be like. And in the end he wasn't."

Then you can't object to this! Anselm screamed in my head.

I said nothing for a moment, then, "That's how you did it, Anselm."

"Did what?"

"You knew that when I piped a curse on parents and children there would be a gaping hole in it—my secret resentment for my own father. It was easy for you to feel the cracks in my work, worm in, take my place, and steal the curse, because *you resented your father too.*"

Anselm's eyes widened mockingly. "You make a very tough counterspell sound like child's play. And what's your cleverness gotten you? A stalemate."

I said nothing for a moment. Then I took my pipe and rolled it across the shingles. It landed at Anselm's feet.

He picked it up. "What now, Hannes?"

I shouted down through the flames, "Gudrun! Can you see me?"

She stopped in the middle of the bucket brigade. "Yes!"

"Throw me my father's flute!"

A moment later, it flew up, end over end, over the edge of the broken roof, and I caught it. The wood was smooth in my hand.

Anselm laughed. "Maybe you missed class on day one, Hannes," he said. "Only guild pipes have power. 'Forged with wisdom, destined for service.' Sound familiar?"

I nodded. "There's one tune this flute can play." I stepped back. "Papa," I said into the smoke wreathing around us, "I've been angry with you long enough. I forgive you."

Anselm's expression changed, and a shudder went through his body. He began frantically playing the Childrule tune.

I shut my eyes and lifted my father's flute to my lips. I played "The Woman of Aerzen," and the flute came alive in my hands. Like a flood, like a fire, the music gushed and tumbled through me. I was carried up and forward on an invisible, rushing Pipeworld wave.

A jumble of music burst from Anselm, then the crackle and roar of a wall of fire just ahead of me in the Pipeworld. Before I had time to think, the wave of water pushed me on, steam hissed, heat faded, and I was flung down with a crash of spray. I shoved my hands forward to catch myself and found the warm skin of Gudrun's mind. I felt for her hand and put my hands around it, feeling hundreds of strings spreading from it in every direction.

Gudrun, I said into her mind.

Hannes, she answered. *Here. Stop the curse.* She put in my hand the strings that controlled the adults of Hamelin. I gently tugged them from the children and let them go.

233

Smoke billowed from the trapdoor now, and flames swept across the roof. Amid the noise and splashing in the street below, Gudrun was shouting, "Hey, everybody! Hannes stopped the curse! The Pied Piper stopped the curse!" Shouting broke out all around, but I didn't listen.

I reached toward Anselm in the Pipeworld. The fingers of his mind were scrabbling for the strings he could no longer find. At last his pipe slipped from his lips, and the Childrule score fell from his nerveless fingers. He sagged like an empty water skin.

I laid the cool pipe against my lips one more time and felt the sleep song come out like warm milk.

Anselm knew he would be asleep in seconds. "Wait," he objected. "Just kill me."

And live with the memory? I answered in his mind. *No, Anselm, I don't want to plan murder or remember it. Six years of hating Bauer was enough poison for me.*

His eyes flashed. Dropping his pipe, he snatched a knife from his boot and lunged, thrusting hard at my chest. I blocked; the blade barely sliced my arm. I saw the moment when the sleep music grabbed him. It would hold him for a good ten or twenty minutes.

Blood spilled from the shallow wound as the dagger fell to the rooftop. Anselm slumped against me, the sleep tune sinking into his mind.

"Speaking of poison," he grinned, pointing at the cut on my arm, "you'll be dead before I wake up." With a gurgling laugh, he fell asleep.

The roar and heat of the fire was all around me as I lowered Anselm to the roof. From the warm shingles, I picked up the Childrule scroll and tucked it safely under my shirt. I took Anselm's pipe and retrieved my own from his belt, stowing them in the pouch at my side. Shouting drifted up from the street, but I couldn't make out the words through the rushing and crackling of the fire, and the dullness of my thoughts as the poison overcame me.

I bent myself under Anselm's arm, and his deadweight lolled over onto me. I stood halfway, feeling he might slide off at any moment, then almost fell before I got my left foot planted. My leg wobbled. I leaned on it carefully and shot my right foot forward. As I coughed furiously in the thick smoke, I tilted my head up to see the edge of the neighboring house's roof, praying that it wouldn't be burning.

The house frame shuddered below me, and I staggered, clutching at Anselm's arms. Already I felt the poison creeping like a mist along my arms and legs.

"Hannes!"

It was Wolf, crawling out of the trapdoor on the neighbor's roof.

My heart sang at the sight of him. I managed three more dizzy steps before Wolf loomed up alongside me. He gave Anselm a look of amazement and fury, then heaved him over his shoulder like a sack. I collapsed against Wolf's arm, and we began stumbling across the shingles.

There was a cracking sound, and the hot roof buckled as we crossed it. Wolf's left foot broke through the roof, and with a yell he went in. His right leg, which had kept him from plunging into the inferno below, lay twisted under him at a nasty angle. As flames sprang up around him, he gasped for a moment, looking dazed. Anselm sprawled as he had fallen. I felt the heat of the shingles against my body and inched up onto my feet. Wolf fumbled for a handhold on the hot shingles and pulled himself, groaning, up out of the ragged hole. Rolling onto the shingles, he beat out the flames on his breeches, then clenched his teeth and took up me and Anselm again, one on each shoulder. His breathing was ragged and painful to listen to as he hauled us slowly toward the neighbor's roof. I bent my will to make my legs walk on their own, dreading to put any more weight on Wolf's destroyed knee, but I could not help weaving.

Twice he fell, twice he bit back a scream as his two pipers crushed the bad leg under him, and twice he picked us back up. By the end he was crawling, and I could not stop my tears as I watched his face and heard his breathing. By now his palms and fingers must be burning on the roof tiles.

At last, like near-drowned men making shore, we reached the neighbor's roof. On all fours, Wolf pulled his double burden to the neighbor's trapdoor. Suddenly, with a great groan of buckling beams, Roth's roof tilted away from us, crumbling into the fires below. We wound our way downward in a blur.

"I have our two pipes and my father's flute in the bag," I managed to say to Wolf, then indicated Anselm with my head. "Don't let him get them."

"Right."

I breathed in slowly as stairs and hallways wavered around me.

"Wolf," I said with effort, "my wound is poisoned."

He grunted. "We'll fix you up."

Then I was out in the street, carried by men I didn't know. Gudrun and Klara, who seemed angry at being left outside, appeared before me with anxious faces.

"Johannes," said Klara, reaching for my hand.

I smiled at her, blinking to clear the blur in my eyes. Everything seemed to be moving. What should I be saying?

"It's good to see you, Miss Hofmann," I said.

I turned to Gudrun, who was sucking on her bleeding lip.

"Gudrun," I said, "you were amazing."

Then their faces faded into darkness.

NINETEEN

The Mayor's Daughter

Monday, June Twenty-sixth, 1284, Hamelin

MY FATHER WAS STANDING, BOWED OVER AND THIN. *I WANTED TO let him lean on me, but I could not cross the stream between us. He was coughing, a rattling cough that terrified me.*

"Come here!" I shouted. "Please cross."

He began to walk toward me. Suddenly I noticed that he was wearing Mayor Hofmann's fur-lined coat. He could never swim across in it.

"Take that off, and then you can cross."

He began unbuttoning it. It took so long that he was sweating. I was sweating. My heart was pounding, as though something terrible would happen if he did not cross soon.

"Please take it off!"

He kept unbuttoning. There was no end to the buttons.

"Come on, Papa—now!"

He shook his head. He was giving up again.

"No!"

My eyes opened in a bed I didn't know. Where was I?

The march. How was my father? Was he marching? In spite of all that had happened in Hamelin, nothing had changed for the steward of the Aerzen manor. He was going to start marching the serfs. I was already late, but I still might have time if something had delayed them.

I sat up, feeling each muscle cry out. On a low wooden table beside the bed, I saw a note: *Sent urgent message during night to steward of Bauer's manor informing of Bauer's arrest & requesting news re estate. Steward says awaiting word of "how matters would be resolved." Plans for march canceled. W. Hofmann.*

I sank back in bed and sighed with happiness. My father was safe. Our side had won. And I was alive.

Then I remembered. Roth was Anselm. In the midst of the slashing daggers, flying shingles, and bursting flames of the night before, I'd had no time to face this loss. Now I wanted to howl and throw things. Roth the friend was Anselm the Rebel. I had never felt with any of the guild apprentices the connection I had felt with Roth. And he had insisted that I call him friend. But he had lied to me and used me and tried to kill me. All along, back to the very first meeting on the road, it had all been planned; I was merely a pawn. I placed moment after moment of our friendship under that light, and it scalded me. All of it, scripted. All the chaos and loss, all the hard things people had said and done to me, the insults, the scars—it all crashed in on me, and I just wanted to be somewhere else, floating down the Weser River in a little boat toward a place where no one knew me, where I would have no responsibilities, no one to rescue, no one depending on me, no one waiting to be injured because of my shortcomings.

"Good morning," said Gudrun, appearing in the doorway. She sat by my bed, hands folded primly. "You're in my room."

Of course it was Gudrun's room. On the windowsill were some dice, several lengths of string, a broken quill, and a thimble; on the chest were two pinecones and a small box painted blue; and on the floor around the bed were dolls.

"They said maybe you wouldn't be able to get out of bed. So Mommy let me make you oatmeal like I did before. Remember?"

Sure enough, Gudrun held a pan in her lap. As she lifted the spoon, the entire contents of the pan rose to greet me.

"Oh, but, Gudrun, I feel magnificent," I insisted, throwing a foot out to scramble for the floor. "Like I slept a week just for fun and woke up ready to run a race."

Her face fell. "But I made this just for you."

"Well, maybe one bite."

She pulled her chair up close, pinched off a lump of her creation from the mother heap, and officiously brought the spoon to my lips. I wrestled it down and felt it making the long trip from mouth to stomach. It brought a sudden memory of the night before, and a sudden awareness of traces of guild piping in my body.

"Guwu," I said, "Awa powo."

"Yes." She tucked hair in place and glowed. "You were poisoned. There's so much stuff you don't know." She grabbed and gathered dolls. Suddenly she stopped, her face twisted together like a rag, and began sobbing.

"Gudi, Gudi, what is it? What's wrong?"

She held up the dolls. They were new. The ones she loved best —the legless doll, the clown, the bear, and the beautiful clay doll— had all been lost in the fire at Roth's. She let me knead her shoulder as she cried.

When all that was left was some sniffling, she wiped her face with a doll in each fist and set out her new troupe. Soon I was seeing and hearing events that I had missed: How the mighty Bauer had fallen from a well-placed stone (in case I'd missed that very important bit). How Bauer and Anselm had both been arrested. How the sisters had made their peace and worked together to organize the bucket brigade. How master pipers had worked over me all night . . .

"Gudrun, when I leave Hamelin I won't be able to tell a story without thinking of your dolls."

"Well, actually, if you can walk and everything, it is time for breakfast."

I smelled ham cooking and felt like I could take up permanent residence over Mrs. Hofmann's kitchen. Gudrun put out her hand to help me out of bed one more time.

The four Hofmanns, who had shared my nightmare, sat with bowls of properly cooked steaming porridge—and there was one for me. Klara brought some butter, and Mr. Hofmann hugged her. He stroked Gudrun's hair as though he could not get enough of the feel of it. Mr. and Mrs. Hofmann beamed at each other's comments like a courting couple.

The first spoonful of porridge, with warm milk and salt on top, comforted me right down to my toes. The ham was tender, blending the flavors of smoke curing and the spices Mrs. Hofmann was so fond of. Coarse black bread seemed to be all the Hofmanns could get in the chaos of the last few days. It had never tasted so good.

"Johannes," said Mr. Hofmann, marveling at the sight of me as though I were the legendary Ant's-hill Treasure, "how are you feeling?"

"Hollow," I said, before thinking how strange it might sound. And in fact, I had been yawning when he spoke to me, staring

239

ahead of me and seeing nothing at all. "I don't mean my stomach —the porridge is wonderful. I mean . . ." I wasn't sure what I meant.

"Of course," said the mayor. He popped a bit of bread into his mouth, and I realized that once again I had been biting my bread instead of breaking it. "You know that Mr. Bauer and . . . Anselm have both been arrested?"

I nodded.

"There'll be a trial as soon as Duke Albrecht can come."

As the mayor said this, I knew that it was because the death sentence was being considered for at least one of the men. Somehow the news did not delight me.

"Mayor Hofmann, how did men from my guild happen to be at your house last night?"

"I think a piper named Friedrich told them what was happening. Anyway, they were here when you were brought back after the . . . fight. They piped all night over the injured ones. The best I could make out, they each took a portion of your poison. With you they seem to have had success."

I suddenly remembered. "Wolf! How is he?"

Their faces clouded over so much, I was sure we had lost him.

"He's very hurt. They've said he'll live, but he's weak . . ."

Gudrun started crying, just sitting there and letting the tears run down without any wiping. I asked if I could go to see him.

When I saw Wolf sleeping, he looked frail, which I had never thought possible. As I stood there, Klara climbed up to the landing beside me.

"We have to go to the jail," she said. "There's something I need to say to Anselm, before the duke comes and the trial starts."

We set out together, not saying too much. It was full morning now, with the sun shining over the town. The events of last night seemed almost impossible.

We were each so full of the night before that we hardly noticed the merchants' homes along Emmern Street. I could already see the last house before the jail. I would go inside, and I would face Anselm, with no fight to distract me and no sleep to shield me from the nightmare of his betrayal. I was going to meet the friend who had become my enemy, the man who had helped me in order to use me, who had saved my life and then tried to kill me. Now by the hard light of day, I would face my betrayer in cold blood.

I clenched my fists at the remembered ring of his infectious laughter, his rich voice. I squirmed at the thought of his well-trimmed red beard, his intelligent eyes—where I had seen the wish for my death.

The moment we rounded the corner and saw the jail, I knew there had been trouble. Dozens of townspeople were milling around. Closer to the entrance, people were pressing against a row of hard-faced men-at-arms to get a look at something, and my heart had an awful premonition of what it might be.

Klara's mouth was open, her eyes wide. Here was the same impulse that had stopped her at our first meeting on the road to Hamelin. She broke into a run.

Curiosity is no match for passion and a sense of authority. Klara wormed her way to the front of the crowd, past the guards, and I followed.

When we burst into the jail, two cell doors were flung wide open. One was empty. In the other, Mr. Bauer lay on the floor, facing the corner, his head a caved-in mass of blood and bone.

When I turned to look at Klara, I saw someone in the doorway. It was Frieda, Mr. Zimmer's daughter and Strom Bauer's girlfriend. Klara reached out her arms toward the girl, who collapsed against her and sobbed.

After a long time, Frieda grew still. I could barely hear Klara ask in her ear, "What happened?"

We learned the answer slowly, backward, in pieces. Any phrase might trigger a burst of tears, trembling, and apologies, and Klara would have to comfort her friend till she could speak again.

Strom's gang had grown fast and wreaked havoc during the Childrule Curse. Strom had foreseen that the jail might be used against them and had used the Childrule to extract a spare set of keys from the jailer.

When it was obvious the Childrule was over, Strom had given the gang a speech about the future ("a very beautiful speech," said Frieda, and dissolved again). There was no real place for them anymore in Hamelin, he said—certainly no place for the sort of freedom they'd grown used to, no place for their leadership skills, and (with a severe look at the timid ones) they would pay a steep price for their pranks. Things would be fine once again if they'd take a short vacation from Hamelin together with the Boss. He, Strom, would personally make sure that all parents were notified. With his wide knowledge of the world outside Hamelin, the Boss would take care of them.

Strom said a few other things of a stirring and comforting nature and then said that those who liked this plan should stick with him, while anyone scared or silly enough to stay behind was welcome to do so now. A few slipped off quietly, but the remaining band was still large.

When they had reached the jail, it was dark. The warden had left his two prisoners safe in their cells and joined every other able-bodied man in Hamelin fighting the fire and coping with the other results of the Childrule Curse. Strom and Frieda left the other children outside and entered the shadows alone.

Strom called through the door, found the Boss's cell, and opened it. Before stepping out into torchlight, the Boss said, "I've taken off my disguise. I look very different. But it's me, and I can prove it."

A strange, whispered conversation between the two of them followed, and in the end Strom came out looking pleased.

"Boss'll bop Father just a little one on the head, then open his door. When he wakes up, the guards'll still be away, but we'll be long gone. Come on!" Strom hurried out to tell the children they would be leaving soon.

Frieda saw the new, different-looking Boss hefting a heavy cudgel he'd found in the warden's office.

"Go on, Frieda," he said. "I'll catch up in a minute. Just a little job to finish up here."

Frieda stood outside the door. She heard the jangling of the keys, the groaning of the old lock, the creaking of the door.

Hello, Father. ("Those were the words he used, I swear!" said Frieda.) Then a question, she couldn't catch it. Voices, but no clear words. An oath, maybe pleading. A loud blow and a cry, a sound of thrashing. *A life for a life,* said the voice. *For my mother.* A bone-cracking blow. *For Franz.* A loud thudding blow. *For me!* A sound of fierce battering, which eventually grew still.

Frieda slid down Klara's body. A long silence.

"When he came out of the jailhouse," she whimpered, "he said, 'I opened his cell door.' Strom said, 'All right, then.' And I knew I had to leave." She wept silently for Strom, for herself, and for the sudden hardness of the world.

Frieda estimated that more than a hundred children, fearing

the consequences of their Childrule games, were trekking across Saxony, preferring life under the exiled Anselm. Our witness twisted her shawl, sniffled, and asked Klara what would happen to them, out there. She looked at the murdered councilman and could not look away.

I looked with her. As Mr. Bauer lay slaughtered and sprawled in a jail cell, I could no longer find the birthmark that would once have ignited me. I walked over, stooped down, clenched my teeth against nausea at the sight of his battered-in face, and closed his eyes.

In a half stupor, I dragged myself to my feet and walked to the other cell. Anselm was gone. But not long ago, he had been here— my pretended friend, my defeated enemy. I looked around at the grimy walls that had failed to contain him and thought of the life that had so invaded mine. Like me, Anselm had grown up a peasant boy; like me he carried that sharp-thorned rose—the beautiful, dangerous gift of piping. He was the dreamer who founded the Unbound movement, the poet who penned *The Piper's Choice,* the assassin who would have murdered me and all the Hofmanns with no second thoughts.

If I could find him now, slam him against a wall, and hammer him with my questions, where would I go from there? Would I force him to ask forgiveness? Squeeze out repentance? Yell at him? Spit on him? Torture him?

Still churning inside, I dragged myself from the jail. We found a friend of the Hofmanns in the crowd to take care of Frieda and walked away through the gawking crowd. I noticed a man with a long scar, the very man I had seen talking to Mr. Bauer on my first day at Town Hall.

Klara asked no questions as I guided her away from her home, around the Market Church and onto Town Square. Without a word, we walked over to the pillory. While Klara touched the wood and iron of the place of punishment, I walked to the old monument. I traced my finger over the severe face of the woman of Aerzen and hummed a line from the song.

"She was right," I said. "A piper from Aerzen led away the children of Hamelin."

"She was right," sighed Klara, "to hate that crusade. Children, for heaven's sake."

"Miss Hofmann, think of it. Your great-grandfather preached for it, and my great-grandfather went on it."

"And we're all still recovering."

"Both our great-grandfathers learned the wrong lesson," I declared. "Some of what passes for heroism is foolishness. But there *are* real heroes, Miss Hofmann."

She smiled at me. "They might even be us."

We made our way home. When we were two or three doors from the Hofmanns', I remembered what was scratching at my belly.

"Miss Hofmann," I said, pulling out the score and showing it to her, "this is the piece of parchment that Anselm and I fought over last night. I never had a chance to tell you—it fell out of Gudrun's clay doll. Do you know how it got there?"

She held it close and began to study it.

"The one side I've figured out," I explained. "It's the tune that Anselm and I—fought over. But look on the other side."

She inverted the scrap to show the short message that had stumped me.

"Oh my goodness—Franz!" She was pointing at the gobbledy-gook signature that had meant nothing to me. "That was his—that was Anselm's servant."

"So does this mean anything to you?"

She examined the inscription, *H hshed E8stn,* and suddenly clapped her hand over her mouth.

"What?"

She pulled me into her house, shut the door, and whispered, "The Hofmann horse!"

"What?"

"Ohhh!" she laughed. "The whole thing is just like Franz! Hannes, it's the treasure!" She danced up and down. "Look, Franz'd always be listening—fixing a buckle or darning a sock, you know—while Anselm talked to me. And Anselm used to point to the bronze horse head in our backyard and say that one day he would bear his beloved away on a fine horse like that one. He'd say things like that—very grand. Of course I never dreamed that all that horse-head talk was about *me*." Her face hardened.

"But, Miss Hofmann, you said treasure."

She put her hand to my mouth as though the walls might overhear us and whispered, "From the Hofmann horse head, go east eight stones."

Within ten minutes Klara and I had stealthily snagged a pry-bar and a shovel from the toolshed and were standing at the Hofmanns' back gate, looking up at the old horse head of Klara's childhood. It was going green from rain and age but still looked grand. The open door of the shed kept us from being seen by family or servants in the house.

With my foot, I counted toward the still-rising sun to the eighth rounded paving stone. Klara and I looked again at the shed door, afraid of being caught and called crazy; then I brought down the crowbar with a *clank*.

Just removing the smooth old stone, so big I was hard put to lift it, was more work than I had imagined. I picked up the shovel. Almost immediately I struck something that was hard, flat, and hollow sounding. Klara knelt and brushed away the black soil to reveal a thick wooden lid. I dug till it was free; we lifted it out and, with one more anxious glance in all directions, threw the clasp and raised the lid.

I had never seen so many coins in one place. And half of the hoard was covered with bracelets, rings, pendants—all of it a quiet fire in the sunlight of a June morning.

I laughed.

"What?" asked Klara.

"It's the Ants'-hill Treasure! The Anselm Treasure!"

For a while we just sat, picking up one jewel after another.

"Anselm became wealthy fast when he started piping for money," said Klara.

"Which the guild forbids," I added.

"Then he took over the city and began confiscating goods, most of it from the councilmen."

"Miss Hofmann," I said, "there's enough here, I think, to free Aerzen *and* to rebuild Hamelin."

———•———

June Twenty-seventh, 1284

The next day, with a large detail of men-at-arms from the Hamelin Town Council, Klara and I rode out toward Aerzen to set my father free. I looked at the waving masses of wildflowers by the road and remembered that day when my future had been bright and simple. Now I was carrying my reward to Aerzen to liberate the serfs as I had dreamed, but nothing in between had happened as planned.

The singing of birds and the clomping of hooves were the only sounds until we reached the place where Klara had rescued me. We stopped. Looking at that place in the dust, marked by the rock wall, brought back in vivid memory the tearing in my mouth, the explosion in my skull, the cruel hands and kind hands that had welcomed me to Hamelin just four days earlier. It seemed like four months.

"Miss Hofmann," I said, "thank you for what you did for me that day."

"I had no idea who I was rescuing," she answered with a sudden grin. After a pause she added, "I thought of something. You know why Franz's clue didn't work?"

I shook my head.

"Because Anselm didn't know how to play. He couldn't be silly. I don't think he ever touched my dolls."

She made a sign to me and to the captain, and the two of us spurred our horses on a little ahead of the soldiers.

"You know," she said quietly, "it's true, what Anselm said. I was attracted to Roth just because he cut a fine figure. When he was Anselm—not rich, not good-looking—I couldn't be bothered. So what does that say about me?"

"Any young lady would have found Roth attractive."

"Just stop it."

We rode in silence awhile.

"All right," I said, "let's face the hard questions. Was I wrong, not killing Anselm when I had the chance?"

"Mr. Piper, the whole world hangs on you, as always." She shook her head. "Remember: I was the one who let him out of the pillory. I don't know. Who gets the blame when a man receives mercy, then does more evil?"

Another silence.

"Mr. Piper, you and I have spent the last week of our lives being blinded by loyalties."

"Yes."

"You had a mission; I had a town. Somehow that made us enemies."

"Yes."

"Mr. Piper, I feel like I'm singing a solo here. Is something wrong?"

"No. Yes. I feel like an idiot." I was staring straight up at the clouds and looking for shapes in them, my head empty as a hatched egg.

"Can you *relax*?" asked Klara. "Honestly, does it exhaust you to make the sun rise every morning?"

"I don't know what you mean."

"Of course you don't. Look." Klara leaned closer to me. "Is there anyone in Hamelin who hasn't been an idiot this week?" She laughed. "I'll tell you what seeing that place in the road reminded *me* of. Kneeling with you on the floor of the banquet room, examining Mr. Lachler. That's where we started, you know."

"Right," I said, with no idea what we had started.

"That was wonderful. It was a day we'd never want to relive, but that moment was wonderful."

"Yes, I see that."

Klara furrowed her brow at me but went on. "And this, right now, going to free the serfs—this is wonderful."

"Of course." I spoke as lightly as I could, but for all Klara's chattering, I saw a problem rolling toward me like a boulder. What waited for me around the bend, after this trip? I imagined myself on the road beyond Hamelin, not marching but pottering.

"'Yes, I see that,'" Klara parodied me. "'Of course.' What's bothering you? I mean, wouldn't today be a good day for being happy?"

"I'm just finding it hard to settle down. For some reason."

"Yes. That's your style."

I showed my surprise, and she explained. "For instance, take the day you got rid of the rats. You were Hamelin's hero; you were my hero. You could do no wrong! But even then I was a little bit afraid of you."

"Afraid?"

"Yes. I thought you might be a machine, not a man."

"Do I look like a machine?"

"Well, right now you look . . . discouraged. Or guilty. Or *something*." She was trying to get me to smile, I could tell.

"Mr. Piper, be at peace."

"Thank you, Miss Hofmann."

"*Thank you, Miss Hofmann.* I really like the warmth in that. *Thank you, Miss Hofmann.*" She actually poked me. "What you need is for someone to tickle you—you know that?"

I said nothing.

"Then of course we have *my* character flaws," she went on. "What I'm glad of, although it hurt like anything, is that I finally did realize, about my father . . ." She was clearly working up her courage to some difficult point. "At first I was way too loyal, blindly loyal, to my father, and Hamelin, and the council. And I was fond of my position. And I was mean to you." She looked down at the dusty road, not at me, and said, "Hannes."

My first name. My nickname, even.

"Hannes. Will you forgive me?"

"Yes." Then I added, "Miss Hofmann."

"Call me Klara."

"Thank you, Klara." And when she laughed again, this time I laughed with her; I really did.

At the manor near Aerzen, we worked with the steward and Mrs. Bauer. We made the purchase in the name of the Pipers Guild and gave the serfs their land. The legalities and dickering took forever. No serfs had been marched or relocated. At the manor house, I saw the man with the long scar. He seemed to be waiting, and Mrs. Bauer seemed afraid of him.

I would bet my hat on it: here was a man to whom Hermann Bauer had owed an enormous sum of money. Today was the deadline, and Bauer was dead. The guild would happily have given Bauer more than he needed in exchange for his serfs. But he had stolen it from me himself.

Afterward, when I came to Marthe's hut, I learned that my parents had left. Marthe would not say another word about it; I had never seen such stubbornness. I was angry at my parents and at Marthe for spoiling what should have been a beautiful moment. But of course there was no way they could have known.

I went to the old grandfather's hut and knocked on the door. When he opened up the door and squinted out at me, I asked him first how my father was able to make a journey.

"Ask 'im yourself." The old man laughed. "He's in Hamelin."

I stared.

When I learned that he, too, was determined to stay mum on the subject, I swallowed my frustration and informed him that he was now a freeman and owner of his own land. He gave me a whiskery hug.

———— • ————

Arriving back in Hamelin, we saw that on Town Square tables had been set out and draped with streamers—red and yellow.

Dozens of tables were set aside for Hamelin's many poor. Today they would eat meat. Men, women, and children bore platters of steaming joints and sliced loaves from Town Hall to the tables. At one of the two high tables, I saw the Hofmann family. Mayor Hofmann wore a circlet on his brow and looked grand as a king. His rich green cloak heaped high about the shoulders and flowed down over a robe of gold. And next to him sat Master Josef, the Pipelord. His beard was bright over the red gown of the guild masters. This would be a St. John's Day the town would never forget.

One of the master pipers was piping a heaped-up bonfire from first spark to fiery blaze, as the crowd roared its approval. He and his colleagues all looked weak. They had saved my life by taking my poison. In the excitement over the bonfires, I approached the high table unnoticed.

"Master Josef, may I speak to you?"

The Pipelord gave me a brisk hug and asked a pair of jugglers if we might duck into their tent for a moment.

"Hannes, how are you?"

I'd never had much stomach for small talk. "Master, why did you send me here alone?"

"We planned for Master Friedrich to follow you to Hamelin."

"I couldn't get to him."

"He came to check on you, and *he* couldn't get to you, either. But he got word to us that something was wrong in Hamelin—as we found here six years back. We came immediately."

I said nothing.

"So," he said, "what happened?"

I shook my head. Now that the Pipelord was finally right in front of me, I couldn't find words for all that blackness, all those images of waste and death.

"Hannes, we've heard stories of what you did here. And here's what the guild says happened: you were magnificent."

"What do you mean?"

"You're the Moses of Hamelin," he said.

I pictured the collapsed and blackened timbers of what had been Roth's house and felt the crushing weight of Anselm's hatred. "But at the time," I said, "all I felt was alone in the dark." I swallowed and closed my eyes. "The things you told me had nothing to do with the Hamelin I found."

He put his hand on my shoulder.

"All I wanted to do," I said, "was free Hamelin, free Aerzen, and become a master piper. That's all. There is nothing complicated in that. There is nothing *bad* in that."

He shook his head.

"Master, I know the pipe is good. Hamelin should have seen it and welcomed me. But to them I was the evil eye. Klara and I should have been allies. But what kept getting in the way was the mission. And Roth—he had nothing against me personally, but he used me and tried to kill me because of *this*." Suddenly I flung the pipe across the tent, where it thwacked against the cloth and clattered onto the flagstones.

The Pipelord walked over and picked it up. He checked it for damage and then played a song I hadn't heard for years. I remembered the words:

John's Day, fine day, day of light,
When we dance away the night . . .

"Johannes, the pipe is about principles. Where there is a principle, someone will eventually get in its way and get hurt. That's not what principles are for, but it is what they do."

He handed me my pipe. "The festivities are starting," he said, and opened the tent's flap.

Mayor Hofmann was addressing the crowd. He praised the midsummer evening, apologized that the plague had delayed the feast of St. John, and linked my name to that apostle, whose feast had fallen during my brief mission to Hamelin.

My master stepped out of the tent and strode quietly to the mayor's side. Klara filled two cups to the brim.

"To the Pipers Guild, who are friends of Hamelin," shouted Mayor Hofmann, "and to the Pipelord, who is a friend of mine." When the two men had drained their cups together, they banged them down. The crowd clapped and whistled as the mayor turned the floor over to Master Josef.

The Pipelord raised a hand. "First let me say: some of you are waiting for word of children who have disappeared. My guild brothers and I feel that sorrow. We've sent a team of the guild's trackers. They're faster and truer than bloodhounds. They've already ridden out to bring your children home. Soon your children will be in your arms, and then we will celebrate again."

He turned and beckoned, saying, "I have come to Hamelin with my brothers of the Pipers Guild."

As though riding on the wave of the townspeople's cheers, a line of men marched past me to the table. Six years ago, when I had been a small, homeless boy pushing a wheelbarrow, these same noble faces, these same embroidered robes, had flashed before me in what seemed like a dream. Now I was seeing it again in Hamelin, that impossible town where anything could happen.

Two long tables now seated the masters of the guild and the members of the Hofmann family. Between the two groups were three empty seats. The Pipelord signaled to me, and I came out of the tent. The applause of the crowd beat on me, and there were rhythmic cries of "Han-nes! Han-nes!" At the high table, Master Josef put an arm around my shoulder.

When he could be heard, the Pipelord raised his voice and said, "I understand Johannes has been useful to Hamelin, helping the townspeople deal with a few threats. In addition, he has used Hamelin's generous reward to buy, in the guild's name, the freedom of a group of serfs near Aerzen. Tonight we celebrate that as well. Johannes's parents have come from that manor as representatives. I call them now to join us at the high table."

Applause rang out again as my parents rose and threaded their way forward through the crowd. My mother looked flustered amid all the finery, noise, and attention. For her, getting back out of focus was more important than our reunion; she touched my shoulder blades, released me, and sank into a soft chair that was like nothing she had ever sat on in her life.

My father shuffled slowly toward me. He put his light hands on my shoulders and looked into my eyes, as though there were no one in Hamelin but us. Putting his mouth near my ear, he said, "I'm proud. Till tonight I had no idea what you'd been doing."

I hugged his wasted body, and he sat beside me.

"In light of these achievements," Master Josef was saying, "the guild recognizes Johannes of Oldendorf's successful completion of all requirements and inducts him as a full member of the Pipers Guild, as a brother and a master piper. Master Johannes, come forward!"

Wild applause broke out, with the master pipers showing more excitement than I had ever seen. One or two even looked teary-eyed.

In front of thousands of people, the Pipelord removed from me the short jacket that had so nearly been skewered by arrows, the jacket that had been pierced by Bauer's knife, the jacket from which Gudrun had wiped mud, blood, and vomit. With his own hands he slid onto me the crimson sleeves of a master's coat. It hung to my feet and covered the two-colored hosen. He shook my hand, and I sat down in the amazing coat between my parents and Gudrun Hofmann, who stroked my new bright sleeve.

"For the second time in your beautiful town," the Pipelord announced, "I have lost an apprentice. The first became a villain and a rebel; the second has become a hero and a master piper. Apprentices must be replaced. The mayor and I have agreed that today I would ask one of your own to be my next apprentice." His eyes ran over the crowd, as though searching for someone. At last the Pipelord turned to the Hofmanns' high table and said, "Gudrun Hofmann, would you be my next apprentice?"

As Gudrun stared at the Pipelord in shock, then went to bow gravely in front of him, the town of Hamelin went wild with surprise, humor, and celebration of something deeper. The two warring sides in a six-year feud were now becoming family.

The mayor rose to speak again. "And now, at last, I think our business is done. It's high time for the feast of St. John to begin! I have never loved my people and my town as I do today. Enjoy this day and this feast with a good heart and a good appetite!"

Amid sounds of benches scraping and conversations launching, I turned to see Gudrun surrendering to Klara her seat by my side. Gudrun cupped her hand to my ear and explained. The last time she had done that, in her bitter attack in the hallway during the Hofmann dinner, now seemed like a month ago.

"Master Josef asked me to sit with him, and, actually, you know, Klara needs something that's *hers*."

The meat, steaming roast pork dressed with currants, was delicious. All around me I heard Hameliners remarking that they had never tasted better. Everywhere I looked I saw people laughing and talking but serious about eating their fill: biting into fragrant links of sausage, wedges of white cheese, and juicy grapes. The bread smelled all the finer, from knowing that Hamelin's fields, mills, granaries, and bakeries would no longer be crawling with rats.

When the bones and scraps were being cleared, Klara glanced over my shoulder, and her eyes showed alarm. I turned and saw Wolf, breathing hard, leaning on a cane. The massive shoulders slouched; the enormous boot dragged as he limped to the high table. Something in his size, in his grim face, in his broken body sent a hush through the crowd like a ripple across a pond.

"Hello, Mr. Piper," he growled, without smiling, and I feared that in his dark eyes I could read the message, *Look what I suffered for you.* He came right up to me, loomed over me like a mountain, and pulled a dagger from his belt. Now even the last child stopped whimpering, and the summer evening was as silent as a grave.

"Johannes Piper, this is for you," he said, and thrust the blade into the table, through the piece of bread I had been eating. "I may not be needin' weapons again. You keep that."

"People of Hamelin," he roared, "you're sittin' at a war feast. A victory was won through courage and skill at arms by a good war captain. His name is Hannes Piper." Wolf's eyes burned as he turned to me. "Hannes Piper, my cane and I would go into battle with you again. Hamelin—" He paused, and a shudder passed through him. "Hamelin has chosen you."

Now Wolf shouted, "Men of Hamelin, will you raise the cup with me and drink to Johannes Piper? Will you?"

A thousand cups were raised and drained. I walked up to Wolf, and even half crippled, he lifted me from my feet in a crushing bear hug. And when he set me on my feet again, my feet realized what they had to do. This celebration had to be a *dance.*

I was a piper, and piping is what pipers do. Piping that causes things: the movement of feet, and of hearts. I took up my pipe, felt its hard metal on my lips. And the first feet that moved were my own. As I began to play, my fingers and my feet in rhythm together, all around me the people of Hamelin entered the stream of the dance.

I danced toward my father. When I was close enough to touch him, the pipe fell to my side.

"Papa," I whispered to him, "I was angry with you . . . Please forgive me." We hugged each other hard. And I thought, *Papa, you are a man; I am a man. You have been crushed; I have been crushed. But even if we are shuffling, we have begun the dance.*

I stepped back from my father, and we looked each other in the eye—two peasants who had tasted brokenness. I reached into my bag, brought out my father's flute, and handed it to him. He lifted it. One long, high note shot forth, so pure our breathing stopped as we waited for it to melt. But this song went on, as though it were fed by the wind and had no notion of stopping. It soared still higher, taking the dancers with it. In a fountain of notes, my father's piping bore all of Hamelin to the mountains. The next thing I knew I was dancing as I'd never danced before—to the music of my father's pipe.

This time my feet stirred toward the Pipelord. He beamed and clasped me again with a smell of skin, leaves, and books. I felt his beard against me, his frailty, and his strength. As I stood before my master, the music rose in me again, tumbling from deep inside, and in harmony with my father, I piped. Now all the pipers joined and piped notes that sounded like freedom, the river of the master pipers' tunes blending in sweet polyphony with the song my father and I had birthed. And Klara was singing, soaring on the high notes, adding words to the music.

> *Ye shall have a song,*
> *As in a holy, solemn night,*
> *And glad hearts, all night long,*
> *As when one goeth with a pipe . . .*

The applause moved to the feet; the guild was dancing; Hamelin was dancing.

I danced over to Mayor Hofmann and bowed to him. With tears in his eyes, he lifted me up and gripped my shoulders. When I opened my eyes again, there was Klara, standing straight ahead of me.

I took a step. She stood her ground. I took another. I reached out and took her hand. Klara Hofmann, the mayor's daughter, curtsied and began to dance with me. Her father and mother stood on either side, clapping in time to the music, saying yes to our dance.

Then, one by one, into the dance glided the gentle harpers. And when the fiddlers' first notes sounded, the last few seated Hameliners came up on their feet, like hounds at the scent of a fox. By the time the drummers picked up the beat, every man and woman on the square, even the elderly, were moving hands and feet.

Gudrun extended her hand to Wolf. He was unmoved as an elephant. Finally, as she insisted, he rose and began a slow shamble.

Impossible things began to happen. Mrs. Hofmann requested a dance of my peasant father. The mayor was dancing with Frieda, the Pipelord with my mother . . . When had the tables been cleared away? When had sunset come and gone, giving way to this long midsummer twilight?

Pipers plunged into complex harmonies, and fiddlers' fingers flew. We danced with no fatigue, floating on the river of that music.

I saw a whirl of color and flying feet; it was my father. Even as I danced, I stared. He was outdancing the young men. There was only one person flying faster—a very large person . . . Wolf. All around me people were hooting for sheer pleasure, laughing. Gudrun reached out her hand toward me. We danced, the jingling clown and the bouncing, legless doll come to life after all. As she stepped away from me, I handed her my pipe. She spun over to the Pipelord and joined him in a duet, getting amazing mileage out of her five notes as he embroidered extravagantly all around her.

The evening, at midsummer, was long. The towering bonfires sent up their showers of sparks in the long twilight as Hamelin danced in health and plenty.

Like a man pushing back full from a platter of delicacies, I stepped toward the edge of the circle. I strode past the last dancer, beyond the bonfires' light. The stars were joining Hamelin's feast at last. Somewhere out under the stars traveled a band of hungry children, led by a hungry man.

The first dark wave swept over me like nausea, and I let it. All the ones I couldn't rescue. A real piper would have saved them, and I had lost them. Zimmer was lost. Bauer was lost. Strom was lost. Anselm was lost. A hundred children might be lost.

Then I saw the dark wave in light of the dance. The message of that whirling, healing music was that I must walk all the way into the pit now, or I would never dance through it. I walked in.

My life as a piper was going to be hard, harder than I had ever imagined. Apprenticeship was over—now the clubs and arrows were real. The grim weariness in the Pipelord's face, watchful for the next attack—now that would be my weariness. I would always be a pilgrim.

I had no tears left. A stillness came. A feeling invaded me, with a shape so unfamiliar, a taste so strange, that only very slowly did I recognize it as happiness.

I stood up and turned toward the bonfires. As I walked back to the dance, I picked out one by one the dancers I loved best. My parents danced together with the Pipelord. There, in a circle, danced Wolf, the mayor, Gudrun . . . and Klara, coming out to find me.

Acknowledgments

dam says thanks:
My father, Keith McCune, taught me storytelling from when I began to talk and let me into his Piper story when *it* was just starting to talk.

Prof. David Wright taught me to try different kinds of writing and made a wonderful experience out of his creative writing class, in which I drafted one of the later chapters of this book.

Fischer Five South, past and present, provided invaluable moral support.

Keith says thanks:
My son, Adam McCune, was simply a joy to work with, a colleague who dreamed creatively, worked masterfully, and brought out the best in his coauthor.

My father, Frederick McCune, always told a fine story.

My mother, Marguerite McCune, always enjoyed my writing.

LB Norton took the time to get to know the manuscript better than we did, helped us polish, and asked insightful questions we had failed to think of.

McCune & McCune say thanks:
Mark Tobey treated us from the first conversation with a dignity we did not deserve.

Andy McGuire applied to the text his fine understanding of good fiction, worked us hard like a good coach, and made the book all that it could be.

Les Stobbe gave important direction and encouragement early in the process.

Dave Lambert led a class on fiction that revealed to us our story's need.

Michael Boyer, the official Pied Piper of Hamelin, was an insightful critic and was immensely informative and encouraging with issues of research relating to Hamelin history and medieval German life. We would like to recognize him and his colleagues at the Hamelin Museum, and to recommend Michael's Web site, www.triune.de, with links to his own novella *Hamelyn: The Legendary Tragedy.*

Julius Wolff wrote the opera about the Pied Piper, *The Burgemeister's Daughter,* which we received from Michael Boyer and translated into Klara and Roth's duet in chapter 12.

Jonas Kuhn's Piper Web site was helpful (www.ims.uni-stuttgart. de/~jonas/piedpiper.html), as were Web sites www. the-orb.net, www. netserf.org.

Valuable aid on questions about life in the Middle Ages was given by the following generous scholars: Alexander Ganse, Melissa Harkrider, Hubert Hoeing, Richard Hoffmann, Duane Osheim, and Helmut Puff.

Our amazing family was the loving environment that made Hannes's development possible. They were our first eager fans and first stern critics.

We owe many people a debt for the creation of this book. If we have failed to mention someone's contribution here, please forgive our oversight.

THE RATS OF HAMELIN TEAM

ACQUIRING EDITOR
Andy McGuire

COPY EDITOR
LB Norton

COVER DESIGN
David Riley & Associates

INTERIOR DESIGN
Paetzold Associates

PRINTING AND BINDING
Dickinson Press Inc.

The typeface for the text of this book is
New Baskerville